D0291937

APR - 2003

A Maze of
Murders

A aze of Murders

C. L. Grace

St. Martin's Minotaur ❧ New York

www.minotaurbooks.com

Library of Congress Cataloging-in-Publication Data

Grace, C.L.
    A maze of murders : a medieval mystery featuring Kathryn Swinbrooke / C. L. Grace—
    1st ed.
      p. cm.
    ISBN 0-312-29016-0
    1. Swinbrooke, Kathryn (Fictitious character)—Fiction. 2. Great Britain—History—Lancaster and York, 1399-1485—Fiction. 3. Canterbury (England)—Fiction. 4. Women physicians—Fiction. I. Title.

PR6054.O37 M39 2003
823'.914—dc21

2002031831

First Edition: February 2003

10 9 8 7 6 5 4 3 2 1

To an excellent nurse and healer,
Helen Dorgan
of Whipps Cross Hospital, North London

"And when a beest is deed he hath no peyne;
But man after his deeth moot wepe and pleyne . . . "
—Chaucer, "The Knight's Tale,"
The Canterbury Tales

"In the Middle Ages women doctors continued to practise
in the midst of wars and epidemics as they always had, for
the simple reason that they were needed."
—Kate Campbellton Hurd-Mead,
A History of Women in Medicine

Historical Note

In 1453 the city of Constantinople fell to the Turks, marking the end of the Byzantine Empire. The fall of this illustrious city sent shock waves throughout Europe. Many legends grew up regarding its collapse even though the city was already weakened by constant attacks whilst the West had provided little support. The last Emperor of Constantinople died, sword in hand, surrounded by his Varangian guard, and a thousand years of glory were over. The fall of this city had a cultural impact upon the rest of Europe. Some of the contents of its gorgeous treasuries and well-stocked libraries flooded into Europe, a powerful influence in the emergence of the New Learning.

By coincidence, only a year after the fall of this city, the seeds of civil strife, the Wars of the Roses, became firmly rooted in English politics when Richard, Duke of York, was proclaimed 'Protector of England' during the alleged insanity of the Lancastrian King, Henry VI. Henry eventually recovered his wits, and York was ousted from power and was replaced by the Beauforts, under the Duke of Somerset, who led the Lancastrian faction in its bloody struggle against the House of York. Somerset, and Henry VI's Queen, Margaret of Anjou, became embroiled in a series of desperate battles throughout England to decide once and for all the question of whether the Crown should be held by the House of Lancaster or York.

Richard of York was killed at the Battle of Wakefield in 1460. However, in 1461, Richard's son Edward won a decisive victory at Towton in Yorkshire. The fortunes of both houses ebbed and flowed for the next ten years. In 1471 Edward inflicted two decisive defeats against Lancaster, at Barnet on the approaches to London and at Tewkesbury in the west country. Edward of York proclaimed himself Edward IV, Henry VI went into the dark and the only surviving Lancastrian claimant was the penniless Henry Tudor wandering the courts of Europe. . . .

List of Historical Characters

THE HOUSE OF LANCASTER

Henry VI: Henry of Lancaster, son of the great Henry V, regarded by some as a fool, by others as a saint, by a few as both. His weak, ineffectual rule led to vicious civil war between the Houses of York and Lancaster.

Margaret of Anjou: French Queen of Henry VI and the real power behind the throne; her hopes of victory were finally quashed by two outstanding victories by the Yorkist forces at Barnet and Tewkesbury in the early months of 1471.

Beaufort of Somerset: Leading Lancastrian general and politician; reputed lover of Margaret of Anjou, killed at Tewkesbury.

Henry Tudor: Last remaining Lancastrian claimant. By 1473, in exile at the Courts of France and Brittany.

THE HOUSE OF YORK

Richard of York: Father of Edward IV. Richard's overbounding ambition to become king led to the outbreak of hostilities between York and Lancaster. He was trapped and killed at the Battle of Wakefield in 1460.

Cecily of York (nee Neville): 'The Rose of Raby'; widow of Richard of York; mother of Edward, Richard and George of Clarence.

Edward IV: Successful Yorkist general and later King.

Edmund of Rutland: Edward's brother, killed with the Duke of York at Wakefield.

George of Clarence: The beautiful but treacherous brother of Edward IV; a prince who changed sides during the Civil War.

Richard of Gloucester: Youngest brother of Edward IV; he played a leading part in the Yorkist victory of 1471.

ENGLISH POLITICIANS

Thomas Bourchier: Aged Archbishop of Canterbury.

William Hastings: Henchman to Edward IV.

A Maze of
Murders

Prologue

"*Kepe wel thy tonge, and thenk upon the crowe.*"
—Chaucer, "The Manciple's Tale,"
The Canterbury Tales, 1387

The chantry chapel of St. Michael and All the Angels in the Franciscan church of Greyfriars in the King's own city of Canterbury was described by one chronicler as "a jewel within a jewel." Greyfriars was a beautiful church with its honey-coloured brick and dark red slate roof. Its windows had been widened and filled with multicoloured glass portraying scenes from the bible. At the height of summer, dazzling in the powerful sun, these paintings took on a life of their own, bathing the inside of the church with a vivid array of glorious colour.

Greyfriars had been widened and extended over the centuries, transepts added, roofs replaced. Its whitewashed walls were now covered with breathtaking pictures and mosaics. On a balmy summer's evening it was easy to believe such a church truly was the House of God and the Gate to Heaven. The marble high altar, with its gold candlesticks, could be glimpsed through the door of the exquisitely carved rood screen which depicted the Crucifixion of Christ and other scenes from his Passion. On that Thursday evening in August 1473, the nave of the church lay quiet, a few candles spluttering weakly in the Lady Chapel to the left of the high altar; on the other side, in a shrine dedicated to St. Francis, two large candles glowed in their red glass containers. A haven of peace except for the pickpocket occupying the Mercy Chair in the main sanctuary. Restless and ill at ease, he sat clutching the arms of the chair, staring up at the high altar, eyes fixed on the crucifix as if begging the good Lord for help.

The pickpocket, known to the bailiffs of Canterbury as Laus Tibi, literally 'Praise-to-Thee,' had forgotten his real name. He vaguely recalled being raised in Gravesend but he had spent most of his life travelling the dusty highways of England earning a precarious living by thieving, pilfering and, above all, cutting purses and picking pockets. Laus Tibi was a greasy-haired, rat-faced, beanpole of a man with pockmarked cheeks and dark glittering eyes. He had joined the pilgrims coming in droves, now that summer was at its height, all keen to worship before the blessed bones of the martyr St. Thomas à Becket in Canterbury Cathedral.

Laus Tibi hadn't been bothered about relics, St. Thomas's bones or acquiring an indulgence which, after death, would release him from the pains of Purgatory. Laus Tibi had slipped through Canterbury's gates like a wolf into a sheep pen. He had come to thieve, to cut purses, filch from the stalls and make a profit before winter set in. He would need money to rest up at some tavern until spring came: pilgrims were like coneys in the hay: they had to be flushed out and caught. It was easy. Pilgrims were so concerned about finding a tavern or a guest house, or staring, mouths agape, at the churches and fine buildings of Canterbury, that they would often forget about the bundles they carried or, more importantly, their purses, wallets and pockets. At first Laus Tibi couldn't believe his good fortune. He took a priest's purse in the marketplace, then a tailor's wallet in a tavern after the man had drunk too deeply of the strong Kentish ale. A young merchant's wife, an embroidered purse hanging from the decorated belt round her slim waist, had been easy prey: the purse had yielded a harvest of one gold coin, freshly minted by the King's treasury in London, some silver pennies and a set of Ave beads. Laus Tibi had sold the latter as a sacred relic to a reeve from Devon. Eventually Laus Tibi had been able to secure a garret in the *Grey Weasel* tavern just off the marketplace: bed and board, pots of ale, and even the attentions of a comely chambermaid.

In the end, however, Laus Tibi had stayed too long; the alarm was raised and the marketplace watched. Laus Tibi closed his eyes and ground his yellowing teeth in anger, his tongue seeking out the abscess just beneath his upper lip.

'I should have taken better care.'

He opened his eyes, stared at the crucifix and felt a stab of guilt. Yet what could a man like him do? He had no trade, no home, no family; it was either steal or starve.

'I should have been more careful,' he repeated.

Laus Tibi's hand stole beneath the filthy linen shirt he had filched from a garden, where it had been drying out over a fence. The pickpocket's dirty fingers traced the outline of the brand mark, "F" for felon, scorched onto his right shoulder three summers ago when he had been caught cutting purses near Smithfield Market in London. If the King's sheriff saw that, little mercy would be shown: Laus Tibi would hang from the crossroads! He had passed such gibbets with their tarred, grisly remains, a chilling warning to lawbreakers. Nevertheless, Laus Tibi had believed, like the gambler he was, that the dice would always fall in his favour—until a week ago.

Laus Tibi had watched that fat priest moving like a bloated carp amongst the stalls of Canterbury marketplace, a fur-lined cloak over one arm, a heavy purse jingling like a bell from the leather belt round his portly waist. Like a hungry fox stalking a fat goose, Laus Tibi had followed. He'd cast his usual cautious cunning to the wind. He never had liked priests. They had no time for him. Very few showed him care, even fewer any compassion. Laus Tibi was determined to take both the cloak and the purse, a crowning achievement! He must have followed his quarry for at least an hour. The priest kept stopping at certain stalls displaying costly hangings and tapestries from abroad. Some hung in front of the stall, others were rolled up and protected under a canvas cloth. The priest was very careful. He would examine the texture, running it between his fingers, and ask the eager trader a spate of questions.

'Was this genuine silver thread?' 'From which mill?'

The priest could not make his mind up. He moved backwards

and forwards. Laus Tibi edged closer. At one stall offering cloth from the looms of Brabant, the priest put down his cloak and moved his belt slightly so the purse which had been hanging on his side was now pushed round to the back. Laus Tibi drew a needlelike knife from the leather sheath strapped to his arm beneath his battered jerkin. The priest was haggling with the stall owner. This was the time! The priest was about to make a purchase, he was oblivious to everything except beating the trader down to accept his price.

Laus Tibi was no longer aware of the chatter and babble of the marketplace, the raucous shouting of the apprentices, the smells from the middenheap, the fragrances of the cookshops and bakeries, the bells clanging or the faint sound of singing from a nearby church. Like a hovering hawk he studied his prey. He quickly stared round: no one was watching him, he could see no bailiff. Laus Tibi decided to close with his victim. He stealthily walked across the mud-grimed cobbles, knife at the ready. One quick cut to sever the thongs holding the purse, he would take that, grab the cloak and escape amongst the crowds in the space of a few heartbeats. . . .

Laus Tibi rose from the Mercy Chair, walked to the entrance of the rood screen and stared down the nave. He could still see the two Franciscans kneeling on their prie-dieus before the Chapel of St. Michael and All the Angels. One of the brothers had taken him down to inspect the chapel and Laus Tibi had marvelled at its beauty. The chantry chapel was really a church within a church. Built against the wall of the north transept, it was screened off from the nave by three intricately carved oaken screens with small windows on either side. The front of the chantry chapel soared up to meet the roof of the transept; it had two oval-shaped windows above a narrow, wooden door, now locked and bolted. Brother Simon the sacristan had let him peer through the grille at the sacred relic hanging in its receptacle from a silver chain.

'According to legend,' Brother Simon had whispered, 'this is the Lacrima Christi, an exquisite ruby formed when our Good Saviour was scourged by the Romans: tears of blood fell to the ground, and these miraculously congealed to form this brilliant stone.'

Laus Tibi had just nodded and peered openmouthed. Oh, to seize such a prize! The ruby was the size of a large pigeon's egg. The good brothers had placed it in a blood-red, golden receptacle: this, in turn, hung on the end of a long silver chain which stretched from the concave roof of the chantry chapel to hang between the door of the chantry and the altar built against the far wall. The receptacle was three-sided, in the shape of a square C so as much as possible of the relic could be viewed; a metal loop on top of this receptacle was used to attach it to the stout silver hook on the end of the chain.

'Why is it here?' Laus Tibi had whispered.

'It belongs to Sir Walter Maltravers.'

The garrulous sacristan had explained while chomping on his gums; he'd felt sorry for this poor felon who had sought sanctuary in his church. When Brother Simon glimpsed him standing so forlornly at the entrance to the rood screen, he'd invited him down. The other Franciscan had not been so friendly but gone and knelt on his prie-dieu, bony face hidden in his hands as if he wished to hide all signs of Laus Tibi.

'You know Sir Walter Maltravers?' the sacristan whispered.

The fugitive thief shook his head.

'He owns Ingoldby Hall on the south side of Canterbury, a very rich lord, a close friend of the King. As a young man,' the sacristan gabbled on, 'Sir Walter was a member of the Emperor's bodyguard at Constantinople.'

Laus Tibi screwed his eyes up and nodded as if he understood, though he had no knowledge of any Emperor or the city with the long sounding name.

'The Lacrima Christi?' he grated. 'How did it get here?'

'Oh, the Empress Helena,' Brother Simon had chattered on, 'mother of the great Constantine, found the Lacrima Christi in Palestine and took it to her son's city. However, when the Turks captured the city over forty years ago, Sir Walter was forced to flee. Rather than allow such a precious relic to fall into the hands of unbelievers, he took it with him.'

'But what's it doing here?' Laus Tibi had insisted.

'Sir Walter bought Ingoldby Hall over three years ago, just as the war between Lancaster and York drew to an end. Prior Barnabas heard about the relic and begged Sir Walter to loan it to the priory for public veneration.'

Aye, Laus Tibi reflected, and so fleece the pilgrims even more than I did!

'Is it safe here?'

'Look around.'

Brother Simon's sharp reply clearly revealed how he mildly regretted inviting Laus Tibi to view the treasure. The jewel was a temptation but well guarded. The chapel was very secure, its high wooden screens were of thick polished oak, its roof had no aperture, the only way in was through the heavy oaken door, secured fast by both clasp and lock. A desperate thief might try and enter through the stained glass window, just above the chantry altar, depicting Michael casting Satan into the fires of Hell, yet the window was held in place by reinforced lead and who would break such beautiful glass? The sound would certainly alarm the priory, and the thief might be able to get in but find it more difficult to get out. Burly lay brothers, armed with stout cudgels, patrolled the cloister garth which the window overlooked; not even a mouse could squeeze into that chantry chapel. Two members of the community were constantly on vigil nearby, either kneeling at the prie-dieus not far from the chantry door, or standing in front of it, allowing the pilgrims to process by, taking their coins for a peep through the narrow grille. Oh no! The Lacrima Christi was secure. . . .

Laus Tibi sighed and leaned against the rood screen door. The sun was beginning to set, Vespers had been sung and the church closed for the day. Nevertheless, the brothers would sustain their vigil until the bell tolled for Compline. Laus Tibi sniffed. Two friars still knelt on their prie-dieus. The felon squinted down the nave to see that one was Prior Barnabas, a sinewy, harsh-faced man with the eyes of a hunting mastiff. The other was Ralph the infirmarian. They would stay until the appointed hour when the Lacrima Christi would be stowed safely away. Laus Tibi felt tempted to go down and have one more look. The brothers had turned the chantry chapel into a gorgeous shrine: thick red turkey rugs covered every inch of the chapel floor. Even the altar cloths, candleholders and candles were of the same ruby red so the entire chapel seemed to glow with some unearthly light. Laus Tibi prided himself on having an eye for beauty, and could have stared through that grille for as long as the brothers had allowed him. The chantry chapel of St. Michael represented everything Laus Tibi had missed in his life: comfort, opulence and luxury. The very air was fragrant with incense and beeswax candles as well as the herb-scented oil used to polish the gleaming woodwork.

'I wonder how much the ruby's worth?' Laus Tibi whispered to himself. 'But where could one sell a jewel such as that?'

Brother Simon had explained how the Lacrima Christi would stay at Greyfriars for the duration of the pilgrim season. Laus Tibi stared down at his battered boots and groaned. The pilgrim season! He felt the brand mark on his shoulder. Where would he be at the end of the pilgrim season? He walked back to the Chair of Mercy in the sanctuary niche, sat down and picked up the wooden platter, absentmindedly drawing the crumbs together. If it hadn't been for that priest—no, no, that wasn't correct: the thief had been greedy and walked into a trap! . . .

Laus Tibi's intended victim wasn't a priest but a market bailiff in disguise. He and his companions had been watching Laus Tibi for days and so the hunter had become the hunted. Laus Tibi had just been about to cut the purse from his quarry's belt when he heard the horn sound behind him, the alarm being raised.

'Harrow! Harrow!' a voice shouted. 'A thief! A thief!'

The false priest had swerved round, a smile on his face, and gripped Laus Tibi's arm, forcing him to drop the knife.

'I have you, sir,' he rasped, his fat, ruddy face laced with sweat. 'I arrest you in the King's name!'

Laus Tibi gave a vicious kick to his shins. The man loosened his grip and, quick as a weasel, Laus Tibi had run, not away from the crowds, but into them. All around horns were blaring, the cry of 'Harrow! Harrow!' being raised. Laus Tibi had knocked people aside. He'd grabbed a cleaver from a flesher's stall, threatening anyone who tried to block his way. He'd run like the wind, slipping and slithering on the cobbles, whilst behind him a posse of bailiffs followed like a pack of yelping hounds. Panting and gasping, heart pumping, his body wet with sweat, Laus Tibi had broken away from the marketplace, but he was a marked man. He had been through such an ordeal before and recognised the signs. People instinctively drew away from him, marking him down as a lawbreaker. A number of apprentices came dashing out from a side street but the sight of the raised cleaver and Laus Tibi's mad, staring eyes forced them to draw back.

'Harrow! Harrow! A thief! A thief!'

Laus Tibi had fled on down alleyways and runnels, the sweat blinding his eyes, the pain in his left side becoming more and more sharp. He could not be taken! Not for him the journey in the hanging cart to the gallows outside the city. He turned blindly, ran down an alleyway and through a half-open gate into a fragrant garden. At first Laus Tibi thought it was some merchant's house but, as he sank to his knees and stared around, he realised he was in the grounds of a priory or convent. Laus Tibi knew the law. He had been caught in York four years earlier and been able to quote the opening lines of Psalm 50: 'Have mercy, Oh God, have mercy, and in your compassion blot out my offence.' He had managed to recite this quotation, the infamous 'hanging verse' which allowed him to claim benefit of clergy. Laus Tibi had been handed over to the church courts for punishment. If he was arrested now, the bailiffs of this great city would make diligent search. He had claimed benefit of the clergy once and escaped scot-free; he could not do so again.

Exhausted to the point of desperation, Laus Tibi had staggered to his feet and begun to run. He felt dizzy, light-headed. He'd knocked a lay brother aside, reached the door of the church and thrown himself inside its cool, welcoming darkness. Pilgrims were milling about; a hand caught at his shoulder, but Laus Tibi shoved this away and staggered up the nave through the rood screen into the sanctuary. He could have cried with relief. At the far side of the sanctuary built into a recess in the wall was a heavy Mercy Seat. Laus Tibi had crawled on all fours towards it, pulled himself up and pressed his hot cheek against the cold stone of the alcove.

Simon the sacristan had appeared, eyes wide, toothless mouth gaping in astonishment.

'Do you claim sanctuary?' he'd gasped in Latin.

Laus Tibi had shaken his head.

'Do you claim sanctuary?' Brother Simon leaned over him so the thief could smell the altar wine on his breath.

'I claim sanctuary,' Laus Tibi stuttered. 'I seek the protection of Holy Mother Church!'

He had performed the ritual just in time. The door of the rood screen filled with angry-faced bailiffs, staves in their hands; one even jangled a set of manacles. They jabbed their fists in Laus Tibi's direction but none dared to cross the sanctuary and lay hands on him. Laus Tibi had sprawled like a dog until Prior Barnabas appeared. Severe and haughty, shoulders back, the Prior had swept out of the sacristy accompanied by a crucifer and confronted the bailiffs.

'You know the law!' Prior Barnabas intoned. 'This man . . .'

'This thief!' the chief bailiff bawled back.

'This child of God,' Prior Barnabas interrupted, 'has, according to statute, and the law of Holy Mother Church, sought sanctuary. If you break that law, you will not only incur the anger of the King but the wrath of Holy Mother Church. Excommunication by bell, book and candle, to be cursed in your eating, your drinking, your sleeping and waking!'

'I know the law!' the chief bailiff rasped.

'Then abide by it!' Prior Barnabas snapped. He brought up the cowl of his brown habit to cover his balding head, slipping his hands up the voluminous sleeves of his robe. Exhausted as he was, Laus Tibi could see the good Prior enjoyed his power, and that there was little love lost between this proud churchman and the city bailiffs.

'Then abide by the law!' Prior Barnabas repeated. 'This man can stay here for forty days. He then has a choice: to surrender himself to your power or take an oath to abjure the realm. I doubt,' he added sarcastically, 'that he will surrender himself, so I will give him a crucifix, two coins, a pannikin of wine, some bread and meat wrapped in linen, then he will have safe custody to Dover.'

'If he ever reaches it!' a bailiff yelled.

'That is not my concern,' Prior Barnabas retorted. 'Now, sirs, this is the House of God. We have pilgrims waiting to see the Lacrima Christi.'

'We all know about that!' the chief bailiff jibed.

'Good!' the Prior remarked. 'In which case you will know of the generosity shown to this church by Sir Walter Maltravers, lord of Ingoldby Hall, close friend of our King.'

The bailiffs decided to retreat. Laus Tibi received some dark glances but the hunting pack withdrew. The thief knew he was safe and settled down to plot what he should do next. . . .

The thief broke from his reverie and turned to stare towards the sanctuary chair. Seven days had passed. He had been given a clean pair of breeches and the friars had been kindly enough, though Laus Tibi suspected the source of this generosity was more antipathy towards the city bailiffs than any compassion for himself. He rubbed his eyes. Prior Barnabas was right. He would have to leave here. But how could he get to Dover? What guarantee did he have that the bailiffs would allow him safe passage? Laus Tibi wandered back across the sanctuary, now awash in gold-red colours as the rays of the setting sun poured in brilliant shafts through the stained glass windows. The marble altar steps glowed in the resplendent light which dazzled in the golden pyx holder. Yet this brought little comfort to Laus Tibi. Night would soon be here. The felon shivered and rubbed his arms. Darkness was already creeping in like a mist. The gargoyle faces at the tops of pillars appeared to spring to life, grotesque images shifting in the twilight. Laus Tibi stared up at the central window displaying Christ in judgement; the late evening breeze, piercing some crack or vent, sent the candle flames dancing.

Laus Tibi returned to his post near the door of the rood screen. The two friars were still kneeling at their prie-dieus. Soon the vigil would be over, the Lacrima Christi would be taken down and ceremoniously locked in its iron coffer. Prior Barnabas shifted on his prie-dieu and whispered something to Brother Ralph the infirmarian, who struck a tinder and lit the sconce torches with a taper on the end of a long pole. Laus Tibi was glad of this light. No matter how beautiful the church was in daytime, at night it became another place, of shuffling sounds and moving shadows. Hadn't the sacristan told him how the nave was haunted by a friar who had committed suicide, hanged himself from an iron bracket down near the corpse door? Brother Ralph, still holding the lit taper, was glaring up at him, gesturing with his hand for the felon to withdraw. Laus Tibi knew the Prior wanted him to stay away from the door so he walked back across the sanctuary and, for a while, stared up at the pyx case carved with its strange symbols. Laus Tibi could not understand the Greek. Brother Simon said that it stood for: "I am the beginning and the end of all things." He was about to stretch up and caress the beautiful gold when a cry from further down the nave made him jump. He hurried back to the rood screen door. Brother Ralph was staring through the grille, gesturing with his hands for Prior Barnabas to join him.

'The Lacrima Christi!' he shouted. 'The Lacrima Christi has gone!'

Laus Tibi stared in horror.

'Nonsense!' Prior Barnabas scoffed. He hurried over to join his colleague, and even from where he stood, Laus Tibi heard his groans of despair.

'Quick! Quick!' Prior Barnabas shouted, almost pushing Brother Ralph away. 'Rouse the community!'

The infirmarian hurried off. Prior Barnabas glanced up the nave.

'And you, sir.' He gestured at Laus Tibi. 'Go back to your chair. You are in sanctuary. Stay in sanctuary!'

Laus Tibi retreated into the shadows. Somewhere deep in the priory a bell tolled, followed by the sound of feet slapping against the hard stone floor, doors being thrown open. Friars thronged down the nave. Laus Tibi returned to the Chair of Mercy in the sanctuary recess. He heard shouts of disbelief, Prior Barnabas giving orders, then the noise faded.

'I hope they don't blame me,' Laus Tibi moaned to himself. 'I had nothing to do with it. How could the ruby be taken from such a place?'

The chantry chapel was sealed; the only way in was through the door, yet that had been bolted and locked. Laus Tibi could hardly wait for Brother Simon to bring his evening meal of bread, cheese and strips of smoked bacon and a leather blackjack of ale. The sacristan was all agog with the news even though he gazed suspiciously at Laus Tibi.

'The Lacrima Christi,' he whispered, 'has truly gone!'

'Gone?' Laus Tibi exclaimed.

'Taken off its hook,' Brother Simon whispered, eyes all fearful. 'The ruby and its holder.' He snapped his fingers. 'Gone like that but with no sign of forced entry.' He leaned closer. 'They say Christ has come back to claim his own!'

The following afternoon, Friday, the eve of the feast of the Transfiguration, Sir Walter Maltravers, Lord of Ingoldby Hall, was about to perform his weekly penance. He had entered the great maze. He knelt down in the shadow of its thick, high hedges and crossed himself. Sir Walter was a vigorous man in his early sixties who prided himself on having the wits and physique of a man thirty years younger. A proud man, Sir Walter, a lord of the soil, confidant and friend of King Edward IV at whose side he had fought in the recent struggle against the House of Lancaster. Maltravers was Dominus of Ingoldby and its surrounding estates, meadowlands, woods, streams full of fat fish, land under the plough, granges and barns. He also owned tenements in Canterbury and a number of houses in Paternoster Row in the shadow of St. Paul's in London. Ingoldby Hall boasted a library which would be the envy of any monastery or abbey. Oh yes, a man rich in the things of the world, Sir Walter had invested money in the Merchants Adventurers and other companies plying the Northern and Middle seas. The Crown owed him money and, even in Rome, Sir Walter's name was held in the highest regard: a man of property, a good friend of the Church. Sir Walter's lined, grim face broke into a sardonic grin.

'Yet what does it profit a man,' he prayed, 'if he gains the whole world and suffers the loss of his immortal soul?'

Sir Walter had drunk deeply of the wine of life. His young wife, the Lady Elizabeth, daughter of the powerful Redvers merchant family, was considered a great beauty with her cornflower blue eyes, perfectly formed face and lustrous golden hair. Sir Walter sighed. The Lady Elizabeth was forever lecturing him that this penance was not necessary. Yet Sir Walter knew the truth: he had lost his soul on that day some nineteen years earlier, thousands of miles away, when he had fought in the Varangian Guard at the side of the last Emperor of Constantinople. Sir Walter placed his face in his hands. He would never forget that day! The Turks had breached the walls; the Janissaries, in their yellow coats and white turbans, came pouring into the city, spreading out through its narrow cobbled streets and across its broad basalt-paved avenues. Churches were put to the torch. Clouds of black smoke hung over the palaces, but still the Emperor and his guard, their armour soaked in blood and sweat, had tried to close the breach. Their cause had been hopeless. The trumpets of their enemies brayed like demons and, even from where he stood on one of the towers, Sir Walter could see the green and gold banners advancing deeper into the city. The Varangians, mercenaries from every nation under the sun, had taken a solemn oath to stand by their master, to die sword in hand and go to their God like soldiers. The Turkish attack had proven too intense. The imperial household troops had broken. Sir Walter had found himself swept down some steps and recognised the Emperor's cause was hopeless. The city was already given over to slaughter. More gates had been opened, and Turkish light horse came clattering through. A black-turbanned Sipahi charged at him, lance lowered. Sir Walter had cut both horse and rider down, but his helmet had been knocked off and a blow to the side of his head had sent him reeling. He'd staggered up the steps of a church, a beautiful Byzantine chapel dedicated to Mary the Virgin. Father John, an English priest known to the imperial household, had been sheltering there. He had tended Sir Walter's wound, hiding in the crypt away from the slaughter being waged all around them. Father John had whispered how the city was doomed, the Emperor was dead, how they could not allow the treasures of the chapel to be seized by the Turks. Together they had filled a chest with plunder: gold coins, jewels, and the sacred relic the chapel held, the Lacrima Christi. Afterwards they had fled through secret passageways and dark caverns which led out under the city. They had been fortunate, making their way to the coast to secure passage on a merchant cog bound for Italy. Since that day Father John and Sir Walter had been inseparable. The priest had argued how Sir Walter deserved to keep the treasure they had seized and so his new life had begun. Sir Walter made little reference to his days in Constantinople and, if he had to, it was always in the most evasive terms.

Now he knelt just within the sole entrance to his sprawling, mysterious maze. The privet hedges blocked out the sun; the lane stretching in front of him seemed like that needle-thin alley he had hurried down so many years ago when he and Father John had escaped from the doomed city. He should never have done that! He should have stood and died beside his Emperor. Now the Furies were pursuing him. The Lacrima Christi had been stolen the previous evening from Greyfriars Church. Was that the work of the Athanatoi—the Immortals? Sir Walter lifted his head and stared up at the light blue sky. It was not yet noon. He would only begin his pilgrimage when Father John came to hear his confession, as he always did every Friday. Sir Walter, dressed only in a hair shirt with a halter around his neck, moved on his knees towards the marble stone bench. His clammy hand appreciated its coolness. He cocked his head and listened. He caught the lilting tune from the arbour of flowers where his wife, the Lady Elizabeth, and her constant companion and maid Eleanora sat making pleasant music together with rebec and flute. She always had an ear for music, did Elizabeth, and had spent hours teaching Eleanora. Other voices caught his attention—the high pitched tones of his steward Thurston, then the deeper voice of his captain of the guard Gurnell who, with his men-at-arms, always guarded the entrance to the maze. Another voice came and Sir Walter sighed in relief. Father John had arrived! Sir Walter knelt back on his heels.

Huffing and puffing, Father John swept by him, sat down on the marble bench and stared at his master.

'I am sorry I am late.' He smiled.

Sir Walter was always struck by how kindly Father John appeared. The priest had been sheltering in Constantinople, where he had secured a benefice at the church of St. Mary the Virgin. For the last nineteen years he had been Sir Walter's constant companion and asked for little except Maltravers's company, a roof over his head and three square meals a day. Well, that had been the case till recently. Sir Walter blinked. He would not think of that!

Father John, as usual, was dressed in a dusty robe, slightly threadbare with a white cambric shirt underneath; his face was grey and lined though laughter wrinkles crinkled his eyes and mouth. The priest scratched his thinning black hair and wiped the beads of sweat from his forehead. He adjusted the purple stole around his neck and leaned closer.

'I was sleeping, my lord. I was dreaming.'

'You drank too deeply of claret,' Sir Walter teased, dropping his voice to a whisper.

'Don't be fearful,' Father John replied. 'No one can hear you.'

The priest gazed into the light green eyes of this man he'd served so well over the last twenty years.

'Walter, you are not at peace.'

'I am never at peace.'

'The killings?' Father John queried.

Maltravers looked away. He recalled the great bloodletting at Towton some eleven years previously, the bloody hand-to-hand combat amongst the frozen hedgerows of Yorkshire when Edward IV and his warlike captains had smashed the power of Lancaster. The massacre of prisoners, the summary bloody executions . . .

'Sometimes,' Sir Walter replied, 'that does concern me, as does my flight from Constantinople. The Athanatoi . . .'

Father John leaned closer.

'Sir Walter, that is nonsense, a cruel joke!'

'Is it?' Sir Walter rasped. 'The Athanatoi were the Immortals, members of the Imperial household. They, at least, stayed by their master's side. They suffered imprisonment, slavery . . .'

'And, according to a silly fable, they now hunt down all who deserted their master. . . .'

'I did not desert him!' Sir Walter retorted.

'I know. I know,' Father John replied soothingly. 'So, put this foolishness away.'

'They are hunting me down.'

'Ridiculous!' Father John snapped.

'They stole the Lacrima Christi last night from Greyfriars!'

'That's not true.' Father John's face was only a few inches from Sir Walter's. 'The Lacrima Christi was stolen by a clever felon, some trickery and mischief at Greyfriars.'

Sir Walter was not listening, he knelt shaking his head.

'You must reconcile yourself,' Father John continued. He touched the hair shirt and the halter round Sir Walter's neck. 'You have asked for absolution and absolution has been given. Nevertheless, every Friday you come into this maze and insist on walking on your knees to the centre to pray before the Weeping Cross.'

'It is only right,' Sir Walter replied, 'during the three hours of Christ's Passion. I do it as an act of atonement.'

'Is that why you bought Ingoldby?' Father John teased, trying to lighten the situation. 'Because of this maze and its Weeping Cross? I much preferred it when you knelt in front of a crucifix in some chapel.'

Sir Walter lifted his head and strained to hear the faint conversation between Thurston and Gurnell, the laughter of his wife and Eleanora, the lilt of the flute.

'You should be with them,' Father John urged. 'Enjoy your wife, celebrate your life. Put away these gloomy thoughts.' The priest steepled his fingers. 'You had to flee Constantinople, likewise the massacre of the Provencales at Towton was not your fault. Constantinople fell nineteen years ago, Towton is well over a decade in the past. Forget such things.'

'And the Athanatoi?' Sir Walter glared at his chaplain.

'The Athanatoi may call themselves that name.' Father John smiled. 'But they're not real. I doubt if they come from Constantinople. It's a cruel joke perpetrated by people who have studied your past. The good Lord only knows how many deeply envy your good fortune.'

'But the proclamations?' Sir Walter protested. 'Posted on the market cross in Canterbury, not to mention that nailed to the door of the cathedral itself!'

'Cruel acts,' Father John said. 'The twisted jape of some malicious jester. Now, Sir Walter, I will hear your confession though I know that it'll be no different from last Friday. *In Nomine Patris et Filii. . . .*' The priest made the sign of the cross and Sir Walter followed suit.

'Bless me, Father, for I have sinned. It is a week since my last confession.'

Father John placed his hand gently on Sir Walter's bowed head and stared despairingly at the green privet across the narrow lane. He was beginning to hate this place. He wished he could leave, yet he was genuinely frightened for the health of his lord's mind. Sir Walter was so businesslike in many ways: a generous, compassionate man, a brave warrior, skilful in council but, when it came to his past . . .

Father John listened to the litany of petty sins and half-smiled. Ingoldby Hall was a paradise with its marble floored chambers, rich fields and fragrant gardens. Sir Walter had come here just after the war and bought it immediately. Was it because of this maze? These tortuous, narrow paths winding through yards of thick green privet? Only Sir Walter knew the way. On one occasion Sir Walter had taken him, twisting and turning, to the centre. Father John had found it a dizzying experience; the paths seemed to go nowhere, the hedges closed in like a trap.

'A man could become lost here,' he'd declared.

Sir Walter had merely smiled. At last they had reached the Weeping Cross, a tall, wooden crucifix, fitted into a stone plinth at the top of three stone steps and surrounded by a pebble-dashed path. Sir Walter had knelt on the step like some pilgrim before the holy sepulchre in Jerusalem. Father John believed the maze represented Sir Walter's soul, a desolate search to find peace.

'Father, I have finished.'

'Of course you have.' The priest smiled.

'And my penance?'

Father John was tempted to order him back to Ingoldby to enjoy a tub of hot water and a cup of chilled Rhenish wine, to join his wife and sing a canticle, yet Sir Walter was stubborn.

'Say three Aves,' the priest whispered, 'and the Salve Regina but, for God's sake man, find peace! Now, I absolve thee from thy sins.' Father John made the sign of the cross. He hoped Sir Walter might stay and talk but the knight was intent on the ritual.

'It must be noon,' he murmured. 'I must be at the Weeping Cross. Tonight, Father, seeing it's the feast of the Transfiguration tomorrow, we'll feast well. Perhaps the Lady Elizabeth will sing?'

'I hope so.'

The priest made to put his hand on Sir Walter's shoulder but the knight, clutching his Ave beads, was already shuffling off on his knees up the grassy path. Father John watched him go, barefooted, that damn halter about his neck. Father John made the sign of the cross, wiped away a tear from his eye and made his way back to the entrance. He did not like to linger here. He was always fearful that he might take a wrong turning, even though the distance was so short, and be caught up in the dark greenness. He glanced once more at his master now lost in his own Via Dolorosa. How did Sir Walter know the way? Did he have a map? Father John looked after the library and had discovered no trace, either there or amongst Sir Walter's private manuscripts. The priest shrugged and made his way out of the maze. Gurnell was squatting on the grass, dressed only in a white linen shirt and dark green breeches pushed into riding boots on which spurs jingled, his war belt slung on the ground beside him. A little distance away were the four men-at-arms wearing the dark blue and gold livery of Maltravers. Thurston, the Manciple, dressed like a friar in his brown robe, was already waddling back to the house. Father John stretched and stared across the broad green meadow to the right of the maze, where Lady Elizabeth and Eleanora sat deep in the flower-ringed bower which stood near the tree-fringed edge of the great meadow, heads together, chattering and whispering. Father

John narrowed his eyes. Eleanora was Lady Elizabeth's lifelong companion.

'More of a sister than a maid,' the lady of the manor had described her.

Father John found Eleanora personable enough, though he often wondered how she and her mistress found so much to talk about.

'Is Sir Walter well?' Gurnell called out.

Father John walked across and stood over the captain of the retinue. Gurnell was a youngish man who claimed to be of Scottish extraction, thickset with thinning blond hair and a rubicund, polished face, a laughing mouth, snub nose and mischievous dark eyes. Father John liked him; from conversations with Sir Walter he knew that Gurnell was not to be judged by his looks. 'A born master-of-arms' was how Sir Walter described him. 'A fighter who likes nothing better than the tang of blood and the sound of battle.' A mercenary who had seen service abroad in the French wars, Gurnell had joined the household two years ago and proved himself to be a faithful retainer.

'The master is well.' Father John smiled. 'But I wish he was at peace.' He took off his stole and kissed the gold embroidery and folded it neatly. 'I don't think he'll find peace at the centre of that maze.'

As Father John returned to his beloved library, Sir Walter continued on his self-imposed pilgrimage. He moved slowly, now and again pausing to whisper verses from the gospel such as, 'Jesus fell for the first time.' He moved on: the lanes became narrower. The hedges seemed to rise like walls blocking out the sun and sky but Sir Walter did not care.

'*Miserere Mei Domine,*' he prayed.

Today the journey seemed to take an eternity as the sounds from the meadow receded. Sir Walter was no longer journeying towards the cross but back down the passage of years to that group of bloodsoaked men standing beside their Emperor under his imperial banner. The image changed to that frozen copse on Towton's bloody battlefield. Sir Walter returned to his prayers. He only half thought of where he was going; he knew the plan of this maze so well it always came as a surprise when he broke free and gazed up at the Weeping Cross. Sir Walter blessed himself and, allowing the pebbles to graze his knees, he lurched over towards the bottom step. He would first pray for those who had died at Constantinople.

'Out of the depths have I cried to thee, Oh Lord!'

For some strange reason he paused as he remembered the Lacrima Christi. Was its disappearance a sign of God's anger? He heard a sound and lifted his head.

'That's impossible!'

He turned and glimpsed the hooded figure, but Sir Walter only had a few seconds of life left. The sharp, two-edged axe cut through his neck, shearing off his head as easily as a maid would snip a flower.

Chapter 1

"And on a Friday fil al this meschaunce."
—Chaucer, "The Nun's Priest's Tale,"
The Canterbury Tales, 1387

Kathryn Swinbrooke stood fascinated by the wall painting just near the corpse door in Greyfriars Church: a group of yellow geese clustered round a scaffold, ready to hang a russet and black fox. The itinerant artist had painted the scene in vigorous dashes and brilliant hues. The more Kathryn studied the geese, the more they seemed like fat, pompous burgesses about to hang a rather hapless-looking felon. Whoever had commissioned it wanted to teach the lesson that the world could be turned upside down and nothing was what it seemed to be.

'True, true.' Kathryn murmured. 'And it never is.'

'Do you think the geese will ever hang the fox? I mean, in this vale of tears?'

Kathryn turned and stared up into the brown, weatherbeaten face of Colum Murtagh, King's Commissioner in Canterbury and Keeper of the royal stables at Kingsmead. Colum Murtagh, Irish warrior, courtier and her beloved! Their vows had been exchanged, the ring bought and the day fixed; on Saturday the feast of St. Bernard, they would confirm their vows outside the church door and become man and wife.

'We were supposed to visit the market this morning.' He touched her face gently.

Kathryn pressed her hand against Colum's brown leather jerkin, her fingers falling to the buckle of his war belt. She peered closer at the white linen shirt open at the neck revealing a silver cross on a golden chain.

'You should have a silver chain for a silver cross,' she murmured. 'But that's my Irishman, nothing ever matches.' She glanced down; his bottle-green leather breeches were mud-stained. She laughed, stepped back. 'Those boots aren't a proper pair.'

'What!' Colum scratched his black tousled hair and shuffled his feet.

'Irishman, you are not even awake! Wrong boots, and your dagger sheath's empty.' She stepped closer and smiled. 'Are you in love, Colum?' She traced the stubble on his cheek. 'Did you sleep deeply and dream of me?'

Colum pulled a face, his deepset eyes twinkling in amusement; they were still heavy with sleep and Kathryn couldn't resist her teasing.

'It was Thomasina.' Colum yawned. 'Chattering like a magpie and dressed like one, in black and white, that's all I can remember this morning, Thomasina whirling round the kitchen like a tempest.'

'She's nervous,' Kathryn murmured as her gaze returned to the painting on the wall.

Colum Murtagh rubbed his face and studied Kathryn out of the corner of his eyes. He had worked hard the previous day training a young stallion out at the stables. Full of fire and light, the horse had a mind of its own. As do you, Colum thought. Sometimes he felt nervous about Kathryn. She was not hot tempered or sharp in speech, it was more her serenity. She stood there, garbed in a dark blue dress with white bands round the neck and cuffs, sensible brown leather walking shoes on her feet; her black hair was combed back and hidden behind a starched white veil which fell down to her shoulders. The veil, braided with small Ave beads, framed Kathryn's face, emphasizing her large, lustrous eyes, the creamy texture of her skin and that mouth which he loved to kiss, now so tight-lipped. She was looking at the painting but her mind was apparently elsewhere. Kathryn shifted her gaze and winked at Colum.

'A beautiful church.'

She moved away further down the nave to the door of the chantry chapel of St. Michael and stared through the grille. The silver chain still hung from the ceiling, its hook-clasp empty. Both the receptacle and the lustrous ruby it once held were gone as if they were plumes of smoke. Kathryn closed her eyes and breathed in, savouring the fragrant smells.

'Quite a mystery.' Colum came up beside her.

Kathryn walked around the three-sided chantry chapel. The wooden screens soared up, each side covered with carved scenes from the bible: Mary and Joseph on a tired-looking donkey fleeing to Egypt, angels hovering above them. Christ being tempted by Satan. An angel offering Christ a chalice during his agony in Gethsamene. Kathryn caressed the wood as she walked round.

'As hard as iron!' she exclaimed. She tapped the floor, examining the dark grey flagstones.

'Some secret entrance?' Colum asked.

'Perhaps.' Kathryn shook her head. 'Though I think not.' She stood back, gesturing with her hands. 'Here we have, Colum, a stout box built in the side of the church, three sides wood, the fourth being the stone wall overlooking the cloister garth. We have already examined that, hard stone with a stained glass window, not a crack or peep exists. Inside, three thick oaken screens. The only possible way into that chapel is through this door.'

Kathryn walked closer, kicking aside her cloak which she had laid on the floor. She peered through the wooden grille, then examined the iron clasps at the top and bottom of the door as well as the heavy lock, the work of some craftsman from the city.

'According to reports,' she sighed, 'the Lacrima Christi was on display yesterday. Prior Barnabas and Brother Ralph the infirmarian kept the vigil before it between Vespers and Compline. During that time the Lacrima Christi was stolen.'

'It could be that thief.' Colum yawned. 'The one crouched like a mouse in the Mercy Chair. He's a pickpocket, he sought sanctuary.'

Kathryn laughed. 'I have met Laus Tibi! He's good at filching purses and pockets but no, this is beyond him. It's too subtle.'

She broke off as the door leading to the cloister was thrown open. Luberon, the kind but pompous clerk to both the Corporation and the Archbishop of Canterbury, came waddling in with all the power he could muster. One hand grasped his writing satchel, the other fingered the gold chain round his neck. He was dressed in a cote-hardie of dark murrey and the way he waddled reminded Kathryn of an angry duck. Luberon's round, shaven face was slightly red, his protuberant eyes even more popping, whilst his snub nose wrinkled like a ferret smelling a rat. Shoulders twitching with annoyance, he glared officiously at Kathryn. He banged the heel of his boot against the floor.

'At last!' he trumpeted. 'They've come!'

'Mistress Swinbrooke, we were delayed.' Prior Barnabas, pushing back his cowl, came round the clerk to greet them.

'The brethren were in a meeting,' he explained. 'We cannot be summoned like boys from a school hall.'

'Father Prior, it's good to see you.'

'And this is Brother Ralph my infirmarian.'

The second friar was a short, pasty-faced young man, his sandy hair cropped close. Kathryn noticed how his fingers were stained with yellow and blue and she wondered what potions the infirmarian had been mixing. Something poisonous? The ring finger on each hand was sheathed in leather; herbalists and apothecaries used these fingers to mix noxious substances.

Prior Barnabas coughed and Kathryn shifted her gaze to his harsh face. A kindly man, she thought, but a strict disciplinarian, with his beaklike nose, prim mouth and hard eyes. Prior Barnabas's face and hands were darkened by the sun. A friar, she thought, who had spent some time in Outremer, perhaps the Holy Land? Or one of the Order's houses in Provence or Sicily?

'I . . .' Prior Barnabas jangled the ring of keys he held. 'I am not too sure why . . . ?'

'I have explained once,' Luberon intervened.

'Then explain again!' Prior Barnabas snapped.

'I'll do that,' Colum offered.

He undid his war belt and laid it on the floor. Prior Barnabas tutted in annoyance, as weapons were not to be worn in church.

'My name is Colum Murtagh. I am King's Commissioner in Canterbury.'

'But the theft of the Lacrima Christi . . . ?'

'The theft of the ruby,' Colum interrupted tersely, 'is a matter for the Crown. The Archbishop and city council have decided that. It was on loan from Sir Walter Maltravers.'

'And he's a member of the King's Council,' Prior Barnabas added wearily. The Prior's gaze shifted to Kathryn. 'I know you, Master Murtagh but . . . ?'

'Mistress Swinbrooke is a physician and an apothecary of the city,' Luberon gabbled. 'She holds an indenture with the Archbishop and with the Crown. She, too, is commissioned to investigate certain matters.'

Prior Barnabas had taken an apparent dislike to Luberon, and jangled his keys noisily.

'Father Prior.' Kathryn stepped closer. 'The Lacrima Christi has been stolen, that is what is important.'

'But how?' The Prior's face relaxed. He gazed at Kathryn. 'Mistress, follow me.'

He walked across to the chantry chapel of St. Michael, pulled back the bolts, inserted a key and turned the lock. The door opened smoothly. They followed him inside. Kathryn looked around. The three wooden screens were carved in the same manner as outside. The door was thick and heavy and hung on four leather hinges, riveted to the lintel. The stone wall behind the altar had been whitewashed, a painting of an adoring angel on either side of the silver crucifix which stood in the centre of the altar. Above this the large door-shaped window was full of brilliant stained glass depicting Michael the Archangel's victory over Satan.

'The walls are secure,' she murmured.

Kathryn knelt down. The entire floor, as well as the altar steps, were covered with ruby red Turkey rugs neatly stitched together to cover every inch of the floor. Kathryn relished the carpeting's warm softness and the thickness of its texture; a quick glance told her that this had not been disturbed. She went and stood on the bottom altar step and examined the silver chain. This hung at eye level and rose up into the darkness where it was fastened to a clasp in the wooden roof.

'This is beautiful in itself,' she whispered.

The chain was finely wrought. She touched the tip of the hook on which the receptacle had hung. It was strong, the point of the hook sharp.

'Prior Barnabas?' she asked. 'The ruby?'

'It was placed in a golden receptacle, the same colour as itself,' the Prior explained. He demonstrated with his hand, finger and thumb extended. 'There was a backing, a piece at the top and a piece at the bottom. The ruby was wedged in between, then hung on that silver chain, clearly displayed for those who wished to pay their devotion.'

'And the ruby itself?' Kathryn asked.

'About the size of a large pigeon egg. It weighed just over four ounces,' Prior Barnabas explained. 'After Matins,' he continued, 'the ruby was removed from its coffer.' He pointed to the iron-bound chest just within the doorway.

Kathryn went and crouched down to look. The coffer was of the hardest wood reinforced with steel bands, and had two locks.

'The coffer can only be opened,' Prior Barnabas explained, 'by myself and one other brother: each lock is different.'

'So, the ruby was put on display after Matins?' Kathryn touched the box. 'And placed back here just before Compline?'

The Prior agreed.

'But last night?'

'The Lacrima Christi was there,' Brother Ralph squeaked before clearing his throat. 'It was there, I saw it. I went back to my prie-dieu, Prior Barnabas was with me. I prayed for a while then I got up once more to look at it. It glowed in the dark, like a mysterious fire. It was ruby-red.' He smiled. 'Well, of course, it would be but there was a darker red inside, two jewels in one.'

'Why did Sir Walter Maltravers lend it to you?'

Prior Barnabas spread his hands. 'Sir Walter is a good friend to the city churches. The ruby, I believe, came from Constantinople. Sir Walter never explained how it came into his possession. Anyway, last spring he came here to celebrate the Maundy Mass. I explained we had no relic; by then I knew about the Lacrima Christi. Sir Walter kindly agreed that, during the pilgrimage season, the sacred ruby could be displayed at Greyfriars for the benefit of the faithful.'

'And you have told Sir Walter of its loss?'

'I sent the messenger myself but Sir Walter will not be disturbed on a Friday.' Prior Barnabas blinked. 'Tomorrow, I fear, I will face his wrath. Yet it is not our fault.'

Kathryn got to her feet and walked back to the silver chain.

'How did you know Sir Walter owned the Lacrima Christi? He did not proclaim it to the city?'

'I discovered that,' Brother Ralph said proudly. 'Just after the feast of the Epiphany. Sir Walter fell ill, he asked for certain powders. I spent three days at Ingoldby Hall. He'd suffered a bad attack of stomach cramps. Anyway, Sir Walter showed me his manor. It contains a small chapel to Mary the Virgin. He opened his coffers and I saw the Lacrima Christi. I have never seen anything so beautiful. Sir Walter was very pleased with my medication. I gave him a herbal potion distilled from bilberries and explained the benefits of eating fruit with each meal.'

Kathryn smiled; the infirmarian was apparently a skilled leech and apothecary.

'So, he loaned the Lacrima Christi out of friendship?'

'You could say so,' Prior Barnabas intervened. 'He said we could hold the ruby from the feast of St. Mary Magdalene until Michaelmas when it had to be returned.'

'And now it has gone?' Colum asked. 'Will your Order pay compensation?'

'How can we?' Prior Barnabas sat on the altar steps and stared up at his visitors. 'We kept it secure. We guarded it. And there's the legend . . .'

'What legend?' Luberon snapped, coming to stand over the Prior. 'What legend's this?'

Kathryn leaned across and tapped the clerk on the shoulder, gesturing with her head that he stand back. Luberon forced a smile and did so. He just didn't like these friars. He carried the Archbishop's commission and he resented having to click his heels before this austere Prior.

'There is a legend,' Prior Barnabas laced his fingers together, 'that when our Saviour was scourged at the pillar he wept bitterly. His bloody sweat and tears fell to the ground, so sacred they formed precious stones which were later collected by an angel.' He ignored Luberon's sharp bark of laughter. 'According to the legend, each of these tears will be gathered up by God's own messengers.'

'And you think that happened here?' Luberon could not help himself. 'Are you saying St. Michael came down and whisked it off to Heaven?'

'What other explanation is there?' Prior Barnabas riposted. 'Master clerk, look around this sanctuary chapel, gaze at the floor, stare at the roof, the window; there is no secret entrance. Put Brother Ralph and myself on oath.' He gestured at the door. 'No one came through that door yet the ruby has gone. The Lacrima Christi has disappeared.' The Prior got to his feet. He winced, rubbed his right thigh and swayed slightly. 'I am sorry,' he muttered. 'But, as you grow older,' he smiled, 'the body protests.'

'Have you talked to that thief?' Brother Ralph asked.

'We have,' Kathryn and Colum chorused together. 'Laus Tibi saw nothing untoward,' Kathryn added. 'He could not have been involved in this mischief.'

'Mischief?' Prior Barnabas's head shot forward like a chicken's, the muscles on his scrawny neck tight. 'Mischief!'

Kathryn stood her ground. 'I don't believe, Father Prior, that St. Michael swooped into this chapel and stole the ruby. If the good Lord wanted a precious stone, I doubt he'd steal it from a church.'

Again Luberon laughed.

'This chapel was robbed,' Kathryn continued more softly, 'by a subtle thief who planned his mischief and carried it through. Now, in the hours before the Lacrima Christi went missing, did anything suspicious happen? Come, come, Father Prior.' Kathryn placed her hand over his. 'You are a priest, a theologian. Ignore the legends: this is the work of man, not God.'

The Prior relaxed.

'I just don't know,' he shook his head, 'how I am going to explain this to Sir Walter. But, Mistress, nothing suspicious happened. The pilgrims come in, they pass by the grille, they place a coin in our sack. Some stay to light a candle at Our Lady's altar, some want to gossip, others cluster round the rood screen when we sing Divine Office. Sir Walter came.' Prior Barnabas glanced up. 'Yes, Sir Walter and his chaplain Father John. They came here late yesterday afternoon. Sir Walter insisted on being treated like any other pilgrim. He paid a silver coin and stared through the grille. The only thing I noticed was, when he walked away, he was crying. He tried to hide it but I could see him wipe his cheeks. Father John was patting him on the arm as if to comfort him.'

'And you don't know the reason why?'

Prior Barnabas stared at this young woman's eyes. How old was she, he wondered? In her 24th, 25th summer? He racked his memory. And hadn't she been married? There was a story but he had forgotten it. Prior Barnabas, despite his bluster, felt uneasy. Were Mistress Swinbrooke's eyes blue or grey? Her gaze was certainly steady. She looked soft and graceful yet he suspected this masked a steely nature and sharp wits. Prior Barnabas hid his own nervousness.

'Well, Father?'

Prior Barnabas swallowed hard.

'I know nothing, Mistress, of Sir Walter's mood.'

'This thief?' Colum walked to the door of the chantry chapel. 'With the strange name?'

'Laus Tibi's a pickpocket, a cutpurse,' the Prior explained. 'Terrified out of his wits.'

'I can see why.' Colum spoke over his shoulder. 'There are bailiffs camped outside every door of this church.'

'The Mayor is determined,' Luberon spoke up, 'that the pilgrim trade does not suffer from felons and thieves. The bailiffs want Laus Tibi hanged as a warning to the rest.'

'He'll stay here the forty days,' Prior Barnabas explained. 'We'll give him some food and a crucifix. He'll take an oath to abjure the realm and walk to Dover.'

Colum stared across at a vivid wall painting depicting two demons raking the coals of Hell. Aye, he thought, and the poor bastard will never reach the port. Colum knew the law. If Laus Tibi left the King's highway he could be arrested and hanged out of hand, the bailiffs would see to that. Laus Tibi's only protection would be to join a band of pilgrims, but who would show him mercy?

'What would any thief do with the Lacrima Christi?' Colum asked.

'It might be sold abroad.' Luberon mopped his face with a dirty kerchief. 'Many would pay good silver for it.'

Kathryn stared up at the light coming through the window. She'd had a busy day with a long line of patients and pilgrims wishing to buy herbs and potions. She had helped Thomasina with the brewing. Wulf, the foundling boy, her little apprentice, had spent the day fighting with Agnes the maid. Kathryn really wanted to sit in the cool of her herb garden but Colum had been most insistent that she came here. She glanced at the two friars. Brother Ralph seemed uneasy.

'I am sorry I couldn't come earlier,' Kathryn apologised. 'But Master Murtagh was out at King's Mead and I had many patients. Did anything else happen on the day the jewel was stolen?'

'We did close the shrine,' Father Barnabas explained, 'between the hours of two and four o'clock in the afternoon. The number of pilgrims declined due to the heat of the day.'

'And the Lacrima Christi?' Kathryn asked.

'It was put back in its coffer in the presence of a number of the brothers.'

'And taken out in the same company,' Brother Ralph added.

'Why?' Kathryn asked. 'Was that usual?'

'Tomorrow is the feast of the Transfiguration,' Prior Barnabas explained. 'The following day is Sunday, with Masses until well after noon.'

'And?' Kathryn asked.

'We decided to close the church for two hours so the brothers could sweep and clean in preparation for the great feast as well as for the Masses on Sunday.'

'But during that time the Lacrima Christi was locked away?'

'It was locked in the coffer,' Prior Barnabas confirmed. 'This chantry chapel was also cleaned. Afterwards the door was locked, bolted and guarded by two of our lay brothers.' He half-smiled. 'Each armed with a stout cudgel.'

'And you rehung the ruby?'

'At about four o'clock. Let me explain, just wait.'

Prior Barnabas left the chantry chapel and hurried off up the nave, leaving his visitors nonplussed.

'I think he's gone to fetch the sacristan,' Brother Ralph stammered.

Prior Barnabas returned, Simon the sacristan beside him, red-faced and out of breath.

'Explain to Mistress Swinbrooke,' the Prior said, 'how the chantry chapel was secured.'

'Oh, very easy.' Brother Simon drew himself up, pleased to lecture these important visitors. 'Before the Lacrima Christi arrived, I hired a locksmith, a craftsman from the city. He fashioned a new lock for the chantry chapel. It's very intricate and cannot be copied, nor can the keys . . .'

'Who is this craftsman?' Luberon demanded.

'Thibault Arrowsmith in Culpeper Lane.'

'Ah yes.' Kathryn smiled. 'Thibault is a Guild Master. You mentioned keys?'

'Yes,' Brother Simon agreed, 'I did. Two keys: one is held in trust by Master Thibault, the other by me.' He pursed his lips. 'I handed that to Father Prior to open and lock the chantry door, and he would immediately hand it back. The opening, locking and handing over the key was always witnessed by myself and other members of the community.'

'And after four o'clock yesterday when the Lacrima Christi was rehung, that key was always with you?'

'Secured by a metal clasp,' the sacristan agreed. 'It was seen by other members of the community. Prior Barnabas had to send for me to unlock the door when the Lacrima Christi went missing.'

'You are sure?'

'Mistress, I know what I know. After the chantry chapel was

locked, I kept that key very safe.' Brother Simon smirked. 'And, before you ask, I've visited Master Thibault: the other key has never left its strong box, I've seen it myself. Master Thibault never visited the Lacrima Christi, whilst he said he'd go on oath before the Council, those keys couldn't be copied.'

Kathryn nodded: Thibault was a craftsman, the lock and keys to the chantry would be unique whilst it was common practice to have one key held in the strongbox of its maker. She stared up towards the rood screen. She needed to think, reflect.

'May I . . . ?'

Kathryn's question was interrupted by a figure bursting through the half-open main door to the church.

'Mistress Swinbrooke! Mistress Swinbrooke!'

Rawnose the beggar, arms and legs flying, rags flapping, hands flailing, hurtled up the nave like a man possessed. His disfigured face was red and sweaty. Kathryn noticed with amusement that he had forgotten both his limp and his crutch.

'Ah, Mistress Swinbrooke.' Rawnose sank to his knees like a supplicant before an altar. 'Oh, Mistress Swinbrooke, thanks be to God I have found you! A messenger has come to Ottemelle Lane looking for Master Murtagh and . . .'

'What is it, Rawnose?' Kathryn crouched down.

The beggar man scratched the large scar on his nose, blinked his watery eyes and rubbed his beer-sodden face.

'Mistress Swinbrooke,' he breathed, 'Master Murtagh, horrible murder!'

Kathryn's heart skipped a beat.

'Oh no, not in Ottemelle Lane,' Rawnose breathed out, and Kathryn flinched at the stench of ale. 'A messenger from Ingoldby Hall was sent by Father John, Sir Walter's chaplain. Sir Walter has been beheaded.' Rawnose's eyes widened at the exclamations of those standing around. The beggarman relished his importance before such an audience. 'Hideously hewn.' He stumbled on the words. 'Head shorn off his shoulders, his blood-soaked corpse still lies at the centre of the maze.' He leaned closer. 'And the head's gone!'

Kathryn told him to calm down. Colum was already refastening his sword belt. Luberon was clicking his tongue and shaking his head in disbelief. At last Kathryn obtained the facts. A servant had come from Ingoldby Hall with the horrid news. Thomasina had sent him back and given Rawnose a penny to bring the news to Kathryn. She patted the tufts of hair on the beggarman's head, opened her purse and pushed a coin into his hand.

'Drink if you must, Rawnose, but eat a hearty meal.' She got to her feet. 'Prior Barnabas, I have other business to attend to.'

The Prior, lost in his own reverie, simply nodded.

'But I was out there,' Brother Ralph declared. 'I went out to Ingoldby Hall this morning to convey Father Prior's apologies. . . .'

'Did you see Sir Walter?'

The infirmarian shook his head. 'No, I was told he was busy, that he was not to be disturbed on a Friday afternoon, so I came back. Oh, *Kyrie Eleison,*' he prayed. 'Oh Lord, have mercy.'

Colum was already striding down the church, Luberon padding behind like a faithful mastiff. Kathryn made her farewells and joined them out near the lych-gate. Rawnose followed and pointed to the bailiffs camped among the gravestones.

'I don't like the look of them,' he muttered.

Kathryn agreed. The bailiffs looked tough, bully boys hired by the Pie Powder Court to enforce good order in the market. There would be a bounty on Laus Tibi's head and these men were determined to collect it. Kathryn shooed Rawnose away and stood with Luberon in the shade of the lych-gate. She heard the door of the church being closed behind them.

'Strange,' Luberon mused. 'First the Lacrima Christi disappears, now its owner has been foully murdered.'

'Do you know anything of Sir Walter?' Kathryn asked.

'A soldier, a crusader.' Luberon shrugged. 'But otherwise . . .'

He started to chatter about Ingoldby Hall and its spacious estates. How Sir Walter had bought it over two years ago. How his wife was a great beauty. He was still chattering when Colum returned with the horses. They mounted and, with Colum leading the way, rode down towards the city lanes to Southgate. The sun was beginning to set. From the bells of the city Kathryn reckoned it must be six o'clock in the evening. Traders and merchants were putting away their stalls. Heavy-eyed apprentices, their throats raw with shouting all day, were busy drinking and relaxing in the shade. Kathryn found it hard to concentrate on the mystery of the Lacrima Christi or this hideous murder. Now and again the lanes became clogged with carts as farmers and peasants made their way home after a good day's trading. Pilgrims from Thomas à Becket's shrine and other holy places were either returning to their hostelries or going down to the green banks of the river Stour to enjoy the evening breezes. A prostitute, caught soliciting during the market hours, was standing in the stocks, a placard round her neck on which the words "Laced Mutton" were scrawled. A man accused of breaking the peace was fastened to a door-hatch next to the stocks. Nearby, a *chaunter pleur*—a travelling musician—sang the most sorrowful songs and wept at the same time. He faced stiff competition from a sly-eyed rat-rhymer who had memorised doggerel poetry and was bawling out the lines whilst a boy went round to solicit pennies from anyone who bothered to listen. Kathryn kept her eyes down. Luberon tried to push his horse up beside her and chatter but the lane was too narrow and few people were prepared to give way. Kathryn glimpsed the sharp white face of a Dominican preacher peeping out from a black cowl, and this jogged her memory. Who, she wondered, had been responsible for that robbery at Greyfriars? And how had it been done? Two knights, their leather jerkins stained with sweat, made their way up from the tourney ground; behind ran their squires, leading pack ponies from which their armour and weapons dangled. Men-at-arms, in quilted jerkins, roistered outside ale houses, cheering at a drunken woman who danced to the beat of a tambour whilst the ale wife fixed a corn cross under the eaves as protection against evil spirits.

At last they reached the city gates. The crowd thronged about, and the din and noise were deafening. People shouted farewells. Pedlars and chapmen tried to catch the eye of customers. Three bailiffs bundled out a group of roisterers, forbidding them to stay in the city after nightfall. At one point Colum had to produce his royal commission and demand that people step aside. They continued on, houses on either side, the noise fading—then they were into the countryside, following the twisting, rutted tracks. Kathryn had often travelled this way to Dover. Now it was full summer, the time of the harvest; she relished the cool breeze and the different shades of green.

'We should come here more often,' she called out. 'Eh, Irishman? Some wine, some dried meat and bread?' She glanced slyly at Luberon. 'You can come too, Simon.'

The little clerk just blushed and flicked away some mud from his cloak.

'They are bringing the harvest in,' Kathryn declared.

In the fields on either side of the trackway, men, women and children worked, taking full advantage of the beautiful weather. The men worked with their scythes, the women and children tossing and raking, or running backwards and forwards with the glee-cup to the water wagon.

'How many miles?' she asked.

'About three,' Colum replied over his shoulder. He reined in and stared up at the overhanging branches of the great oak tree. 'It is good to be away from the city. To feel the sun and breeze, eh? They say this weather will last long, though we'll pay for it with a harsh winter.'

'So speaks the voice of doom,' Kathryn retorted.

Colum laughed and, digging his heels in, moved on. They reached the crossroads, past the black-tarred, empty gibbet and along the track leading to Ingoldby Hall. They arrived at its high, redbrick curtain wall and followed this round to the main gates. These were shut and guarded by armed retainers under a master-of-arms, a cropped-haired, stern-faced man in a black leather jerkin with a war belt strapped across his chest. He apparently recognised Colum from what he called 'the war years' and shook the Irishman's hand.

'This, Mistress Swinbrooke, is Gurnell,' Colum explained. 'A good soldier and a reasonable swordsman.'

The two men engaged in banter until Gurnell remembered himself.

'You'd best go on.'

They went through the gates and up the winding path lined by ancient sycamores onto the smooth green field stretching in front of the manor house. Ingoldby Hall was built of grey stone under a black slate roof; it rose three stories high, a majestic mansion with its pointed gables, mullioned glass and elegant bay windows. Already the servants were proclaiming the death of their master. Some of these windows were open and black drapes hung out. The main entrance door, reached by a flight of steps, also had black cloth pinned to it with ashes strewn on either side.

'A wealthy place,' Kathryn murmured.

'It's really four houses in all,' Luberon explained, 'each constructed round a central courtyard. The first owner fought with Henry the Fifth at Agincourt and built Ingoldby with a war chest full of ransom money.'

'He must have captured many Frenchmen,' Colum joked, dismounting.

'War has its own profits,' Luberon quipped. 'There are fine oak galleries whilst the ground floor is of hard stone and tiled.'

Liveried servants hurried up to take their horses. The main doors opened and Manciple Thurston came out, his face tear-streaked, hands all a-flapping. Apparently distracted, he half-listened to Colum's instructions.

'Do you want refreshments? Do you want refreshments?' he spluttered. 'The mistress is within, but she is in her chamber. The shock, the brutality, oh so much blood!'

Kathryn grasped Thurston's hand; it was ice cold.

'You should drink some warm wine yourself,' she soothed. 'Now, sir, take us to this maze.'

The Manciple led them around the side of the house. They crossed a well laid out garden with stone benches, latticed fences, fountains, beehives and a dovecote: it boasted a herber and a small apple orchard, flower arbours and gaily decorated pavilions, all bound by a high wickerwork fence. They went through a side gate, along a path and round to the back of the house. Kathryn caught her breath: there was a bank, cut by steps in the centre, which ran down to a wide open meadow, as broad as any market place, circled by trees which rose darkly against the blue-red sky.

'This must have been the demesne,' Luberon murmured. 'The manor lord's own estate.'

The meadow was rich with lush grass. Kathryn reckoned it must be at least a mile wide and perhaps a little longer in breadth. In the centre stood the maze. Kathryn had never seen anything like it before. The maze rose like a dark green square, at least three yards high, each hedge as broad as any footpath in the city.

'The entire maze,' Luberon explained, 'covers a square ninety yards by ninety. The builder of Ingoldby Hall used box and hawthorn to create it.'

The Manciple started offering refreshments again but Kathryn, fascinated by the sight, went down the steps. She had heard of similar mazes in Normandy where French knights, unable to go on Crusade to Jerusalem, would build a maze and use it as a means of resolving their vows. Some would go through on their knees, dressed in sackcloth, heads stained with ash and dust. Others would stay at the centre of the maze for two or three days living on water and dry bread. She had been in stone mazes but these had been constructed as childish affairs, nothing like this.

Kathryn walked across the grass, Colum and Luberon hurrying behind her. A priest came out of the entrance to the maze. He was dressed in a simple robe of dark blue, a purple stole around his neck, ivory ave beads wrapped round his gnarled fingers. He had a tired, lined face, he spoke softly to the retainers, telling them to step aside.

'I am Father John.' He blinked red-rimmed eyes and tried to steady his voice. 'I am Sir Walter's chaplain.' He gazed at the sky. 'Soon it will be dark, the corpse is still there. I have told everyone else to stay away. Oh,' He forced a smile. 'You must be Mistress Swinbrooke and . . . ?'

Kathryn made the introductions.

'Come, come.'

The priest was intent on not wasting time. He led them into the maze. Kathryn swallowed hard, as she had a slight fear of confined places and, although it was a warm August evening with the sun still strong, these narrow tunnels and lanes possessed a quiet brooding menace. Now and again she would start as some bird burst from the thicket on either side of her. She stopped and pressed a hand against the hedge and realised how clever the gardeners had been who constructed this maze: crouching down, she had to almost press the side of her face against the ground to glimpse the roots.

'Oh yes.' Father John stood and watched her. 'The man who planted this maze knew what he was doing. The bushes are close together, so as they grew they interwove. You cannot tell one from the other. Have you seen the hedgerows in Normandy, Mistress? Sir Walter claimed they were better defence than a stone wall.'

Kathryn rose to her feet and brushed the grass from her gown.

'At least three yards high,' she murmured.

'And a yard wide,' Father John added.

'Could you walk along the top?' Kathryn asked.

'No, you'd have to use planks,' Father John explained. 'Or you'd sink in, and the branches are sharp.'

He walked on, giving Kathryn no choice but to follow. Luberon trotted, gasping and spluttering, after her, determined not to be left behind. Father John twisted and turned. Kathryn noticed how scuffed the grass was. She was going to ask how Father John knew the maze so well when Colum nudged her sharply and pointed to the ground. A coil of thick rope snaked along the path.

'Who put this down?' Kathryn asked.

'It was my idea,' Father John replied, not stopping. 'When the alarm was raised, nobody could find the centre. We had to use boards to cross the hedges and, once we reached the Weeping Cross, I ordered great coils of rope to be brought. We fastened them together and marked out the pathway; even then it took hours.'

Kathryn thought they'd never stop twisting and turning but, at last, one pathway led into a clearing. She glimpsed the cross, the steps and pebble-dashed path around it. The blood-caked cadaver lay like a bundle of soaked rags; here and there were footprints of splattered blood. Father John followed her gaze.

'I am sorry,' he muttered. 'When the servants found the corpse, they were upset, they didn't know . . .'

'Is that where it was found?' Kathryn asked, lifting the hem of her dress and moving round to stand close to Sir Walter's bare, grass-stained feet.

'It was pulled slightly back,' Father John said.

'I'd be grateful,' Kathryn gestured at the stone benches on either side of the entrance, 'if you'd sit down.'

As her companions did so Kathryn stared at the severed cadaver: the hair shirt was soaked in blood, its arms out, slightly twisted. She knelt and examined the vein-streaked legs. The flesh was cold, the muscles hardening. The soles of the feet were marked with pieces of grass and twigs. Pulling back the sleeves of her gown, Kathryn turned the corpse over and tried not to flinch as more blood seeped out. The entire front of the corpse was soaked in gore. Kathryn took out the small wooden scraper she always carried with her. Leaning forward carefully, she cleaned the blood-encrusted knee, examined the scraper and sighed at the little fragments of soil and stone. She got up, placed the wooden scraper by the corpse, and walked over to Father John.

'Tell me, chaplain, Sir Walter performed this ritual once a month?'

'No.' The priest shook his head. 'Whenever possible, every week at noon on a Friday, the hour on which Christ's Passion began. He would enter the maze dressed only in a hair shirt, a halter round his neck.'

'Halter?' Kathryn walked back and stared down. 'I can see no halter. It must have been taken with the head?'

Father John nodded. He was shaking slightly.

'Father John.' Kathryn crouched down and rested a hand on his knee. 'You are still filled with horror at your master's death, and this will affect both your wits and your heart. He was murdered. I need to know what happened.'

'Sir Walter came here every Friday.' The priest put his head in his hands; his voice sounded hollow. 'He was dressed in a hair shirt and halter, no sandals on his feet. He carried ave beads.' He pointed towards the corpse. 'They are still there somewhere about his person.'

Kathryn rose to her feet and stared back at the corpse.

'The cut is clean,' she half-whispered. 'The head was sheared off like an ear of corn. Sir Walter reached the cross.' She continued speaking her thoughts aloud. 'He knelt down just before the bottom step. He may have turned but the assassin took his head as easily as plucking an apple off a tree. . . .'

was making little sense of the mystery which confronted her. Colum lounged on a chair beside her. She felt a stab of envy, for his gaze kept going back to Lady Elizabeth Maltravers who sat opposite them in a gilt-edged, thronelike chair. Lady Elizabeth was truly beautiful. She was dressed in widow's weeds, a luxurious black gown which fell down to just above her ankles, her little feet sheathed in ornate purple slippers with silver buckles. She wore a black veil which emphasized the pallid beauty of her oval-shaped face, and her eyebrows were plucked, though it was the eyes which fascinated Kathryn, so blue, innocent, almost childlike. Lady Elizabeth had been crying but had now composed herself. She sat opposite, rosary beads wrapped round one hand, the other holding a Book of Hours in a purple, jewelled cover.

Kathryn could only guess at Lady Elizabeth's age. Certainly she was younger than Kathryn, no more than twenty-two summers: her marriage to Sir Walter must have been a May-December wedding. Kathryn quietly pinched herself at the envy which had prompted such a thought. The woman sitting on a footstool at Lady Elizabeth's feet was also fascinating. She, too, was dressed in black except for the white veil covering her hair. She was olive-skinned with large dark eyes and a full red mouth; her hair raven black. Was she English, Kathryn thought? Or of French or Italian extraction? She had the look of the daughter of the Moon people, those travellers who wandered the roads in their gaily coloured carts. She had been introduced as Lady Elizabeth's principal maid Eleanora; now she leaned protectively against her mistress's chair, one hand on the arm as if she was ever ready to clutch Lady Elizabeth's wrist. Kathryn had met the rest: Father John the chaplain, Thurston the Manciple, and Gurnell the master-at-arms, who sat flanking Lady Elizabeth. The only person who intrigued the physician was the white-faced, red-haired man who sat just behind the lady of the house: he had been introduced as Edward Mawsby, a distant kinsman of Maltravers who had acted as the dead lord's secretarius. Mawsby was definitely nervous: his long, white face, bloodless lips and watery green eyes betrayed his agitation. He sat, head bowed, plucking at a loose thread in his costly jerkin. Luberon, sitting on the far side of Colum, leaned over and picked up his goblet and slurped from it noisily, then returned the cup with such force that the wine slopped out. A faint smile crossed Lady Elizabeth's face. Mawsby's head went down. Colum breathed out loudly, the usual sign that the silence was becoming oppressive. Kathryn wanted that. Beyond those windows, across the fresh green meadow in the shadow of that sinister maze, Lord Maltravers had been killed, his head cut off like that of a common criminal. Someone in this room, intimately connected to Maltravers, must know more than they'd conceded: and she needed time to think, to reflect!

'Mistress Swinbrooke.' Lady Elizabeth's voice was soft and cultured. 'You keep staring about. If you wish, I can show you the rest of the house.' She smiled sadly. 'Even the King, when he visited here last summer, was greatly enchanted. He called it a fairy castle.'

'A beautiful place,' Kathryn agreed. 'But, my lady, one in which a hideous murder has taken place, though I cannot understand the how or why.'

Kathryn glanced sideways at Luberon, who had picked up his writing tray and was absentmindedly filling in one of the letters he had drawn.

'Your husband, Sir Walter, rose this morning,' Kathryn declared. 'He broke his fast, tended to some business and then, as he did on any Friday, just before noon, entered that maze to carry out a penance. Is that how you described it, Father John?'

'I have told you the truth,' the chaplain replied. 'And I find it difficult to repeat now my lord is dead. Sir Walter was born in Chepstow, he became a man-at-arms and fought in France, then, as mercenaries do, drifted across Europe. He fought with the Teutonic knights beyond the Rhine. He visited Cracow . . .'

'And finally entered Constantinople two years before the Turks laid siege to it?' Colum interrupted.

'Sir Walter,' Father John agreed, 'was a master swordsman, a strategist. He joined the Emperor's bodyguard, his personal retinue, and became an officer in the imperial household troops. You know the story? Constantinople was besieged and fell to the Turks. Sir Walter did his duty but was forced to escape; that is where I met him. The Byzantine Empire was finished. Constantinople was given over to pillage. Sir Walter and I seized certain treasures and fought our way out.' He paused to sip at his wine cup. 'Sir Walter journeyed to Italy. He campaigned with the Condottieri and made powerful friends in the banking houses of Milan and Padua.'

'Yes, yes.' Kathryn held up her hand. 'He then returned to England and attached his fortunes to those of the House of York. He fought for the King in the recent civil war and played a part in the great Yorkshire victory at Towton. About three years ago he bought Ingoldby Hall, the same year he married Lady Elizabeth.' Kathryn smiled. 'He had no enemies?'

'Rivals.' Lady Elizabeth turned slightly in her chair. She pointed to a shield fixed high above the fireplace displaying the arms and heraldic devices of Maltravers. 'Sir Walter was a powerful lord, he had rivals who were envious.'

'But the Athanatoi were different!' Kathryn gazed at Father John. 'According to you these were former officers of the household troops of the Emperor of Constantinople who were captured, sold into slavery but later ransomed.'

'That's the accepted story,' Father John replied, 'what I heard some ten years ago. But Europe's full of such fanciful tales.'

'These fanciful tales?' Kathryn insisted. 'Tell me again.'

'Since the fall of Constantinople,' Father John tried to keep his voice steady, 'the courts of Europe were rife with gossip about how the Emperor, who died on the walls of his city, was betrayed and abandoned. The survivors of his bodyguard allegedly took a sacred oath: they would keep their names and identities secret, but hunt down those they considered traitors.'

'And Sir Walter was considered one of these?' Colum asked.

'So the gossips said.'

'But they posed no threat to Sir Walter?'

'I think it was just idle chatter.' Father John shook his head. 'Chaff in the wind. Many people could not accept that Constantinople had fallen and looked for secret reasons. In truth, the city was weak, its power had shrunk whilst the might of the Turks could not be resisted. Sir Walter did his duty. He fought hard and bravely but he was only flesh and blood, not an angel from Heaven. Those treasures he brought from the ruined city he regarded as fair payment for his work.'

'So, these tales about the Athanatoi, "the Immortals," ' Kathryn gestured, 'were just rumours, gossip?'

The chaplain agreed.

'Until about a year ago,' Kathryn continued, 'when Sir Walter began to receive these threats?'

She picked up the strips of parchment from the table beside her. Each strip was made of two sections glued together and written in different hands. On the top one, an ominous salutation: "THE ATHANATOI SEND WARNING TO SIR WALTER MALTRAVERS, TRAITOR AND THIEF." The second part was a quotation from the scriptures: "THOU FOOL, THIS NIGHT THY SOUL SHALL BE REQUIRED OF THEE". Kathryn tapped it with her finger.

'This was the last one?'

'It was posted on the door of Canterbury Cathedral.' Gurnell spoke up. 'One of the monks found it early in the morning; another was fastened to the market cross.'

'Ah yes.' Kathryn picked up a further sheet of parchment consisting of two pieces glued together. The salutation was the same but the quotation was different: "THE WAGES OF SIN IS DEATH."

'And how many of these did Sir Walter receive?'

'In the last year,' Lady Elizabeth pushed away her footstool, 'about eight or nine. Some he destroyed.' She pointed at the parchment strips on the small wine table next to Kathryn. 'Others were kept.'

Kathryn collected these. The greeting was always the same, ending with a strange crudely drawn "A" which she recognised as the first letter of the Greek alphabet. They were written on the same type of parchment, the same ink, the same hand. The quotations were different; the parchment strip was more costly, the writing extremely neat like that of a professional scribe. She noticed how the quotation strips were the same length and breadth though they all carried different threats: "THE NIGHT COMETH, WHEN NO MAN CAN WORK." And "BE NOT DECEIVED: GOD IS NOT MOCKED. FOR WHAT A MAN SOWS HE ALSO SHALL REAP." "THE LOVE OF MONEY

IS THE ROOT OF ALL EVIL." "BEHOLD I STAND AT THE DOOR AND KNOCK." And, finally, from the Book of Revelation; "I LOOKED AND SAW A PALE HORSE AND THE NAME OF HIM THAT SAT ON IT WAS DEATH."

'They all imply a threat,' Kathryn remarked, 'that vengeance was coming, that Sir Walter had good cause to be afraid. Were they ever sent to the house?'

'Never!' Thurston the Manciple spoke up.

Kathryn could see that he had been drinking heavily; his speech was slurred.

'They appeared in different parts of the city.'

'Of course.' Kathryn intervened. 'Where they would be first seen by some official monk or priest and, of course, Sir Walter was a powerful man so they would be sent here immediately. Was Sir Walter frightened?'

'My husband feared nothing.' Lady Elizabeth's voice was clipped. 'Except damnation.'

'Was there any other threat?' Colum demanded. 'Any assault? Robbery?'

Silence greeted his words.

'So, nothing at all,' Kathryn concluded.

'Nothing.' Lady Elizabeth's voice was hard.

Kathryn watched Eleanora. She had sat like a statue but now she noticed how the lady-in-waiting slightly tapped her mistress's wrist as if to comfort and soothe her.

'Did Sir Walter discuss these threats?'

Lady Elizabeth shook her head.

'Yet he felt guilty?' Kathryn was determined to elicit the truth. 'He must have done, otherwise that penance every Friday?'

'Mistress Swinbrooke.' Father John joined his hands as if in prayer. 'Mistress Swinbrooke, Sir Walter was a good soldier, a christian man. He gave generously to the poor. He adorned churches. He did feel guilty about what had happened some nineteen years ago as well as killings carried out at the battle of Towton. He sometimes wondered if he should have died beside his Emperor, if he could have prevented later bloodshed. I advised him to accept God's will. The Friday penance was a way of Sir

Walter purging his soul. Just before noon he would enter the maze. I would hear his confession and shrive him. I do not wish to break the seal of the sacrament. However, I assure you Sir Walter had nothing on his conscience except the events of one day which occurred nineteen years ago and the massacre of some mercenaries at Towton during the civil war. He carried out his penance in a hair shirt, a halter round his neck. He would walk on his knees through that maze and pray before the Weeping Cross. He would then come back the same way.'

'But he only owned Ingoldby Hall for about three years?' Kathryn asked.

'True,' Father John replied. 'Before that Sir Walter performed his penance in a church or before a shrine; Our Lady's at Walsingham or St. Cuthbert's in Durham. During his military service, when possible, he would carry out his devotions in his tent or at whatever hostelry he was staying at, kneel before a crucifix and ask for God's forgiveness.'

'Do you think he bought Ingoldby Hall because of the maze?'

'I know he did.' Mawsby pulled his chair a little closer to Lady Elizabeth's. 'I took the indenture for its purchase and sent letters to Sir Walter's goldsmiths in London. My kinsman was greatly smitten by Ingoldby. A worthy residence for Lady Elizabeth, but, yes, I believe the maze was the reason Sir Walter paid the high price without demur or question.'

Kathryn smoothed out a crease in the folds of her gown. Luberon's pen was squeaking: he was making notes, not so much for her but the letter he would send to the Archbishop who, of course, would pass it on to the King. Once again she studied the people in the room. She had established a number of facts: first, Sir Walter was a very wealthy man but one riven with guilt. Second, he was a lonely man, although surrounded by his riches and married to a beautiful woman less than half his age. Third, he lived in the past. Perhaps the only person who really knew him was his chaplain. Fourth . . . Kathryn chewed the corner of her lip. She had attended many deaths, and found that sometimes the grief of relatives was unbearable. But there was a coldness here, a detachment, even from the chaplain, Father John. Lady Elizabeth was in mourning but not grief-stricken. Was this shock? Had they accepted Sir Walter's death and the horror which surrounded it? Or did they see it as something distant, separate? The result of Sir Walter's private demons?

'My husband was a lonely man.' Lady Elizabeth gazed beseechingly at Kathryn. 'I speak for all my household: Sir Walter was kind and generous but was often like a man lost in a dream.'

A murmur of agreement greeted her words.

'He was secretive,' she continued. 'One never knew what he was thinking. Sometimes, and I have spoken about this to Father John,' she blinked, 'I wonder if he wanted to die? As if he had supped deep of the cup of life and found it wanting?'

'Is that true, Father John?'

'Yes, yes.' The priest measured his words carefully. 'When I listened to his confession, I believed Sir Walter would have preferred to die in battle. During the King's recent campaigns—'

'I know what you are going to say,' Colum interrupted sharply. 'Sir Walter was always in the thick of the fighting.'

'Yet he did not wish to be murdered.' Kathryn made her voice decidedly harsh. 'Whether a man wishes to live or die is one truth, his murder is another. Sir Walter was barbarously murdered at the centre of that maze.'

Her words did not please Lady Elizabeth or her entourage. Father John made to protest but Lady Elizabeth made a cutting movement with her hand.

'And you think his assassin is in this house?'

'That could be another truth,' Kathryn replied. 'So, I must ask a very difficult question but one which the Archbishop or the King's Justices might ask. Who would profit from Sir Walter's death?'

Lady Elizabeth's head went down, and when she glanced up, red spots of fury showed on her cheeks. She gestured towards an elmwood chest.

'A copy of Sir Walter's will, although it has yet to be approved by Chancery, can be studied. I am his heir, Mistress Swinbrooke. Yet, I remind you that I am of the Redvers family, merchant princes of London and elsewhere. The dowry I brought to our marriage was considered to be a fortune. I did not need Sir Walter's wealth.'

'My lady, do not take offence, I did not say that. I asked a question: who profits?'

'The will,' Lady Elizabeth continued, fighting hard to control her temper, 'makes generous bequests to everyone in this room. But, there again, Mistress Swinbrooke, no one in this room had to wait for Sir Walter's death. You had only to ask; my husband's response was always generous.'

'I can vouch for that.' Mawsby spoke up. 'I fought for the House of Lancaster and had to flee abroad to Antwerp. Sir Walter arranged for a pardon to be issued and offered me employment.'

Colum abruptly sat up in his chair as if to study Mawsby more closely. Kathryn wondered if the red-haired, pale-faced man had been trying to hide, but from what?

'Very well.' Kathryn composed herself, knowing that the next questions would provoke even more hostility. 'Sir Walter entered the maze. He was shriven by Father John and made his lonely pilgrimage. Was he the only one who knew how to thread that maze?'

'The only one,' Father John confirmed. 'It was a mystery to us.'

'Fine,' Kathryn interposed. 'Sir Walter enters the maze. He should have returned, what, an hour later? But he did not. How was the alarm raised?'

'Sir Walter was a soldier,' Father John replied. 'When he finished his devotions before the Weeping Cross he always sounded the horn he kept there.'

'But no horn was found?' Colum asked.

'It has gone,' the chaplain replied.

'So, an hour or so after Sir Walter entered the maze . . . ?'

'I became concerned.' Gurnell spoke up. 'I heard no horn. I carry one as well. If something important happened I would sound the horn to alert Sir Walter.'

'So, about two hours after midday.' Kathryn paused. 'Yes, it would be about then, wouldn't it, that the alarm was raised?'

'I tried to enter the maze,' Gurnell confessed. 'But Father John said it was futile. You've been through it, Mistress. The lanes twist and turn. You could become lost for days. Lady Elizabeth was informed. I sounded the horn time and again but there was no answer, so Father John had wooden boards brought from the stable and laid them across the top of the hedges. At first it was difficult but, I'd say within an hour, I had reached the centre.'

'Was it hazardous?' Colum asked.

'Master Murtagh, you have crossed ravines, ditches, gorges, moats. We had to move slowly. One board being laid down after another.'

'Tell me.' Kathryn picked her wine cup from the table and moved it slowly, watching the bubbles wink and burst. 'Can the maze be seen from the top of the hall?'

'No.' Gurnell shook his head. 'If you go up, even to the garrets, and look down the maze is well constructed. The hedges are very thick at the top so they look closely packed. It's like gazing at a forest, or a thickly wooded copse: you can see the leaves, the branches, but not the paths beneath. The only thing which can be glimpsed, very faintly, is the top of the Weeping Cross. I can take you up, you will see what I mean.'

Kathryn shook her head.

'So, this maze was only known to Sir Walter?'

'He loved it.' Lady Elizabeth smiled bleakly. 'He called it his great secret, a way to purge his mind, to feel that he was making reparation. I knew some of his story but not all the terrors which tormented his soul.'

'Is that true, Father John?' Kathryn ignored the Lady Elizabeth's look of annoyance.

'No one knew that maze, or Sir Walter's mind.' Father John shook his head. 'I once asked Sir Walter how long it would take a man to walk from the entrance to the centre. He replied how he'd measured it once with an hour glass, only a quarter of the sand had passed through. And yet,' he shrugged, 'servants have tried it for a jape or jest and became panic-stricken. This was when Sir Walter first bought Ingoldby. After that, he gave strict orders, no one was to enter the maze.'

'I once fought Yorkists,' Gurnell observed, 'along the warren of alleyways in Southwark. That was easy compared to the maze.'

'I know,' Kathryn agreed. 'I went in there and experienced it myself.' She glanced around. 'The world seems cut off, nothing but a dark greenness, an oppressive silence. Whose idea was it to lay the ropes?'

'Mine,' Gurnell replied. 'We had boards put over the hedgerows until I reached the centre. I took coils of rope with me and, helped by a retainer, moved to meet another who came through the entrance.' He grinned, scratching his head. 'Some confusion but, at least we met. It took about an hour.'

Kathryn stared down at the ring on her little finger. A brilliant emerald in a gold setting, a gift from Colum. I should be preparing for my marriage, she thought. My wedding day approaches but I am now in this maze of bloody murder. Kathryn fought against the burst of temper seething inside her. It was always like this, the lies, the masks, the riddle of half-truths and hidden desires which surrounded every murder.

'How did Sir Walter learn to thread the maze?' Colum asked. 'Is there a map, a manuscript?'

'Sir Walter owned a fine library,' Father John replied. 'But I have never found any manuscript or document about the maze, nor would Sir Walter tell how he found out.'

'The former owners?' Kathryn queried.

'The hall had been left vacant for about six years,' Lady Elizabeth replied.

Kathryn noticed how Eleanora was now heavy-eyed. Had the woman fallen asleep?

'The former owners,' Lady Elizabeth repeated, 'were Lancastrians. A widower, Sir Thomas something, I forget now. Both he and his son died in battle.'

'I see,' Kathryn replied. 'So, his estates were forfeit and the Crown sold them to Sir Walter? Did you ever ask him the secrets of the maze?'

Lady Elizabeth shook her head. 'I asked him when we first moved here but he pressed his finger against my lips.' She blinked quickly. 'He said I was not to ask again.' She tapped the psalter lying in her lap. 'I respected his wishes.'

Kathryn glanced sharply at Colum, gnawing his lip, a sign of growing impatience.

'And the Athanatoi?' Luberon's voice came out as a squeak.

Mawsby sniggered. Luberon coloured and cleared his throat.

'These Athanatoi?' he repeated. 'Do they exist?'

'As I have said,' Father John eased himself in his chair as if in pain, 'such old legends are like the whispering of dry leaves.'

'But do they exist?' Luberon insisted. 'The Athanatoi?'

'I don't think so,' Kathryn intervened. 'Until today, no one attacked Sir Walter. The Athanatoi are just a name. I'd be very surprised if they are flesh and blood.'

She refused to be drawn by the puzzled looks and hurried whispers amongst them.

'So, who murdered my husband?' Lady Elizabeth stared archly across. 'Sir Walter had a great influence at court.' She paused. 'And so do I. I will ask for a Royal Justice to be sent down.'

'My lady, if a Royal Justice arrives, he will ask the following questions: where were you all between the hours of noon and one o'clock today?'

Kathryn glanced out of the window. The evening was drawing on, still beautiful and golden but soon darkness would fall. And what then? Would she return to Ottemelle Lane?

'I asked a question,' she repeated quietly.

'My maid and I,' Lady Elizabeth spread her hands prettily, 'were in the arbour of flowers, on the edge of the great meadow to the right of the maze entrance. I saw my husband go in. We remained there, playing musical instruments. Ask my household, Gurnell, Thurston, Father John.'

A chorus of agreement greeted her words. The rest followed suit, explaining their movements: Thurston was busy in the kitchens; although a Friday, it was the eve of the Transfiguration and a household banquet was being arranged. Gurnell remained on guard near the maze, as he always did; Lady Elizabeth and her maid vouched for him as did Thurston. Father John was in the library whilst Mawsby had been sent into Canterbury to buy some cambric cloth. He only returned after the alarm had been raised. Kathryn stifled her disappointment.

'My lady.' Kathryn picked up her cup and moved it from hand to hand. 'Would you object if I took lodgings tonight at Ingoldby Hall?' She ignored Colum's sharp intake of breath. 'I am sure I shall be safe.' Kathryn kept her voice steady. 'As you may appreciate, I need to question the servants.'

'They were all busy in the kitchens.' Lady Elizabeth smiled. 'But, to answer your question, Mistress, you will be my honoured guest. I'll certainly find you more congenial than a Royal Justice.' Lady Elizabeth's smile faded. 'Mistress Swinbrooke, everyone in this chamber can vouch for where they were when my husband was killed, barbarously murdered. None had a grievance against Sir Walter. Yet,' Lady Elizabeth's voice rose, 'someone entered the maze and carried out that hideous deed. If you search for answers so do I.' She tightened her lips, her blue eyes hard. 'Who killed Sir Walter? Why? And so barbarously? I have had his remains moved to the death house but there's no . . .' She couldn't bring herself to say 'head.'

Kathryn stared pityingly across. Lady Elizabeth was acting the grand lady; nevertheless, the horror of Sir Walter's death would soon make itself felt in this luxurious mansion: it would cast a long, cold shadow over these opulent surroundings.

'Did Sir Walter have any enemies?' Colum broke the silence. 'I mean, in the days before his death, were there any other threats or abuse?'

'The Vaudois woman.' Eleanora's head came up, no longer heavy-eyed, her face tense and watchful.

Kathryn caught a slight trace of accent and wondered if Eleanora was of Spanish or Portuguese extraction.

'The Vaudois woman,' Father John explained, 'is mad, witless. She was once the mistress of the former owner of Ingoldby Hall; his wife died, and she was a local girl who moved into the hall. She gave the lord a son, but both were killed in battle. After their deaths and her disgrace, she and her daughter moved into a small hunting lodge near the hall.'

'Are they dangerous?' Kathryn asked. 'This mother and daughter?'

Father John gestured with his hand. 'No. The daughter is

slightly simple, the mother is witless. She does not even know who Sir Walter was. She thinks her lover and son will return from the wars and often wanders up to the hall demanding to see them.'

'Sir Walter gave strict instructions she was not to be abused,' Lady Elizabeth declared. 'Even so, when Sir Walter would go out and ask her to be taken away she would shout threats and curses. The woman is confused. Sometimes she believes that her lover and son are sheltering here, even that Sir Walter had killed them. Mistress Swinbrooke,' Lady Elizabeth suddenly broke off and rose to her feet.

Kathryn, followed by Colum and Luberon, did likewise. Lady Elizabeth rubbed her brow, her fingers fluttering round the white band which circled her beautiful throat.

'I do not feel well, and there are things I must do.'

'I understand.'

Lady Elizabeth nodded, whispered a few words to Thurston, and swept out of the chamber.

A short while later Kathryn sat on the top step leading down to the great meadow, her gaze fixed on the entrance to the maze.

'I have never seen anything like that,' she whispered.

'I have heard of similar in France and the Low Countries.' Colum scratched his chin. He sniffed the air. 'What's that fragrant smell?'

'From the kitchens,' Luberon said. 'The cooks are making potted swan.' He smacked his lips. 'Claret and butter, mace and nutmeg, small rolls of well cooked bacon.'

'You are hungry, Luberon,' Katyrn teased.

'I am also inquisitive,' the clerk replied, munching on a piece of bread seized from the kitchen. 'The stories we heard were correct. Everyone was where they claimed to be. Thurston was in the buttery making sure the milk and cream were kept cool from the heat. One maid took a cup of malmsey to Father John in the library. Mawsby definitely went to Canterbury whilst Lady Elizabeth and Gurnell never left the great meadow.'

'You shouldn't stay here, Kathryn.' Colum abruptly changed the subject. 'And, if you do, so shall I. Do you remember that hideous business at the Friars of the Sack? You have no one to protect you.'

'There, my passionate Irishman.' Kathryn squeezed his calloused hand. 'Sir Walter had his household to protect him but he still died. I'll be safe. Anyway, you've got to mend the drenching horn for that sick mare.'

'Aye,' Colum agreed. 'And the blacksmiths are out to shoe the yearlings. I have to make sure they do it properly and don't drink too much smithing ale.'

'What's that?' Luberon demanded.

'Part of the custom,' Colum replied. 'For every yearling they shoe for the first time, the blacksmiths demand a quart of ale. I have seen them so drunk they can hardly stand.'

'Why?' Kathryn asked. 'No, not about smithing ale. Why should Sir Walter be killed so barbarously? Decapitated, his head taken? The killer must seethe with hate.'

'Could it have been a hired assassin?' Luberon asked. 'It must have been a man.'

'Nonsense,' Colum intervened. 'I have seen women in Ireland with a scythe or a sharp blade take a man's head off in one clean cut. The blood,' he continued. 'The assassin must have been drenched in blood.'

He ignored Luberon's exclamation of disgust as the clerk took the bread away from his mouth.

'Blood from a severed neck spurts high like water from a fountain.'

'Yet,' Kathryn declared, 'we found no bloodied clothes on the ground, either in the maze or around it. Nor, indeed, was there any trace of the killer. The ground must have been scuffed and torn by the servants searching for their master's corpse as well as bringing up those planks to lay across the tops of the hedgerows.'

Luberon returned to his munching. Kathryn stared across the great meadow. It must have been late in the evening; the sun was now dipping into the west, filling the sky with bursts of scarlet-gold, and the shadows of the trees lengthened across the grass. She repressed a shiver as she recalled a childhood tale of how, at sunset, the gargoyles slithered down from their pillars and crept across the churchyard to meet evil goblins and wood sprites from the trees. She wondered if her father had ever come to Ingoldby. Now she was here she recalled scraps of gossip about its grandeur and the maze, yet the place had been nothing but a name to her.

'Murder will out,' Colum remarked.

'Don't start quoting Chaucer,' Kathryn replied.

'Women desire to have sovereignity,' Colum teased.

'I am not the Wife of Bath,' Kathryn retorted. 'But, to quote the poet's words: "the sword of sorrow" certainly hangs over Ingoldby. So strange,' she mused loudly. 'They are all shocked, disgusted by Sir Walter's death but . . .'

Kathryn watched a raven swoop over the grass and land a few feet away to dig at the grass with its yellow, swordlike beak.

'You don't think Sir Walter was loved?' Luberon asked, swallowing a mouthful of bread quickly.

'I think he was respected,' Kathryn replied. 'But he was a stranger to his own household. I believe the older he became the more he lived in the past.' Kathryn paused. I used to do that, she reflected, after my marriage with the drunkard Alexander Wyville; her Father dying, then Wyville joined the Lancastrians, going off to war. She had lived in a dream until Colum had arrived, swaggering into her house like sunlight bursting through a darkened chamber. Yet, even now, betrothed to this man she so passionately loved, preparing for her wedding day, the darkness of the past would occasionally draw her back. She recalled vividly Wyville's flushed face, his ale-drenched breath, and the nagging suspicion, despite every confirmation to the contrary, that he may not have died and been buried in some pauper's grave in the west country. Kathryn rose to her feet.

'Colum, leave the cob here. You must go back to Canterbury. Tell Thomasina what I am doing and ignore her protests. Ask her to fill a saddlebag with some fresh clothes, my green woollen cloak, and my writing satchel.'

Colum got to his feet and turned her face gently with the tip of his finger. Luberon, who'd always been fascinated by Kathryn and quietly doted on her every word and touch, glanced away in embarrassment.

'Kathryn.' Colum's puzzlement deepened. 'You look pale.'

She shook her head. 'Nothing, nothing at all. I will be well. Hurry now.'

A short while later Kathryn accompanied Colum and Luberon down the winding path towards the main gate. This had now been opened, and they stood aside to allow a wine cart, pulled by two drays with hogged manes, to rumble by. Kathryn was giving Colum further instructions about what was to happen at Ottemelle Lane when she heard a scream. A woman appeared through the gates garbed in a long, red gown, its sleeves tattered, the ragged hem hanging above dirty bare feet, a mass of grey hair falling down to her waist. She was thin-faced and yellow-skinned with high cheekbones. As she ran towards them, Kathryn noticed the spittle at one corner of her mouth and the wild, frantic look in the staring eyes. Another woman, a cowl pulled over her head, hurried after.

'In God's name!' Colum breathed.

The grey-haired woman stopped and fell at their feet, head bowed. Kathryn noticed the leaves and twigs sticking in the coils of her grey hair.

'Have you seen him?' The woman's face came up. She wiped the spittle on the back of her hand. 'Have you seen him? My son? My master? So many,' she blinked, 'riders galloping about. Have they brought messages from the war?'

Kathryn's hand went out to stroke her face but the woman recoiled.

'You must be the Vaudois.' Kathryn crouched down and stared into those mad, blood-flecked eyes. 'We bring no news, Mistress.'

'You must.' The woman's bony hand grasped Kathryn's. 'So much excitement.'

'She means no harm!'

Kathryn glanced up. The other woman had pushed back her cowl to reveal a dark brown face framed by a mass of unkempt auburn hair. She was comely but her gaze was rather vague, and her mouth hung slack. She was better dressed, with sandals on her feet, and Kathryn smelt fresh herbs.

'She is the Vaudois woman?' Kathryn released the old woman's hand and got to her feet.

'She is.' The young woman's voice had a marked Kentish twang. Her eyes were now more guarded, her face more determined. 'She's been excited all day. Talks of messengers coming and going, of news from the great hall.'

'You've heard what happened?' Colum asked.

'Aye, I've heard. My name's Ursula.' She forced a smile. 'Sometimes my mother is quiet, she helps me, but today . . .'

'The news must have disturbed you?' Kathryn asked.

'I hated Ingoldby!' Ursula spat the words out. 'Sir Thomas, its former owner, used my mother. He and my brother were strangers to me. Theirs was a man's world of iron and fire, of armour and sword.' She grimaced. 'But I am sorry for Sir Walter's death. He was kindly enough. He sent us delicacies and money. The news is all abroad now. A bloody death, but that's what happens to the men of war, mistress, they all die bloody deaths. Those who live by the sword die by the sword.'

'And you know nothing of Sir Walter's death?' Luberon became all efficient.

'Plump man! Appleman!'

Ursula raised her mother up and drew her away.

'I live in peace and I go in peace. What would the likes of us have to do with Sir Walter?' She turned and walked down the lane, stopped and looked over her shoulder. 'Wars come and wars go,' she intoned. 'And as the tree falls so shall it lie!'

Her mother tried to break free but Ursula held her close, chattering softly.

'I wonder if she speaks the truth?' Luberon murmured.

'I think she does.'

Kathryn watched the women disappear through the gate.

'Ursula looks after her mother. I wager she knows a great deal about men. Of soldiers coming in the dead of night, their bellies full of ale and hearts full of lust.' She seized Colum's arm. 'But not you.'

They walked on. At the gateway Kathryn made her farewells. Luberon mumbled something about going on ahead, and led off both his horse and Colum's. The Irishman seized Kathryn's face in his hands and kissed her passionately on the lips.

'You will be safe?' His breath was hot on her face, his eyes no longer crinkled in amusement. 'I believe you, Kathryn. If the Athanatoi existed, and they wanted Sir Walter's death, they could have struck before.' He let go of her face and grasped her hand, pulling her close. 'Which means that in that manor house there is someone with a heart as hard as steel and black as hell who will kill and kill again, though God knows why. Keep yourself safe.' He raised his hand. 'I think I should . . .'

'I think you should go, Colum.'

Kathryn blew him a kiss and, turning on her heel, walked back up the trackway. The trees on either side now lay silent, the shadows deepening, the evening silence broken by the sounds of the coming night. She was glad when she reached the green, and was about to climb the steps when the horn sounded. A stable boy, still carrying a leather bucket slopping with water, came hurrying round the corner. He dropped the bucket and for a while stood staring.

'What's the matter, boy?'

'You'd best come, Mistress. Master Thurston sent me. There's been another death!'

Kathryn hurried up the steps and grasped the boy's hand.

'Death?'

'One of the maids.' The boy stammered, his face frantic with fear. 'In the mere, beside the old tower, drowned they say!'

Chapter 3

"What is this world? What asketh men to have?
Now with his love, now in his colde grave. . . ."
—Chaucer, "The Knight's Tale,"
The Canterbury Tales, 1387

The corpse looked hideous. Once so comely, the young woman's face was now coated with a veneer of green slime and filthy water that clogged her eyes, nose and mouth. She was drenched in black mud and Kathryn had to use the edge of her own cloak to clean the maid's liverish face. Kathryn pulled away the water-soaked hair to reveal half-open eyes.

'She's been in the water some time.' Thurston, crouching on the other side of the corpse, gazed tearfully at Kathryn.

Others joined them, all agog with curiosity, whispering and muttering amongst themselves. Father John pushed his way through and, kneeling by the corpse, made the sign of the cross and recited the words of absolution into the dead woman's ear.

'What is it?'

Lady Elizabeth stood back along the path, Eleanora beside her. Each had thrown an ermined-lined wrap around their shoulders, for the evening breeze had turned a little cold.

'It's Veronica.' Father John clambered to his feet. 'She must have slipped and fallen into the mere. She's dead, my lady. She must have been in the water for hours.'

'What was she doing here?' Kathryn asked, but Thurston just shook his head.

She glanced across at the mere, a broad, dank, evil-smelling pool. The bushes and trees on either side were leafless and withered as if some miasma from the water had drawn all life from them. Kathryn stared at the nearby tower covered in moss and lichen. The encircling ivy even covered the arrow-slit windows, climbing as high as the turreted battlements.

'What is this place?' Kathryn asked.

Father John rose and went to give further details to Lady Elizabeth.

'I don't know.' Thurston blinked and stared up at the tower fearfully. 'They say it was built by the Normans and cursed by a witch. We always regard it as derelict land. The mere is fed by a rivulet, sometimes that's choked off.'

'And what would Veronica be doing here?'

Thurston shrugged. 'She was a chamber maid. She had no reason to be here.'

'There are no flower beds or herbers?' Kathryn demanded. 'No washing or drying to be done here?'

Thurston shook his head. Kathryn heard Lady Elizabeth make her farewells as Father John shooed away the other servants. Afterwards the priest knelt by the feet of the corpse to recite the psalm for the dead: "Out of the depths have I cried to you, Oh Lord. Lord hear my voice. Let thine ear be attentive . . .'

And let my wits be sharp, Kathryn reflected. She finished cleaning the dead woman's face and rose to examine the mud-splattered edge of the mere.

'Who found her?' she asked over her shoulder.

'I did.' Thurston had remained kneeling. 'I was looking for some kindling for the kitchen.' He pointed to the half-open door of the tower. 'We keep it in there. I came round. At first I thought a bundle of cloth had been dropped in the mere, until I saw the hair.'

'So, she was floating on the top?'

'Yes, slightly on her side, with her back to me.'

Kathryn studied the ground; any chance of studying footprints was lost now that the alarm had been raised.

'What's wrong?' Father John broke off his praying.

'Mistress Swinbrooke, this could have been an accident. Sometimes the mere seeps over, soaks the ground and renders it slippery, perhaps Veronica stumbled . . . ?'

Kathryn returned to the corpse and examined it. She could detect no mark of violence. She began to knead the girl's head very carefully with her fingers and discovered a large bump just beneath the left ear. Kathryn turned the corpse so it lay fully on its belly. She ignored the water which gushed out of the mouth and nose and, taking her own comb and a small pair of scissors from her wallet, combed the thick, black hair aside. She cut some of the hair so she could see the swollen contusion more clearly, still soft to the touch and filled with blood.

'What is that?'

'As I suspected,' Kathryn replied. 'Master Thurston, do you have a rag?'

Thurston handed over the one thrust through his belt. Kathryn cleaned her comb and scissors and put them back.

'What did you suspect?' Father John asked.

'That Veronica met someone here—who, or why, I don't know, but that person killed her. He or she took a piece of kindling from the tower storeroom and, when Veronica wasn't looking, inflicted a powerful blow to the back of her head.'

'But wouldn't that kill her?' Thurston protested.

'No, no, it didn't.'

Kathryn examined the girl's hands: they were soft and small, the nails neatly pared.

'There was no struggle. I can tell you what happened.'

Kathryn got to her feet and, avoiding the edge of the mere, made her way into the musty storeroom of the tower. Thurston followed and, mumbling his apologies, quickly lit the fat tallow candles on a rusty plate on a ledge near the door. The storeroom flared into light. At the far side were steps built into the room leading to the first floor; between that and the door, bundles of kindling had been neatly tied and stored, one on top of the other, dry bracken used to fire the ovens as well as logs for the great hearths of the mansion.

'What are you looking for?' Thurston demanded.

'Some trace of our killer, but there's none. I suggest the killer met Veronica here. They had their meeting. Veronica believed she was talking to a friend.'

Kathryn walked back outside. Father John was still kneeling by the corpse.

'Very well, Thurston.' Kathryn smiled, waving him forward. 'You pretend to be Veronica.'

The anxious-faced steward obeyed.

'Now.' Kathryn came up behind him. 'The killer took a pole or stick from the tower and struck Veronica here.' She touched the Manciple's thin-haired head just behind the left ear. 'Veronica staggered forward, half conscious. The killer finished the task by giving Veronica a push with the pole. The poor maid stumbled into the mere. Perhaps she struggled awhile but the blow had been cruel: her mouth and nose filled with water and she drowned. The assassin watched her death throes, then hurled the makeshift weapon into the mere and fled.'

'But why?' Thurston turned round. 'I'll have to report all this to Lady Elizabeth.'

'How old was Veronica?'

'About seventeen summers.'

'She had no enemies?'

Thurston grimaced. 'She was a chamber maid, a merry girl. She lived for the next dance or juicy piece of gossip. She has family in Canterbury but moved here to take service with Sir Walter.'

'And she had no paramour?'

'No, a good girl, clean living and pious. Whenever possible she attended Mass in the chapel. She saved her pennies and entrusted them to me.' Thurston's eyes grew more tearful. 'I'll have to go into Canterbury to tell her family. You've finished with the corpse?'

'I can do no more,' Kathryn said quietly.

'In which case I'll fetch a cart.'

'Is there anything?'

Thurston turned back.

'Is there anything?' Kathryn repeated. 'You didn't tell me. Why someone should kill this pretty maid?'

'If I knew, Mistress, I'd tell you. But I'll make careful search.'

'Do you think the murders are linked?' Father John had made his final benediction and rose to his feet, knees cracking. He rubbed these carefully. 'I'm getting old and the cold never seems to leave me. Mistress Swinbrooke, do you think the two deaths are connected?'

'I don't know.'

Kathryn gazed around. The day was now dying, the shadows shooting longer. Soon it would be dark; she shivered slightly as she recalled Colum's warning.

'Mistress Swinbrooke! Mistress Swinbrooke!'

Kinsman Mawsby now stood at the edge of the path gesturing at her. He stared at the corpse and quickly made the sign of the cross but came no closer.

'Mistress Swinbrooke, Lady Elizabeth has sent me. I am to show you to your chamber.'

Kathryn thanked Father John, who said he would stay by the corpse until Thurston returned. Kathryn followed Mawsby along the path through the side gardens and into the mansion through a postern door, which led into the cavernous kitchens, scullery and buttery. The air was full of steam and sweet smells. Meat was roasting on the spit which a young boy turned, his face brick red. Now and again he would jump to his feet and baste the meat with a ladle of sauce. Kathryn studied the servants: the bakers, cooks and scullions. They were all busy and red-faced, moving pots and pans, chopping meat and vegetables, putting the newly baked bread into baskets, all apparently involved in the countless tasks of such a large household. Kathryn, however, caught their quick glances, the furtive looks, the sense of fear.

'Mistress Swinbrooke!' Mawsby had now reached the far side of the kitchen.

Kathryn went across as if to join him but paused and, picking up a large pan and heavy ladle, clashed the two together. The effect was immediate; the hubbub of noise died and even the spit boy left his post.

'You have heard the news?' Kathryn ignored Mawsby's exclamation of annoyance. 'First Sir Walter was barbarously murdered, now the maid Veronica.'

Her words were greeted by moans and cries of disapproval.

'She was murdered,' Kathryn continued. 'God rest her soul and that of Sir Walter's. God will give them peace but he will also demand justice for such hideous deeds. I ask you now, on your allegiance to the King and your duty to the law, did any of you see, hear or notice anything untoward this day? Either out in the great meadow or here in the house where Veronica worked? If you did, you must speak to me.' Kathryn put the pan and ladle down. 'Thank you for listening. I am sorry for the distraction I caused.'

'Was that necessary?' Mawsby hissed as soon as they were out of the kitchen.

'As the King's Commissioner!' Kathryn snapped.

Mawsby sighed, wiped his hands on his jerkin and caught at Kathryn's arm.

'Mistress, I did not mean to give offence.'

Kathryn studied this young man's face, his sharp green eyes under a mop of red fiery hair, the long face and almost milk-white skin.

'Have I met you before, Master Mawsby? Do you know me, Master Luberon or the King's Commissioner Master Murtagh?'

Mawsby pulled his mouth. 'I don't think so.'

You are lying, Kathryn thought, I must ask Colum if he's ever met you.

'I'll show you to your chamber.' Mawsby offered.

They went down a passageway into the main hallway, where servants were lighting candles and lamps. Mawsby took her up the great wooden staircase; the railing and newel, carved in the finest oak, gleamed in the candle light. The wooden boards had been covered with strips of the best Turkey carpet, which deadened sound and made Kathryn feel as if she were walking in a dream. The same wooden wainscoting as in the solar had also been built against the whitewashed walls of the stairwell. Above these hung paintings, their gilt frames covered in black crepe as the house mourned Sir Walter's death.

The first gallery was magnificent; shiny wooden panels reflected the light from large candle wheels hung on chains from the ceiling.

The floorboards were covered by thick rugs. Capped braziers stood between the doorways to chambers; these would be fired and scented when the weather turned cold. Mawsby explained that this was where Sir Walter and Lady Elizabeth had their chambers and chancery.

'I must go there.'

Mawsby paused, one foot on the step leading to the second gallery.

'Go there?' He knitted his brows. 'You would go through Sir Walter's private papers?'

'If I deem it necessary, Master Mawsby. I am also skilled enough to detect if those papers have been interfered with before I begin my search.'

'But there's nothing . . .'

'That will be for me to decide. I think you should appraise Lady Elizabeth of my intentions.'

Kathryn was about to ask him when the funeral would take place but then recalled that headless corpse; Lady Elizabeth and Father John would insist that the body not be coffined until that grisly relic to the murder was found. She followed Mawsby up the staircase. The second gallery was more shadow-filled with capped candles burning at either end. Mawsby opened a door and explained how the chamber overlooked the front of the house, and would she need anything? A maid would be sent up. Kathryn absentmindedly thanked him and asked if he would light the candles and oil lamps. The bed was a four-poster protected by heavy blue curtains. She pulled these back to find that the sheets and bolsters were crisp and clean. She walked to the window and knelt on the small seat in the alcove and stared out through the mullioned glass. Darkness was falling, but Kathryn could still make out the maze, and she recalled Gurnell's explanation of how the hedgerows clustered close together, blocking any signs of the paths. In fact, the maze crouched like some sinister animal in the darkness. She opened the small window door to let in the evening breeze. Mawsby had now finished lighting the candles.

'Is this comfortable for you, Mistress?'

Kathryn stared at the coloured drapes on the walls, the triptych depicting Christ and his mother, the large, black, wooden crucifix. There was a coffer, a large chest at the end of the bed, a writing table and a high-backed, cushioned chair.

'It's very comfortable. My thanks to the Lady Elizabeth.'

Mawsby bowed and left.

Kathryn bolted the door behind him. She went and lay down on the bed and dozed until a servant brought up fresh napkins, a water bowl and jug for the lavarium.

'Would the mistress,' the maid asked, 'like to eat in the great hall?'

Kathryn refused so the maid offered to bring up some wine, bread, meats and a dish of vegetables.

'The onions and lentils are covered in a fine sauce,' the cheery-faced girl added. 'Sir Walter's cooks.' Her smile disappeared as she recalled what had happened. 'Er, well . . .'

'I am sure the cooks know their sauces.' Kathryn smiled. 'And how to broil bream and roast a haunch of venison. I'll let you choose for me. Your name?'

Kathryn undid her purse and held out a silver piece. The girl gasped. Kathryn thrust the coin into the palm of her hand.

'My name is Amelia.'

'A pretty name for a pretty face,' Kathryn replied. 'Amelia, look after me well.'

The girl, breathless with excitement, assured her she would. A short while later she ushered up Colum's messenger from Ottemelle Lane, an ostler from a nearby tavern. He gently placed the saddle bags on the top of the chest and, closing his eyes, gabbled out the message Colum had given him.

'Mistress, everything is fine. Thomas . . .'

'Thomasina?'

'Ah yes, Thomasina.' The young man did not even open his eyes. 'Thomasina sends her love, all is quiet. For once she agrees with the Irishman, you should have come home. She will ask Father Cuthbert at the Poor Priests' Hospital to help with your patients.'

He added a few other items of local gossip: how Ragwort had bought himself a new set of hose and Goldere, the spotty-faced clerk, had become so drunk he had fallen into a horse trough. At last he finished. Kathryn said there was no reply, gave the lad a coin and closed the door behind him. She opened the saddle bags and took out the change of clothing and undergarments, smiling at how Thomasina had put in small herbal sachets of perfume to keep them fresh and sweet-smelling. She placed the contents in the chest and the small writing satchel on the table. She pulled out the capped inkpot, the sharpened quills, pumice stones, strips of parchment, the small weight to keep the parchment level and the ruler she used when writing. As she did so, Kathryn half-listened to the sounds of the house; a bell tolled the sign for the evening meal. Sir Walter's death had taken the household by surprise: it would take at least a day before the formal ritual of mourning was inaugurated with its fast and death watches. The requiem would probably take place in the cathedral. Sir Walter, being a powerful landowner, must have left instructions for his burial under the cold flagstones as close to the great shrine of Sir Thomas à Becket as possible.

'Your body is mutilated,' Kathryn whispered, 'and your soul gone to God. Who will seek justice for you? Or for your maid Veronica?'

Kathryn still felt refreshed despite the tumult of the day. She would have sat down and begun her reflections, listing what she had learnt as she would the ailments of some disease or malady. However, Amelia was eager to prove that she was worth the silver coin and brought up a tray of food. Kathryn laughed at the quantity.

'I asked for a meal, not a feast,' she teased. She gazed into the wine jug. 'And if I drank all that I'd be still sleeping at midday tomorrow.'

She sat down and ate what she could, Amelia coming back to fuss her. Once Kathryn was finished, the maid took the tray away but left the wine cup full to the brim. Kathryn bolted the door. Ingoldby Hall may have been a splendid mansion, full of treasures, but it was also a haunt of murder. Kathryn couldn't forget Lady Elizabeth and her household. How calm they seemed, grieving but not desolate or despairing. Was that their fault or Sir Walter's?

Did he lead such a secluded life, keeping everything sub rosa, his private thoughts to himself? Kathryn arranged her writing materials and brought across two of the beeswax candles to provide more light. She began to write down her conclusions.

Primo—Sir Walter Maltravers, a self-made man, a warrior, a soldier who had fled Constantinople and used the treasures he had taken to amass a fortune. He was well respected by Church and Crown. A man with powerful friends yet a lonely one. A man obsessed by an incident which had occurred twenty years earlier as well as the bloody affrays during the recent civil war. A man who, perhaps, often thought about his own death and judgement. Riven by guilt; Sir Walter had carried his Friday penance out whenever he could but today, at the centre of that maze, the penance had ended with his own hideous death. Was there a connection—Kathryn's quill raced across the parchment—*between Sir Walter's death and the disappearance of the Lacrima Christi? Am I wrong?* Kathryn wrote, *Do the Athanatoi exist? Who sent those warnings? Why were the strips of parchment so different in colour, texture and handwriting styles? Did this mean there were two assassins? A group? What other evidence existed for such a secret society, apart from court gossip, Sir Walter's own fears and those sinister threats?*

Secundo—The maze: how did the killer enter and leave that maze unnoticed? No one knew its secret routes except Sir Walter but the killer must have been waiting for him there, taken his head like an executioner, before mysteriously vanishing. Yet he, or she, must have been blood-soaked carrying that severed head, not to mention the weapon used. Who could it be? Everyone could guarantee where they were and what they were doing. A hired assassin? But, if that was the case, such a person would still need help from someone in the household. And how did Sir Walter discover how to thread the maze, yet no one else could? No reference existed to any map or charter. Was there some secret document?

Tertio—Why did the murder take place in the maze and in such a barbaric way? Why not poison in a cup? Or a stiletto in the dark? Kathryn lifted her head and breathed in deeply. Of course, such simple means were also dangerous. To the killer, this maze was a perfect place for murder. Sir Walter was a veteran soldier, he would be carrying no weapons nor could he cry for help. Kathryn returned to her writing.

Quartro—So, what did happen? If the killer stayed in the maze after the murder then he, or she, would have been seen by Gurnell when those planks were placed across the hedgerows. The killer could either hide or escape immediately, though carrying a severed head and a bloody sword, whilst the assassin's boots and cloak must have been stained with blood. Kathryn brushed the quill round her lips and watched the candle flame. Her father had confessed that, whenever he looked at a candle flame for a long time, he fell into a trancelike state.

'God rest you,' Kathryn murmured.

She wondered what her father would have made of Colum and her plans to marry him. She put the quill down, rose and went to stand by the window. Night had fallen. On the steps below braziers had been lit: cresset torches, fixed on long poles, flared against the blackness and bathed the edge of the great meadow in light. Kathryn could still make out the dark mass of the maze. Was Sir Walter's severed head still there? Beneath one of the hedges together with the sword or axe wrapped in some blood-soaked cloak? And those responsible? Lady Elizabeth and Eleanora had played music in their bower until the alarm was raised. They had seen Gurnell, and Gurnell had seen them, whilst the guards would have noticed if their Master-at-arms had disappeared for any lengthy period of time. And Father John in his library? Kathryn pressed her hot cheek against the mullioned glass. Did some secret passageway or tunnel exist running from the hall to the maze? The old ruined tower showed the estate had been cultivated for centuries. Ingoldby probably stood where a small castle, farm, or manor house had been built. So, what did happen? What was the cause for such a grisly killing?

'Hate,' Kathryn murmured.

Whoever had taken Sir Walter's head had a soul full of hate. She was about to return to her writing when there was a knock on the door.

'Who is it?'

'Mistress Swinbrooke, it's only me, Father John.'

Kathryn pulled back the bolts, opened the door and Father John slipped into her chamber.

'You are not fearful of your reputation, Mistress Swinbrooke?'

'I am more concerned about my soul, Father.'

The priest laughed. Kathryn ushered him across to the small stool against the wall near the writing desk and offered him the wine cup.

'Did you expect me, Mistress Swinbrooke?'

'Yes and no; you puzzle me, Father. Your master is dead. Your face looks drawn and your eyes red-rimmed, yet your grief seems controlled.'

'I watched when you were questioning us,' Father John remarked. 'Were you surprised at our restraint?' He shrugged. 'Don't be, you have the measure of Sir Walter. A good man who kept his heart and feelings hidden behind the thickest armour. Sometimes I think he wished to die.'

'What was he so anxious about?' Kathryn sat down on the stair. 'Sir Walter was very worried?'

'Sir Walter was always worried.' Father John took the wine cup, sipped from it and put it back on the table. 'I have broken my own rule.' He smiled. 'Never drink wine after nightfall. Yes, Sir Walter was a worried man. Only years after he fled Constantinople, when its Emperor's last stand became part of the chivalry of the west, did he fully realise what he had done.'

'But you don't believe in the Athanatoi, do you?'

Father John shook his head. 'According to legend and fable, Mistress, the greatest Christian city of the East fell because of betrayal and cowardice. That's nonsense; Constantinople was a doomed city from the start of the siege. Its empire had shrunk to an area within bowshot of its own gates. The West sent no help whilst the Turks were as many as grains of sand on a sea shore. No, Mistress Swinbrooke, I don't believe in the Athanatoi. Tittle-tattle, the only place they truly existed was in Sir Walter's imagination.'

'But those written warnings were real enough. Why did they begin so recently—they were recent?'

'Ah yes.' Father John rubbed his face. 'Sir Walter hardly discussed them: I always suspected those scraps of parchment had nothing to do with Constantinople! Someone heard about the legend and, out of cruel envy or some other sinister reason, decided to exploit it.'

'Who? Why?'

'God knows, Mistress, I don't.'

'Did they worry Sir Walter?'

'They nourished his guilt, his anxieties, his worries.'

'But why now, why did they come now?'

'Mistress.' Father John lifted his face. 'I truly don't know. I even suspected Sir Walter sent them himself—some dark twist in his mind.'

'Did he have other worries?'

'You know he did.' The priest smiled. 'You have read Chaucer's *Canterbury Tales*, Mistress? Do you remember the poet's description of a knight? "Parfait et gentil"? Sir Walter tried to be that, even when he fought with the King at Towton.'

'Ah yes, Towton.' Kathryn replied.

She'd often heard of that battle fought on a freezing Palm Sunday along the wild moors of Yorkshire some eleven years ago. The young Edward IV, seeking vengeance for the defeat and death of his father and brother at the earlier battle of Wakefield, had stormed north with his Yorkist warlords. He had met the Lancastrian at Towton. A bloody, violent battle had lasted all day and ended with the deaths of thousands upon thousands. The news had swept Canterbury, and Kathryn's father had been shocked at the hideous cruelties perpetrated after the battle. Colum himself had been there and rarely talked about it. He still suffered nightmares from that bloody conflict in the freezing fields and woods followed by hideous massacres around the river Swale.

'I was there in the royal camp.' Father John curled his fingers together. 'Sir Walter had taken part in the pursuit. He surrounded and captured a group of French mercenaries from Provence who had fought for the house of Lancaster. They had taken refuge in a copse. By then Sir Walter was tired of the bloodshed. He offered the mercenary captain and about sixty of his followers their lives, if they laid down their arms. The Provencals agreed.' Father John paused. 'I very rarely speak of this. There must have been at least sixty mercenaries. They surrendered their swords and banners. Sir Walter was called away to another part of the battle field, a royal summons. When he returned his troop had taken the law into their own hands. . . .'

'The Provencals?'

'Yes, mistress, the Provencals were massacred. It was like a slaughter yard, their blood streamed across the frozen ground. Their heads had been taken; some had been fixed on poles, others tied by the hair to the branches of trees. Sir Walter was furious but the captain of the troop argued that the Provencals had tried to seize their weapons and fight their way out: his men, hardbitten veterans, all took oaths swearing this was the truth. Sir Walter suspected different but could do nothing. He complained to the King but our noble lord was not in a giving mood. Edward dismissed them as mercenaries fighting against the realm's legitimate sovereign, caught in open revolt against the Crown. The King refused to be moved, so for the last eleven years, Sir Walter blamed himself.'

'Could Maltravers's death be connected to that massacre?'

The priest tightened his lips. 'Perhaps. Ask your betrothed, he was at the battle. The massacres after Towton are known to many but very few tell the truth.'

'Was Mawsby at Towton?'

'In his time Mawsby was a good soldier. An aim-crier, he commanded a troop of archers under Beaufort.'

'So, he was a Lancastrian?'

'Dyed in the wool,' Father John confessed. 'But so was Gurnell. He was captured at Towton but took the oath and changed sides.'

'What else?' Kathryn covered the priest's hand with hers.

'Sir Walter was also worried about his health. Last winter he suffered gripes in his belly and blood in his stools. I asked him to see a physician. He visited the infirmary at Greyfriars. Brother Ralph provided some comfort and assistance, as did Father Prior.'

'So, there was a relationship between the good brothers and Sir Walter?'

'Oh yes, didn't you know?' Father John laughed sharply. 'Father Prior, Brother Ralph, not to mention one or two other brothers in their Order, all supported one side or the other.'

'As priests?' Kathryn exclaimed.

'Oh no!' Father John scratched his balding pate. 'In 1461 two great battles took place in the north: Wakefield, where Edward the Fourth lost his father and brother, and Towton. What happened in those bloody struggles forced many to reflect on their lives. I know a number of churchmen, secular and religious in Canterbury, who took a vocation for the priestly life because of what happened at those battles.'

'The Lacrima Christi?' Kathryn asked.

'Ah, Sir Walter believed he held that in trust. He was only too pleased to loan it to the Franciscans who had helped him. . . .'

'But its loss? I understand you and Sir Walter visited Greyfriars yesterday, that Sir Walter became upset?'

'Memories.' Father John smiled thinly. 'Sir Walter was touched to see the ruby being publicly venerated again after nineteen years. However,' he added, 'Sir Walter also believed its theft was due to the work of the Athanatoi. He was very upset, but it being Friday, he refused to meet the Prior's messenger.'

'And who do you think stole the ruby?'

Father John pulled a face. 'A clever felon; that chantry chapel was secure. I pressed against the door and it held fast. Brother Simon the sacristan made great play of showing us how the sole key was firmly in his possession.'

Kathryn stared down at the piece of parchment on the table; the Lacrima Christi would have to wait. She was not surprised by Father John's admission about the friars' past. Colum meeting Gurnell at the gate was an apt example of how close the brotherhood of soldiers was. She'd heard many stories about men like Gurnell who had fought for either party, changing sides or, as in the case of Prior Barnabas, leaving the world of war for the order and tranquility of some religious house.

'Did Prior Barnabas often come here?'

'No. He has been Prior for about eighteen months to two years. Brother Ralph, his infirmarian, was a more frequent visitor.'

'And Gurnell?' Kathryn decided to exploit the opportunity of the priest's visit.

'A good soldier, loyal to Sir Walter. He will probably stay and serve the Lady Elizabeth.'

'And Mawsby?'

'More shadow than substance,' Father John retorted. 'I hardly know the man, secretive and withdrawn. A soldier and a clerk, a rare combination, Mistress. He and Gurnell served Sir Walter well.' Father John half-smiled. 'Thurston the steward is also an old Lancastrian. He's a local man who knows Ingoldby well. Sir Walter found his assistance invaluable.'

'Did Thurston fight at Towton?'

'No, but he lost two sons there.'

'And the Lady Elizabeth?'

'Ah.' Father John smiled. 'She is what she appears: spoilt, beautiful, self-possessed and, yes, I'd say selfish. She saw her marriage to Sir Walter as a good match.'

'Did Sir Walter love her?'

'As much as he could anybody. He hoped for a son but she never conceived. Their relationship was amicable. Sir Walter never discussed her. Sometimes I think he was worried about her but he never told me the reason why.'

'And Eleanora her maid?'

'Ah, a strange one. Her mother's English but, I believe, her father is from northern Spain, Burgos? The Redvers family sold English wool there. The world of trade is as close as that of soldiers. Eleanora was raised with the Lady Elizabeth. She's her companion as well as her principal lady-in-waiting. Eleanora helps Thurston with the management of the household.'

'And you?' Kathryn leaned back in the chair. 'Why have you come to tell me this, Father John?'

'I don't really know. Except,' he narrowed his eyes, 'I guessed you'd come looking for me, Mistress Swinbrooke. I could tell that from your face. Then that poor maid Veronica was murdered. Ingoldby had its own tranquility but even here evil has burst through.'

'Even here?'

'This was a refuge, Mistress, or so I thought, for Sir Walter but,' the priest tapped the side of his head, 'Sir Walter was never at peace. He used to tell me stories about the ancient Greeks, how they believed the Furies pursued those who had offended the gods. Sir Walter believed he was pursued by the Furies and it looks as if they have caught up with him. . . .' He sighed, rose and patted Kathryn gently on the shoulder.

He was almost at the door when Kathryn called out.

'Father John!'

He turned, his hand on the latch.

'Why did you stay with Sir Walter?'

He smiled. 'You should have been a priest, Kathryn. You have two questions haven't you? Let me see.' He walked back, head to one side, his eyes not so gentle. 'You have asked me one question: why I stayed with Sir Walter. Because he saved my life in Constantinople. If it hadn't been for him, I would have been captured or killed. They would have shown a priest no mercy. And your second question, Mistress, is what was I doing in Constantinople? I would like to say I was on pilgrimage but that's not true. I was once a soldier. I, too, fought with the great lords.' He blinked. 'I killed a man, so I fled across the Narrow Seas.'

'You were a priest at the time?'

Father John nodded. 'In my youth, Kathryn, I attended the Halls of Cambridge. I studied the Trivium, the Quadrivium, Logic, Philosophy and Theology. I became a Master in the schools but the lure of war has always attracted me. The man I killed had powerful kin. I felt bitter. I fled, arrived in Constantinople and served in a church there, not as a priest, more as an assistant or helper. The Patriarch wouldn't allow a priest of the Latin rites to exercise his functions. Anyway, I served at that church and, every day I used to gaze at the Lacrima Christi.' He smiled. 'And plotted to steal it.'

'What?' Kathryn exclaimed.

'Oh, it wasn't for the wealth. I could see the city was going to fall: all its icons, paintings, statues and sacred relics would be destroyed. I thought if I could take the Lacrima Christi, escape and travel to Rome, I could use it to further my own ends. Perhaps seek pardon and absolution from both King and Church.'

'But Sir Walter stole it?'

'No, he took it to a safer place. He vowed he would never sell it for profit. The other treasures were different. Anyway, Sir Walter saved my life. We travelled to Rome and I arrived back in England.' He grinned. 'With letters from so many cardinals you'd think I was a saint! A royal pardon was issued.' He spread his hands. 'Now, you have my story.' He made to go, but then began to speak again. 'I once read that we are all linked by invisible threads. Is the story true, Mistress, that you were married to Alexander Wyville, a Lancastrian?'

Kathryn held his gaze. 'Alexander Wyville was a Lancastrian, a Yorkist, whatever you wanted him to be, Father. He was also a drunkard and a wife-beater, a man who lived behind a mask. Now his body lies in a pauper's grave in the west country and his soul has gone to God.'

Father John turned away.

'I like what you say about masks, Mistress. We all wear them but they cannot hide the truth.'

'Pilate asked what was truth? With Christ's help,' Kathryn replied, 'I'll find it.'

Father John sketched a blessing in the air and quietly left. Kathryn sat and reflected on what he had told her. Was there any loose thread there? Anything she could tease out to unravel this mystery? Kathryn was not surprised by what she had learnt. Sir Walter had been a man who had armoured his soul and feelings against the outside world, a man oppressed by sin. But who had murdered him? Kathryn rose and went to the door. She opened it and crept out into the passageway. She glanced down the gallery. On shelves and ledges more candles glowed, capped or hidden behind pottery and glass; soon they would burn out. The passageway was empty, though she heard the scurry of mice and the dark shape of a cat came sneaking up the stairs and padded gently along the gallery. Kathryn closed the door and bolted it. She felt safe and secure, her investigation was incomplete. She had faced attack before but not now; after all, she had learnt nothing to accuse and indict a possible suspect, so what danger could she pose? She crossed and sat on the edge of the bed. To calm herself Kathryn went through the preparations for her wedding day. The church would have to be decorated, and flowers laid round the font and up in the sanctuary. The church was her choice: St. Mildred's was where she had been baptised and her parents buried. The list of guests was long. Kathryn tried to recall if there was anyone she had omitted. For some reason she kept thinking of Alexander Wyville.

'Go away!' she whispered. 'Just go and leave me alone!'

Her stomach curdled. Too much meat and wine, she thought. Kathryn pulled back the curtains and lay down on the bed, resting herself against the bolster and staring up into the darkness. She missed her house in Ottemelle Lane: Thomasina clattering about, Wulf and Agnes chasing each other up and down the stairs, Colum stitching some leatherwork or, even better, trying to draw up the accounts for King's Mead. He was good with his numbers and letters but always wrote with his tongue sticking out of his mouth. Kathryn drifted into sleep. When she woke she thought the clanging was part of some nightmare: the running feet, the cries and shouts, both from the gallery and from below. Kathryn hastily pulled herself off the bed and ran to the window. Servants, carrying torches, were hurrying towards the maze where a great fire was burning, orange-tongued flames leaping up to the night sky. She heard a pounding on the door and ran across, pulling back the bolts. Amelia, heavy-eyed with sleep, leaned against the lintel, a blanket wrapped round her shoulders.

'Mistress, you had better come.'

'A fire?' Kathryn asked.

'Aye, a fire, Mistress, and started mysteriously!'

Chapter 4

"Thanked be Fortune and hire false wheel,
That noon estaat assureth to be weel. . . ."

—Chaucer, "The Knight's Tale,"
The Canterbury Tales, 1387

Kathryn grabbed her cloak, pulled on her soft walking boots and followed Amelia down the stairs. The house was now in an uproar, sleepy-eyed servants and retainers hastily dressing themselves. Kathryn went through the main door and out onto the steps. Gurnell and some of the guards were there, swords drawn. Father John, looking rather pathetic in his white nightshirt, also came hurrying down. Gurnell lent him his cloak. Thurston was shouting and screaming at the servants to bring water from the well. Kathryn stood before the steps and stared through the darkness: it seemed as if the rearmost hedge of the maze was fully alight, the flames roaring up to the night sky. She went down into the meadow and started as an owl, disturbed by the fire and noise, swooped over her head, a dead mouse in its beak. Someone bumped into her, and she hastened along the side of the maze and round the corner. She felt a blast of heat, caught the stench of oil whilst floating ash tickled her throat and nostrils. A gust of smoke made her cough and splutter; she moved away, rubbing her eyes. A further glance proved her first suspicions were correct: the rearmost hedge had been soaked in oil, and torched as a farmer does stubble. Servants were already throwing buckets of water on the flames; others brought sheets and old blankets, rakes and spades to beat the flames out. Only then did Kathryn become aware of something else. Three of the servants had moved away from the fire and were gaping into the darkness. One raised his hand and shouted. Kathryn couldn't understand his accent. She followed his directions, aware of Gurnell and Thurston beside her. Just beyond the pool of light thrown by the fire, Kathryn glimpsed a spear shaft or pole dug deep into the soil, a severed head on top. The fire roared, the light shifted and Kathryn glimpsed the ragged neck, gaping mouth, half-open eyes and straggly hair framing a liverish-white face.

'In God's name!' she breathed.

Father John pushed by her. He took off the cloak and, even as the other servants drifted towards the gruesome spectacle, removed the head. He wrapped it tenderly, plucking out and throwing the pole into the darkness. Attempts to fight the fire now faltered as Father John, bearing his grisly burden, hastened back to the house. On the steps leading up to the porch a group had gathered. Kathryn could make out Lady Elizabeth and Eleanora surrounded by armed retainers. Father John hurried by them. Kathryn heard a scream as Thurston arrived, shouting orders at the servants to fight the fire. Kathryn, pulling her cloak about her, walked into the darkness. She found the pole, one end sharpened, the other crusted with blood. Kathryn gingerly picked it up. It was one of those poles used by farmers as a garden stave to allow a tender plant to grow.

'Are you well, Mistress?'

Kathryn turned. Thurston was standing behind her, great hands hanging by his side. In the poor light he looked ominous, threatening.

'No, I am not,' Kathryn retorted and, walking forward, thrust the pole at him.

The fire was now under control but a whole swathe of the rear hedge stood charred and burnt.

'How did it happen?' Kathryn asked.

'I was doing my nightly rounds.' Thurston coughed and spat. 'I smelt burning and saw the smoke but it's harvest time, Mistress, such fires are common. Only sometime later did I see the flames and raise the alarm. It was started by oil,' he continued in a rush.

'The hedge is dry. After all, the sun is hot and it's been weeks since we had rain.'

'So, whoever it was,' Kathryn concluded, 'took a pannikin of oil.' She noticed how the grass was burnt and added, 'Yes, it would be dry as tinder. The oil is poured, a torch is thrown and we are all brought out here to see the grisly spectacle.'

'I don't know who did it,' Thurston wailed. 'I saw no one, nothing suspicious. I have duties to do.' The Manciple was talking to himself; Kathryn wondered if this was a pretence or if his wits were really disturbed.

'Lady Elizabeth has returned to her room.' Gurnell came out of the darkness. He carried sword and dagger as if expecting some assailant.

Kathryn stared at the sword. Gurnell, apologising, resheathed his weapon and stretched out his hand.

'Mistress, you can do nothing here. You'd best come in.'

Kathryn watched this man of war, eyes bright with excitement, chest slightly heaving, his loose shirt, open at the neck, displaying glistening beads of sweat. Kathryn recalled what Father John had told her. She was surrounded by men of war, soldiers who had spent most of their lives fighting.

'Do you miss the heat of battle, Master Gurnell?'

The words were out before Kathryn could think. Gurnell's hand fell away, he stepped back.

'Mistress.' He looked perplexed. 'Are you well?'

'I am well, Master Gurnell. My sleep's disturbed but my wits are sharp. That fire was started to bring us all out here to see the head displayed on the pole, so the assassin must have started it. That's what you do in war, isn't it? Spike the heads of traitors on London Bridge? We had our fair share in Canterbury.' She paused. 'And at Towton. You were there with Lancaster, weren't you?'

Gurnell faced her squarely.

'Mistress Swinbrooke, I'll be honest and as blunt as you are. I am a soldier, a self-confessed mercenary. I fight for gold and silver and, when that runs out, so do I. I couldn't give a fig if the great Cham of Tartary sits on the throne of England.' Gurnell spat the words out. 'I am one of the worms of the soil, son of a peasant, grandson of a peasant. I had two choices in life: to break my back over a plough or pick up a sword and fight.' He wiped the sweat from his throat. 'Aye, I was at Towton. I fought bravely enough for my silver. Lancaster's line broke and we were in full retreat. Edward of York issued an order, kill the nobles, spare the commoners; that's why I am here today.' He leaned closer. 'I was given a choice: change sides and receive fresh clothing, a hot meal and some pennies or hang from a nearby elm tree. Now, Mistress physician, which would you choose?' Gurnell spoke passionately, tears in his eyes.

'I am sorry,' Kathryn apologised, extending her hand. 'My world is more comfortable than yours, Gurnell, I sometimes forget.'

Gurnell's harsh face suddenly broke into a smile as he grasped her hand.

'You've a tart tongue, Mistress. I hope you speak to that Irishman as bluntly as you do to me.'

'Even harsher.'

Gurnell laughed and, taking her gently by the elbow, led her back to the house. Kathryn stared up at the sky.

'It's a beautiful summer's night,' she murmured. 'Look at the stars, Gurnell, the harvest moon.'

She heard a sound at the far edge of the meadow as a russet dog fox, a rabbit hanging from its jaws, padded arrogantly towards the trees.

'Yet death is all around us.'

Kathryn glanced back. Smoke still billowed about; the odd spark rose; ash, floating gently on the night breeze, drifted towards them to stain face and clothing.

'I need a drink.'

Gurnell coughed and led her on.

'To answer your question, Mistress, the spiking of heads was common. When the King's father and brother were killed at Wakefield, the Lancastrians spiked their heads above Micklegate Bar in York and put paper crowns on them. After Towton Edward removed the heads and replaced them with Lancastrians'.'

Kathryn paused at the foot of the steps. Lady Elizabeth had withdrawn, and only two of Gurnell's retainers remained, carrying torches and, swords drawn, guarding the rear entrance to the manor house.

'Where is Mawsby?' Kathryn asked.

Gurnell demanded the same from one of his guards.

'Oh, he is busy with Lady Elizabeth,' the fellow replied, gesturing with his head. 'The mistress asked him to stay. They have gone inside now, taking some mulled wine in the solar. Lady Elizabeth was crying.'

'Shall we join them?' Gurnell asked.

Kathryn climbed the steps: Gurnell still touched her elbow, a gesture of friendship she appreciated.

'No,' Kathryn declared. 'Master Gurnell, I need to think, though I would appreciate a glass of that mulled wine.'

They entered the house and Gurnell led Kathryn down passageways to a small, whitewashed chamber with clean rushes on the floor. In the centre stood a trestle table with benches on either side. A crucifix was nailed to the far wall and beneath that was a battered dresser with a pewter jug and some cups.

'This is where the labourers break their fast in harsh weather,' Gurnell explained.

Kathryn sat on a bench. Gurnell left and returned with a steaming pottery jug. The spiced wine smelt delicious. He placed two pewter cups on the table, filled them to the brim and drew two napkins from his belt. Kathryn wrapped hers round the cup and sipped gratefully. The wine was good, a rich claret from Bordeaux spiced with ginger, nutmeg, cloves and a little sugar. Gurnell sat opposite. The light in the room was quite strong: a number of squat, tallow candles glowed fiercely beneath their metal caps. Kathryn pointed to one.

'Maltravers must have been a very wealthy man to provide light, even during the hours of darkness.'

'Very wealthy,' Gurnell agreed, watching Kathryn intently.

Kathryn blushed slightly and returned to her cup. Something about Gurnell reminded her of Colum: the calm watchfulness, the direct gaze, blunt speech, the slight hint of mockery in his voice. Gurnell, as if sensing her embarrassment, got to his feet, undid his sword belt and placed it on the floor.

'This chamber is also used by the night watchman.'

'So, the house is patrolled and guarded at night?'

'Oh yes. Old Thurston never sleeps. He says he only needs two or three hours.'

'Are there watchmen in the grounds?'

'No, the house is secured and locked. Sometimes the huntsmen and verderers go out looking for poachers but Sir Walter was very indulgent. He always claimed he'd never miss the odd pheasant or deer; the only thing he objected to was when they poached out of season.'

'But could someone leave the manor house unnoticed?'

'Oh, it's possible. There are enough postern doors and side entrances. We don't guard against that.' Gurnell laughed. 'It's people trying to break in.'

'But the assassin must have left the house.' Kathryn looked around for an hour candle. 'What time is it, Master Gurnell?'

'About two hours after midnight.'

'So, the fire must have been started just after midnight? The assassin goes out, retrieves the severed head, digs that pole into the ground and places the head on top. The hedge is soaked in oil, the tinder struck.'

'That could have been done yesterday evening just after dark,' Gurnell objected. 'That's what I would have done.' He held Kathryn's gaze. 'Prepared everything under the cover of darkness, then slipped out later to light the fire. No one would dream of walking in the darkness beyond the maze, especially after what happened.'

Kathryn sipped from her cup. 'Yesterday afternoon, Master Gurnell, you were guarding the entrance to the maze. You never left?'

'Never.'

'Could someone have climbed the rearmost hedge, slipped into the maze and waited for Sir Walter?'

'That's possible but they would have been glimpsed by the Lady Elizabeth, if not while entering then certainly when leaving. Indeed, Mistress, once they were in, how could they find their way to the centre?'

'Are there secret passageways,' Kathryn asked, 'here in the Hall?'

'There is a passageway from the cellars out under the great meadow.' Gurnell put down his cup and held up his hand to fend off Kathryn's exclamation. 'I assure you it's well known to servants. However, a fall of earth has blocked it and the previous owner built a makeshift wall against it. Even if it was open, I am not too sure whether it led to the maze or elsewhere.'

'So, you were at the entrance to the maze? Lady Elizabeth and Eleanora were in the flower arbour to the right of the entrance. Mawsby was in Canterbury. Father John was in the library, Thurston busy in the kitchen. Were there any other visitors or strangers here?'

'That infirmarian Brother Ralph. He came to speak to Sir Walter. I think he brought the Prior's apologies about the Lacrima Christi, but Sir Walter was adamant: he would receive no guests on a Friday.'

'Was Sir Walter furious at the loss of the Lacrima Christi?'

'He grieved but he said the ruby was too precious to sell on the open market. He was confident it would be returned. Perhaps he was distracted by other matters. None,' he added hastily, 'that I know about. To answer your earlier question,' Gurnell continued, sipping at his cup, 'for the assassin to climb a hedge in the maze, he would need ladders. He would certainly be seen through a window from the manor. Even if he did enter, he would have to know that maze like the back of his hand.'

'Is there a map?'

Gurnell shook his head. 'None that I know of. Sir Walter never spoke of one.'

'And the Athanatoi?'

Gurnell tapped the side of his head.

'Only what was in Sir Walter's mind.' He glanced suspiciously at her.

'You mentioned Towton?'

'Yes I did.' Kathryn smiled. 'I had been talking to Father John . . .'

'Perhaps these Athana . . .' Gurnell stumbled over the word.

'Athanatoi,' Kathryn finished, 'had something to do with Towton?'

'It's possible,' Gurnell agreed. 'You see, Mistress, in the eyes of the lords the likes of me and mine are nothing.' He was clearly struggling to hide his feelings. 'I plough the lord's fields and fight his battles. If I have sons, they will do the same whilst my daughters will take their pigs out to snout for acorns. On a holy day I am given some ale so I can drink myself stupid.' Gurnell blinked. 'I can count to twenty and recognise the letters of the alphabet, but that's all. The lords are different. They believe God especially created them, their blood is sacred . . .'

'You sound bitter.'

'No, just truthful.' Gurnell leaned across the table, wetting his lips. 'I fought in Italy once, Mistress, eight months for the city of Siena. They had the blood feud there. Eye for eye, tooth for tooth, life for life. It's the same with the great ones here. Many died at Towton; perhaps Sir Walter had the blood feud invoked against him? Perhaps some Lancastrian heard the story about the Athanatoi and thought he'd use it against Sir Walter?' He shook his head. 'But I don't know.'

'Yet the warning letter only appeared recently?'

'Perhaps that person was biding his time.'

There was a knock on the door; a tousled-haired boy came in. He peered at Kathryn and gestured at Gurnell.

'You must come, sir.' The boy scratched his chest. 'The Lady Elizabeth wishes to speak to you.'

'If the mistress calls,' Gurnell winked at Kathryn, 'then Gurnell must jump.'

He left the chamber. Kathryn finished her mulled wine and followed suit. The house had fallen silent; Kathryn made her way back up the stairs. She had almost reached the second gallery when a figure stepped out of the darkness. Kathryn staggered back with a cry.

'It's only me, Mistress.'

Thurston lifted the lantern he carried. In the poor light his face looked like that of a gargoyle, staring eyes, puffy cheeks, lips slobbery from too much ale and wine.

'What do you want?' Kathryn snapped.

'I didn't mean to startle you, Mistress.' Thurston stepped back. 'I came to speak to you.'

Kathryn followed him up onto the gallery and into a cushioned window seat. She looked quickly through the glass; the fire had died but she heard servants talking below.

'The mistress has put a guard out there,' Thurston remarked. 'But why close the door of the stable when the horse has gone? Father John has ordered the body to be coffined, he will dress it himself. It's to be taken down to Canterbury tomorrow. Sir Walter's death watch will be conducted in the chapel of St. Thomas à Becket, I am sure the Archbishop will agree.'

'I am sure he will,' Kathryn agreed, thinking of old Bourchier, the wily Archbishop of Canterbury who had survived the civil war by pleasing everyone and offending nobody. 'You wanted to see me, Master Thurston?'

'That young girl,' Thurston remarked, 'Veronica, drowned in the mere. She disappeared early in the evening. Those who worked with her said she had become secretive. She finished her tasks and slipped out of the kitchen. No one knew where she was going.'

'And?' Kathryn asked. She suddenly felt weary. 'There is something else?'

'As I have said, Veronica was a comely girl, of good family. Her father had bought her a locket on her feast day. Veronica treasured that. Earlier in the day she claimed she had lost it and slipped away to look for it.'

'Did she find it?'

'Yes, yes, she did,' Thurston replied. 'And her companions heard no more of it. I thought I should tell you.'

Kathryn thanked him and continued down to her own chamber. She'd left the door open and stepped warily inside. She first checked the room: the bed curtains, the wine cup. Kathryn was about to bolt the door when she looked down at the writing table. The candle had burnt out; perhaps it had been extinguished by a servant? The piece of parchment had certainly been moved. She remembered leaving it under some weights, but these had been pushed away so the manuscript now curled. Had Thurston been in here? Mawsby? Father John? Gurnell claimed he couldn't read, but was that the truth? Kathryn bolted the door, slipped off her cloak and boots and eagerly lay down on the bed, pulling the coverlet up over her head. She tried to compose herself by thinking of Colum, then wondered how long she could stay here. Try as she might, the image of that severed head, its half-closed eyes and ragged neck, drifted like a nightmare through her mind. Who ever had done that, she reasoned, was full of hate. To kill an enemy was one thing, to dishonour his corpse another. Who could be responsible? Was it Gurnell? Was he the assassin who prepared everything as soon as darkness fell? Where had the head and pole been kept? Out in that copse which divided the great meadow from the curtain wall of the manor? Kathryn pushed the coverlet away. Staring between the curtains, she glimpsed the darkness beyond the window; soon it would be dawn. She lay down and drifted into sleep.

Kathryn slept late that morning. She would have attended Mass in the manor chapel but, from the sounds below, she realised the daily routine of the hall was well under way. Amelia brought her fresh water and a napkin, followed by a tray bearing a blackjack of light ale, some bread, cheese, a pot of butter and an apple freshly sliced. Kathryn ate, went to the garderobe and came back to wash and attire herself for the day.

By the time Kathryn had left her chamber the manor was busy; servants and chamber maids hurried up and down the stairs. They were friendly enough and one even offered to take her down to the great hall for some food, but Kathryn had decided to walk this manor and discover more for herself. The main rear door was open; maids swept the steps while ostlers and stable boys brought out buckets slopping with water so they could be washed and scrubbed. Kathryn excused herself and went down the steps. It was about ten in the morning and it promised to be a beautiful day. The sky was light blue and the sun was strong, though a refreshing breeze still stirred the branches of the trees. Birds swooped over the grass and already the crickets were beginning their usual monotonous song. Doves flew from the nearby cote, flashes of brilliant white against the sky. The air was sweet with the smell of flowers and the lucid cooing of wood pigeons. Nevertheless, the tumult of the night before had marked the great meadow. Buckets, rakes and spades still lay about. Kathryn walked along the side of the maze and inspected the damage. The fire was now fully doused, though the rearmost hedge and the grass around it were a black cindery mess. Kathryn decided not to enter the maze: the guide rope still lay there, one end trailing out of the entrance, but she felt uncomfortable and uneasy. She turned to look at the hall, its windows shimmering in the morning sun. Was someone watching her? As she walked the perimeter of the maze, she noticed how the grass beside the hedge was long and lush; its close proximity to the prickly branches had saved it from the scythers' cut. At one point she crouched down, pulled the grass aside and tried to stare through. The maze had been cunningly laid. The roots of the hedges were thick and hard, planted so close together they were almost impenetratable. At one time Kathryn started as a rabbit, attracted by the lush grass on either side of the maze, fled like a shadow at her approach. Try as she did, Kathryn could find no gap, no weakness in this wall of closely interwoven prickly branches. An evergreen, the hedge would keep its leaves even in winter. At one point Kathryn leaned against it; the hedge supported her weight. She realised that anyone who tried to use ladders, certainly at the front or sides, would be easily glimpsed. The weakest point was the rear hedge facing the line of trees which divided the meadow from the curtain wall: any approach to this might be glimpsed from the arbour of flowers where Lady Elizabeth and Eleanora had sat. Kathryn walked across and sat down in the arbour.

'Yes,' she murmured. 'Anyone who approached the rear of the maze would be seen by them.'

She looked back towards the hall to confirm that anyone who tried to scale the maze with a ladder certainly risked being seen. Kathryn sighed in exasperation. She rose and walked towards the line of trees behind the maze, a thick copse of hollybush, oak, sycamore and beech, growing closely together, almost linked by the bracken and bramble which grew in such profusion. Kathryn tried to force her way through, but the thorns and branches caught at her clothes.

This must have been part of the ancient forest, Kathryn reflected, staring up at the outspread branches of the trees. If anyone did climb the curtain wall, they would have to struggle through here and across the grass. She returned to the great meadow and stared at the arbour of flowers, a pretty place, its wooden trellis work almost covered by a rambling rosebush. Kathryn walked back to the hall. Thurston stood near the door. She asked if she could see the house for herself and Thurston, distracted by other matters, mumbled his assent. She visited the chapel, an elegant, well furnished room with small square windows, whitewashed walls and black wooden benches. A simple marble altar stood at one end, covered with crisp white linen cloths. The floor was tiled, its lozenge-shaped red and white stones highly polished. Triptychs adorned the walls. Kathryn recognised one as the Theotokos—Mary Mother of God, a famous painting which, according to tradition, had been painted from life by the evangelist St. Luke. The symbols on either side of the triptych showed it was Byzantine: similar paintings adorned the sanctuary, a testimony to Sir Walter's stay in that great city.

Kathryn crossed herself and sat down on one of the benches. There was no rood screen so she could clearly view the sanctuary: the bronze candlesticks, the silver pyx hanging on its chain and the glowing red sanctuary lamp in its jar fixed to the wall beneath. Kathryn wondered if the Lacrima Christi had been kept here. She closed her eyes; that was another problem awaiting her. The theft of the sacred ruby was truly puzzling. The chantry chapel of St. Michael was as fortified as any strong room, its door bolted and locked. The precious ruby had been guarded by two brothers and, when taken down, placed in an iron-bound coffer with two locks. So how had it simply disappeared from the end of its chain?

'I can see no . . .'

Kathryn caught herself speaking aloud. She wondered why Colum hadn't arrived and decided to continue her investigation of the house. She learnt from a servant carrying linen cloths into the chapel that Father John and the others were busy. Sir Walter's corpse, together with that of Veronica the maid, were now being dressed, sheeted and coffined. They were to be taken down to Canterbury later in the day. Sir Walter's corpse would lie in the cathedral chantry chapel whilst Veronica's remains were to be handed over to her family.

'And the Lady Elizabeth . . . ?' Kathryn asked the servant.

The fellow just shrugged. 'I am responsible for the laundry, Mistress,' he replied tartly, 'not the doings of the great ones.'

Kathryn walked into the great hall with its heavy beamed roof draped in banners depicting the arms of England, France, Maltravers and Redvers. More paintings, icons and crucifixes adorned the lime-washed walls of this clean, long chamber with its vaulted roof. It boasted a raised dais at one end, choir stalls for musicians and a heavy oaken lectern where wandering scholars or chanteurs might entertain the household. The hall's long windows were filled with glass, the paving stone floor washed and scrubbed. Servants were laying out the trestle tables and benches, shooing away the dogs, excited by the smells from the nearby kitchens of freshly baked meats, spices and sauces. An orderly place despite the yelping of the hounds and the clatter of platters. The servants gazed askance at her, and Kathryn was about to leave when one plucked at her sleeve.

'Mistress, are you a physician? I am Hockley.' The man's weatherbeaten face broke into a gap-toothed grin. 'I understand you are a leech, an apothecary?'

'Some people say I am.' Kathryn smiled. 'Why, are you ill?'

'We have our ailments, Mistress.' The man shuffled his feet. 'Lady Elizabeth has instructed us not to leave the manor. Brother Ralph the infirmarian, perhaps he won't return, not with this business over Sir Walter? We thought . . .' Hockley's voice faltered.

'I'll tell you what,' Kathryn replied. 'You have a small refectory where the night watchman stays?'

Hockley nodded.

'And a medicine chest?'

Kathryn was ushered like a queen out of the hall down the

passageway to the room where she had seen Gurnell the night before. A medicine chest of elmwood was quickly brought. Kathryn pulled back the lid to find that it was well stocked.

'I'll need some wine, the type used for cooking,' Kathryn advised, 'as well as some honey, salt and hot water in a bowl. Oh, I'll also need napkins and a knife.'

Kathryn wondered if Lady Elizabeth would object but, then again, this would be one way of repaying the household for its kindness. Kathryn soon found herself busy. Some of the grooms had suffered burns the previous evening. She washed and cleaned these, mixing the honey, wine and salt together, binding the wounds gently with strips of linen. Thurston arrived and watched for a while but didn't object. One maid suffered from the rheums, streaming mucus inflaming her nose and throat. Kathryn showed her how to gargle with a mixture of salted water and honeysuckle. She used house leek to dress a leg ulcer and fashioned a makeshift splint for a disjointed wrist. Most of the ailments were mild, like belly gripes, for which she simply advised what to eat and what to avoid. One of the grooms who complained of violent pains, she told to visit Father Cuthbert at the Poor Priests' Hospital in Canterbury. Nobody objected to her work, and Kathryn wondered whether her patients were more keen to meet her than have their ailments cured. She had finished by noon and asked Hockley, who had assumed the role as her assistant, to refill the chest and clean the table. Some of the servants offered to pay but Kathryn just shook her head and said she would accept no return in money or kind.

The news of her work quickly spread so by the time Kathryn continued her journey round the house, she was greeted with smiles and nods despite the growing funereal atmosphere. Black cloths now draped most of the paintings. Even tables and chairs were adorned with a black fine lawn. Where possible, candles and lights were extinguished and windows opened, an old tradition so the souls of the departed could more easily begin their journey back to God. A funeral fast had also been imposed: one meal a day, and that would be at noon.

Kathryn, however, did not feel hungry and was determined on

her quest. Some of the chambers were locked, but the library on the ground floor at the far side of the house was both open and empty. It was a long, spacious room with soaring bookshelves at right angles to the walls. Kathryn marvelled at the richness of its contents. Books backed in leather or calfskin, others with jewel-encrusted covers, were stacked on the shelves. Some were so precious they were chained and padlocked. The books were arranged according to subject: Theology, Philosophy, Lives of the Saints, Sermons, Histories, even a small section on Medicine and Astrology. Kathryn took some books down: sermons of Chrysogonus and other Fathers of the Church, *The City of God* by St. Augustine, the *Summa Theologica* of Thomas Aquinas and *The Secret History of Procopius*. A beautiful edition of the bible was chained to an elaborately carved book stand, its reading ledge carved in the shape of a soaring eagle. There were books in Arabic, Froissart's *Chronicles*, even a copy of Edward Grim's firsthand account of the murder of Thomas à Becket. Kathryn, distracted, ignored the sounds of the household as she went up and down this chamber of treasures.

The library was well lighted, with rounded windows filled with plain glass under which stood carrels and writing desks for scholars. The far end of the library was bathed in the light from a glass-filled oriel window just above a huge oaken table with a matching high-backed leather chair. The table was clear of books and manuscripts; it bore only a writing tray with quills, inkpots and pumice stones. The floor before it was not of polished oak but elaborately tiled in white squares within a green border. Strange red geometric drawings adorned it, surrounding a blue cross in the centre. Kathryn sat down at the desk, undoubtedly Sir Walter's, and stared round the library with its shelves, coffers and casket. She'd probably find nothing in here. Personal papers and manuscripts would be kept in Sir Walter's chantry. She recalled Mawsby's close-guarded eyes: undoubtedly Sir Walter's kinsman would have been through his dead lord's papers and, if there was anything untoward, kept this to himself. Kathryn believed she had the measure of Mawsby, a sly, secretive man; so where else could she go? Kathryn rose, came round the desk, crouched down and studied the geometric design on the tiled floor; she recalled Father John's words about a secret passageway. A sound further down made her glance up sharply: the library door stood half-open. Had someone been lurking there, silently watching? Kathryn sighed, rose to her feet and went into the kitchen. The cook and bakers were now busy cleaning the oven, washing down tables. She was greeted cheerfully enough. Kathryn asked for the cellarman and the spit boy pointed to her former assistant Hockley sitting on a stool cradling a tankard of ale. He welcomed Kathryn effusively, offering to share his tankard, but, as Kathryn had earlier treated him for an abscess on the mouth, she politely declined.

'I understand a secret passageway runs under the hall?' she asked.

'Oh, there is.' Hockley gestured with his hands. 'And more than one. It's like a rabbit warren.' He pointed to the floor. 'According to local lore, a castle once stood here.' He leaned closer, and Kathryn tried not to flinch at his stale breath. 'A robber baron lived here, one of those involved in Becket's murder and a lot more, smuggling, receiving stolen goods . . .'

'Will you take me down there?' Kathryn asked.

'I'd be delighted to.'

Hockley led her out through a door into a cobbled courtyard with a well in the centre and outhouses and store chambers facing onto it. He led her across, through a postern door, and turned immediately right, jangling a bunch of keys, then opened a door and took Kathryn aside. He lit two lanterns, handed one to her, unlocked another door, and led her down steep steps into what he called his "warren of tunnels." Kathryn reached the bottom. The passageway before her, dark, narrow and musty, stretched into the darkness. The stones on either side were of a different type from that of the hall, roughly hewn and sharp edged. The cellarman told Kathryn to be careful. The ground beneath was mud-beaten, and Kathryn realised she was in the crypt of the old castle. Caverns and chambers stood off the passageway, some with air grilles high in the walls looking out onto the central courtyard. The cellarman explained these were storerooms for tuns of wine, logs, tools and huge barrels of ale. He led Kathryn deeper into the darkness, their footsteps sounding hollow, voices echoing eerily. Kathryn felt cold and rather wary. The tunnel floor was uneven, the ceiling was low and the light from the lanterns made their shadows dance round them as if they were being visited by ghosts from the past. They turned a corner; there were no more store-rooms but two further tunnels, one leading off to the right, the other to the left.

'Come along here, Mistress.'

Hockley led her to the left. The passageway was even narrower, its ceiling brushing Kathryn's head, and eventually they reached the end, where the tunnel was sealed off by a red brick wall. The cellar man patted it.

'Sir Walter repaired that, just after he bought the house.'

'Why?' Kathryn asked.

'Ah, the rest of the tunnel beyond is dangerous, filled with rub-ble. No one is too sure where it goes.'

Kathryn crouched down and examined the wall carefully. It was the work of a master mason, a hard stone face with thick mortar between each line of bricks.

'It would take a battering ram,' Hockley explained, 'to break that down.'

'Yes.' Kathryn wiped her hands together. 'It would.'

'Well we'd best go back,' her companion declared. 'It's one meal a day and I haven't had mine yet.'

Kathryn gratefully agreed: the narrowness of the tunnel, the silence, the flickering light and dancing shadows made her uneasy. They returned to the main passageway, Hockley chattering away, when Kathryn heard an echo further along. She paused, one hand on Hockley's arm.

'I heard something.'

'Nonsense!' he retorted. 'I have the keys to the cellar. No one can come down here without my permission.'

'But you left the door open?'

'So I did,' Hockley replied. 'Mistress, are you afeared?'

'I heard a sound,' Kathryn insisted. 'If it's another servant why don't they greet us?'

'You'd best stay here.'

Before she could stop him, Hockley went further up the passageway, lantern raised.

'Who's there?' he called.

Again Kathryn heard the sound. She couldn't place it—it sounded like a creak, as if a rope was being tightened. She peered past Hockley. Was that a shape? Again a sound, a footfall. Hockley, too, became alarmed. Kathryn glanced to her left, where one of the storerooms was used for grain sacks piled on wooden slats.

'Master Hockley, you'd best come . . .'

Hockley turned. A sound broke the silence, like a bird's whirring wings. Hockley was coming towards her but abruptly started forward as if pushed in the back. He paused, swaying on his feet, a stricken look on his face. One hand went out, and the lantern crashed to the ground, extinguishing the candle. The cellarman buckled to his knees and fell on his face. Kathryn glimpsed the stout, feathered quarrel in his back. She heard that sound again, a crossbow; its cord was being pulled back! Blood was already gushing out of Hockley's nose and mouth, and his body twitched a little. At another sound, Kathryn threw herself to the left into the storeroom even as the death-bearing crossbow bolt sliced through the air to smash against a wall. Kathryn grasped her lantern and gazed round. She was trapped.

'Who are you?' she called out. 'What mischief is this?'

She was desperate for anything to distract her assailant. She lifted the lantern and could have cried with relief. She thought the cavern was unprotected but now she could see better. It had doors pulled back, nothing more than flimsy wooden slats like those to a makeshift stable. She dragged at one but the bottom bolt dragged along the ground. Kathryn hurriedly pulled this up and swung it over, then dragged the other across. She looked for a bar but quickly realised the doors were secured by wooden slats on the outside.

Kathryn looked around for anything to keep the doors from being pushed back. Feverishly, careful not to tip the lantern on the floor beside her, Kathryn heaved and pushed at a wooden pallet leaning against the wall. She pulled this free to barricade the door. She had hardly finished when she heard a footfall, and the door was tried. Kathryn pressed against the pallet. Her assailant threw his or her weight against it but the makeshift barricade held. The attacker drew away. Kathryn used the breathing space to drag across another pallet as well as a half-filled sack. The attack was renewed, the door kicked and banged. Kathryn, drenched in sweat, gazed fearfully around. The tallow candle was burning dangerously low. How long could she stay here? She went deeper into the cavern and her hand brushed the neck of a sack and the rough parchment tag used to inscribe its weight and contents.

Kathryn glanced up at the grille. Her assailant could wait or even return. How many people knew she had come here? She recalled how, when she had crossed the yard, servants were sitting round the well, a few sunning themselves on benches. Kathryn made a decision. The assailant was already hammering at the door. Kathryn piled the sacks together, sweating and cursing, and used the smaller ones to build a makeshift ladder so she could reach the air grille. She opened her pouch and used a small knife to cut the tags free. Kathryn grasped the lantern horn and climbed the makeshift pile of sacks. She opened the lantern, used the candle flame to light the tags and pushed these through the grille, fervently hoping that someone in the courtyard would see the smoke. The grille stood in a small recess; Kathryn used the ledge to build a small fire. One burning tag was placed on another: the tongue of flame grew, the smoke drifting through the narrow openings between the iron bars. Kathryn strained her ears. Every household was vigilant against fire. Would there be any cry of "Fire! Fire!" or the alarm bell rung? Only faint sounds from the kitchen drifted across. The battering on the door continued. Kathryn placed more of the precious scraps onto the glimmering flame. One must have been soaked in oil or grease for it spluttered and a trail of blackened smoke drifted through the bars. Behind her the pallet was being pushed back. More scraps of parchment fed the flames. Kathryn's heart was beating like a drum, her legs trembling in fear. Suddenly she heard a cry; the smoke had been glimpsed.

'Fire! Fire!'

She jumped down from the sacks even as someone outside ran across the cobbles with a pail of water which sluiced through the grille. Scullions in the kitchen began to bang pots and pans. A bell tolled, an abrupt clanging, warning of danger. Kathryn screamed.

'Fire! Fire in the cellar! Fire! Fire!'

Kathryn glimpsed a face pressed against the bar.

'Quickly!' Kathryn urged.

The man outside must have misunderstood for more water poured through. Kathryn continued to scream and yell even though that sinister hammering had ceased. She sat on the floor, arms across her chest. She heard footsteps, faint at first, exclamations of surprise as her rescuers came across Hockley's corpse. One voice she recognised.

'Colum!' she shouted. 'Colum!'

She summoned up her strength and staggered across the cellar floor, pulling the sacks away from the pallet. The door was pushed open. Kathryn caught a dizzying glare of torchlight and then glimpsed Colum and Gurnell with swords drawn. Kathryn wanted to throw herself into the Irishman's arms, but instead she just stood, hands hanging down, fighting hard to curb the terror seething within her.

Chapter 5

"O wombe! O bely! O stynkng cod
Fulfilled of dong and of corruption! . . ."
—Chaucer, "The Pardoner's Tale,"
The Canterbury Tales, 1387

Mistress Swinbrooke, I am truly sorry for what happened. If I found the culprit . . .'

Lady Elizabeth Maltravers gazed over her shoulder at Gurnell, but her master-of-arms shook his head.

'Ingoldby Hall,' Lady Elizabeth continued, 'is built over a warren of tunnels, a veritable maze in itself. We did not find your assailant, but poor Hockley is dead and his murder must be avenged.' She leaned forward, her beautiful face ivory-white, her blue eyes looking darker due, perhaps, to the shadows which ringed them.

'You should have been safe, Mistress Swinbrooke, though I wish you had asked for my advice. I would have insisted that Master Gurnell, or someone of my livery, accompany you. I am also grateful for your work. I understand you have ministered,' she smiled, 'to the needs of some of my servants. I must repay you.'

'My lady, your hospitality is kindness enough.'

Kathryn cradled the cup of warmed posset; the wine had begun to cool and she no longer needed the napkin. In fact, she felt rather foolish. She had managed to retain her poise until Colum had escorted her to her chamber. For a while she had just lain on the bed, shivering, composing her mind, calming her heart and cursing her own stupidity. Amelia had brought a bowl of hot broth, freshly baked bread and a small goblet of fortified wine. Kathryn was certain that it contained an infusion of camomile to soothe her wits. Despite her dishevelled clothes, Kathryn slept for a short while and woke feeling better. She had risen, washed and changed, ignoring Colum's constant tapping on the door, shouting out that she felt better and would be with him soon. The Irishman had lost all of his lazy charm: when she left the chamber, he was pacing the gallery, fingers tapping the hilt of his sword, ready to enter the tourney ground against Kathryn's mysterious assailant.

'I shouldn't have left you here. You shouldn't have gone down there!'

'Should! Shouldn't!' Kathryn riposted. 'Master Murtagh, if I only did what I shouldn't do.' She forced a smile. 'Perhaps I shouldn't be marrying you!'

Colum looked perplexed.

'I am only teasing!'

Further discussion was prevented by Amelia, who came pattering breathlessly up the stairs announcing the Lady Elizabeth would like to see them both in her chamber. They'd quickly composed themselves, and now sat in high-backed chairs before the great mantelpiece in Lady Elizabeth's opulent chamber. Kathryn had never seen such rich elegance: eye-catching paintings in gold gilt frames, gleaming wooden panelling, Turkey carpets of deep blue on the polished wooden floor. Coffers and chests, a large ornate four-poster bedstead of dark oak draped and hidden by thick blood-red curtains with golden tassels. Baskets full of flowers gave off a pleasing fragrance which mingled with the smell of beeswax polish. There was a writing desk beneath one of the oriel windows. A beautifully carved lavarium and a large aumbry, one door hanging open, revealing the wealth of the clothes and cloaks stored within. There was even a beautiful silver mirror within a wooden frame attached to one desk which was littered with cosmetic jars and small phials of perfume.

Lady Elizabeth and Eleanora sat opposite. Both were dressed in costly black mourning robes with white bands at the collar and sleeves, dark blue petticoats peeping out above stockinged feet.

Lady Elizabeth's sandals were of deep purple, decorated with small ivory buttons; Eleanora had pushed her feet into wooden clogs which looked rather incongruous in such elegant surroundings. Each wore a dark veil laced with a silver lining. Lady Elizabeth sat on a thronelike chair while Eleanora, on a quilted stool beside her, cradled a book of herbs. Gurnell and Thurston stood behind their mistress: both men looked anxious-eyed, agitated at this hideous attack upon an honoured guest. Kathryn was certain that each had caught the edge of Colum's tongue. The Irishman would not have chosen his words carefully but emphasized how an attack upon Kathryn was an attack upon the Crown and that was treason, hence Lady Elizabeth's heartfelt apology.

'How could it have happened?' Colum demanded.

'How could any of their dreadful deeds have occurred?' Eleanora spoke up, her tone clipped, eyes challenging. She seemed to have taken a distinctive dislike to Colum. She placed the book of herbs on the floor. 'Mistress Swinbrooke, we, too, are afeared. I gather you do not believe in the Athanatoi?'

Kathryn glanced at Gurnell, who looked embarrassed.

'I do, whatever they call themselves.' Eleanora continued fiercely. 'They wish vengeance against the Maltravers name.'

'How could it have happened?' Colum repeated, deliberately ignoring Eleanora's outburst.

'Easy enough,' Gurnell replied shamefacedly. 'Beneath Ingoldby Hall,' he walked forward, fingers splayed, 'run tunnels and passageways, the cellars and dungeons of the ancient castle which once occupied this spot. Some are used, most are blocked off.'

'And entrances?' Kathryn asked.

'Hockley used the one we all know,' Gurnell conceded. 'But there are others. One from the old tower out near the mire, and there's a third which can be entered from a storeroom near the stables.'

'And you saw no one?' Kathryn demanded of him.

'Mistress, it was as difficult to catch any of the rats which scuttle there. By the time we reached the passageway it was empty, apart from poor Hockley's corpse. We saw no one.'

Colum agreed.

'But why?' Kathryn mused loudly. 'Why attack me unless I've discovered something important?'

'In which case, why was my husband murdered?' Lady Elizabeth demanded. And poor Veronica?'

Kathryn could only shake her head. She realised this discussion could easily slip into bitter argument. She stared down at her hands, her fingers were cut, probably from when she had climbed those rough sacks and attempted to light that fire. Small, white welts marked her knuckles where she had been slightly burnt.

'You were most fortunate, Mistress,' Lady Elizabeth remarked. 'And I thank God for your escape.'

'And the crossbow?' Colum demanded.

'We have a small armoury,' Gurnell replied, 'as well as those weapons used by the huntsmen and verderers.'

'Lady Elizabeth . . .'

Kathryn had decided to seize the opportunity, but paused at a knock on the door. Mawsby and Father John came into the chamber. They were cloaked and booted. Mawsby wore black as a sign of public mourning. Father John had donned a white chasuble, a purple stole round his neck, a psalter in his hands.

'My lady, we should be leaving.' Mawsby bowed.

Lady Elizabeth leaned back and closed her eyes.

'I have made my farewells,' she whispered. 'Father John, see my husband's corpse into Canterbury. The good monks have laid out the funeral hearse and candles. You have money for the offerings?'

'Mistress, that is all taken care of,' Mawsby intervened. 'A second casket has also been arranged for the maid Veronica. Once we have handed Sir Walter's corpse to the monks at the cathedral, we shall meet the girl's family.'

Lady Elizabeth was about to say something but then shook her head. She picked up her mother-of-pearl ave beads from her lap and began to thread them through her fingers.

'You'd best go.'

Both the chaplain and Mawsby bowed and left. Kathryn was tempted to observe the protocols and excuse herself, but would such an opportunity ever present itself again?

'Lady Elizabeth, I must talk to you confidentially.'

'Mistress Swinbrooke, I have hardly slept. My husband's corpse is coffined and on its way to the Cathedral.'

'And his soul demands vengeance,' Kathryn added. 'God's justice, not to mention the King's, must be done.'

Eleanora offered her mistress a goblet of wine. Lady Elizabeth declined, gesturing for Gurnell and Thurston to leave, but once the door closed behind them, Lady Elizabeth whispered to Eleanora, who then rose and served more wine. Kathryn sipped hers but decided she had drunk enough and placed the cup on the small checkerboard table beside her. She nudged Colum gently, a signal to remain silent and guard his tongue. Lady Elizabeth raised the goblet to her lips and stared across at Kathryn.

'I suspect what you are going to ask me, Mistress, so let me help. I am young enough to be my husband's daughter. My family, as you know, are powerful merchants in the city of London. My father has a finger in every pie, be it wood from the Baltic, herrings from the North Sea, flax from the Low Countries or wine from Spain and Portugal. He has friends at the courts of Castile and Aragon, which is how I met my lady-in-waiting, Mistress Eleanora. We grew up together.' She smiled. 'Two young women in the iron world of men. I wished to have a good match. Sir Walter was personable and the King approved. So, why should I object? Is it not the lot of us women to do what our menfolk demand?'

Kathryn bit back her reply just in time. Lady Elizabeth sipped from her goblet like a cat would a bowl of cream, the ave beads hanging from her wrist like a bracelet.

'We married just over three years ago, a May-December marriage. I did not love Sir Walter but I thought that in time, I would do so.'

'And did you?'

'I came to respect him. He was an honourable man, though one lost in his own world. If he was here he would be courtly and chivalrous. He would talk to you about medicine or the city of Canterbury. He would show Master Murtagh his horses. But his true soul?' Lady Elizabeth wetted her lips. 'Sometimes it was like being married to a man who had his face hooded, his eyes hidden. Oh, he indulged me.' She forced a smile. 'Our marriage was like many a marriage, a life based on friendship.'

'Did he talk to you about the past?' Kathryn asked.

'Very little.'

'And the Athanatoi?'

'On a number of occasions he told me what had happened, but the details were vague, like a man recalling a dream.'

'And the battle of Towton?' Kathryn ignored Colum's sharp gasp of surprise.

'Towton was a bloody scar on his soul,' Lady Elizabeth replied fiercely. 'Go down to the cathedral, Mistress, or travel to that of York. You'll find a host of fat priests who received my husband's gold to say Masses for those slain. Yes, that was a nightmare, one he never forgot. But that was Sir Walter.' Lady Elizabeth put the cup down, her gaze shifting to Colum. 'I have met Edward of England and his warlords: George of Clarence, Richard of Gloucester, Hastings, Howard and the Rivers gang!' The words were spat out. 'You must have met them too, Mistress Kathryn. They waded to the throne in pools of blood and don't give it a second thought. Sir Walter was different: a good soldier but of a gentle disposition.'

'Did anyone threaten your husband?'

'I have answered that, Mistress. Not to my knowledge.'

'And your husband's illness?'

'He had stomach trouble last winter. Brother Ralph from Grey-friars was a great help. Before you ask,' Elizabeth continued archly, 'that may be one of the reasons why Sir Walter loaned the priory the Lacrima Christi.'

'And what will happen now its been stolen?'

'Sir Walter was angry but not too upset.' Lady Elizabeth closed her eyes, then opened them. 'He muttered something about God's justice being done. I gather from Father John that the relic was taken from a church in Constantinople. To be honest, Mistress, I don't think my husband really cared.' She wound the ave beads and pressed them into her hand as if weighing them.

'But I do! I shall petition the Crown to issue proclamations to all sheriffs, portreeves and market bailiffs: those who trade in precious stones will be warned about handling stolen treasure.'

'Will you stay at Ingoldby?' Colum pulled himself up in the chair as he spoke. He'd been sitting quietly, head down, eyes half-closed, though Kathryn knew he'd been listening intently.

'Master Murtagh, my husband has yet to be buried. I will be announcing a decision very soon.'

'And your husband's papers?' Kathryn asked.

'Ah!' Lady Elizabeth raised one finely plucked eyebrow. 'That is the reason for these questions, is it not?'

'I must go through your husband's papers. I must examine a copy of his will, even though it has not gone through Court of Chancery. There may be something there. A small thread, perhaps a clue to all these mysteries?'

'Master Mawsby,' Lady Elizabeth replied briskly, 'is only accompanying Father John down to Canterbury. He'll be back later this afternoon. You have my permission to go through all papers and documents, memoranda and accounts, kept in my husband's writing office. Now, Mistress Swinbrooke,' Lady Elizabeth smoothed the pleats of her gown. 'I must also prepare to leave. I wish to keep the death vigil over my husband's corpse. The good monks at Canterbury have said I and Eleanora may rest at their guest house. You are welcome to stay here this evening. But I do ask—in fact, I beg you—that tomorrow we be left alone. My husband's funeral requiem will be sung at eleven and, for the rest of the day, I shall be entertaining the principal mourners. I have to see craftsmen about Sir Walter's tomb. Chantry Masses have to be sung.'

Kathryn rose to her feet, Colum likewise.

'And one more thing.' Lady Elizabeth poured the ave beads into a beautiful quilted bag. 'If you go anywhere in this manor,' she pointed at Colum, 'your beloved goes with you!'

Kathryn walked to the door.

'Oh, Mistress Swinbrooke?'

Kathryn turned. Lady Elizabeth had risen from the chair and come towards her. With a surprising gesture she grasped Kathryn's hands and pulled her close. The physician smelt her fragrant perfume and stared at this beautiful woman's face framed by its sombre veil. Lady Elizabeth reminded Kathryn of a painting her father had brought from Italy; that serenity, those well spaced, calm blue eyes and skin without blemish.

'I am sorry if I was sharp. You may envy me, Mistress Swinbrooke.' She let go of Kathryn's hands and gestured round the room. 'But in truth I envy you. I have made my own searches about Alexander Wyville and this, your Irishman.' Her voice had a slight lilt to show she intended no offence.

'Envy me, my lady?'

'You are mistress in your own house,' Lady Elizabeth replied. 'Skilled in your own profession. You are about to marry a man of your own choosing, a man you love. Isn't it strange, Mistress Swinbrooke, how I, who have everything, can still envy you?'

Kathryn glanced at Colum who simply winked and hid his own embarrassment by moving close to the door.

'Be careful,' Lady Elizabeth urged. 'What happened this morning must not happen again.'

Once they were out in the gallery, Colum slipped his arm through Kathryn's and brushed his lips against the side of her face.

'Are you not fortunate?' he teased.

'Irishman, always remember I'll be mistress in my own home.'

Colum continued his teasing as they made their way downstairs. They went into the great hall where some bread and meat had been laid out. Kathryn and Colum shared a platter and sipped at the watered ale before going out to the rear of the house and down the steps to the great meadow. They walked across to the arbour of flowers where Lady Elizabeth and Eleanora had sat on the day Sir Walter was murdered.

'You should have been more careful,' Colum admonished as they took their seats.

'And you, Irishman,' Kathryn dug her elbow into his ribs, 'shouldn't have been late. Some trouble at King's Mead?'

'No, Greyfriars.' Colum sucked on his lips. 'Do you remember the cutpurse, Laus Tibi? Well, the good brothers opened the church this morning . . .'

'He's not dead?'

'No, he's vanished.'

'What?' Kathryn spun round.

'I know it's impossible,' Colum said. 'The sacristan will take an oath over the blessed Host. He locked that church; not even a small mouse could enter. The bailiffs guard every entrance, yet when Brother Simon opened the door of his church this morning, Laus Tibi had drunk his wine, eaten his food and vanished like incense smoke. Neither hide nor hair of him remained.'

'Impossible!' Kathryn declared. 'First the Lacrima Christi and now Laus Tibi? How could he . . . ?'

'Well, he has. The bailiffs are beside themselves with rage. I interrogated each and every one of them. There was good silver on Laus Tibi's head and they were determined to arrest him. I searched the church. No windows broken, nothing forced, gone like a thief in the night. The good brothers are most apologetic. They allowed Laus Tibi to wash, eat and drink. During the day he used a privy just outside the sacristy. At night he was given a jakes pot which was the first thing emptied when the church was opened.' Colum laughed abruptly. 'Indeed, that's the only trace left of him. A half-full jakes pot but no Laus Tibi. Luberon has ordered a search to be made of the markets. The city gates are watched, but when I left, Laus Tibi's disappearance was still a mystery.' Colum stretched his legs. 'By the way.' He grinned at Kathryn. 'I went a-wandering through Canterbury. I called in to see Thibault the locksmith. . . .'

'And?'

'He fashioned the lock to the chantry chapel, as well as two keys; they could not be replicated. One of them was stored in his strongbox and never left it.' Colum spread his hands. 'Thibault claims that lock couldn't be forced. He also assured me that Brother Simon was very proud of carrying the other key and would not let it out of his sight.'

'So, the mystery remains?'

'Yes. Now, this attack upon you?'

'Oh, I've reflected on that,' Kathryn confessed. 'It was easy enough. Someone learnt I went down to those cellars, and the assassin must have followed; two people in the light of a lantern are an easy target. If Hockley hadn't been there,' She grasped Colum's hand, 'that quarrel would have taken me.'

'But why?' Colum leaned back against the turfed seat. 'You carry the King's seal, Kathryn.'

'It means,' Kathryn explained, 'that I did something which frightened the assassin.'

'If the assassin's here?'

Kathryn looked askance.

'Remember the good brothers at Greyfriars. They have a link with Ingoldby Hall. Brother Ralph was here the day Maltravers died, and Prior Barnabas had to explain how the Lacrima Christi was stolen.'

'A friar committing murder?'

'Judas betrayed Christ. Remember, dear physician, we don't yet know what the motive is. My favourite tale is the Pardoner's . . .'

'*Radix Malorum est Cupiditas.*' Kathryn finished the sentence, raising her eyes heavenwards.

'In "The Pardoner's Tale" thieves fall out and kill each other,' Colum mused. He grasped Kathryn's shoulder, squeezing it gently.

She pulled away. 'I don't want any of your Irish riddles!'

'Don't be sharp, sweetheart.' Colum edged closer and put his arm round her shoulders.

'I did miss you,' Kathryn whispered. 'I always miss you, Colum, not because of the danger.' She poked him gently in the stomach. 'But because of your riddles. The attack on me was a mystery.' She sat up, hands in her lap. 'I am sure,' she declared, 'I did something this morning, or last night, which alarmed the dark soul of this assassin but, for the love of me, I don't know what.'

She then told him everything that had happened: the death of Veronica, which Colum had learnt about from servants; her conversation with Gurnell and Father John; her impressions of Ingoldby Hall and the hideous scene which had aroused the manor household during the night. Every so often Colum interrupted with a question.

'*Radix Malorum est Cupiditas,*' he repeated as she finished. 'Deep desire is the root of all these evils, Kathryn, a love of money or a love of something else.'

'More the hatred of a gargoyle's soul,' Kathryn replied. 'So many at Ingoldby have good reason to hate.'

She told Colum about Gurnell, Mawsby and Thurston—how they had been linked to the recent civil war. Colum whistled under his breath.

'I believe every man in this kingdom had a part to play in that bloody struggle,' he declared. 'Look at Greyfriars, both Brother Ralph and Prior Barnabas experienced the horrors of war—but Towton?' Colum's face became grave. He mouthed the name softly.

'You've talked about it occasionally.' Kathryn brushed his hair. 'Sometimes, when you've drunk a little more ale than you intended. You often ask Father Cuthbert to offer a Mass for those who died there.'

'Towton was bloody! Kathryn, you have to experience battle to understand it. You're not brave but full of fear. Towton was the very pit of hell. Misty and cold, hard ground and frozen rivers. If the enemy didn't kill you the bitter wind froze your blood. I was terrified, Kathryn! Banners flying, horses neighing, the clash of arms, eyes glaring at you through helmet slits. Men in armour, blood pouring out through every slit and gap. Men, unhorsed, drowning in mud, screams and yells. Englishmen begging for mercy but showing none. I was near the King. Edward was fearful that the Lancastrians would try to outflank him through Wrenshaw or Castlehill Woods, a favourite strategy of Beaufort the Lancastrian commander. So I was sent to scout the battlefield. I saw hideous scenes, Kathryn; we'd ceased being men and become wolves tearing at each other. I heard vaguely about what Maltravers's men did to the foreign mercenaries, but it was just one story amongst many. They say twenty-five thousand men died that day.'

Beads of sweat appeared on Colum's forehead.

'Do you think Towton lies at the root of all these murders and deaths?' Colum asked abruptly. 'It's possible,' he continued, not waiting for an answer. 'Many hatreds were born that day. Our armies were composed of three sections: the great lords, the commons, and men like myself, Gurnell, Mawsby and Thurston's sons.

We are the mercenaries, the professional soldiers. We, in turn, can be divided into two further groups, those who fight for money and those who fight for the cause. I fought for the cause: Richard of York once saved me from a hanging on Dublin's fair walls. Gurnell, I suspect, is a sword-seller, a man who will fight bravely enough, till the silver runs out or the battle is lost.'

'And Mawsby?'

'Mawsby fought for the cause of Lancaster. I keep a roll of those indicted by the King's lawyers. Mawsby's name was on it. Maltravers must have paid dearly for his kinsman's pardon, though Edward of York is now in a more forgiving mood.'

'Because he's King?'

'No,' Colum grinned, getting to his feet. 'Because most of his enemies are dead. You say Maltravers fell ill of a stomach ailment?'

Kathryn shook her head. 'I don't know what Brother Ralph thought was the cause, but the sickness disappeared.'

'Come.' Colum stretched out his hand and Kathryn grasped it. 'I want to walk that maze again!'

They strolled across the grass into the maze. The guide rope still lay there, so Kathryn found it easy to thread the maze. The paths lost their air of menace, the hedges no longer seemed to crowd in on her. Soon they reached the centre and stood on the small path leading up the Weeping Cross, its steps still stained with blood. Kathryn sat on the stone bench. This was a serene place with the brooding Christ hanging on the wooden cross, the weatherbeaten steps, the dark green of the hedgerow, the sun full and strong. Butterflies danced and chased each other, bees hummed lazily whilst, in the grassy verge, crickets continued their monotonous clicking.

'Maltravers came here that Friday,' Kathryn declared, staring across at Colum sitting on the top step. 'He knelt down. The assassin was waiting for him. One clean swipe.' She mimicked the movement with her own. 'The assassin grasped the head, rolled it into a sack, then disappeared like dew under the sun. Who could it have been, Colum? Everyone has given a good account of their movements that day. . . .'

'And that includes Mawsby,' Colum interrupted. 'I asked Luberon to make careful search amongst the market bailiffs. Mawsby is well known to the stall-holders in Canterbury. He was definitely seen that morning in the city.'

'Mistress Swinbrooke! Mistress Swinbrooke!' A girl's voice carried faintly from the maze.

'That will be Amelia.' Kathryn got to her feet. 'Let's see what she wants.'

They walked back, following the guide rope. Amelia was standing near the entrance hopping from one foot to another, wringing her hands, her face all woebegone.

'What's the matter, girl?'

'You were very kind. You've been very kind to us.' The words tumbled out. 'One of the stable lads told me how you tended the burns on his hand. He said you were very kind, that I was wrong not to tell you. I didn't mean to tell a lie. I was just . . .'

'Hush now,' Kathryn said, grasping the girl's hand.

Amelia gazed fearfully at Colum as if he was the figure of Death itself.

'I'll be in no trouble will I?' Amelia stared wild-eyed. 'But I didn't steal it. Veronica said I did.'

'What did Veronica say? Slowly now.'

Amelia closed her eyes and took a deep breath.

'Veronica lost her locket. She claimed I had stolen it. I was angry and denied it. Veronica later found it and apologised.'

'Where did she find it?' Kathryn asked.

'I am not too sure, possibly her chamber. I live in a small garret at the top of the hall, at the back overlooking the great meadow.'

'And Veronica's?'

'Hers was at the front.'

'Is that all?'

Amelia looked fearfully over her shoulder. 'I must get back.'

Kathryn gazed across where Eleanora was directing the maids who were bringing out small coffers and saddlebags, piling them high at the top of the steps.

'I have duties.'

Kathryn let go of her hand. Amelia stepped back and, spinning on her heel, ran towards the hall.

Kathryn and Colum stayed a while speculating on what they had learnt, watching Lady Elizabeth's retainers bring out more baggage and household goods in preparation for their mistress's journey to Canterbury. Laurel branches were stacked on either side of the door as a sign of mourning, and by the time Kathryn and Colum reentered the house, strips of black lawn had also been pinned to the lintel. Kathryn showed Colum the library; they were seated close together at the great black table when the door opened and Mawsby came swaggering in.

'Master Murtagh. Mistress Swinbrooke.'

The red head went down in a mock bow. Mawsby's boots were dust covered and he trailed a cloak over one arm.

'You are a strange man, Master Mawsby.'

Kathryn's blunt remark caught their visitor unawares; he stepped forward, face perplexed.

'Mistress, you have a tart tongue.'

Colum cleared his throat threateningly.

'I meant no offence,' Maswsby added. 'I know you, Master Murtagh, as well as you know me.'

'You were at Towton?' Colum asked.

'Aye, and Wakefield and Barnet. I missed the bloody massacre at Tewkesbury.' Mawsby listed the hideous battles of the civil war. 'By then King Henry's cause was lost and I'd taken ship across the Narrow Seas.'

'You were an archer?' Kathryn asked.

'No, Mistress, a master bowman, a good soldier. Do you find that strange?'

'You walk like a soldier,' Kathryn explained. She pointed to the war belt strapped round his waist and added, 'You dress like one.' She gestured around. 'Yet you are a scholar, Lord Maltravers's secretarius?'

'I studied in the Halls of Cambridge.' Mawsby replied. 'I disputed in the schools and received my bachelorhood.' His smile faded. 'Then my father and brothers were killed in the West Country fighting for Lancaster.'

'When Lord Maltravers was killed,' Kathryn asked, 'where were . . . ?'

'I returned just after the alarm was raised,' Mawsby interjected. He turned as if distracted by the sunlight beaming through the window, and watched the dust motes.

'Do you know why Lord Maltravers was killed?'

'Murdered, Mistress. My master was murdered. I know of no threats.'

'Did you find it easy here?' Colum asked, getting to his feet and helping Kathryn up.

'To serve Lord Maltravers?' Mawsby pulled a face. 'He was a distant kinsman, a kind man. The war was over, Murtagh. I fought, I did my best. I couldn't kick my heels in the slums of Paris for ever and a day. I know nothing of Lord Maltravers's death, no more than you do.'

'Even though you were his secretarius?'

'Mistress Swinbrooke, I served in the armies of Lancaster. I worked alongside men whom I drank with, ate with and fought with. Men who told me about their wives and sweethearts, their children, their dreams. Ask Murtagh here, what are they to me now but dreams? When you're a soldier, you keep your friends, as well as your enemies, at sword-length.' He gathered his cloak to hide his agitation. 'The Lady Elizabeth will soon be leaving for Canterbury. You have asked to see Lord Maltravers's papers; I am to help you.'

He didn't wait for them but walked away, leaving Kathryn and Colum no choice but to follow. They reached the hallway, busy with servants and climbed the main staircase to the first gallery. Mawsby undid the small ring of keys he carried on a belt hook and led them to a door at the far end of the gallery. He unlocked this and ushered them in.

Maltravers's chancery or writing office was as comfortable and luxurious as the rest of the manor. Light poured in from a large bay window, illuminating the design on the quilted seat beneath, where golden lions fought silver unicorns against a bright blue background. Some of the walls were wainscoted; the rest, where shelves had been fixed, were lime-washed. Chests and coffers stood

113

about, lids thrown back, rolls of parchment spilling out. There was a wooden, open-fronted case, its shelves packed with ledgers and calfskin books. Rolls of parchment, all tied neatly in red ribbon, were stacked in order along the shelves. Underneath these stood a large, rounded tub full of freshly scrubbed bundles of parchment. Two small writing benches carrying inkpots, pumice stones; paper knives and large black jars full of quills were arranged against the far wall, whilst the large, black desk, with its red leather surface, was positioned to catch the light from the window. The chancery reminded Kathryn of her own, with its smell of ink, vellum, parchment and cured polished leather. It was a comfortable chamber from where Maltravers could manage his many affairs, both at home and abroad.

Kathryn's attention was caught by a silver tray just within the door, bearing three silver chased cups and an elegant wine flagon. The flagon cap was of polished silver and on top of this sat a gold chased pelican, its silver beak pecking at its chest to provide blood for its young. Kathryn ran her fingers gently over this.

'Exquisite,' she murmured.

'A gift from the good burgesses of Ghent when Lord Maltravers went into exile with King Edward.' Mawsby pointed to the highly ornate cross hanging on the wall above the wooden panelling. 'That, too, was a gift. Lord Maltravers loved this room. He would spend a great deal of time here or in the library. Would you like some wine?' He pointed to the tray. 'Lord Maltravers always insisted that this jug be filled with the richest burgundy.'

Kathryn and Colum demurred. Mawsby, with more than a hint of sarcasm, gestured at Kathryn to sit in the large thronelike chair behind the desk, and explained how the chamber was organised.

'Most of the documents are household accounts, trading ventures, bills of sales, indentures, memoranda and land charters.'

Mawsby went across to a large coffer reinforced with steel bands and undid the two locks.

'These are what I term Lord Maltravers's personal documents.'

He scooped out the contents, brought them across and placed them on the desk. He sauntered off to sit in the window seat, humming softly beneath his breath as Kathryn and Colum, rather self-consciously, undid the red and blue ribbons and began their search. The light from the window was very good. Kathryn refused Mawsby's offer of candles and tried to concentrate on what was before her. Maltravers was a skilful writer with correspondents as far north as York and Carlisle as well as abroad: there were letters to friends in Paris, Orleans, Rome, Dordrecht, Mons, even Cologne. Other items, dark and shiny with age, contained prayers, lists of goods bought or sold, memoranda, even a small journal Maltravers had kept when he'd visited the eternal city.

The documents included letters from the King and his ministers. Kathryn felt as if she were eavesdropping on the chatter of the court—who was in favour and who was out. She looked over reports from spies and Judas men. One interesting document described the itinerary of the last Lancastrian claimant to the throne, Henry Tudor, now in exile abroad. Kathryn became immersed in her task. Sounds from the household drifted into the chamber, and she heard noises from the stables as sumpter ponies were prepared for Lady Elizabeth's journey to Canterbury. Once again they refused Mawsby's offer of wine, so the secretarius poured a cup for himself and returned to the window seat. The song he was singing was now more distinct and clear, and Kathryn recognised it as one of the great troubadour carols:

> "The rose which
> basks under
> wanton lips,
> Her tender laughter
> is not so sweet. . . ."
> "When darkness falls
> And night winds chill the air."

Mawsby laughed as Kathryn finished the song for him.
'You like the troubadours, Mistress Swinbrooke?'
'My father did. Many visited Canterbury.'
Kathryn returned to her task. Occasionally, she rose to look at other documents on shelves or in the bookcase, but Mawsby was correct: the locked coffer contained what was personal and private

to Maltravers. Kathryn sifted the more interesting documents into a small pile.

First there was a roll of dead, inscribed *Missae Pro interfectis, Apud Towton*—'Masses for the slain at Towton'; it contained a list of names given to a chantry priest whom Maltravers paid to sing requiems. Kathryn scrutinised the names: the dead were foreigners, Spanish and Italian but mostly Provencales. Kathryn realised they must be the mercenaries whom Maltravers's men had massacred after they'd sued for terms at Towton. Kathryn also found a map, only to realise it described the cellars and tunnels beneath the Hall. A quick study explained the arrogant ease of her assailant, for the cellars had at least five entrances in different parts of the manor.

'No wonder you escaped!' Kathryn murmured.

'Look at this.' Colum tossed across a small, yellowing scroll. It was written in doggerel Latin but gave a description of the Lacrima Christi, its size and shape as well as the legend behind it. How it had been rescued by the Empress Helena and brought to Constantinople. However, during the Fourth Crusade, the Western knights had pillaged the city, and the ruby was stolen and taken to Assisi in Northern Italy. Here it had been venerated as a sacred relic before the ruby was stolen again by a group of mercenaries who took it back to Constantinople and sold it to the imperial court.

Kathryn placed this with the rest of the documents. She was about to move on when a small, calfskin tome caught her eye, a book of meditations. She opened it to find that it contained nothing more than a list of quotations from the bible:

"Thou shalt love the Lord thy God . . ."

"Sufficient for the day is the evil thereof."

"A man reaps what he sows."

The writing was all in the same hand. Kathryn had seen similar books drawn up so the reader could reflect and meditate upon two or three simple texts from Scripture, but the quotations reminded her of those warnings Maltravers had received.

'This is strange,' she murmured.

'What is?' Mawsby asked. He rose and came up behind her. 'Is there another book like this?'

'I don't know. Perhaps in the library.' Mawsby's voice was slightly thicker. 'But they are common enough.'

'Those warnings,' Kathryn explained, 'sent to Lord Maltravers by the Athanatoi, the quotations from Scripture, were cut from a book like this; that's how it was done. Another strip of parchment bearing the warning was glued on top.'

'Lord Maltravers or Father John would have soon found out if any book had been damaged or cut like that,' Mawsby retorted.

'True, true,' Kathryn murmured. 'Nevertheless, I'll bear that in mind.' She glanced up: Mawsby's face was flushed with wine. 'Did Sir Walter ever discuss these warnings, why they should appear so recently?'

'No.' Mawsby pulled a face. 'Sir Walter thought it was the work of the Athanatoi, I considered it to be some wicked trick by an envious rival.'

Kathryn returned to the manuscripts, then glanced quickly over her shoulder. Mawsby was back in the window seat. The secretarius seemed distracted, cradling his cup and staring out of the window like a lovelorn squire. Footsteps echoed outside in the passageway. The door opened and Eleanora swept into the room. Kathryn and Colum rose to meet her. The lady-in-waiting was now attired for travelling, soft black leather boots on her feet, a cloak of midnight-blue about her shoulders. Kathryn noticed she now wore a silver chain round her neck with a golden rose on the end; this contrasted sharply with her sombre funeral weeds.

'Master Mawsby, you are finished?' Eleanora spoke haughtily. 'Our mistress is about to leave.'

'And I am to go with her,' Mawsby responded wearily, getting to his feet.

He picked up his cloak and sword belt and waved Kathryn and Colum to the door. Kathryn glanced at the pile of parchments she had singled out.

'Mistress, trust me, they will be there when you return.'

Eleanora led them out into the gallery and down the stairs back to the hallway. Lady Elizabeth, seated elegantly on a chair just inside the doorway, was ready to leave; she caught Kathryn's eye and lifted her hand in greeting.

'I think they would like us to leave,' Kathryn whispered. 'But we'll let them go first.'

Through the open door came the neigh of horses, the cries of ostlers and the creak of carts. Horns blew, people ran up and down stairs. Eventually, under Mawsby's direction, Lady Elizabeth and her entourage swept through the main door, Kathryn and Colum following. Despite the occasion the cavalcade was a colourful one, gaily caparisoned palfreys for Lady Elizabeth and Eleanora, soldiers in armour, heralds with banners. Mawsby and Thurston took up position alongside their mistress. Gurnell organised the cavalcade and, to the sound of braying horns and the calls of those being left behind, Lady Elizabeth and her entourage left in a haze of dust.

Chapter 6

"Trouthe is the hyeste thyng that man may kepe."
—Chaucer, "The Franklin's Tale,"
The Canterbury Tales, 1387

A short while later Kathryn and Colum also rode through the main gates of the manor house, turning onto the rutted lane which would take them past the hedgerows and copses to the crossroads and the main road into Canterbury. Kathryn decided to visit the Vaudois woman, and they eventually found the narrow lane which ran like a needle under a canopy of trees down to a large wood-and-plaster hunting hodge. The house was much decayed, the outside flaking, tiles missing from the roof. Kathryn recalled the tale of how each tile on a roof was supposed to be the resting place of a soul waiting to escape from Purgatory.

'In which case,' she murmured, 'there will be very few ghosts here!'

She wondered how the inhabitants fared when the weather changed and the rain clouds swept in across the downs.

The scene which greeted them was pleasant enough. The front door was open and the Vaudois woman, dressed in her red shift, was seated on a log just outside the door. She was cradling a corn dolly wrapped in swaddling bands. She sat, rocking backwards and forwards, crooning over it. Kathryn and Colum's arrival did not disturb her. Ursula, her face brick red, came hurrying out, hands and arms white with flour. She stopped and stared at Kathryn, then peered round her at Colum hobbling the horses.

'We didn't expect visitors.' She gestured at two logs, smooth and tarred, which served as seats round a makeshift table. 'I'll bring you some ale. I make good ale.'

Kathryn agreed and Colum sat down. The Vaudois woman lifted her head and smiled, her strange eyes crinkling as she peered at them.

'Baby's asleep,' she crooned. 'He's been fast asleep for some time. But you talk, you tell me, has the messenger returned? That man galloping hard along the lane bearing news from London?'

'Hush, Mother!'

Ursula brought out leather blackjacks of ale and handed them to Kathryn and Colum. She stood in the doorway just behind her mother, one hand resting protectively on her shoulder. Kathryn sipped at the bittersweet ale. Colum murmured his approval and, lifting the blackjack, toasted Ursula.

'Your kindness is appreciated.'

'You are Irish,' Ursula retorted. 'We had Irishmen here at the time of the troubles; fierce men they were, but they never hurt me or Mother. They just took our chickens and drank our ale.'

Kathryn, cradling her blackjack in one hand, stretched out and gently caressed the Vaudois woman's lined cheek.

'Lady, I have come to ask you questions.'

'Ask no questions, get no lies,' the Vaudois replied. 'Though you have a soft touch, Mistress. I had a soft touch. Skin, he said, as soft as shot silk.' She had forgotten about the doll and now touched the tendrils of her straggly hair. 'Black as ravens' wings, skin white as snow.' The Vaudois moved her head. 'Do you think we'll have snow, Mistress? Or is it still too warm? But he's gone now.' The Vaudois blinked. 'Now my body has grown old with nasty sin.'

'We've come about the maze,' Kathryn told Ursula. 'No one but Sir Walter knew the path through?'

'Aye,' Ursula agreed. 'And in times past only the old lord knew. He kept it a secret, he did.'

'No secret from me,' the Vaudois woman harshly interrupted. 'Told me all his secrets, he did, whispering them into my ear.'

Tears filled her eyes. 'Love-filled nights, perfume-drenched sheets. Do ghosts come back, Mistress?'

'Perhaps he will,' Kathryn replied ignoring Ursula's sharp intake of breath. 'Perhaps he'll come and walk the maze again?'

'Oh, that would be nice,' the Vaudois simpered. 'We used to take wine and bread in there.'

'How did he find his way around?' Kathryn asked. 'Didn't you ever get lost?'

'Oh, he knew the way, did the master, his own little conceit, he called it. I once asked him the secret, do you know what he said? He replied in fanciful Latin: *"Sub pede inter liberos."'*

'Underfoot amongst the children,' Kathryn translated.

'That's what he said. Now hush now.' The Vaudois remembered the doll she carried. 'He'll wake soon and I'll have to take him for a walk.'

'Can't you go?' Ursula asked. 'I am sorry but visitors only excite her.'

Kathryn and Colum finished the ale, thanked Ursula, remounted their horses and left.

'What do you think of that?' Colum asked as they rode back onto the trackway.

'Sub pede inter liberos,' Kathryn repeated. 'Underfoot amongst the children. Now, that's a riddle to puzzle an Irishman's wits.' Kathryn turned to make sure the saddlebags strapped behind her were secure. 'I'd like to go to Greyfriars first.'

'And so you shall,' Colum replied.

They rode in silence. The spires of the cathedral and the black and red tiled roofs of the city rose into view. The road became busy as pedlars and chapmen, tinkers and farmers, a day's trade finished, now left for home or other towns, a noisy, cheerful throng. Carts piled high with goods or full of children trundled by. Families, who had spent the day in the city, sat under the shade of trees. Pilgrims, grasping sturdy staffs, walked determinedly on to Dover. A group of men-at-arms, resplendent in their royal livery of blue, red and gold, clattered by clearing the road. One of them recognised Colum and called a greeting, but was gone in a cloud of dust before the Irishman could reply.

They entered Ridingate. The day's trade was drawing to an end, stalls were being dismantled: the scavengers were already out with their heavy carts clearing the open sewers of ordure and dung, removing the flyblown rubbish heaps. Kathryn was pleased. Time and again she had petitioned the Council, reminding them that the cleaning of the streets was essential, especially in summer. When they asked her why, she couldn't give a reason except what her father had told her, as well as what she had read in manuscripts, how verminous flies lived on such refuse and spread infection. The dogman was also busy with his heavy cage and wooden cart to collect unwanted curs and mongrels. A group of scholars from the cathedral school scampered by, hitting each other with their battered leather satchels. The boys paused to watch a grinning match between two peasants: each contestant wore a horse collar, and the loser would have to don hop shackles for a while. The stocks and pillories were full of those who had broken the market regulations, the rotten produce, seized by the bailiffs, tied round their hapless necks.

Colum rode ahead, forcing his way through the throng. Pilgrims and visitors, farmer peasants, desperate to get home, purse-proud merchants in their costly cote-hardies. Kathryn was reminded of a shoal of fish, the different colours, people fighting for room in the narrow streets with their overhanging signs. The lower stories of these buildings jutted out so low, riders had to be careful they didn't strike their heads. Eventually they had to dismount and lead their horses. On one occasion Colum produced the royal seal to force a passage through a group of merchants who had surrounded some hapless chapman trading in the city without a licence. A funeral procession forced them into the doors of a house, the priest going before it chanting prayers like a child would a rhyme, the boy, staggering behind him, swinging a thurible which gave off grey puffs of incense.

Eventually they reached the quarter Kathryn was familiar with, up Beer Cart Lane, past the Poor Priests' Hospital and across the bridge before turning north into Greyfriars. They entered by a postern gate, and Kathryn had to shout at the rather deaf lay brother before they were allowed passage through. Another brother hurried up to apologise, took their reins as they dismounted, and promised he-would look after the horses.

'I would be grateful if you would tell Father Prior that we are here.'

They made their way to the priory buildings. In the cloisters the almoner was tending to a group of beggars, distributing the free clothing the priory held: shoes, sandals, breeches and jerkins, whatever the good brothers had collected in their begging forays throughout the city. They entered the church by the corpse door. Kathryn found the incense-filled nave refreshing after the hurly-burly of the city. The sun poured through the stained glass windows so they seemed to glow and burn in a variety of colours: fiery red, dark green, light blue and mother-of-pearl. Candles flickered on altars and before statues which stared stone-eyed down at this feast of light beneath them.

Kathryn and Colum crossed the church, genuflected towards the pyx and made their way to the chantry chapel of St. Michael. The church was now deserted. A few visitors still stood in the doorway, but the lay brothers had rung the bell, and further up the nave the choir was practising a low, melodious chant. The words of the *Magnificat* carried softly through the incensed air like whispers from another world: "My soul does glorify the Lord. My spirit rejoices and God is my Saviour." The choir was preparing for the great feast of the Assumption. Kathryn guiltily realised that she had missed Mass, so caught up had she been in the affairs of Ingoldby Hall. She pressed against the door of the chantry chapel; it was still locked and bolted so she peered through the wooden grille. The chapel was as she had seen it before with its red turkey carpets and altar cloths. The silver chain still hung forlornly from the beam; its hook, shaped in the form of an S, winked in a sliver of light. Kathryn gazed at this intently.

'Why, Colum?'

'Why what, Kathryn?'

'Why did they take the receptacle?'

'Perhaps that, too, was precious. Perhaps the thief thought it was easier?'

They heard a door open further up the church. Prior Barnabas,

Brother Ralph hurrying behind, padded softly down the nave towards them. The Prior had his hands hidden up the sleeves of his voluminous grey gown which flapped around him. Both friars were clearly not pleased at their unexpected visitors.

'If you had told us you were coming, Mistress Swinbrooke.' Prior Barnabas stopped and bowed. 'However, I understand you have been at Ingoldby Hall. A hideous business. More deaths, I understand?'

He explained how Lady Elizabeth's retainers had visited the church a short while earlier to see what progress had been made in recovering the Lacrima Christi.

'And has there been?'

The Prior's dark eyes in his lined, leathery face remained flint hard. He shook his head.

'How can there be?' Brother Ralph spoke up, his pasty face all tight with annoyance. 'If we knew where the Lacrima Christi was . . . ?' He let his words hang in the air.

'Can you open the chantry chapel?' Kathryn asked.

'Yes, I hold the key now.'

Prior Barnabas unlocked the door. Kathryn entered, her boots sinking deep into the thick, soft red carpet. She felt as if she were entering a different world; the red carpet seemed to glow as well as deaden all sound. She walked up the altar steps and closely examined the silver chain. She gave it a slight tug to find that it was strong and held fast. The same was true of the hook; one end went through the chain while the other was used to hold the precious relic.

'Was this chain specially bought?' she asked.

'Of course,' Prior Barnabas retorted. 'Brother Crispin, our almoner, ordered it specially from a craftsman in the city.'

'And the relic-holder?'

'Again, Brother—'

'Crispin purchased it.' Kathryn finished the sentence for him. 'I was wondering,' she continued, 'why the thief simply didn't take the ruby out from its receptacle?'

'It was held secure,' Prior Barnabas explained. 'The thief would have had to pull.'

'So.' Kathryn tapped the hook. 'It would have been easier just to unhook both container and ruby?'

'Of course,' Prior Barnabas hurriedly agreed.

'And Brother Ralph?' Kathryn looked round the Prior at the infirmarian; he stood in the doorway, peering back down the nave as if anxious to go. 'Do you or any of your brothers have any idea how this ruby was taken?'

'Such questions should be directed to me,' Prior Barnabas declared pompously. He moved slightly as if to avoid Kathryn's searching gaze.

'Prior, I mean no offence. A precious relic, a costly ruby has been stolen. I believe Brother Ralph kept the vigil with you. I would like to have words with him, about the theft, and with Brother Simon the sacristan about the disappearance of your sanctuary man, Laus Tibi.'

Prior Barnabas's face relaxed. 'A wily rogue, Mistress. Somehow or other he slipped from the church. Brother Ralph!' he called over his shoulder. 'Ask Simon to join us.'

A short while later the fussy, bleary-eyed sacristan came hurrying down the church, his loose sandals flapping against the flagstones. He still carried a candle knife used for trimming the wax.

'What is it now? What is it now?' he exclaimed.

'I wish to refresh my memory.' Kathryn sat down on the altar steps and stared up at these three friars. 'The Lacrima Christi was in this chapel, barred and locked, secure against any thief. On the day it was stolen it was taken down for a while,' she pointed to the iron-bound coffer in the corner, 'and placed in there. Later on Prior Barnabas rehung both the container and its precious burden.' She pointed at the silver chain. 'It hung there like a pyx does before the altar. Prior Barnabas locked the door to the chantry chapel, the bars were pulled across, and the keys were handed to you, Brother Simon. Prior Barnabas and Brother Ralph maintained their vigil until it was discovered that the Lacrima Christi was stolen. What actually happened, Brother?' She pointed at the infirmarian.

'Oh, quite easy. I have been through it many times.' Brother Ralph almost chanted his words. 'Father Prior was at the prie-dieu, I was kneeling behind him. My knees were beginning to ache so I rose for a short walk. I passed the door and peered through the grille. I could see the chain and the hook but nothing else. I thought my eyes were deceiving me so I called over Father Prior. He immediately—'

'I immediately,' the Prior intervened, 'sent Brother Ralph to raise the alarm and fetch the keys.'

'I brought them.' Brother Ralph raised a hand. 'I watched you unlock the door and pull back the bolts, and so did the other brothers.'

'I went inside,' the Prior continued. 'Well, the chantry chapel was as you find it now.'

'And the sanctuary man?'

'Ah,' Prior Barnabas replied. 'He was standing near the door to the rood screen, eyes popping, mouth gaping. I told him to go back.'

Kathryn rose to her feet; the friars stood aside as she walked up the nave. The choir had stopped singing and dispersed. Kathryn walked up through the screen door and across the broad sanctuary. The Mercy Chair was built into a recess in the wall on the left, just behind the high altar. She went across and sat down in the chair as the others followed her in. Kathryn watched the incense haze and recalled the legend that these were really angels passing through the church.

'Did Laus Tibi have a hand in that robbery?' she asked.

Prior Barnabas genuflected towards the pyx and sat on the bottom of the altar steps, head slightly turned as if distracted by something else.

'That's what they say.' Brother Simon spoke up. 'He must have been a cunning rogue, Mistress. I brought him his food last night: bread, cheese and some wine. He was sitting there all forlorn and miserable. I served him food and locked the church.'

'You are sure every door was secured?'

'At the end of Compline,' Prior Barnabas explained, 'the doors are already locked, except for those which lead through to the sacristy and to the priory, two thick oaken doors, Mistress, locked and barred from the other side. When we rose at dawn the next day to sing the Divine Office the doors were still locked and bolted.' The Prior pointed down to the choir stalls on either side of the approach to the sanctuary. 'The brothers had filed in, the singing had begun. Brother Dominic the Subprior whispered he couldn't see the sanctuary man. Once Divine Office was finished I ordered the church to be searched, but there was no trace of Laus Tibi. The bailiffs outside had kept strict watch; their anger can only be imagined.'

'They even stopped brothers leaving the church,' Brother Ralph explained, 'just in case the thief had stolen one of our cowled robes. It wasn't till midday they realised the bird had flown its nest.'

Kathryn shook her head.

'And you searched the entire church?'

'Mistress, if a sparrow was hiding we'd have discovered it.'

Kathryn turned to the sacristan. 'Brother Simon, I would be grateful for your help. I need to talk to your colleagues on another matter.'

The sacristan looked at the Prior who nodded. Kathryn sat picking at a loose thread on her gown.

'Well, Mistress?'

'Were you ever in Constantinople?'

Prior Barnabas blinked. 'I was, and so was Brother Ralph and a number of brothers in our community. You must remember, Mistress Swinbrooke, before it fell to the Turks, Constantinople held great shrines. I wager at least six score men and women in Canterbury, of a certain age, visited that fabulous city.'

'So, you both went there as pilgrims?'

'Not together,' Brother Ralph attempted to joke. 'I wanted to be a physician. The hospitals of Constantinople, their leeches and apothecaries were famous.'

'And you, Father Prior?'

'A wandering troubadour.' The Prior tried to be offhand. 'Once I was an armourer.' He shrugged. 'Like carpenters, glaziers, free men with skills.' He emphasized the words. 'Or mercenaries.' He glanced quickly at Colum. 'We follow our path wherever it leads.'

'Have you seen the Lacrima Christi before?'

'No,' Prior Barnabas retorted.

'Or met Lord Maltravers?'

'Not until I came here.'

'Brother Ralph, you tended Sir Walter last winter, when he had stomach gripes?'

'I did,' the infirmarian agreed. 'He suffered blood in his stools, vomiting and retching. I treated him with certain herbs and regulated his diet. After a number of weeks the symptoms ceased.'

Kathryn smiled at this pasty-faced infirmarian who, despite his nervousness, was probably a very good leech and a skilful physician.

'How did you treat him?'

'As I said, different herbs, camomile, peppermint . . .'

'Was it an infection?'

Brother Ralph shook his head. 'Mistress, I cannot say. In my studies I have found the humours of some people are hostile to certain foods. You've read the same?'

'I've heard of the theory,' she replied.

'Certain foods,' Brother Ralph continued, immersed in the subject he loved, 'disturb the balance of humours in specific individuals. Surely, Mistress, you have met people who take one goblet of wine and suffer mawmsey?'

'I have met many who have taken ten cups and suffered the same symptoms.' She smiled.

'Sir Walter's belly may have been hostile to certain foods,' Brother Ralph continued. 'I told him to fast for three days, drink clear spring water and, in the future, avoid milk, cream and certain breads. Sir Walter followed my diet and claimed he was much better.'

'But the blood?' Kathryn asked.

'Perhaps a fistula in his anus?'

'And the day Sir Walter died?' Colum intervened.

'That was my responsibility,' Prior Barnabas replied. 'I was so embarrassed at the loss of the Lacrima Christi, I despatched Brother Ralph to Sir Walter, to offer him our apologies.'

'But he refused to see you?'

'I'd heard of his Friday penance.' The infirmarian shrugged. 'But

I had forgotten. I must have arrived at Ingoldby Hall just before noon. I was met by Thurston and Father John; they were courteous enough, though they showed their displeasure at the loss of the sacred ruby.'

'Did you notice anything untoward,' Kathryn asked, 'in your journey to and from Ingoldby or whilst at the hall?'

'No.' The infirmarian went and picked up a small stool from the far side of the sanctuary, came back and sat down. 'A beautiful morning, Mistress. I took a cob from the priory stables. The roads were empty, the hall peaceful and quiet, servants going about their duties. I went round to the rear door; Lady Elizabeth was in the arbour of flowers. Sir Walter was out in the great meadow. Father John was most insistent that he should not be disturbed.'

'Ah yes, Father John.' She glanced up at the Prior. 'Did Sir Walter ever come here to be shriven?'

'I absolved him on two occasions. But, as you know,' the Prior added hastily, 'the seal of confession means I cannot discuss what he told me in the sacrament.'

'So, he told you something?'

'Sir Walter was a very worried man. He suffered dark thoughts.'

'Did he ever discuss the Athanatoi?'

'I've heard the rumours but Sir Walter was . . .' The Prior paused. 'Certain people, Mistress Swinbrooke, have a melancholic disposition. Brother Ralph talked of an imbalance of the humours. I used to urge Sir Walter to pray more, put his trust in Christ.'

'But you had heard of Sir Walter's reputation?' Colum asked. 'Were you at Towton, Father?'

'Yes and no,' the Prior replied. 'That's where I met Brother Ralph. Leeches and armourers follow armies. I would say we were on the fringe of the battlefield. Neither he nor I could give a fig for the House of Lancaster or York.'

'Did you know each other then?'

'It was only when we came here that we shared our experiences, but I saw the battlefield. The dead piled high.' The Prior blew his lips out. 'Men groaning and shrieking, the wounded being despatched. Men hanging from the branches of trees. It was Palm Sunday. I could never forget those hideous sights on such a holy day. I journeyed to London and decided to enter the Order. Brother Ralph had travelled on to Carlisle and made the same decision. The good brothers in London let me stay for a while. I proved to be a good scholar so they sent me to our Mother House in Italy. I returned and served in a number of our communities. Eighteen months ago I came here.'

'Brother Ralph, did Sir Walter ever talk to you?'

'Oh, gossip and chatter. Sir Walter was a closed book: you only saw the covers and the edge of the pages lying within. I liked the man, even respected him, but I no more knew him than I do you, Mistress Swinbrooke.'

'Father Prior, did you buy that pyx?' Kathryn pointed to the round silver casket holding the sacred host. 'I noticed the Greek symbols on it.'

'No, that was a gift from Sir Walter. Now, Mistress, we do have other . . .'

The door leading into the sanctuary burst open and Brother Simon came through, cloak flapping.

'Father Prior! Father Prior!' he gasped. 'You must see this!'

'See what?'

'Come on! Come on!' Brother Simon turned and called to someone in the sacristy.

A burly, thickset man came shuffling into the sanctuary. He was dressed in a costly cote-hardie, though this was buttoned wrongly in an attempt to hide the rather grimy shirt and hose beneath.

Kathryn got to her feet.

'Yes?' Father Prior asked. 'What is so urgent?'

The man opened his leather bag and took out a shiny red piece of plate formed like a square C with a clasp on the top. Kathryn recognised what it was even as the Prior took it from the man's hand.

'It's the receptacle,' Brother Ralph exclaimed, 'which held the Lacrima Christi!'

The Prior was turning it over and over in his hands. He passed it wordlessly to Kathryn. It felt heavier than it looked. A piece of red, precious metal, fashioned by craftsmen, it would encase the Lacrima Christi and hold it in place on three sides, allowing the sacred ruby to be seen in all its beauty. The receptacle was about five inches long and three inches broad. The clasp at the top was a thickset circle of red bronze from which it could hang on the silver hook.

'Where did you get this?'

'I trade in precious metals, Father.' The man's lower lip jutted out, his fat face red and fiery. 'I didn't know what it was. . . .'

'So, how did you find out?'

The man picked up the edge of his cloak and mopped his face. 'I am trying to be honest.'

Brother Simon hurried away and came back with a pewter cup of water. The trader drank this greedily; when Father Prior offered him Brother Ralph's stool, he sat down gratefully.

'I own a shop near St. Thomas's Hospital. Early this morning a well dressed man came in. Well, he looked well dressed: good leather jerkin, hose pushed into his boots, he wore a cloak, its cowl half pulled over his head. I can't truly recall what he looked like but he offered this for sale. He claimed he'd been given it in Dover in payment for work done. The metal's quite precious, and I thought that if I couldn't resell it perhaps I could refashion it. I gave him two silver pieces.'

'In which case you would have made a very good profit,' Father Prior intervened.

'Oh, I was very proud of my purchase. Then into my shop came this clerk, pixie-eared and bright-eyed. He saw it in my scales and asked for a closer look. I let him see it and the fellow began to laugh. He explained how he'd gone to Greyfriars to view the Lacrima Christi. Didn't I know it had been stolen and that this was the receptacle in which it was set?'

'When was this?' Kathryn asked.

The trader looked at her keenly. 'You are a strange friar, Mistress . . . ?'

'Answer the question!' Colum barked.

'I'll answer it for him,' Kathryn replied. 'You realised it had been stolen yet you'd paid good silver for it.' Kathryn came across and patted the man's arm. 'Eventually, your conscience told you to do the right thing?'

The trader looked at Kathryn lugubriously.

'Two silver pieces,' he mumbled mournfully.

'Brother Simon will take you to our almoner,' Prior Barnabas ordered. 'We will give you half of what you paid as well as remember you and yours in tomorrow's Mass.' He sketched a blessing in the air.

The trader looked pitifully at Kathryn, then longingly at the receptacle.

'Next time,' Kathryn advised, 'pay more attention to strangers who sell you precious metals. Could you describe him?'

'As I said, not very well; lean-faced, balding, well attired though shifty-eyed.'

'Shifty-eyed?' Prior Barnabas asked. 'And you never wondered . . . ?'

The trader just stared back. 'I'd best get my money.'

He followed Brother Simon out of the sanctuary.

'Well, well, well.' Kathryn smiled. 'Laus Tibi will be giving praise to God. He managed to escape from sanctuary and, somehow or other, got hold of the receptacle which held the Lacrima Christi.' She sighed. 'I can't find any logical reason to explain his good fortune. Father Prior, you are sure that Laus Tibi had nothing to do with the chantry chapel of St. Michael's?'

'As God lives,' the Prior replied, 'no.'

'At night,' Colum remarked, 'he could have wandered this church at will.'

'What profit would there be in that?' the Prior replied. 'Doors are locked and barred. The chantry chapel of St. Michael likewise and the sacred ruby safe in its coffer.' He paused as a bell, deep in the priory, tolled. 'I have other duties. . . .'

Kathryn and Colum thanked him. The Prior left. Brother Ralph, tactfully as possible, ushered the two guests down the nave and out through the half-open front door.

A lay brother had brought their horses round; he now lay sunning himself whilst the horses cropped the long grass.

'I was really enjoying myself.' This beanpole of a man sprang to his feet, dusting down his grey gown. He rubbed his stomach.

'Time for the evening meal. Man may not live by bread alone.' he grinned. 'But sometimes it helps.'

And he disappeared through the door of the church, slamming it behind him.

'A sea of mystery.'

Kathryn stared up at the white puffs of cloud. The blue sky was beginning to darken. Beyond the lych-gate a boy pushing a noisy wheelbarrow bawled at someone to get out of his way. From the marketplace came the faint sound of the horn, the signal for the end of the day's trading.

'Do you know, Colum, one mystery I've never solved: Gurnell said that Sir Walter kept a horn at the centre of the maze. He always sounded it as a signal, but on that day no horn was sounded. Was it because Sir Walter didn't have time, or had the killer already taken it? It's disappeared and never been returned. And there's something else.' Kathryn paused. 'Whilst riding into Canterbury I realised Gurnell guarded the entrance to the maze. He was seen by other guards, but they were lazing in the sun. Lady Elizabeth also said he remained there, but if he knew how to thread that maze, couldn't he have disappeared for a short while to do his bloody-handed work?'

'Possible,' Colum agreed, unhobbling the horses and wrapping the reins round his wrists. 'We'll walk, Kathryn, yes?'

'For a while let's just stay here,' Kathryn urged. 'This graveyard is so peaceful. Now, Father John and Master Thurston . . .'

'What about them, Kathryn? Like that lay brother my stomach is grumbling.'

'Well, Thurston said Father John was in the library,' Kathryn continued. 'He took him refreshment there. So, for a while, the only people who could guarantee Thurston's and Father John's whereabouts were each other. This is so perplexing.' She stamped her foot. 'Is it possible that Sir Walter was killed not by one person, but by a conspiracy of many? Like cunning men in the market place who put a silver piece under one of three cups and then fool the onlookers. Am I looking in the wrong direction? Did Sir Walter's household plot his murder and do they now protect each other?'

133

'Why not include Lady Elizabeth and Eleanora?' Colum replied.

'Again that's possible. I have yet to see a copy of Sir Walter's will, but apparently, they are all to benefit from his death.'

The bell of the priory began to toll again.

'An end to your silence, Kathryn.' Colum stretched out his free hand. 'We must go.'

Kathryn, lost in her own thoughts, walked beside him as they left for Greyfriars and, turning left, made their way back over the bridge and through the half-emptying streets. Kathryn was unaware of her surroundings. She heard her name being called and Colum exchanging greetings with passersby. They reached her house in Ottemelle Lane and the Irishman playfully tweaked her ear.

'Kathryn, we are home.'

'Yes, yes, of course we are.'

Kathryn pushed open the door and immediately Wulf the young foundling came racing along the passageway, arms extended, face smeared with butter and honey. He leapt at Kathryn, throwing his arms round her waist. Behind him trotted Agnes the maid, bright-eyed, her cheeks flushed, and then came Thomasina, Kathryn's nurse and maid, all a-smiling, her white wimple billowing out like the sails of a ship.

'Just in time,' Thomasina called. 'I have had enough of the teasing of these two.' She peered through the half-open door. 'Ah yes, and the Irishman with his horses. Come, Mistress Kathryn, come on in.'

'How can I resist a greeting like that?' Kathryn replied.

Thomasina pushed by Agnes, grasped Wulf by the scruff of his neck, and tearfully embraced Kathryn as if her mistress had just returned from a pilgrimage to Jerusalem.

'I have missed you,' she whispered. 'And it's always dangerous, these sudden, horrible murders. . . .'

Kathryn was surrounded by soft flesh; the smell of lavender, flour and soap tickled her nostrils. By the time Thomasina stood away her eyes were dry as she turned her fierce glare on Wulf.

'Born to tease,' she accused. 'If not poor Agnes then me!'

Kathryn thought "poor" Agnes was enjoying every second of it but she held her peace as Thomasina led her into the stone-flagged kitchen. Everything was in place: a small fire burnt in the mantelled hearth, the windows overlooking the garden had been thrown open, and the broad, black oaken table had been scrupulously scrubbed and cleaned. Cutting boards, pots, skillets, and pans hung from hooks on the whitewashed walls. The bread basket had been pulled up under a beam to protect the fresh batch of loaves from the ever present mice. Thomasina had been busy at the cutting table, slicing leeks, shallots and other vegetables. A thick wedge of bread almost covered in butter and honey lay precariously on the side; Wulf immediately grasped this and, ignoring Thomasina's screech of disapproval, thrust it into his mouth. The boy was a foundling, and Thomasina, despite her gruff appearance, treated him as tenderly as a son. He responded, copying Colum, with a constant stream of teasing.

'Now, now, now.'

Thomasina made Kathryn sit at the kitchen table and immediately served her a tankard of cool rich ale drawn from its tun in the nearby buttery. Bread, cheese and sliced apple followed. Kathryn knew she had to eat and drink, for the alternative wasn't worth considering. Once Kathryn had begun to eat, Thomasina cleared Agnes and Wulf out of the kitchen and chattered like a squirrel on a branch, divulging all the gossip of the parish. How Goldere had spent an hour in the stocks for being drunk. How Fulke the tanner had organised a pissing contest as he needed the urine for his vats.

'He bought the cheapest ale he could,' Thomasina snapped. 'Quite a number of the men were sick. Oh and Alicia, the one who is pregnant, she came down, I felt her belly. I think the child's in the wrong position. I sent her to Father Cuthbert. Henry the sackmaker claimed to have a lump in his throat. I sent him to Father Cuthbert as well.'

I am sure you did, Kathryn reflected. If Thomasina had one great love of her life, apart from Kathryn, it was Father Cuthbert; their relationship dated back many years.

'Venta the wise woman. Oh no.' Thomasina screwed her eyes up and scratched her red cheek. 'No, she didn't come. I saw her in the street. She was asking about the wedding. I have been down to St. Mildred's church. I want flowers round the font, church ale near the door. If the weather is good, we could have the feasting in the graveyard.'

Kathryn laughed.

'And perhaps in the evening,' Thomasina continued remorselessly, 'chosen friends.' She emphasized the word. 'I don't want any of the Irishman's bog-trotting friends. Chosen friends,' she repeated, 'will attend the wedding banquet at the *Chequer of Hope* inn.'

Kathryn recognised it as one of the best taverns in Canterbury.

'I have been down to see Mine Host: he's to supply the best pork and beef, not the saltiest he can find in the market. . . .'

On and on Thomasina went. Colum came in, filled a blackjack of ale and went out into the garden. Kathryn sat half-listening to Thomasina, but her mind drifted back to Ingoldby Hall, that shadow-filled maze and the growing suspicion that the black-souled assassin, whoever it was, might kill again.

Chapter 7

"The smylere with the knyf under the cloke . . ."
—Chaucer, "The Knight's Tale,"
The Canterbury Tales, 1387

The guest house refectory of Canterbury Cathedral was a two-storied wood and plaster building. On that particular night its thick paned windows glowed with light, for the powerful Lady Elizabeth Maltravers, together with principal members of her household, resided there. Lady Elizabeth had attended the churching of her husband's corpse. The coffin now lay on its trestles in the chantry chapel covered in a black and gold drape surrounded by purple candles. These funeral lights would glow all night as the Lady Elizabeth, or the good brothers, maintained a litany of prayers so that, whatever his sins, Sir Walter's soul might find peace in Paradise. Lady Elizabeth had ceased her vigil and was now with Gurnell, Thurston, Father John and her lady-in-waiting Eleanora, preparing to dine in the long, narrow refectory.

It was a simple, stark chamber, befitting a monastery with its heavy black-beamed roof and plaster white walls decorated with the occasional crucifix or devotional painting. A trestle ran down the centre with benches on either side, though a cushioned chair was placed at the top for Lady Elizabeth. The brothers had swept the refectory and laid down fresh rushes strewed with mint and other herbs. The nearby kitchen had been busy preparing roast duck, quail and strips of spiced venison. The lay brothers had served the meal on pewter dishes, giving each of the guests a white napkin. They had left the wine on a side table and, after the guest master had intoned the Benedicite, quietly withdrawn. Lady Elizabeth now allowed herself to relax. She pulled back the veil covering her face and picked delicately at the food, lost in her own thoughts. Thurston and Gurnell served the wine whilst Father John, aware of the growing tension, simply stared down at his platter of well cooked venison.

'My Lady.' He glanced up. 'The day went as well as it could, I mean in the circumstances.'

'In the circumstances, Father, yes it did.' Lady Elizabeth sipped at her cup and stared coldly over its rim at the priest. 'I am glad we are here,' she continued, 'as there are matters we must discuss.'

She paused as Mawsby entered the refectory, bowed, poured himself a goblet of wine and sat down beside Father John. Thurston served him food from the main platter while Lady Elizabeth stared in annoyance at the latecomer.

'As I was saying.' Her voice rose. Eleanora's hand went out to stroke her hand but this was gently pushed away. 'We have matters to discuss. No, no, not matters of the will. Sir Walter's made it very clear. You are each to receive a generous bequest and you may, if you wish, continue at Ingoldby for a while, though I shall be returning to London.'

'What matters, my lady?'

Father John picked at his food.

'You know very well,' came the tart reply. 'Mistress Swinbrooke is of the firm belief that one of us is responsible for Sir Walter's death.'

'She has not said that,' Father John said.

'She has implied it.' Mawsby pointed his knife at the priest. 'It's in her eyes, the way she looks at you.'

'Aye, she's a shrewd woman,' the priest agreed. 'And she moves round the hall like a ghost.'

'My house, Father,' Lady Elizabeth declared, but then her face softened. 'Though I agree she has sharp wits and a keen mind.'

'So keen she may cut herself,' Father John quipped.

'She was attacked,' Gurnell stated.

Silence greeted his words.

Lady Elizabeth cleared her throat. 'The day my husband Sir Walter was murdered we all knew where we were, though that's not the full truth, is it?'

'What?' Mawsby's head came up. 'My lady, I was in Canterbury.'

'So you say. So you say. But, Master Gurnell, is it not true you entered the maze?'

'Well, yes.' Gurnell dropped his meat knife, hand going out to the goblet of wine. He lifted it hastily to his lips and slurped. 'You know I often do; I am intrigued by its mystery. But I came out again.'

'Yet you were so distracted,' Lady Elizabeth retorted, 'that you forgot to listen for the sound of the horn?'

'Well, yes, but . . .' Gurnell's voice faltered.

'And you, Master Thurston. Did you not bring out refreshments to the guards and follow Master Gurnell into the maze?'

The Manciple, his face red with anger, glared at his mistress.

'Of course I did, but Gurnell was just in the entranceway. I told him I had left a tray on the grass, that he'd best drink . . .'

'And Father John?'

'Mistress, what are you saying?' the priest replied coolly.

'You did come down from the library and speak to Master Gurnell?'

'But I then returned to the library.'

'And have you told Mistress Swinbrooke all this?'

'They are matters of little consequence,' Gurnell spluttered. 'My lady, where are you leading us? None of us could follow Sir Walter into the maze, and even if we could, who here would want to murder him? He was a good lord, a generous master.'

'I am simply making a point,' Lady Elizabeth declared. 'I agree with Mistress Swinbrooke. The murderer must have been one of Sir Walter's household. I have, therefore, decided that after my husband's will has been approved by the Court of Chancery, I will be dismissing my household.' She lifted a hand to quell their protests. 'You will all receive generous bequests, and that includes you, Eleanora.' She ignored her lady-in-waiting's gasp of protest. 'I do not feel safe,' Lady Elizabeth continued. 'Indeed, I warn you, none of us should feel safe, until this matter is resolved.'

Lady Elizabeth grasped her knife and cut the venison. She paused, picked up a small manchet roll and crumbled it on the pewter dish.

'You know my wishes in this matter.' She forced a smile. 'But now we will eat a funeral meal.' She lifted her goblet in a toast and the rest, sullen-faced, followed suit.

The meal continued in silence, Lady Elizabeth making it very clear that she wanted no idle chatter. Thurston cleared the platters and brought around the dish of small pastries and comfits the brothers had left on the side table. Wine cups were refilled. The sombre meal continued. Gurnell, drinking heavily, grew more withdrawn and heavy-eyed. Mawsby tried to talk to Father John, but the priest failed to respond, whilst Thurston sat staring into his wine cup as if it could determine what the future held. Eleanora was crying softly, and when Lady Elizabeth tried to comfort her, she morosely turned away. The meal was almost ended and Father John thought Lady Elizabeth was going to deliver another speech when his mistress suddenly pushed away her chair and made to rise, clenching her fists, her beautiful face contorted in pain.

'Oh, *Domine Miserere!*' she whispered. 'Oh, Lord, have mercy!'

Eleanora screamed, springing to her feet, and tried to support her mistress. Lady Elizabeth, lost in her own pain, was clutching her abdomen. Her headdress became loose and fell to the floor, her golden hair spilling out. The others, surprised, simply stood and stared as Lady Elizabeth gripped the edge of the table and tried to pull herself up. She had almost done so when another spasm caught her and, hands flailing, knocking her goblet to the floor, she collapsed once again. The sound of her lady-in-waiting's screams rang through the refectory, alarming the brothers who had been cleaning in the nearby kitchen. They hurried in to find Lady Elizabeth stretched out on the floor, a hideous gargling sound coming from the back of her throat, her household standing about.

'My mistress has been poisoned!' Eleanora cried. She stared accusingly around. 'Someone has poisoned my mistress!'

* * *

Kathryn sat in her writing office, filling in the ledger of payments received.

'As well as those owing,' she whispered to herself. The sums were petty. Kathryn's profits accrued not so much from the patients but potions and powders, the remedies she sold from her apothecary's chamber further down the passageway. Kathryn put down her quill. The house was now quiet. Wulf was sitting out in the garden, staring up at the stars, Agnes and Thomasina busy in the kitchen. Kathryn welcomed the distraction from the murderous riddles which had plagued her mind since she had arrived from Ingoldby Hall. News had soon spread that Kathryn was back in her house, and a line of patients promptly appeared.

'As quickly,' Thomasina declared, 'as bees to the honey.'

Helga, the rotund wife of Torquil the carpenter, maintained she was pregnant, but Kathryn quietly believed it was more wishful thinking than a happy event. Molyns the baker had burnt his arms then tried to treat himself; the wounds had begun to suppurate, and Kathryn had to clean these with salt, wine and honey. Edith and Eadwig Fulke, the tanner's twins, had arrived as deaf as posts.

'We can't hear!' they had yelped. 'We have gone deaf!'

'When did this happen?' Kathryn asked as solemnly as she could.

'We can't hear you,' Eadwig had shouted. 'That's why we are here.'

Kathryn had carefully examined their ears and consulted the leech book. She had warned Fulke about the dust in his shop which, somehow or other, irritated the noses and throats of his family.

'It's a build-up of fluids,' she tried to explain.

The twins, alike as peas in a pod, had simply sat dolefully, staring round-eyed, unable to comprehend.

'You have hardened wax in your ears,' Kathryn shouted.

'We are not candles,' Edith had replied.

'No, no, you have wax.' Kathryn tried to stop her laughter.

Wulf, alarmed by her shouts, came down and stood grinning in the doorway of her apothecary chamber until Kathryn glared at him. She had done her best to clean the ears of both girls and prepared a mixture of oil, stirring in cloves and cinnamon. She gently heated this and, using a small funnel, had tried to pour some of it into the ears of the hapless girls, explaining how the wax must be softened whilst they could help by blowing their noses. Kathryn's best efforts, however, had ended in farce. Wulf was eventually despatched to bring their mother so Kathryn could explain what had to be done, only to find that Fulke's wife was in no better condition than her daughters. Other patients were arriving and Kathryn had to usher the mother and daughters into the kitchen for Thomasina to treat in a loud booming voice, as well as prepare certain potions to take home. The most intriguing case of the evening was Stephen the sackman, a hearty young man whose wife had just given birth to vigorous twin boys. Stephen had been the proud father but tonight he had shuffled in and sat on the stool like a man ready to be hanged.

'What's the matter, Stephen?' Kathryn had asked.

The man scratched his tousled head and muttered something. Kathryn studied him quickly, his strong hand and firm fingers, the neat hose and leather jerkin. She'd always liked Stephen, with his merry ways and open face. He was good-hearted and generous, a skilled craftsman. Farmers and merchants came from all over Canterbury, as well as the villages beyond, to buy Stephen's sacks. He never cheated or used base material, and he contributed to the parish by fashioning clothes for beggars and those who came demanding relief.

'Stephen, what is the matter? You look hale and healthy to me! Judith your wife is well? The boys?'

'I was drinking in the *Fastolf*,' Stephen's head came up. 'Goldere the clerk made a merry jest,' he spat the words out, 'that my wife was a by-leman!'

'Oh no!' Kathryn groaned. She recognised this old wives' tale: how, if a woman conceived and bore twins, she must have fornicated with another man.

'If you believe that, Stephen,' Kathryn declared, 'then you are a great fool and you do your wife a grave injury: a wickedness which you should confess and be shriven.'

'I know that,' he spluttered. 'But one womb . . . ?'

'Listen, Stephen.' Kathryn grasped his hand. 'Your wife bore twins because her womb conceived twice over.' She smiled. 'Like a fruitful tree. So you tell Goldere that if he spreads such a jest you will box his ears; your wife conceiving twins means you are a man twice over. Tell Goldere that he shows as much knowledge about life as he does about writing, which is nothing. Ask him to come and see me. I will educate him and box his ears as well.'

Eventually mollified, Stephen left much happier and a little wiser. Kathryn saw to other patients. Colum had gone out to King's Mead then returned for the evening meal. He was up in his chamber trying to mend some piece of saddlery, eyes intent, tongue sticking out of his mouth as he worked.

Kathryn pushed the ledger away and drew across the sheet of vellum on which she had written down all she had learnt about Ingoldby Hall.

Primo: The murder in the maze. Who, how and why?

Secundo: Veronica's murder. Who and why?

Tertio: The slaying of Hockley. Who and why?

Kathryn paused and tried to recall why the assassin had regarded her as so dangerous. What had she done except visit the maze and walk that murder-haunted manor? The assassin must have seen her, but what had she done to alarm him or her? She had found no manuscript in the library, no clue behind these hideous murders. Kathryn returned to her writing. *Quarto: Were these murders some rotten fruit left over from the massacre at Towton some twelve years earlier?* What was the Italian word for a blood feud? Oh yes, a vendetta. Had Maltravers been responsible for deaths which he now had to pay for? Or were the roots of this much earlier in Sir Walter's escape from Constantinople? She returned to her first question. The maze! If only she could discover how the murderer had entered. What had the Vaudois woman said? *"Sub pede inter liberos."* Underfoot amongst the children? That's how Thomasina described Wulf, always underfoot. But there were no children at Ingoldby Hall! Kathryn threw the quill down in exasperation and put her face in her hands. And then, of course—she took her hands away—there was the business of Greyfriars. According to appearances, the thief Laus Tibi had escaped from sanctuary, and it was probably he who had taken the receptacle to that craftsman. So, was the thief involved in the disappearance of the relic? But how?

Kathryn heard a knock on the door, and Thomasina answered it. She could tell by her maid's cooing and soft words that it could be no other than Father Cuthbert from the Poor Priests' Hospital. Kathryn rose as the chamber door opened. Father Cuthbert, eyes screwed up against the candle light, came into the chamber. Behind him was Thomasina, fingers all a-fluttering ready to take his cloak. He handed that over to her and Thomasina held it as she would a child.

'And would Father like some ale?' she asked. 'And he did look hungry?'

Father Cuthbert settled for a blackjack, and Thomasina reluctantly withdrew. Kathryn ushered the priest to the chair beside her desk.

'You look well, Father.'

'In other words, I haven't changed, Kathryn—the same mop of white hair, the same bony frame and lined old face!'

'But those dark eyes are full of life,' Kathryn retorted, kissing him gently on each cheek. '*Pax tibi Pater,* peace be with you.'

'*Et pax tecum filia,* and peace be with you my daughter.' Father Cuthbert put his elbows on the arms of the chair. 'You are ready for the great wedding day?'

'I still have nightmares about Alexander Wyville.'

'Tush Kathryn. Be he in Heaven, Hell or Purgatory,' Father Cuthbert smiled, 'or in London, he's dead to you. Live your life, woman. Colum's a good man. The banns have been read. I am looking forward to dancing with Thomasina.'

'I heard that.'

The maid bustled into the chamber, carrying two tankards: one she placed in front of Kathryn, the other she almost pushed into Father Cuthbert's hand. She went back and stood in the shadow of the doorway.

'Do you remember, Father, many years ago how we danced? Nimble and merry, two souls under the stars!'

Kathryn couldn't make out Thomasina's face but she caught the deep sadness in her voice.

'And we'll dance again, Thomasina, on the greens of Canterbury as well as in the halls of Heaven.'

Father Cuthbert didn't turn round but raised the tankard to his face. Thomasina coughed and closed the door softly behind her.

'Oh, that man you sent to me.' Father Cuthbert didn't lift his head: he, too, was lost in the past.

'What about him, Father?'

'I came to tell you that the lump in his throat was a small fish bone. I dislodged it.'

'Did you come to tell me that, Father, or flirt with Thomasina?'

Father Cuthbert glanced up, a smile on his lips though his eyes were sad.

'We are, Kathryn, prisoners of our past, that's what St. Augustine called us: souls haunted by dreams, images, memories, not only of life on earth but of what God intended us to be.'

'You are sad? You've come to share this.' Kathryn tried to keep her voice light.

'No, no, I heard about the business at Ingoldby Hall. You know how servants chatter. You sent one of them to me.'

'Oh yes,' Kathryn recalled.

Father Cuthbert put the blackjack of ale on the ground beside him and leaned forward, grasping Kathryn's hands between his.

'I worry about you, Kathryn, especially when you examine these brutal, mysterious deaths. They say there was an attack upon you. No, no, listen.' He let go of her hands and picked up the blackjack of ale. 'I am an old priest, Kathryn. I have heard the confessions of hundreds, perhaps even thousands. I have absolved sins you can't imagine, heard of hideous cruelty, but I always recognise one very important fact. The men and women who come to be shriven acknowledge they are sinners: they seek absolution. They are determined on reparation. However, in my life, I have also met people who don't give a fig about God or the devil, about right or wrong. They seem to have no conscience. They will do what they want, carry out some heinous deed to achieve their ends. That's what's happening at Ingoldby. Sir Walter has been barbarously murdered and you have interfered, so you must be stopped.'

'Do you know anything about Sir Walter?' Kathryn asked.

'No, I don't, so don't change the subject.' Father Cuthbert smiled. 'I heard about his murder in the maze and I knew something of that. Ah!' He lifted a hand. 'Now I have your attention. You are going to ignore my advice anyway, aren't you?'

'You know about the maze?'

'Not about that maze,' Father Cuthbert replied. 'Do you remember Peterkin the poacher?'

'How can I forget him?' Kathryn laughed. 'The eternal source of fresh meat! Do you remember when he was caught with two rabbits in a bag, he claimed they must have crawled in there to die?'

Father Cuthbert joined in her laughter.

'Well, Peterkin's a very sick man now. He coughs bloody sputum but I've made him comfortable at the hospital. We have good conversations, Kathryn; oh, the stories he can tell about the countryside. I'd heard about the maze. Now Peterkin could steal through any hedge or fence, so I asked him if he wanted to enter a maze, but not through the entrance, how would he do it?'

'And?' Kathryn asked.

'Peterkin laughed. He said if you climbed over the hedge you'd be seen whilst you certainly can't climb through it! Peterkin explained how the weakest part of the hedge was the base.'

'But that's not true,' Kathryn declared. 'The roots are deep set, close to each other.'

'Not necessarily, Kathryn. Peterkin claimed he could penetrate any hedge. First, there's often a gap between the ground and the bottom of the hedge. Secondly, the roots seem to be planted close together, but that can often be an illusion.'

Kathryn recalled what she had seen at Ingoldby Hall and shook her head.

'Perhaps a slim Peterkin could weasel through—but a man with a sword?'

'Ah no, Kathryn. Peterkin insisted you must search for two

weaknesses: a gap between the roots and one between the bottom of the hedge and the ground. Remember, such gaps are often hidden by the long grass and weeds which sprout under hedgerows. What you do then is take a saw and cut through each root, forcing it apart, widening the gap.'

Kathryn closed her eyes. 'But these hedgerows are evergreens. The sap flows all year and the trunk of the hedge would be difficult to sever.'

'No more than an oak tree for a woodman,' Father Cuthbert explained. 'I would examine that maze again, Kathryn. Peterkin added that sometimes a hedge can begin to die so the trunk of the hedge is easier to cut.'

Kathryn couldn't recall seeing anything like that at Ingoldby. She was about to ask Father Cuthbert if he wanted his blackjack refilled when there was a pounding at the door, followed by Thomasina's exclamations. The noise even roused Colum upstairs, and he came clattering down. Kathryn excused herself and left the chamber as she recognised Mawsby's voice.

'I'm here, Master Mawsby. What is the matter?'

The secretarius pushed by Thomasina, his face flushed, eyes gleaming.

'Master Mawsby, you've been drinking!'

'Aye, mistress, but I'm sober enough now. You must come to the guest house at the cathedral: Lady Elizabeth has been poisoned!'

'Poisoned?' Colum came up behind Kathryn. 'What makes you so certain? Is she dead?'

Mawsby shook his head. 'A leech amongst the monks says she must have vomited the noxious substance. She is weak but well and has asked for Mistress Swinbrooke.'

'We'd best go,' Kathryn whispered.

'Is it safe?' Father Cuthbert stood in the doorway of the apothecary's chamber.

'If you say your prayers, Father, I'll be safe.' Kathryn kissed him gently on each cheek.

She hastened upstairs and quickly put on hose and a stout pair of walking boots. She grabbed her cloak and the walking cudgel kept in the corner. Mawsby and Colum were waiting for her outside in the street. The night air had a slight chill now it was fully dark; the lanterns on either side of the doorway threw bright arcs of light.

'Shall I come?' Thomasina called.

'Look after Father Cuthbert.'

Thomasina needed no second bidding, shutting the door quickly behind them.

'I came by foot,' Mawsby explained, hastening ahead.

'Is Lady Elizabeth in any danger?' Kathryn hurried up beside him.

'I don't think so, Mistress, but . . .'

'Who was at the dinner?'

Mawsby listed the principal members of the household.

'And what were you talking about?' Kathryn asked.

'It's strange you ask, Mistress.' Mawsby paused to ease the stitch in his side. 'The Lady Elizabeth questioned us on our whereabouts the afternoon her husband was killed.' He held Kathryn's gaze. 'She agrees with you, the assassin must be a member of her household. She caused some upset, especially when she announced that we were all to leave her service as she does not feel safe.'

'Will she stay at Ingoldby?'

'I doubt it,' Mawsby replied, hurrying on. 'The hall holds ill memories for her.'

Colum caught them up, still trying to strap his war belt securely about him. They crossed Bridge Street, past the Guild Hall and the *Chequer of Hope* tavern into Palace Street, through Christchurch Gate into the cathedral grounds. Kathryn ignored the street scenes, the patrolling bailiffs, the revellers outside taverns, those dark shadows hovering at the mouths of alleyways and runnels. She wanted to ask Mawsby more questions but the secretarius was clearly discomfited. She paused to catch her own breath and stared up at the dark mass of the cathedral: crenellations and spires, buttresses, roofs, windows gleaming in the bright night. Here and there Kathryn glimpsed the glow of a candle. The awesome sanctity of the place always impressed her, that fragrant smell of incense which persisted whatever the weather or the hour. Time and again her father had brought her here, especially in the winter months when the pilgrim season had ended, and they'd both marvelled at the lustrous beauty of Becket's shrine.

Kathryn, Colum, and Mawsby went up the paths past the Bell Tower and into the monastery precincts, a place of shadows and fiercely burning cresset torches. Now and again a monk would slip by, silent as a shadow. They crossed the cloisters, down paved passageways. Suddenly a beautiful voice, some soloist rehearsing for the feast of the Assumption, sang out a hymn to the Virgin Mary.

'To you most favoured Lady.
Gloria, Gloria . . .'

Kathryn would have loved to listen but Mawsby, apparently oblivious to his surroundings, urged her on. They crossed a grassy patch of ground towards a half-open door of a two-storied building, the light pouring out. The brother inside introduced himself as the guest master and took Kathryn up the wooden staircase to a chamber on the first floor. Lady Elizabeth was in the simple cot bed, the bolsters piled behind her. She was dressed in a white nightgown edged with blue piping, hair falling down to her shoulders. She was pale, her skin white as the driven snow, and her eyes seemed larger.

'I'm glad you came, Mistress. I apologise.' Bereft of any haughtiness, Lady Elizabeth stretched out a hand towards Kathryn.

Eleanora, on a stool near the bed, got up and moved to a bench beside the wall. Kathryn sat down on the vacated stool and took Lady Elizabeth's hand. Colum stood, embarrassed, in the doorway, Mawsby behind him.

'Please wait for me downstairs, Colum,' Kathryn murmured. 'In fact, I'd like you to collect Father John and the rest. I need to speak to them in the refectory.'

Colum was only too pleased to close the door against Lady Elizabeth's glare. Kathryn rested her fingers on the young woman's wrist.

'A little quick but nothing alarming.' She then stood up and pressed her fingers against the soft neck. 'I am trying to measure the beat of your blood.' Kathryn smiled down at Lady Elizabeth. 'It's good and strong. Are you in any pain?'

Lady Elizabeth tapped her stomach. 'A soreness,' she explained.

'That would be from the retching.'

Kathryn pulled back the coverlet. Lady Elizabeth did not resist as Kathryn placed her ear against her stomach, listening intently.

'Your humours are certainly agitated.' Kathryn sat down on the stool. 'But you have no pains elsewhere? No burning at the back of the throat, sores or blemishes on the skin?'

'None.'

'Stretch our your hands,' Kathryn ordered.

Lady Elizabeth obeyed.

'Squeeze your fingers into a fist. Good! You have no lack of strength in your legs or feet?'

'None,' Lady Elizabeth replied.

'Do you feel hungry?'

Lady Elizabeth's fingers went to her mouth. 'I will not drink wine for some time.' She half-laughed in embarrassment.

'Tell me what happened,' Kathryn demanded.

'I had finished my vigil before Sir Walter's coffin. I returned to my own chamber. The brothers said that supper was ready and I went down to the refectory. I do not want to repeat what I said to my household.' She glanced quickly across at Eleanora sitting on the bench, head down. 'I ate reasonably well: slivers of duck and venison, a manchet loaf smeared with butter.'

'And that tasted well?'

'Thurston served me from the main platter. I felt no discomfort. I do have a delicate stomach, Mistress Swinbrooke. Afterwards we had some pastries and comfits. I remember drinking the wine a little faster than I should have done.'

'What wine?' Kathryn asked.

'From a jug, kept on the dresser.'

'As you drank, Lady Elizabeth, did you notice any distaste? Think carefully.'

Lady Elizabeth closed her eyes. 'I remember drinking the wine and thinking that it was rather sharp, acrid, but that may have been my own humours. Then I felt nauseous. At first just a a little, but then this pain shot through.' She opened her eyes.

'Mistress Swinbrooke, it was like a knife being turned. I couldn't sit still. I wanted to get up. I could feel my gorge rising. I wanted to vomit but found it difficult. I remember collapsing to the floor amidst screams and yells. The pain ceased but then returned. I was violently sick.' She pulled a face. 'I must apologise to the good brothers.'

'And no one else suffered any discomfort?'

'No, Mistress, they did not! Mawsby may have told you the news. I am becoming afeared of my own household. Was I poisoned?'

'With a sudden upset like that,' Kathryn replied, 'and symptoms suffered by no one else, I suspect so. The acrid-tasting wine was probably tainted. What saved you was the retching and vomiting. Your belly violently purged itself, hence the soreness now.'

'Will it remain?' Lady Elizabeth clutched at the coverlet.

'No, no. What you need to do is drink a great deal of pure spring water. Eat nothing till the morning and then limit yourself to dry bread. You may experience a little discomfort as your belly settles, a bile in your throat and mouth but don't be alarmed. Dry bread and water and you'll be well enough to attend the Requiem Mass.'

'What poison?'

'I don't know.' Kathryn shook her head. 'How many leaves on a tree, Lady Elizabeth? I have, in my own apothecary's chamber, belladonna, foxglove, deadly nightshade, at least two types of arsenic. I can go into the cathedral grounds and collect herbs and plants, mushrooms and berries which can stop the heart and kill within a few heartbeats.'

'But could I still be in danger from what I drank?'

'No,' Kathryn reassured her. 'My father once told me a story he'd read in the ancient chronicles of Rome. How the Emperor Claudius was poisoned but managed to purge his stomach by tickling his throat with a feather.'

'And he survived?'

'Well, yes he did, my lady. So the next time they poisoned the feather!'

Lady Elizabeth laughed.

'Your belly has been cleansed. What concerns me is how that noxious substance was administered.'

Again Lady Elizabeth closed her eyes. 'I thought about that myself, Mistress Swinbrooke. On one occasion Thurston took my cup across to refill it. On another Gurnell fetched the jug. There was movement around the table.'

'And the nearest person?'

'That was me!' Eleanora's voice cut across.

Kathryn turned round. Eleanora sat still as a statue, though her face blazed with anger.

'I did not poison my mistress's cup, nor did I see anything untoward!'

Kathryn nodded and turned back.

'Lady Elizabeth, you must excuse me. I shall ask the infirmarian to prepare powders, something to soothe your stomach and ease the cramps.'

Kathryn left the chamber and one of the lay brothers took her across to the guest house. The austere refectory was still ablaze with light. Colum sat at the head of a table, the others on benches on either side. They all rose as Kathryn entered. Colum offered her his seat then stood behind her.

'You are all cloaked and hooded,' Kathryn observed.

'We are to return to Ingoldby Hall,' Mawsby explained. 'Lady Elizabeth says she does not wish us to stay here tonight. We can, if we wish, return tomorrow morning for the Mass.'

'I would have liked to stay,' Father John spoke up.

Kathryn noticed the flush marks high in his cheeks; his eyes were bright, his speech rather slurred.

'Forgive me, Mistress.' He blinked and wetted his lips. 'But I have drunk too much wine.'

He slumped against the table and put his face in his hands, talking to himself. Kathryn half-heard the words 'Too much to bear.'

'Where is the cup Lady Elizabeth drank from?'

Colum went across to the side table and brought back a simple pewter goblet.

'No wine?' Kathryn asked.

'In her convulsions Lady Elizabeth knocked it from the table.' Colum sniffed and handed it to her.

Kathryn also smelt it; there was the odour of wine and something else, a sharp acrid tang which she couldn't place, and a slight touch of mint. Had that been used to mask the poison? She asked Colum to bring a candle over, and scrutinised the inside of the cup, but she could detect nothing. Kathryn moved her chair and stared down at the floor.

'The good brothers cleaned the floor,' Thurston slurred, his face heavy with drink. 'Faugh!' He waved his hand. 'The stench was offensive. I did not envy them their task. They cleared the rushes, took them out for burning and scrubbed the floor. I never thought fresh rushes would smell so sweet.'

Kathryn rolled the cup between her hands.

'Do any of you know how this noxious substance was administered?'

'We have been through that time and time again.' Father John took his hands away from his face. 'Haven't we, Gurnell?'

The master-of-arms agreed.

'From the little I have learnt,' Mawsby declared, 'the poison must have been administered towards the end of the meal, but there was movement around the table, people getting up, platters being cleared, wine being poured. Look at the cups, Mistress, they are all the same. They were brought back and forwards to the table.'

'Yes, that's it!' Gurnell snapped his fingers. 'Do you remember, Thurston, rather than bring the jug to the table, you took the cups away to fill them?'

'So?' Thurston stared hot-eyed. 'What are you implying?'

'He's implying nothing.' Kathryn intervened. 'Except that hands moved over cups.'

'You'd see powder falling into a goblet,' Father John declared.

'How do we know it was powder?' Kathryn retorted. 'Some substances come in no more than little pellets, easy to drop into a brimming goblet and dissolving as quickly as sugar.'

'But wouldn't Lady Elizabeth notice?'

'Wine is a good mask for poison, especially burgundy: its deep red colour would hide any change and its fullness any taste, at least for a while.'

Silence greeted her remarks.

Kathryn pushed back her chair. 'The hour is growing late, sirs; you have a journey to make.'

They all rose, collected cloaks and war belts and trooped out of the refectory. Colum closed the door behind them.

'Another mystery, eh?' He came and sat on the edge of the bench.

'Yes, a mystery. Any one of them could have poisoned Lady Elizabeth's wine.'

'Or her lady-in-waiting?' Colum added.

'But why their mistress?' Kathryn tapped her fingers on the table. 'True, she made an announcement about them leaving her service, but that came as a surprise. Why should they strike now at Lady Elizabeth?'

'Perhaps a blood feud?' Colum offered. 'In Ireland the blood feud was root and branch; men, women and children, no one was spared.'

Kathryn leaned over and ruffled his unruly hair.

'Root and branch, eh, Irishman?' She tweaked his cheek. 'The good Lord knows I am marrying a bloodthirsty man.'

Colum got up, leaned down and kissed her passionately on the lips, his hand caressing her side.

'And one who loves you,' he murmured as she pulled away. 'Next time you go to Ingoldby I shall be with you.'

He went to kiss her again but Kathryn coyly withdrew.

'No, I am not playing the reluctant princess, Irishman.' She chuckled. 'But I don't want to give the good brothers a fright. They have had enough tumult for one evening. So, sit down.' Kathryn leaned her elbows on the table. 'Why Lady Elizabeth? Did they strike at her as they struck at me—because of something she might know? The assassin brought the poison into this refectory. He or she was intent on murder long before Lady Elizabeth spoke.'

'Unless,' Colum observed, 'Eleanora knew what she intended to say. She appears devoted to her mistress and would not be happy if she was separated from the Lady Elizabeth. Should we question her?'

'Perhaps later.' Kathryn rose and pushed back the chair. 'I promised Lady Elizabeth some powders. She thinks they are to settle her stomach but they'll make her sleep. Let nature take care of itself.'

They left the refectory and returned to the infirmary. The brother who served as leech and apothecary was busily sifting powders into small jars in the light of a squat tallow candle. A cheery-eyed, merry-faced man, he was only too willing to discuss the different properties of certain powders, and fetched what Kathryn wanted. She sat on the high stool, the pots of angelica, burdock and white poppy on the table before her. Kathryn asked for the Leech Book.

'I keep it well locked away.'

The monk smiled and went across to a cupboard, pulling back the bolts at top and bottom. He inserted a key then whispered a curse.

'Silly, silly man!' He withdrew the key and opened the cupboard. 'I thought I'd locked it but I hadn't.'

He searched for the Leech Book and brought it out with a cry of triumph. Kathryn just stared.

'Kathryn?' Colum asked. 'Are you well?'

Colum seldom saw his beloved speechless, but now she sat as if shocked, mouth slightly open, face slack, eyes intent on the Leech Book.

'I wonder?' she whispered.

Now the infirmarian was alarmed.

'Mistress?' He touched the side of her face with the back of his hand. 'Mistress Swinbrooke?'

'Isn't it strange how God's good grace makes itself felt? How we are to look at the little things of life?'

'Kathryn,' Colum warned.

'I am well,' she said briskly shaking herself from her reverie. 'Brother, I would like this mixture, stirred into a glass of pure spring water. It must be stirred vigorously so it dissolves. Ensure Lady Elizabeth drinks it. You must also tell her only to eat and drink what is tasted by yourself.'

The brother was surprised but agreed. Kathryn thanked him and, absentmindedly clutching her cloak, walked out into the cobbled yard beyond.

'What now, Kathryn?'

'Why Irishman, bed!'

'Together?'

'On our wedding night for ever!' Kathryn laughed.

Chapter 8

"The gretteste clerkes been noght wisest men . . ."
—Chaucer, "The Reeve's Tale,"
The Canterbury Tales, 1387

Much to Colum's annoyance, Kathryn insisted on walking the magnificent, shadow-filled cloisters. She went round and round, refusing to be drawn into conversation. Occasionally she'd pause to stare at some grave-eyed statue or peer up at a hideous gargoyle sculptured with a monkey face and devil's horns.

'Did you know, Colum,' she asked, increasing his exasperation, 'that sometimes these gargoyles have the faces of those monks the stonemason didn't like?'

'Kathryn, what are we doing here?'

'Why, thinking, Colum, and before I act, I want to be sure.'

Kathryn sat on the stone plinth and stared out across the cloister garth, a stretch of green grass which shimmered in the moonlight endowing the rose bushes in the centre with a spiritual aura.

'Roses bloom full at midday, don't they?'

'Aye, and all God's creatures are in bed by midnight,' Colum retorted.

He glanced round the cloisters, a sea of moving shadows as the light from the cresset torches danced in the night breeze. Here and there a cowled figure slipped from a side door. A cathedral bell boomed and, from the choir stalls of the cathedral, drifted the words of the last hymn of the day: "*Salve Regina, Mater Misericordia*—Hail Holy Queen, Mother of Mercy."

'You are right.' Kathryn sprang to her feet dusting off her gown. 'There's work to be done, Irishman, and sufficient for the day is the evil thereof.'

Kathryn and Colum left the cloisters, going out of the cathedral grounds and back down the emptying streets of Canterbury to Ottemelle Lane. Once she'd returned to her house Kathryn became very busy, bustling in and out of the apothecary chamber, lighting candles, pouring Colum and herself stoups of hot milk laced with nutmeg. Thomasina, who had fallen asleep in the high-backed chair before the hearth, woke heavy-eyed.

'Do you know what Kathryn is doing, Irishman?'

Colum just shrugged and sipped at the stoup of milk.

'She's never been the same since you arrived,' Thomasina declared. 'She's to be married but doesn't give it a second thought. I've got to tell her, Oswald the pewterer came here—'

'Who?' Kathryn came back into the kitchen.

'Oswald! He thinks his wife is pregnant.'

'Oh no!' Kathryn breathed.

'Oh yes.' Thomasina grinned. 'And he's suffering from mother-pains again.'

'Mother-pains?' Colum queried.

'A rare condition.' Kathryn laughed. 'No one knows the cause but some men, when their wives are expecting, suffer birth pangs.'

'Nonsense!' Colum whispered.

'My father met a number of cases,' Kathryn continued, 'and so have I. Oswald is now our peritus, our expert on the matter. He's given birth to no less than three children in his time. You did explain, Thomasina?'

'For the hundreth time,' Thomasina replied. 'I gave him some water mixed with sugar and honey. I told him it was a special cure. I stirred in some camomile and peppermint. He drank it and pronounced himself better. I gave him my lecture, like any master at his podium at Cambridge, how it is the woman who gives birth. God bless her!' She glared at Colum. 'The man's work is already done. Now, Mistress, what are you . . . ?'

Kathryn, however, had already left the kitchen. Thomasina,

mystified, followed her. Kathryn became like this when she was working on a problem or a disease or ailment which baffled her. Much to her surprise Thomasina found Kathryn consulting a book on the life of St. Francis of Assisi as well as fiddling with the key and lock to her apothecary chamber.

Kathryn finally retired and rose early the next morning, coming down to the kitchen to break her fast on bread and watered ale. A messenger arrived from the cathedral to say that Lady Elizabeth had slept well, felt much better and sent Mistress Swinbrooke her sincere thanks as well as a small purse of silver. Kathryn seemed distracted, unconcerned about this; she was about to leave for Greyfriars when a second knock on the door sent Thomasina fluttering down the passageway.

'If it's a patient,' Kathryn called, 'I cannot help. Tell him, or her, she'll have to wait.'

Thomasina returned to the kitchen, a dark-haired man following. Kathryn didn't recognise him: his hair was cropped short and he wore a rather frayed linen shirt with a small cote-hardie over it, and dark blue hose pushed into battered black boots. He carried a small leather bag in his hand and stood at the entrance to the kitchen gazing sad-eyed at Kathryn. His red face was unshaven and he kept nervously scratching his stubbled chin.

'Mistress Swinbrooke, I am Thomas Bishopsgate.'

'What can I do for you, Master Bishopsgate?'

The man cleared his throat and shook the leather bag.

'I must have words with you, Mistress.'

'Sir, I am sorry. I do not know you. I have business elsewhere.'

'Ingoldby Hall?' the man replied. 'The great manor house of Sir Walter?'

Kathryn beckoned him forward to sit on the bench.

'You wish something to eat or drink, Master Bishopsgate?'

The man agreed to some ale and bread smeared with honey.

'I live in Radegund Street near St. John's Hospital,' he explained. 'My daughter, Veronica . . .'

'Oh yes.' Kathryn sat down in the chair at the top of the table. 'Master Bishopsgate, I am so sorry. . . .'

'We buried her yesterday evening. Afterwards I thought I should come and see you. They say that you will find who murdered my Veronica?'

'In God's good time.'

'I hope so.' Bishopgate's hand shot out and he grasped Kathryn's, squeezing it tightly. 'She was a comely maid. I own a small ale house. I put silver away for her dowry. I did not want her to work with me, have customers pawing at her bosom, so I sent her to the great house. She was happy there.'

'If God is good,' Kathryn replied, 'I will find your daughter's killer and that person will hang from the gallows. They will answer to the King and to God for such a hideous deed.'

'Good, but I have not come for vengeance.' Bishopsgate chewed softly at the bread, savouring the honey. 'I am hungry,' he whispered. 'I couldn't eat last night. Well, Mistress, as you may know, they brought my daughter's corpse back and a sack of her possessions. I went through them.'

He opened the small leather bag and pulled out what Kathryn thought was a dark green napkin stained at one corner. Bishopsgate unrolled it, laying it flat on the table. Kathryn's heart skipped a beat. It was a mask, a small sack really, with holes cut for the eyes, nose and mouth. When she picked it up and examined the edge she found the dark stain was crusted blood.

'I've looked at it myself, Mistress.' Bishopsgate pushed the mask towards her. 'I asked myself, why should my daughter have a foulsome thing like that? Perhaps some mummer's game? Then I studied the stain: the blood is dry but quite fresh. My girl Veronica never liked blood. If that was hers she would have washed it.'

'Can I keep this?'

'Of course.' Bishopsgate pushed some more bread into his mouth, chewing noisily, slurping at the ale.

'How did you find this?' Kathryn asked.

'Oh, she had clothes neatly folded, a kirtle, hose; it lay there, between them.'

He paused as Colum came into the kitchen. Kathryn made the introductions. Colum examined the mask.

'Like a hangman's,' he murmured. 'But theirs is red, not green.'

Kathryn studied it. The fabric was of serge, two parts stiched together. Had it been specially made? Or was it a small bag cut to form a mask?

'Tell me, Master Bishopsgate.' She folded the mask up and pushed it to one side. 'Did Veronica ever talk to you about Ingoldby Hall?'

'Ah, Mistress, only chatter and gossip.'

'Yes, but what chatter?' Kathryn leaned across the table. 'You know how it is, Master Bishopsgate, in these great households. If I ask questions the answers are polite but not satisfactory. No one dare speak, they do not want to be dismissed.'

'But why was my daughter killed?'

'I don't know, Master Bishopsgate.'

'She wasn't involved in that bloody affray, was she?'

'No, of course not,' Kathryn reassured him, though secretly, she could not say. 'Did she talk about Ingoldby?' she repeated.

'Oh yes. She said that Sir Walter was a good man but secretive. Lady Elizabeth was the great, well, the great lady. Veronica really had little to do with either of them. She did chatter about the rest. How Master Gurnell used to visit the Vau . . .'

'The Vaudois woman?'

'Ah, that's right.' Bishopsgate lifted his tankard. 'Veronica said he was sweet on that woman's daughter. Veronica didn't like Thurston: in his cups he used to damn the King and all the House of York.'

'And Father John?'

Bishopsgate screwed his eyes up. 'Something, but I've forgotten.'

'Did she ever mention Mawsby, a distant kinsman of Sir Walter?'

'Yes but not much. Ah, that's it, Father John!' He exclaimed. 'Veronica overheard bitter words between him and Sir Walter.'

Kathryn glanced quickly at Colum.

'Over what?'

'It was recent,' Bishopsgate answered. 'For our Saviour's sake, Mistress, I can't remember. It was just chatter. She told me it took place on the eve of the feast of Our Lady of Mount Carmel.'

'That's about the middle of July?' Kathryn wondered aloud.

'Well Mistress.' Bishopsgate finished the tankard and pushed back the platter. 'I must be getting back.' He pointed to the mask. 'I made enquiries. They told me about you. I don't want to go up to the Hall so I thought I'd best hand this over.'

Kathryn shook his hand and Thomasina showed him to the door. Colum picked up the green mask and threw it from hand to hand.

'It would fit over a man's head or, there again, a girl's thick hair. Do you think it has any significance?' Colum asked.

'It may have nothing to do with Veronica's death or anyone else's,' Kathryn replied. 'However, Master Bishopsgate believes this mask did not belong to his daughter, and why should a chambermaid possess such a thing? We must ask ourselves, was it placed in her chamber deliberately? Or did Veronica find it? If she found it, why didn't she show it to someone? Let me have another look, Colum.' Kathryn spread the mask out on the table. 'See, Colum, the blood stain at the end, the part which should hang over the chin so; someone with bloody fingers took it off.'

'The killer?' Colum asked. 'The one who murdered Sir Walter? The handle of his sword or axe would be bloody.'

'And he'd pull it off,' Kathryn murmured. 'He'd grab that part between his finger and thumb and pull it up. But what's it doing in Veronica's possessions?' She beat her fists on the table. 'Colum, you are to come with me to Greyfriars. I wish to—'

She was cut off by another pounding on the door. Thomasina had hardly answered it when Kathryn heard her scream of protest, followed by the sound of running footsteps and a stable boy she recognised from Ingoldby Hall burst into the kitchen.

'Mistress, Father John sent me! You must come quickly!' The lad fought to control his breath. He snatched the stoup of ale Thomasina gave him, but more of it splashed over his face than down his throat.

'Take your time, boy. Is it Lady Elizabeth?'

'Oh no, mistress, she's still in Canterbury!'

'Of course,' Kathryn agreed. 'The Requiem Mass.'

'They had to force the door of the writing office,' the boy burst out. 'Master Mawsby went there last night. Mistress, he's dead! Lying all ghastly, his face like a ghoul. Father John thinks he's been poisoned. He has asked for the body not to be removed, not until you come. He asks you to do so swiftly.'

Kathryn was already on her feet demanding her cloak. Colum ran down the passageway shouting that he'd get the horses. Kathryn, grasping her writing satchel, followed the boy out. Colum brought round the horses and they were soon clear of Canterbury, Colum setting a fast pace until they reached the gates of Ingoldby Hall. Ostlers and grooms were waiting for them in front of the house. Thurston looked as if he had spent the night drinking. Bleary-eyed and unshaven, he came shuffling to meet them and took them through a side door into the servants' buttery where Father John and Gurnell were waiting. Both men were agitated and anxious-eyed. Gurnell looked as if he had slept in his clothes, and Father John confessed he had not even celebrated his Mass and had given up any thought of joining his mistress in Canterbury.

'Does Lady Elizabeth know?' Kathryn asked.

'No, Mistress, she's in the cathedral with Eleanora and some of the maids,' Gurnell explained.

'I think it's best,' Father John interposed, 'that the Requiem Mass be sung undisturbed. Gurnell and I will go down to meet her as she leaves Canterbury. Mistress, I would like you to look at the corpse so it can be moved. Lady Elizabeth is in a delicate state. Such a sight must not greet her, there will be guests . . .'

He made to lead her out but Kathryn grasped his arm.

'No, Father, first tell me what happened last night.'

'We left Canterbury late. We had all drunk too much, deeply aggrieved by what had happened. The ride back soothed us, a beautiful starlit night. We arrived at Ingoldby Hall and went our different ways. Mawsby said he had certain matters to attend to in the chancery; that's where he always was.'

'Who has keys to that?' Kathryn asked.

'Why, Lady Elizabeth and Mawsby. The mistress now holds Sir Walter's keys.' He shrugged. 'I went to bed, so did Gurnell.'

'I made sure the manor house was safe,' Thurston declared.

'Watchmen were set. Every door was locked and bolted, all windows closed. We didn't want any outlaw or wolfshead to think the dreadful events here would offer easy pickings.'

'And?' Kathryn asked.

'I rose this morning,' Father John declared, 'and went to Mawsby's chamber. The door was open, the bed untouched, so I went along to the writing office. Mawsby had drunk a great deal, perhaps he had fallen asleep. I knocked and knocked. Thurston joined me. We received no answer so we went outside but the casement window overlooking the garden was firmly shut.'

'I searched the hall,' Gurnell explained. 'I sent servants out through the gardens shouting for Mawsby. I became alarmed over what had happened in the refectory at the cathedral. Mawsby's horse was still in the stables.'

'So you went back to the chancery?'

Father John breathed out noisily and nodded. 'I gave the order for the door to be forced. The crashing and banging must have been heard in Canterbury. It's a strong door, Mistress. At last we broke it down. It had been bolted and locked from the inside. Mawsby was sprawled on the floor. Near his hand was a wine cup, most of it had been spilt over the carpet. I think you'd best see for yourself.'

Kathryn agreed.

They went up the main staircase along the gallery. The door to the chancery, pulled from its leather hinges, now leaned against the wall. Inside Kathryn found it much as she had left it the previous afternoon, except for Mawsby's corpse, and next to his fingers the spilled wine cup, its dregs staining the floor. Kathryn crouched down. A pool of vomit mixed with a white froth stained Mawsby's face, turned ugly by the contortions of death. His eyes were half open, his mouth gaping, and his skin had a strange liverish hue. The muscles of the corpse felt tense and hard. Kathryn turned the body over. The front of Mawsby's jerkin was also stained whilst his tongue was caught between his teeth. Leaning down, Kathryn sniffed at his mouth and then at the wine cup. She pulled a face, feeling the shoulders and neck of the corpse.

'Definitely poison.' She rose to her feet.

'What type?'

'At a guess, monkshood; it's deadly and fast acting.'

She picked up the goblet gingerly between her fingers and recalled admiring it the previous day. The inside was of dark pewter. Kathryn went across to the side table, picked up the finely embossed wine jug and sniffed the sweet tang of the richest burgundy. The other two cups also bore wine dregs. She examined these but could find no trace of any noxious substance.

'Did anyone drink with Mawsby?' She stared at all three members of the household. 'There's a wine jug almost full, dregs in two cups, with a little poisoned wine left in Mawsby's.'

'I never came here last night,' Father John declared. 'I was too tired.'

The other two were equally emphatic in their denials. Kathryn walked round the chamber; resting on the window seat, she peered through the paned glass. The handles of the small door window were securely in place. Kathryn gazed round the room. Two of the walls faced the outside. She examined the two inside walls.

'If you are looking for some secret entrance,' Father John plopped down on the chair, 'you'll find none, Mistress. Mawsby stayed here all night.'

'Watchmen have patrolled the grounds,' Gurnell added. 'They saw candles burning late into the night.'

Kathryn stared around. All the candles had now burnt down, each of their holders encrusted with snow-white wax. She went across to the desk and recognised the manuscripts she and Colum had put aside the previous day. A large indenture had been spread out, a copy of Sir Walter's will. The writing on the document was clear and distinct, the Latin words perfectly formed: this must have been the last draft, for small amendments had been made, but nothing significant.

'Mawsby must have been examining this,' Kathryn murmured. 'He goes across and fills himself a goblet of wine. He drinks it and continues reading. He begins to feel the effects of the poison.' She pointed to the door. 'But it's too late. Monkshood strikes like an arrow. He collapses, suffers some convulsions, loses consciousness, and slips into death—a hideous way to die!' she added. 'When you dress his corpse, Father, you will notice liverish marks on his belly, red, almost mulberry in colour.'

Kathryn examined the corpse, feeling the head, but she could find no blow or cut. She went back, sat at the desk, and pulled across a copy of the will, reading the clauses carefully. Sir Walter had been a generous man: there were bequests to chantry chapels for priests to say Masses for his soul and legacies to principal retainers, whilst the bulk of his wealth went to Lady Elizabeth. Kathryn was about to push it away when she caught one correction. Sir Walter had inserted a clause about his library but made a change from 'liberos' to 'libros.' Kathryn became so engrossed with this that she sat staring at it until Colum lightly touched her shoulder.

'What is the matter?'

'Nothing, nothing for the moment.'

She quickly finished reading the will, rose from her chair and went across to the side table. She examined the two used cups and the amount of wine in the jug, sniffing carefully.

'According to the evidence,' she turned, 'Mawsby must have entertained two other people here last night.'

'But that's ridiculous!' Gurnell stepped forward. 'Ask my men, I retired to bed. I was exhausted. . . .'

Thurston and Father John also gave their explanations.

'And Mawsby would never allow anyone else into this chamber,' Father John added, 'except Lady Elizabeth. But the only person who came into this room last night was Mawsby, no one else.'

'Then who filled the wine jug?'

Thurston shrugged and left the chamber. Kathryn went and knelt on the window seat and stared out of the window. Truly perplexing, she reflected. Here is a man who locks himself in a chamber yet is found poisoned the following morning. No one else came in; the three other principal members of the household can account for their actions. Lady Elizabeth is lying sick at Canterbury whilst it would be ridiculous to think of Eleanora riding through the countryside at night and somehow stealing into this chamber. Did Mawsby commit suicide? According to the evidence he was busy in here, possibly without a thought to the future. She closed her eyes and tried to remember the properties of monks-hood: a deadly potion; the claret would have masked it.

'Mistress Swinbrooke?'

She opened her eyes. Thurston had returned to the room. Kathryn smiled when she recognised Amelia, who looked frightened out of her wits.

'Have I done wrong, Mistress?'

'I don't know, why is she here?' Kathryn asked Thurston.

'Amelia brought up the wine jug last night.'

'Yes I did,' the maid replied breathlessly. 'I took it from the cask of the best Bordeaux, that's what the master always wanted in this chamber. I filled a jug and brought it up here as Master Mawsby had asked.'

'And how was he?'

'Oh, Mistress Swinbrooke, he was tired! He seemed distracted. I filled the jug.' She pointed across to the beautiful pewter wine container. 'I filled it right to the brim.'

'And the other cups?' Kathryn asked.

'Mistress, I didn't touch them.'

'Was there any wine in the pewter jug?'

Amelia shook her head. 'No, no, I remember that. Master Mawsby said there wasn't a drop left so I filled it. There were only two or three candles burning and it was dark. I made sure I didn't spill any, then I left. Master Mawsby locked and bolted the door behind me.'

Kathryn thanked and dismissed her.

'Are we finished as well?' Thurston grumbled. 'The mistress is returning; she will be bringing guests.'

Kathryn walked across and examined the door; a beautifully carved piece of oak, it had hung on a number of thick leather hinges, but both its lock and bolts had been broken.

'Can we go?' Thurston pleaded.

'Yes, yes, you can but, Father John, I would like you to stay.'

Kathryn waited until the footsteps of the others faded, then took the priest to the other side of the chamber. Colum stayed and guarded the doorway.

'Mistress?' The priest forced a smile. 'I must be honest, I am very, very tired.'

'Was Mawsby the type of man to take his own life?'

'Never!'

'Where is his chamber?'

'On the stairwell leading up to the second gallery.'

'Did you visit Mawsby last night, Father?'

The priest shook his head. 'Master Mawsby and myself, well, we were friendly enough, but that's because we lived under the same roof.'

'Did you resent his closeness to Sir Walter?'

Again the faint smile. 'I can see the path you are following, Mistress, but you are wasting your time.'

He raised his head slightly. Standing so close to him, Kathryn realised how powerful his eyes were, with his deep, penetrating stare.

'Let me read your mind, Mistress. I was Sir Walter's chaplain, confessor and companion for the last twenty years. Yet perhaps I don't mourn him as I should.'

'The thought has crossed my mind, Father. However, that could be said of all of you, though I suspect Sir Walter played his part in that.'

The priest shifted his gaze. 'I don't mourn him as I should. I am a priest. Other people prepare for life, I prepare for death and what comes afterwards.'

'Yet you quarrelled with Sir Walter?'

The priest stared at her.

'Last July,' Kathryn continued, 'they say angry words were exchanged between you?'

'Because I asked to leave him,' the priest replied quickly. 'Mistress, I have lived my life. I wanted to prepare for death. I told Sir Walter that I was thinking of entering a monastery, taking the vows of a monk. I want to be away from the hurly-burly, the clatter of arms, the chink of cups. I want to prepare. Don't you understand?'

And, not waiting for an answer, Father John strode across the room. He stopped at the doorway, crossed himself and came back.

'I don't mean to give offence, Mistress.'

'None taken.'

The priest pointed at the corpse. 'One of the seven acts of mercy is to bury the dead. In justice to him and fairness to my mistress . . . '

'You may have the body removed,' Kathryn declared. 'I am finished here.'

Kathryn, followed by Colum, left the chamber. They walked along the polished gallery up the stairs at the far end. The door to Mawsby's chamber hung half-open; Kathryn pushed this aside and stepped in. In many ways it reminded her of Colum's room, a typical soldier's; everything was neat and orderly. A gold embroidered coverlet was pulled up over the bolsters. A small black table stood beside the bed with a six-branched candelabra. There were shelves on the walls for pots and caskets, and two large chests beneath, along with a table and writing chair. The books on the table included a bible, a psalter, and the copy of a chronicle which Mawsby must have borrowed from Sir Walter's library. She and Colum carefully went through the contents of the coffers and chests. Kathryn felt rather guilty, yet all she found were a few letters and some keepsakes. The rest was nothing significant.

'Are you searching for anything in particular?' Colum asked.

Kathryn went across and pulled back the shutters of the window, then picked up a lute and a roll of parchment from a corner shelf.

'Nothing,' she remarked. 'This is the song Mawsby was humming to himself in the library.'

'How do you think Mawsby was poisoned?'

'I don't know.'

Kathryn left the chamber and continued up the servants' gallery. This was not so grand but simply a long passageway with large windows at either end. The walls were whitewashed and unadorned except for the occasional crucifix. Leading off the passageway to the left were thin, narrow rooms. Kathryn peered into one; all it contained was a cot bed, a stool, table and chest with pegs driven into the walls. Most of the rooms were empty, the servants busy preparing for their mistress's return from Canterbury. Abruptly a door opened and Amelia came out.

'Why, Mistress?' She wiped her hands on her skirt.

'Ah Amelia, I thought you'd be busy below?'

'I asked Master Thurston's permission to tidy my chamber,' the maid gabbled.

'May I have a look?'

Amelia stepped back, pushing the door open. Kathryn walked inside. The chamber was no different from the others, with white-washed walls, a truckle bed and a few sticks of furniture. The window was square shaped, high in the wall; Kathryn had to step on a small ledge beneath to peer out. Below her stretched the great meadow and the dark green mass of the maze. She glimpsed the top of the Weeping Cross and the meadow behind it running down to the line of trees and bushes. Kathryn realised how, even from here, the maze was still an impenetrable mystery. She could detect no trace of any path as the hedges seemed to close in, blocking any view. Kathryn stepped down, wiping the dust from her fingers. She left the chamber and Amelia closed the door and made to hurry off.

'One more thing.' Kathryn smiled. 'Or should I say two?' She opened her purse and took out a coin and thrust it into the girl's hand. 'Would you be surprised, Amelia, to find a green mask amongst Veronica's possessions?'

'A mask?'

'Yes, like a hangman's,' Colum remarked, 'which covered the head and face with slits for the eyes, nose and mouth.'

'Oh Lord, have mercy!' Amelia shook her head.

'What I want to know is, would you be surprised if we found such a mask in Veronica's belongings? You cannot remember her taking part in some mummer's play or revelry?'

'By Heaven and all its angels!' the girl replied. 'Of course not, Veronica was a quiet girl.'

'But you still thought she may have had your locket?'

Amelia coloured. 'I only said that because she was always admiring it. It was wrong of me.'

'And last night,' Kathryn asked, 'you are sure there was no one in that chamber apart from Master Mawsby?'

'Mistress, I went in, I filled the jug, I left and the door was locked and bolted behind me.' The girl gazed fearfully down the passageway. 'I really came back up here,' she patted the pocket of her skirt, 'to collect my Ave beads. I am afeared, Mistress, these hideous deaths, some servants are leaving. Now I must go.'

Kathryn watched her leave hastening along the passageway and clatter down the stairs.

'Time is running out,' Colum observed, 'like sand through a glass. Amelia is correct. Servants are leaving. Lady Elizabeth will soon disband her household.' He put his arm round Kathryn's shoulder. 'I watched you downstairs.' He pulled her close and his lips gently brushed her hair. 'And I wondered, what is all this to us, Kathryn?'

'It matters,' she replied. 'I wouldn't be a good physician if I only studied the ailments and never searched for a cure or, in this case, the cause.'

'And?' Colum asked.

'We are not animals, Colum. One night out in the great meadow I saw a fox trotting by with a rabbit in its mouth. It reminded me of a wall painting in St. Mildred's Church depicting death as an eagle swooping on its quarry. Now that I understand, I must accept that death is part of life—but murder? Swooping down to take a life before its time, without God's consent?' She gently pushed away his arm. 'It matters, Colum, but come, I want to show you something.'

They went downstairs and out through a side door. Kathryn had to ask a servant to direct them, but eventually they stood beneath the bay window of Maltravers's chancery.

'What are you looking for?'

Kathryn examined the strip of grass which divided the path from the wall of the house.

'An imprint of a boot or shoe.'

'What?' Colum crouched down beside her.

'It's possible,' Kathryn tweaked the end of his nose, 'that Mawsby invited someone into his chamber. This person poisoned the wine, without Mawsby knowing, then left secretly.'

'And Mawsby politely closed the window behind him?' Colum teased.

'Possibly.' Kathryn tried to hide her confusion. 'Monkshood takes a little time to work but there's nothing here except . . .' She edged further onto the grass and plucked a few blades. 'That's wine.' She sniffed at the grass. 'Someone was here and spilt wine.' She gently held one blade of grass and scratched at the stain with a finger nail and peered closer.

'Anyone could have done that,' Colum muttered.

Kathryn got up, clutching her writing satchel. She walked to get a clearer view of the maze.

'I'd love to know your mystery,' she murmured. 'And, perhaps, I will. . . .'

Kathryn was about to go back into the house when she caught a flash of red from the line of trees. At any other time Kathryn would have thought she was mistaken, that she had seen only a trick of the sunlight. But she stared and caught it again, between two bushes, then it disappeared. Grasping her writing satchel, she raced down the bank across the great meadow, Colum hurrying behind her, shouting in alarm. They passed the maze and reached the line of trees and bushes. Kathryn held a hand up. At first there was nothing, then Colum heard the snap of twigs and the crackle of bracken.

'I thought this was close grown?'

'I put my faith in Peterkin the poacher,' Kathryn replied. 'There's not a hedge which can't be penetrated.'

She left the lawn and began to push aside the bushes; bracken, brambles and nettles blocked her way. Kathryn paused, recalled what she had glimpsed, and tried once more, pushing her way through the undergrowth to the two bushes between which she had glimpsed the splash of red. The bracken caught at her gown. Colum, muttering and cursing, drew his sword and began to hack either side. Kathryn reached one bush and edged along.

'I thought as much!'

The small area between the bushes was trampled down. Kathryn forced her way through and found herself on a winding path over a foot broad, a clear trackway through the undergrowth. In winter, after snow or rain, it would be muddy and slippery, but now the ground was firm underfoot. Kathryn felt as if she were entering an ancient forest with only patches of sunlight, the occasional call of a bird, and a sinister sound of rustling from the cool, green darkness, well sheltered from the strong sun. Colum, mystified, followed. The trackway turned and twisted. At times Kathryn had to walk sideways so her clothing wouldn't be caught by the brambles. The path led to a small clearing of moss-covered ground which stretched to the curtain wall of Ingoldby Hall. Kathryn walked along this and stopped at one place.

'See, Colum, the cracks and crevices. Even I could climb it.' And she began to gingerly make her way up.

'Kathryn,' Colum pleaded. 'Get down please. I can do it.'

'It's not often I climb a wall,' she called back. 'When I was a girl, I used to raid Widow Gumple's orchard. The apples were sour but I loved her to chase me.'

Kathryn, scratched and perspiring, at last reached the top of the wall and pulled herself up. Beyond was another grassy verge, trees and bushes, and through these she could see the trackway leading up to the crossroads and the road to Canterbury. Kathryn was about to climb down when she glimpsed the red threads caught in the sharp stones on the top of the wall. She picked these up, grasped them in her sweaty hands and made her way down. Colum, impatient, grasped her by the waist and helped her then, turning her around, pulled her close.

'You enjoyed that didn't you? Colour to your cheeks, a sparkle to your eyes?'

'That's not the wall, Irishman, it's you!'

Colum kissed her fully on the lips, hands gently caressing her back. Kathryn, unresisting, rested her head against his chest.

'It's a wonder no one saw us,' she murmured.

'Oh, I am sure they did.'

'In which case, Irishman, I don't want to be caught playing naughty with you in a wood.' She gently pushed him away.

Colum would have continued to tease her but Kathryn held out her hand so that he glimpsed the red threads.

'The Vaudois woman?'

'Yes, the Vaudois. I am sure she was here just now. I wager she knew this path like Sir Walter knew the maze. A poacher's trackway or, indeed, for anyone who wants to leave or enter the hall without being noticed.'

'Could she have been the murderer?'

Kathryn put the red threads into her wallet and adjusted her headdress.

'Remember what you said, Colum. A woman can swing an axe or sword as deftly as any man. Is the Vaudois as mad as she pretends to be? Did she have some grudge against Sir Walter? Does she know her way through the maze?'

'But, if that's the case,' Colum said, leaning down to pick up Kathryn's writing satchel and hand it to her, 'how did she enter the maze?'

Kathryn chucked Colum under the chin.

'One day I must introduce you to Peterkin the poacher.'

'You've mentioned him before.'

'Let me show you something.'

Kathryn and Colum left the copse and stood on the edge of the great meadow. Kathryn stared at the rearmost hedge of the maze, with its blackened, shrivelled branches, then let go of Colum's hand and walked across. She crouched, and saw that the fire had been so intense some of the roots and stems had been burnt through. Nothing more than charred stakes were left, the branches above a mere tangle of dead bracken. Kathryn rose and went along the side. Every so often she would kneel, pull back the grass and peer carefully.

'What are you looking for?' Colum demanded.

Kathryn recalled doing this the morning she had been attacked at Ingoldby.

'Well?' Colum insisted.

Kathryn broke from her reverie and explained Peterkin the poacher's principle, how somewhere along this hedge, there must be a place where the trunks of each hedgerow allowed a small gap. Colum joined in the search and eventually found a place where a gap of at least a foot stretched between the roots of the hedges which formed the maze.

'It's wide enough,' he murmured. 'But the branches come down low, no more than nine inches above the ground. A child could squeeze through—but a fully grown man or woman?'

They continued their search and found other places.

'And, even if they got through,' Colum asked, 'what then?'

Kathryn clambered to her feet and stared back at the darkened copse with its secret paths.

'*Inter liberos sub pede.* The Vaudois woman misled me. Was it an accident or deliberate? You see, Colum, in Latin liberos stands for children, but "Underfoot amongst the children" didn't make sense. However, libros is the Latin for books. I realised that when I was examining Sir Walter's will.' She winked at Colum. 'So, now, the Vaudois's comment means "Underfoot amongst the books," and I think that library holds the key to the maze.'

'A manuscript? A map?'

'*Sub pede,*' Kathryn murmured. 'Under foot.'

Chapter 9

"Though clerkes preise wommen but a lite,
There kan no man in humblesse hym acquite
As womman kan."
—Chaucer, "The Clerk's Tale,"
The Canterbury Tales, 1387

Kathryn closed the library door, drawing the bolts across. They had met Father John in the corridor and he had offered to help, but Kathryn had tactfully refused. Tugging at Colum's sleeve, Kathryn led him along the polished wooden floor to the far end of the library. She paused just before the stone mosaic which covered a huge square of the floor in front of the broad writing desk.

'*Sub pede inter libros,*' she repeated. 'Under foot amongst the books.'

Colum stared appreciatively at the manuscripts and calfskin covered tomes on the shelves and stands.

'I haven't seen a library like this since I guarded Richard of York, but Kathryn, finding a map amongst these books will be like finding berries amongst brambles.'

'That's what I thought.' Kathryn pointed down at the mosaic. 'It's not amongst the books but underfoot.' She placed the writing satchel on the floor and crouched down. 'See, Colum, the green border, the white squares, the blue cross in the centre and what appears to be haphazard red lines, a decorative motif which pleases the eye but doesn't intrigue the mind.'

Colum crouched down and studied the mosaic.

'Sweet Fintan's bones! It's the cross, Kathryn! That's the Weeping Cross; the green border simply marks the confines, but these white squares and red lines indicate the hedges or paths. It's the maze!'

'Underfoot amongst the books,' Kathryn repeated. 'The man who laid out the maze and built this beautiful hall did have a map which he used for this mosaic, then he destroyed the map. It's an illusion really,' she continued, 'Strange geometric symbols, but notice,' Kathryn moved to the bottom right hand corner, 'there's only one entrance, one gap.' She traced her finger along the white squares of the mosaic. 'These mark the path, the red indicates the hedges, the blue cross lies in the centre, whilst the green border marks the great meadow. Once you realise what this mosaic represents, it's very easy to thread the maze! What we do, of course, is start at the centre. Colum, pass me one of those pots of ink.'

Colum fetched the copper container. Kathryn shook it gently, lifted the cap, dabbed a finger in and began to trace a path leading from the blue cross. Sometimes she went wrong but eventually her finger, twisting and turning as it stained the miniature white tiles, reached the end.

'Thurston will complain,' she breathed, getting to her feet and wiping her fingers on a yellow cloth used for dusting. 'But now we know how to solve the mystery of the maze. Sir Walter discovered this and so did our assassin.' She took a small writing tray with a piece of vellum and traced the path she had delineated on the mosaic. 'I once heard,' she murmured, 'that if you get lost in a maze, you keep turning left to reach the centre and turn right to get out, I'm not too sure if that's true. . . . ?'

'But the assassin didn't enter the maze by its entrance,' Colum declared. 'Gurnell told us that was guarded.'

'You are correct,' Kathryn said. 'But we have just resolved the problem. The assassin committed this map to memory, learning it by rote. He or she didn't enter the maze by its entrance.' She smiled at him. 'Like Peterkin the poacher, the assassin searched for a weakness and found it in the rearmost hedge.' She put down the writing tray and raised her hands to describe it. 'There was a gap between two of the hedges, large enough for someone to enter. In the days, even weeks before Sir Walter's death, that gap was secretly widened. The assassin either cut through the base of the hedge, or worked to lift the bottom of the hedge further up, in order to create a hole large enough to go through.'

'But wouldn't that be noticed?'

'No.' Kathryn shook her head, emphasizing the points on her fingers. 'Firstly, it was at the back of the maze where people don't go. Secondly, the grass and weeds grow long and thick around the maze, too close to the hedge for a scythe. Thirdly, the assassin would make sure that his handiwork was carefully hidden; branches can be pulled down or pushed together. Fourthly, no one's looking for that gap, so why should they find it? Even if they did, as people keep saying, getting into the maze is easy but, if you don't know the way, you are really walking into a trap. Our assassin entered the maze by that secret entrance. Once inside, the murderer knew the paths, and he, or she, easily reached the centre and hid near the Weeping Cross. Sir Walter entered the maze to carry out his penance. He reached the centre, the assassin struck, took his head and left.'

'But who?'

'It could have been anyone. Did Gurnell wander off and creep along the far side of the maze, turning right along the rear hedge to this hidden place? Might Father John have done it? Thurston?'

'Or the Vaudois woman?'

'Yes, the list of suspects is long. Did the murderer take Sir Walter's head, place it in a leather sack and hide it somewhere in the maze along with the hunting horn as well as the sword or axe used for the killing blow?' Kathryn rubbed the side of her face. 'This is only a theory, a hypothesis.'

'But what makes you think it was at the back of the maze?'

'The fire! At first I thought that was used to alarm the household, a sinister pointer to Sir Walter's head placed on the pole.'

'It was,' Colum declared. 'But it was also a way of destroying evidence, to prevent someone like you stumbling across that secret entrance.'

Kathryn picked up the writing tray and finished the details of the map.

'Yes, my wild Irishman, that's what happened. The assassin entered by the back of the maze, then used that fire to hide the secret entrance. The details of how he or she got in,' she shook her head, 'I still don't know.'

Kathryn finished drawing her map and placed the parchment on the desk so the sun pouring through the window would help dry the ink.

'Lady Elizabeth will return soon.'

'Aye, she will, and we must be gone.'

Kathryn sat down at the desk to study her map, now and again getting up to compare it with the mosaic. Once satisfied, she took the yellow rag and began to remove the ink stains. Some had begun to dry but she did her best.

'Fetch some wine please.'

Colum left the library and returned with a small jug. Kathryn used the contents to finish her cleaning.

'Take it back to the kitchen, Colum. Put the rag amongst the rubbish and tell one of the maids to clean this jug carefully.' She stared down at the streaked floor. 'Perhaps the assassin will notice, but he or she is going to find out anyway. . . .'

'Why?' Colum asked.

'Because we are going to enter that maze again using this map. I want to test this part of my hypothesis.'

Colum hurried off to the kitchen and came back. Kathryn was still staring down at her crude map.

'If we get lost . . . ?' Colum inquired as they left.

'If we get lost,' she replied impishly, 'then just imagine it, Colum, you and I, all alone, lost in a maze. What on earth will we do with ourselves?'

His hand went out to grasp her arm but she danced away, hurrying ahead along the polished floor to the main door of the manor. The sun was now at its zenith, the great meadow and that sinister maze sleeping under the late summer heat, and even the birds sheltered in the coolness of the trees. No one was about as Kathryn and Colum went down the steps, across the meadow and into the maze. Colum picked up the guide rope as they walked. When they reached the centre, he threw it down the steps near the Weeping Cross. Kathryn used the map to follow the path which would lead to the rear hedge. Once or twice she made a mistake and became lost but, eventually, they reached the swathe of charred hedgerow. Kathryn, peering through the branches, glimpsed the copse at the far end of the meadow.

'We stumbled and fumbled,' she remarked, 'yet it did not take long. The assassin would have moved more speedily. Now, Colum, we must return to the Weeping Cross and using this map,' Kathryn tapped the vellum, 'find our way out. I wager our assassin must have secretly practised walking these paths.'

Kathryn felt apprehensive but confident that her hypothesis was correct. They returned to the Weeping Cross easily enough and began their return along the needle-thin, shade-filled lanes, the hedgerows pressing in around them.

'It reminds me of going through a forest,' Colum whispered. 'The trees closely packed, the bracken growing waist high whilst the silent darkness hides an enemy, arrow notched or crossbow ready.'

'But not here,' Kathryn replied. 'Just the phantasms of our minds. The fears of our souls. Isn't it strange, Colum?' She paused at a corner. 'Doesn't this awake childish fears, of lonely dark corridors, of empty passageways? No wonder Sir Walter chose this. A man lost in his own dreams, a remorse-filled past. He would feel at home here, cut off from the rest of the world.'

'Let's get out,' Colum said. 'I do not like this place.'

Kathryn used the map she had drawn; two mistakes set the panic bubbling within her but, eventually, they turned a corner and reached the entrance. The great manor lay silent before them. Occasionally Kathryn glimpsed a face at the window but she didn't know whether it was someone watching or one of the servants busy at their tasks. They returned to the stables, where ostlers and grooms lounged on benches sunning themselves, waiting for the cavalcade to arrive from Canterbury.

'We will not make our farewells,' Kathryn murmured.

Colum agreed, secured their horses and, a short while later, they left Ingoldby Hall.

'I would like to go to Greyfriars.'

Kathryn reined in the gentle cob, patting its neck. She listened to a thrush's lucid song ringing out through the hazy summer air, and she could also hear the faint cries of the harvesting parties in the fields beyond the hedgerow.

'But first we'll visit the Vaudois woman.'

'Could she truly be the assassin?' Colum asked.

'All things are possible.' Kathryn gently urged her cob on. 'She may be old but she's wiry enough. She knows the secret path through that copse and, perhaps, how to thread that maze. I certainly want to question her. Was she there the day Sir Walter was killed? More importantly, what was she doing there watching us this morning? Is she as mad as she pretends to be?'

They reached the small turning, down the narrow lane leading to the old hunting lodge. The Vaudois woman was sitting on a log some distance from the house, busily fashioning a chain of flowers, rocking backwards and forwards, humming under her breath. At first she didn't see or hear their horses; when she did, she jumped to her feet and ran towards the house. Instead of going inside, she sat down on the bench just near the door, acting like a child who had been caught where she shouldn't have been. Colum and Kathryn dismounted and hobbled their horses. The Vaudois woman had changed her red dress to one of dark blue, buttoned high at the neck. Kathryn noticed the scuffed brown boots on her feet; good protection, she thought, for someone walking a cobbled trackway, climbing a wall and following that secret path through the undergrowth.

'Mistress, we greet you.'

The Vaudois woman's head went down, and she stared at Kathryn from under her eyebrows.

'You've changed.' Kathryn picked up a stool near the outside table and sat down near her.

'Not changed,' the woman mumbled. 'Still waiting.' Her head came up. 'Has the messenger arrived?' She brought her hands together, imitating a rider urging on his horse.

'You know the messenger hasn't come,' Kathryn replied. 'This is not the first time I have seen you today, Mistress. I glimpsed your red gown in the copse near the great meadow of Ingoldby Hall. You crossed the trackway and climbed the wall, didn't you? You followed a secret path. You were watching me and Master

Murtagh until I saw you, then you hurried away?'

For a short while, a few heartbeats, the empty, vacant look disappeared: the cunning, knowing gaze in the Vaudois woman's eyes alarmed Kathryn. She had made a mistake! This woman was not fey or witless, she had moments of lucidity, of reasonableness, as her soul drifted in and out of its own dark, tangled nightmare.

'You often climb that wall, don't you?' Kathryn continued. 'You go and sit and watch the maze? What's happening in the manor house? You see it as your house don't you? Your property? Did you resent Sir Walter? Baulk at his kindness?'

'I go home sometimes,' the Vaudois replied, 'to see that all is well. No harm done. I was queen there once.' She combed her iron-grey, straggly hair with her fingers. 'I used to eat on the lawn, white wine cooled in the cellars, the most succulent of meat.' She pressed her hands against her belly. 'I was beautiful then.'

'Were you there the day Sir Walter died?' Colum, standing behind Kathryn, asked. He studied the Vaudois woman's wrists and arms. This woman, who could climb a wall and thread so skillfully along a woodland path, would have little difficulty with an axe or sword, especially if her heart burned with angry revenge at the new lord of Ingoldby.

'Did you see Sir Walter as an usurper?' Kathryn asked.

'Beautiful wife,' the Vaudois woman replied. Her gaze held Kathryn's in a frank, knowing stare. Something in her face, a steely malevolence, chilled Kathryn. 'Beautiful wife,' she repeated, her voice tinged with sarcasm. 'Long, gold hair like mine used to be, or was mine black as night?'

'Were you there?' Kathryn asked.

She heard a sound inside the house and the sweat on her back prickled like ice-cold water. She rose to her feet. Colum caught her alarm, his hand going to his sword. Ursula emerged through the doorway. The Brabantine crossbow had been primed and ready, the stout cord wound back, the cruel barbed bolt in its niche. Ursula held it with one hand; in the other she held a second arbalest, its cord pulled taut. She stood in the doorway and carefully placed the second arbalest against the lintel. Using both hands Ursula pointed the arbalest at Kathryn's chest, ready to release the lever, to loose that hideous bolt, to shatter flesh and bone. Ursula's hair was tied back, her face calm, her eyes deadly calculating in their intent.

'Mistress Ursula.' Kathryn stepped back. 'Mistress Ursula,' she repeated. 'This is foolishness. We mean your mother no harm.'

Ursula simply lifted the arbalest a little higher, her gaze full on Kathryn.

'Irishman, take your hand from your sword. Do not doubt me.' She gestured with her head to the back of the house. 'We have a garden, a few apple trees, some herbs, a few flowers, but there are also some graves. Do you know that?' She smiled at Kathryn. 'Irishmen,' she whispered. 'They came here during the troubles when the great ones were marching up and down with banners flying. They wanted to take a chicken or two.' Ursula half-smiled. 'They thought they'd also take us, mother and daughter. Kings on the dung heap they were, three of them.' She gestured with her hand. 'They sat at that table drinking our ale, preparing, as they laughed, for a night of roistering. I killed all three! Two with the crossbow, and the third was so drunk all I had to do was slit his throat. Mother helped me strip and bury them. We sold their weapons and possessions to a passing pedlar. They wouldn't leave us alone, you see.'

Kathryn stood rigid. She was aware of Colum's rapid breathing, of her own fear; her throat was so dry she could hardly talk, her legs felt weak, the heat was so oppressive yet she dare not move. She had met violence: Alexander Wyville had been violent and, before he lashed out with fists or belt, his face was the same as Ursula's, tight and drawn, that hate-filled gaze, the voice mockingly soft. Ursula would kill, and kill again, and not spare a second thought. Kathryn heard Colum move.

'Please!'

Ursula clicked her tongue. 'What are you going to do, Irishman? Come between me and your leman? The bolt will be in her soft chest even as you move. Try and draw that sword; perhaps you have a knife in the top of your boot? Stand away, Irishman! Stand away!'

Her voice rose to a scream as Colum walked a few paces. Kathryn turned her head. Colum didn't gaze back, his eyes intent on Ursula.

'If you hurt her, Mistress,' his voice came softly, 'I will take your mad head and that of your mother's!'

Ursula stepped back as if to keep them in full view, the arbalest still raised, not trembling, no flicker of uncertainty in her eyes.

'You have come on to this land. You accuse my mother. Is that the way it's going to go, eh? Yes, you saw her there this morning. She often enters Ingoldby and stares at what was hers, what rightfully should be hers.'

'There's no crime in that.' Kathryn found her voice. 'No harm has been done.'

'No!' The arbalest pointed straight at her. 'You will come back, won't you? Sir Walter has died, a great lord of the land. That maid died. Oh yes, I hear all the stories! We thought we'd live peacefully here.'

Kathryn found her panic beginning to recede. Something had startled this woman, alarmed her so much she was prepared to kill.

'Oh yes,' Ursula continued. 'I have heard the noises at night.'

'What are you talking about?' Colum interjected.

'Shut up, Irishman! Come Mistress.' She mocked Kathryn. 'You'll return with warrants and soldiers, you'll arrest my mother.'

Kathryn's gaze shifted to the Vaudois woman sitting on the bench, feet apart, hands on her knees, a malicious smile on her face, rocking herself backwards and forwards as if savouring every moment of this.

'You'll arrest my mother and me for the murder. You'll point to the wall, the secret trackway through the copse. You'll argue my mother took a two-edged axe from a leather sack, that she entered that maze and killed Sir Walter.'

Kathryn drew a deep breath to calm herself.

'I know the lawyers. They are clever little men with their pointed noses and fur-edged gowns, the ones who took Ingoldby from her and drove us out. They will say my mother's heart was full of vengeance, that she knew the maze, she'd learnt its secret paths and that she was mad enough to crawl back one night, place

Sir Walter's head on a pole and burn that hedge. Oh, yes, we saw the fire and you, Mistress, dashing about like a rabbit, backwards and forwards, busy, busy.'

'How do you know it was a two-edged axe?' Kathryn asked.

Ursula blinked. 'Clever, very clever you see.' She turned her head slightly sideways. 'But that's the way it will go.'

'What are these sounds at night?' Kathryn asked, as a second wave of panic threatened to engulf her. She played with the loving ring Colum had given her. 'Mistress, for all I know you are as innocent as a dove. I simply came here to ask some questions.'

'She has a nice ring,' the mother rasped. 'Look at the ring, Ursula. Can I have that?' The Vaudois woman got to her feet. 'I used to have a ring like that but they took it from me.' Her face turned ugly. 'Turned out in my shift like some common whore! Sir Walter, all kind and gentle, allowing us to stay here in the old hunting lodge; a goose at Christmas, a hare for the pot at Easter.' Her upper lip curled like a dog snarling. 'Me!'

The Vaudois glared at Kathryn's ring as if it represented all she'd once owned and lost. She brushed by her daughter. Kathryn stepped back. The Vaudois, ignoring her own daughter's exclamations, hurled herself at Kathryn, clawlike hands going for the ring finger. Kathryn grasped the woman's wrists, pulling her between herself and Ursula who was now screaming, arbalest chin high. Out of the corner of her eye Kathryn glimpsed Colum coming forward at a crouch, sword snaking up. The crossbow snapped, a whirr and the Vaudois almost slammed into Kathryn, her face all shocked, eyes staring, mouth open as if to scream. Ursula was yelling. The Vaudois's grip slackened. Blood bubbles appeared in her nose, a trickle spurted from the corner of her mouth, her eyes fluttered as she crumpled to the ground.

Ursula was now picking up the second arbalest, only this time it was no longer pointing at Kathryn but towards Colum, who'd slipped on the cobbles. Kathryn wanted to scream. She stared down. The Vaudois was lying sideways, blood gushing out of her mouth, the ugly quarrel embedded deep between her shoulder blades. Further screams as Ursula moved to avoid Colum's sword but the Irishman cut, slicing deep into her neck, severing the blood cords. Ursula staggered away. The arbalest slipped from her grip as her hands went out as if to staunch the wound. She crashed against the side of the house, gave a loud sigh and crumpled to the bench, then rolled off that onto the ground beside her mother. Colum stood, resting on his sword, fighting for breath. Kathryn felt as if the whole world was moving; the sunlight seemed to have gone. She staggered to the stool and sat down, arms wrapped across her middle, her breath hot and shallow as if someone was suffocating her. Colum touched her. Bile filled the back of her throat, bubbling like sour wine. Kathryn moved her feet. Was there strength in her legs? And why did she feel so cold? Colum gripped her and dragged her to her feet; moving her to the grassy verge beside the house, he gently made her sit down, then returned with a pewter bowl.

'It's wine.' Colum's voice sounded as if from a distance, as if he was shouting down an alleyway.

'Kathryn, drink the wine.'

She did so but gagged and retched. Colum took the wine bowl out of her hand. Kathryn lay down upon the grass, so cool and green! She felt as if she was back in the small orchard at the back of her own house. Lying down, away from the heat, her eyelids felt heavy. Colum was moving around but she didn't care what he was doing. She must have drifted into a shallow sleep, and when she suddenly woke, her feet felt free. She rolled over and glanced up.

'My boots! You've taken my boots!'

Kathryn sat up; her headdress lay on the grass a distance away. The hem of her gown was wet, whilst her boots were on the stool. There was no sign of the corpses, just pools of blood glistening near the doorway where the Vaudois had collapsed. Colum crouched down; his face looked leaner, younger, eyes watchful.

'I took your boots off, Kathryn, they were splashed with blood, the same for the hem of your dress. Here, I found a small cask of vinegar.' Colum touched the blotches on her dress. 'I also washed your hands and face. I became frightened. You were sleeping, your face was like that of a ghost.' He grinned. 'It's good to see the colour return and the life sparkle in those beautiful eyes. Both the women dead. I have moved their corpses to the back of the house and placed them under a sheet. Kathryn, can you stay here? I must return to Ingoldby Hall. I'll have Gurnell's retainers guard this place until I send men from King's Mead . . .'

'No, no.' Kathryn grasped his hand; it felt warm to her cold touch. 'Don't leave me, Colum, I feel better. What I need is dry bread and watered wine, make sure the water is fresh. There's a rain butt at the side of the house.'

Colum left briefly and returned with a wooden platter. The bread looked dry, though it was wholesome enough, probably a day old. Kathryn ate it slowly and sipped at the watered wine. She no longer felt cold or nauseated. She stretched out her fingers, curled her toes, recalling what her father had taught her about the effects of deep fear. She stared around: things no longer moved, the shabby hunting lodge, the open door, the bench, the broken cobbled yard, the disused bucket. A peaceful scene except for the blood drying in the late summer's afternoon.

'I feel better. Colum, what on earth caused that?' She felt the anger well within her. 'We meant no harm. We did no harm. We simply came to ask questions; that cut, you took her. . . . ?'

'In the neck,' Colum retorted harshly. 'Here.' He pressed Kathryn's neck. 'Just above the bone.' Colum plucked a blade of grass and began to chew on its edge, eyes never leaving her. 'Kathryn, she meant to kill you. They meant to kill us both. You are a physician, Kathryn. You look for the small things, the symptoms. What is missing, what is out of place! You pluck at loose threads. You are sharp witted and keen. You. . . .' Colum closed his eyes searching for words. 'You are self possessed! The more we investigate such bloody business, like those we have done in the past, the more skilled you become. I admire you, Mistress Swinbrooke.'

'Are you trying to seduce me, Irishman? Flattery will achieve everything.'

'No, I am trying to explain,' Colum replied heatedly. 'I describe what you are whilst I know what I am.' He edged a little closer, pressing a forefinger against her lips. 'I am a soldier, Kathryn. I am like Mawsby and Gurnell, a master-at-arms. I love horses, their stabling, their management, what they are to be fed, their different seasons, but at the end of the day, I am a soldier, I kill people. Because I do that, I sometimes recognise other killers when I meet them. Ursula and her mother, although at first they hid it well, were full of hate and resentment. Perhaps they were right?' He pulled a face. 'Perhaps they had good cause to be? They nursed grievances like a man does a wound which never heals.'

'I don't blame you for killing Ursula.'

Colum glanced away. 'She was a woman,' he murmured, 'though that doesn't change anything. Ursula was going to kill me and, above all, she was going to kill you. I recognised that, as soon as she came through that doorway.' He gestured with his hand. 'I've searched the back of the house. I have found the corpses of at least three others buried in quick lime. She was going to put a bolt in your heart and, if she could, one in mine. They would have stripped our corpses. . . .' He left his words hanging in the air.

'But why?' Kathryn insisted.

'I've searched this benighted place,' Colum replied. He rose to his feet, stretched out his hand and helped her up. 'You feel well?'

Kathryn drew a deep breath.

'Where are the horses?'

'They became agitated at the smell of blood. I moved them further down the lane. They are cropping at the grass. Come, I must show you this.'

Kathryn put on her boots and followed Colum round the house. They passed where he had laid the two corpses under a tawdry canvas sheet. The flies were already buzzing over the dark blood stains seeping through. The garden at the back of the house was overgrown; here and there plots and patches had been cultivated. Amongst the small copse at the far end Kathryn glimpsed mounds of earth against which a mattock and hoe leaned.

'You've been very busy.'

'I wanted to make sure.' Colum put an arm across her shoulder. 'I felt guilty. I wondered if Ursula had just been boasting. Yet it's true, they have killed before. Now, look at this.'

Colum led Kathryn round a rambling hawthorn bush, the grass scorched with fire. In the centre lay a mound of black ash and white cinders; a few tendrils of dust and smoke still curled up. Colum picked up a stick and raked amongst the ashes, pulling out the blade of a two-edged axe, its wooden handle burnt away. He sifted amongst the ashes again and dragged out pieces of blackened fabric. Some had been reduced to ash, others were only partly burnt. Kathryn stooped down and pulled the axe blade towards her; it was about a foot broad, its winged blades nine inches long.

'Good steel,' Colum remarked. 'They burnt the handle, they probably intended to throw the blade away in some mere or bury it in the garden.'

Kathryn picked up a piece of the half-burnt cloth. The fabric was very coarse, one end strengthened with close set stitching.

'Stephen the sacker,' she murmured. 'I'd recognise his handiwork anywhere. This is one of his sacks.' She glanced at Colum. 'Of course,' she breathed. 'The axe was used to kill Maltravers and the decapitated head placed in a sack which Ursula was trying to burn.'

'So, are they the killers?' Colum asked.

'It's possible that the Vaudois woman climbed the wall carrying that axe and sack. Somehow, she entered the maze and, with her daughter's help, killed Sir Walter. Later that night they brought the head back, set it on a pole and burnt the rearmost hedge of the maze to hide their secret entrance.'

Kathryn walked away. She stared up at the sky; the blue was darkening. She reckoned it must be midafternoon, and only now did she become aware of the sun and the heat, the distant call of a bird. She closed her eyes. The attack had been so sudden! She cursed her own foolishness. Whenever she questioned people about murder, some bloody-handed work, she must remember she might be talking to the assassin who'd only kill and kill again to hide bloody secrets.

'Kathryn, are you well?'

She opened her eyes. 'The Vaudois woman didn't kill Mawsby, nor did Ursula. I have no direct proof, except I can't imagine them creeping into Ingoldby to poison wine. My conclusion is more a matter of logic.' she declared. 'They were just two poor souls caught up in their own mist of hate and revenge, and they were also fearful. Do you remember what Ursula said about the sounds at night?' Kathryn walked over, kicking the axe and sacking with the toe of her boot. 'The assassin used these in his bloody execution of Sir Walter, then brought them here, not to hide, but to incriminate those two poor women.' Kathryn paused. 'They discovered them and became alarmed and frightened. You can follow their logic, twisted though it was. Two women living by themselves with the will to murder as well as the means. Any sheriff's court would have them guilty, they'd have hanged at the crossroads in the blink of an eye.'

'So, who brought these things here?'

'I don't know, Colum. I want to be away from here, I don't even want to enter that house.'

'I've been through the old hunting lodge,' Colum replied. 'I could see nothing untoward, just the remains of two pathetic lives. I had no choice,' he added as an afterthought. 'Kathryn, I truly didn't.'

They walked back down the lane and unhobbled the horses. Kathryn stayed whilst Colum rode swiftly back to Ingoldby Hall and returned a short while later with four of Gurnell's retainers. He left instructions about what they were to do, then he and Kathryn rode into Canterbury. The closer they got to the city gates the busier the roads became. Now, late in the afternoon, many traders had sold their produce and were eager to get back to use the rest of the day. The crowds milled about them as they entered Ridingate and rode up Watling Street. Colum wanted to return home but Kathryn demurred.

'We have other business at Greyfriars, perhaps not so bloody, at least I hope not! First, Colum, we must eat, I don't want Thomasina questioning me about how pale or gaunt I look.'

They stopped at the *Rose of York,* a newly furnished tavern in an alleyway off Beercart Lane; its kitchens had a good reputation. Kathryn ordered parsley bread and a dish of custard lombard whilst Colum had strips of pheasant in a sauce of spiced apple and oats. The ale was newly brewed. The tavern was a pleasant eating house, its round tables carefully scrubbed. Kathryn and

Colum occupied a seat just near the window overlooking a small herber and carp pond.

'Will you tell me what happens at Greyfriars?'

Kathryn wiped the corner of her mouth with a finger.

'It's best if I surprise you.'

'So, you know where the Lacrima Christi is?'

'No, I don't.'

'Or Laus Tibi?'

'No, I don't.'

'Oh Kathryn!' Colum banged the horn spoon against the platter.

The tavern master sitting on a stool feeding crumbs to a pet weasel started to his feet, but Colum shook his head so the fellow sat down.

'The Lacrima Christi is not very far away,' Kathryn murmured. 'Laus Tibi, however, will be over the hills and miles away. He's probably safely ensconced in some tavern at Dover, where he is considering a sojourn abroad until the market bailiffs of England forget his name and face.' She leaned over and gently caressed Colum's cheek. 'I know you, Irishman. You have a hot temper and the words come spilling out faster than you want. Anyway, let's test my theory.'

They finished their meal, collected their horses from the stables and walked through the busy lanes and streets towards Greyfriars. Here and there Kathryn met a patient or a friend from the parish, but she didn't pause to chatter, claiming her business was urgent. The paths and alleyways were busy, particularly with pilgrims who, according to custom, would spend the morning in the cathedral and the afternoon seeing other sights of the city. Rich merchants perspired in their heavy, embroidered robes, their wives loudly complaining at the press and push. Tinkers and chapmen offered ribbons and geegaws for sale, badges or small statues of Becket or other saints. One enterprising chapman had rosary beads round his neck, shouting loudly how they had been blessed by no less a person than the Pope himself. Another offered dirty scraps of parchment which he claimed bore special prayers to the martyred archbishop copied down by a visionary. Kathryn had a sharp eye for the false leeches who peddled medicines and advertised them as elixirs of good health and a long life. One, a pockmarked individual popularly known as Toadwort, who had been driven from Kathryn's quarter, suddenly recognised the physician and disappeared like a whippet up an alleyway.

'So, you are feared as well as liked?' Colum joked as they turned into a small tavern to stable their horses.

'Oh, that's Toadwort,' Kathryn explained. 'Most false leeches are harmless. Toadwort's different. I have seen him sell foxglove for a bad cough and water hemlock for the rheums. He advertises them as a cure.' She handed the reins to Colum. 'In a way, he's correct, they cure all ills—you die!'

Colum pulled a face and led the horses away. Kathryn walked back to the tavern gate and peered down the lane. Toadwort had reappeared but, as soon as he glimpsed Kathryn, he stepped back into the darkness of a narrow runnel.

'I must see Luberon,' Kathryn declared as Colum returned. 'The bailiffs must seize the likes of Toadwort, they should at least have a licence before they sell their rubbish. Now, come on!'

They walked through the streets and into Greyfriars. A porter led them in. Kathryn did not go to the church but asked the lay brother to take them round the grounds of the priory, taking special note of the different doors and entrances. She was busy doing this when Prior Barnabas, accompanied by Brother Ralph and Brother Simon the sacristan, came striding through a door towards her.

'Mistress Swinbrooke, you did not tell us you were coming.' The Prior stopped and studied her carefully. 'You look pale, rather dishevelled.'

'We have had some excitement,' Colum replied. 'Prior Barnabas, I need a scribe to write an urgent letter for me. Perhaps a lay brother could take it out to my serjeant, Holbech at Kings Mead?'

'Of course, of course,' the Prior murmured. 'Come with me.'

He led them through the cloisters and into the scriptorium, a large barnlike room with plain white walls and a hard wooden floor. The brothers were busy at their carrels under the window

192

using the full light of day. Colum dictated a short letter which a beak-nosed scribe swiftly took down. Once he had finished, Colum asked Kathryn to check it. The piece of vellum was then rolled, the red wax imprinted with the priory seal.

'The Vaudois woman!' the Prior exclaimed as he led them out of the scriptorium. He paused to hand the sealed scroll to a lay brother. 'Ask Bruno to take that down to Kings Mead,' he ordered. 'The Vaudois woman,' he continued, 'and her daughter Ursula, they are both dead?'

'An unfortunate accident,' Kathryn replied. 'In fact, Father, I would like to ask you a favour: their corpses have to be coffined, churched and buried. You have a place here?'

'We have the Poor Man's Plot,' the Prior answered.

'There will be three other corpses,' Colum added.

'What?' the Prior exclaimed.

'God in Heaven!' Brother Ralph declared. 'Has there been a battle out at the old hunting lodge?'

'Five corpses in all,' Kathryn replied. 'Master Luberon will pay any reasonable expense. However, Father Prior, I haven't come about the Vaudois woman. I need to see you and Brother Ralph in the chantry chapel of St. Michael.'

'I . . .' The Prior seemed confused. 'I cannot see why?'

'Oh, I can, Father Prior. I have solved the mystery. I need to see you and your infirmarian alone.'

The sacristan was dismissed. Prior Barnabas, head bowed, shoulders hunched, led them into the church. He unlocked the door of the chantry chapel, drew back the bolts, and they stepped inside. Kathryn immediately sat down on the altar steps. Colum leaned against the door whilst, at Kathryn's insistence, Prior Barnabas and Brother Ralph sat on small stools next to him.

'You know where the Lacrima Christi is?' Brother Ralph asked.

'No, I don't.' Kathryn shook her head. 'But I do know how it was taken!'

The Prior's eyes widened, his face fearful. Brother Ralph stirred uncomfortably on the stool.

'My father and I used to often debate, as the scholars do in the schools at Oxford,' Kathryn continued. 'I would ask a question, such as, does God exist? Prove it. My father would reply with a different view, that if he could prove that God existed, God would cease to exist, for how can a finite mind comprehend that which is infinite? You have heard the famous disputation?'

Prior Barnabas nodded.

'Or, if challenged,' Kathryn continued, 'to prove God's existence, you counter it with a similar question for your opponent to prove that God doesn't exist.'

'What has this to do with the Lacrima Christi?'

'Oh, I am just making the very important point, Father Prior, how it all depends on how you look at the problem in order to resolve it.' Kathryn rubbed her hands together. 'Take Laus Tibi: everyone thinks he disappeared from the church.'

'Well, he did.'

'No he didn't, Father Prior. He disappeared from the priory and you should know. After all, you all helped him, just as you helped yourself to the Lacrima Christi!'

Chapter 10

"My theme is alwey oon, and evere was—
Radix malorum est Cupiditas. . . ."
—Chaucer "The Pardoner's Prologue,"
The Canterbury Tales, 1387

W hat?'

Prior Barnabas would have leapt to his feet but Kathryn gently pushed him back on the stool. Colum came away from the doorway as Brother Ralph, white-faced, put a restraining hand on his superior's arm.

'That's my theory and I will explain it,' Kathryn continued. 'Let's take our rogue Laus Tibi, a cutpurse, a thief, a felon whom the bailiffs want to lay by the heels. Laus Tibi was destined for exile or a hanging, probably the latter. He has taken refuge, penniless, hungry, dirty and fearful in this church, yet he has the arrogance and skill, apparently, to walk through solid brick wall and escape the vigilance of his would-be captors.'

Prior Barnabas sat, hands on his knees, gazing intently at her. Now and again he would move his head as if fearful of Colum standing behind him.

'When Laus Tibi disappeared,' Kathryn went on, 'everyone immediately thought he had escaped from the church. Such a sly cutpurse! Such a cunning man! If he can escape from sanctuary, evade the vigilance of the bailiffs, surely he's the man who stole the Lacrima Christi? This suspicion hardens when the receptacle for the sacred ruby is later sold to a city trader for a goodly amount. Everything points to Laus Tibi, but let's examine the basic theory.' Kathryn paused, pulling back the sleeves of her gown. She was happy to talk, give vent to her feelings, even though the bloody events out at the old hunting lodge still haunted her. 'Laus Tibi didn't escape from the church,' she explained, 'because he couldn't escape from a church locked, barred and guarded! Everyone looked at the church, that's where Laus Tibi was sheltering.'

'What are you saying?' The Prior's voice was thick, though Kathryn could see she had hit the mark.

'Laus Tibi didn't escape from the church.' Kathryn gestured with her hands. 'Laus Tibi escaped from the priory.'

'Kathryn!' Colum warned.

'No, Colum, think of it. Laus Tibi is shivering in the Sanctuary Chair. All the doors to this church are barred, locked and guarded; however, the priory isn't.'

'But the sacristy door?' Brother Ralph stuttered. 'That's locked.'

'It's barred and locked from the outside,' Kathryn agreed. 'And the night Laus Tibi escaped, someone simply unlocked the sacristy door, drew back the bars and, dressed in a robe and a deep cowl, possibly a mask over his face, glided into the sanctuary and approached Laus Tibi. In a gruff voice this apparition tells Laus Tibi to rise, that his day of deliverance is at hand. He brings a fresh batch of clothes, some food, silver and the beautiful receptacle for the sacred ruby.'

'Wouldn't Laus Tibi protest?' Colum asked.

'Would a bird weep for being rescued from a cat? Oh no,' Kathryn exclaimed. 'Laus Tibi must have thought he was experiencing a vision. He doesn't know who his benefactor is, he doesn't really care. He strips in the sanctuary and dons his new clothes, all covered by one of the priory's dark grey habits and cowl. He has money, the precious receptacle and a stout walking stick. His mysterious benefactor explains that, if he sells the receptacle, he will make even more money. Laus Tibi's deliverer then leads our jubilant felon out of the sanctuary, through the sacristy and into the priory buildings.'

Colum, fascinated by Kathryn's story, came over and, uninvited, sat down on the floor beside the Prior.

'But wouldn't Laus Tibi be wary? Suspicious?'

'Would you?' Kathryn laughed. 'It's a serious crime to take a man out of sanctuary, to provide him with sustenance. To give him what really belongs to a sacred relic. Why should he fear such an accomplice?'

The Prior's head went down.

'Laus Tibi would skip like a lamb on a May morning! The priory is silent and dark, the good brothers asleep. Even if one did wake and glimpse two figures in robes and cowls, what would he think? That two of his community are going about some priory business.' Kathryn gestured at the Prior. 'You were Laus Tibi's liberator whilst Brother Ralph acted as your guard, spying out the land, making sure all was safe.'

The infirmarian stared back, pale-faced and glassy-eyed.

'Laus Tibi, like Peter delivered from Herod,' Kathryn continued, 'suddenly finds himself taken through a postern gate of the priory, well away from the bailiffs busily camped in the cemetery on the far side of the buildings. I have walked the precincts of this priory: the bailiffs were like foxes watching three rabbit-holes, not realising there were six.'

'Of course,' Colum agreed. 'No bailiff would dream that a member of the Greyfriars community would dare help a convicted felon to escape.'

'You have said it,' Kathryn replied. 'Laus Tibi is a free man. Fast as a ferret down a hole, he puts as much distance between himself and Greyfriars as possible. Dawn breaks, he goes to a barber to be shaved and washed. He sells the relic-holder to our craftsman and, enriched even further, Laus Tibi heads for the city gates. He has new attire, is freshly shaven and cleansed, and strides out like a lord of the soil. No one would ever dream he was the same dirty, harassed felon who should be cowering on the Chair of Mercy in the sanctuary of Greyfriars. Laus Tibi is probably now in Dover or one of the Cinque ports, if he hasn't already fled across the Narrow Seas to Calais or some other city in Christendom. Father Prior?'

Prior Barnabas lifted his head. He was haggard, anxious-eyed. Brother Ralph mouthed wordlessly, a sheen of sweat lacing his face.

'Of course, the bells chime and the community rises to chant its praises. Laus Tibi has escaped. But how? The sacristy door has been relocked and bolted. The church is searched but the felon has gone and the mystery deepens.'

'You have no proof of this!' Prior Barnabas interrupted.

'Tell me, Father, how many of the community hold keys to the sacristy door? How many of the community can unlock the store cupboard where you keep clothes to distribute to the poor? How many of your community would dare even to contemplate liberating Laus Tibi?

Katherine paused.

'That's where I made my real mistake when formulating my hypothesis. I simply couldn't imagine a prior of a leading Franciscan community helping an outlaw to flee justice. Why should I suspect you, especially when I kept thinking that this outlaw had fled the Church? In fact, he fled to the Priory! It was only when I concluded that you were the only possible person to have stolen the Lacrima Christi that I realized you were responsible for Laus Tibi's escape. No one else could have done that. Indeed,' Kathryn spread her hands, 'how many would have a motive for doing so?'

'And that motive?' Prior Barnabas's voice was weary as if he knew what Kathryn was about to say.

'Why, the Lacrima Christi, of course. There's no doubt that the receptacle for the sacred ruby can be traced back to Laus Tibi. The felon was freed to divert suspicion, as well as to allay the real thief's anxiety.' Kathryn paused at the sound of footsteps. 'Colum, make sure no one approaches the sanctuary chapel. I don't want to embarrass Father Prior more than I have to.'

Colum went out. Kathryn stared up at the silver chain, listening to Colum's voice as he informed Simon the sacristan that Father Prior and Brother Ralph were far too busy to be disturbed. Once Colum returned, Kathryn pointed to the silver chain.

'Now, we come to the Lacrima Christi, the sacred ruby which is supposed to hold the blood of our Saviour.' She shook her head. 'I don't know if that's true or not but it is a stone of great price and I have read its history. The Empress Helena took the Lacrima Christi from Jerusalem and gave it to a church in Constantinople.

Two hundred and sixty years ago crusaders sacked Constantinople on their way to Jerusalem. They seized the ruby and brought it back to the west. It found its way to one of the great Franciscan churches in Assisi. From there it was stolen once again, probably at the orders of the Emperor of Constantinople who wanted such a sacred relic back. The Lacrima Christi is returned to its original owner until the fall of that city to the Turks when it was seized by Sir Walter Maltravers and his chaplain Father John. Now you, Father Prior, were never in Constantinople. However, you may have known of Maltravers long before you entered the Order or he bought Ingoldby Hall. You did, perhaps, learn about Sir Walter's escape and the legend of the Athanatoi. After all, two kinds of people in particular rub shoulders with the lords of the soil: armourers and Franciscans. Tell me, Father,' Kathryn paused. 'Here in the presence of Christ, am I lying? Put your hand on a crucifix and say that I am lying.'

'I am waiting for you to finish,' the Prior grated, 'and then I shall speak.'

'You are a zealous man, Prior Barnabas. I suspect you were a very good armourer. When you became a Franciscan, you immersed yourself in the history, traditions and spirit of your Order. By your own admission you travelled to Assisi. You would know about its churches and the relics they held, or once held. You'd read the manuscripts and chronicles in their libraries and you learnt about the Lacrima Christi allegedly having been stolen from the Franciscan Order. When you were appointed to head this house as a Franciscan Prior, devoted to poverty, you must have resented the likes of rich Maltravers holding a precious ruby, a sacred relic which, in your eyes, truly belonged to your Order.' Kathryn leaned over and tapped the Prior's shoulder. 'Prior Barnabas,' she whispered, 'you or Brother Ralph can challenge, whenever you wish, whatever I say.'

The Prior had regained some of his composure, but Kathryn noticed the beads of sweat on his upper lip and the way he kept stretching his fingers, a nervous gesture as if to relieve the anxiety seething within him.

'Naturally, as a leading ecclesiastic of the city,' Kathryn continued, 'you would get to know Maltravers better. He fell ill. Brother Ralph was sent out to Ingoldby Hall. You learnt all the rumours and stories about this royal favourite and his beautiful new wife and you decided to punish him.'

'I was not responsible for his illness,' Prior Barnabas retorted.

'No, Father Prior, you would not harm a man, at least not physically—though you did dream of securing that ruby.'

'The Athanatoi!' Colum exclaimed. 'You were the Athanatoi!'

'He certainly was,' Kathryn agreed. 'Whoever sent those messages to Sir Walter was a scholar with a rudimentary knowledge of the Greek alphabet and an even deeper knowledge of scripture. Somewhere in this priory is a book of meditations, a list of texts from the scriptures. You, Father Prior, cut an appropriate one out, scrawled a message on another strip of parchment and glued the two together. Being the Prior of Greyfriars, you can go wherever you wish: you leave one at the market cross,' Kathryn waved her hands, 'on the door of the cathedral or anywhere else. . . .'

'Why did you do that?' Colum intervened. 'To punish Maltravers?'

Prior Barnabas held Kathryn's gaze.

'Yes to punish him,' Kathryn declared, 'but more to stir his guilt. You knew what kind of a man Maltravers was, with his anxious mind and troubled soul: a penitent ready to do reparation for what he regarded as the hideous sins of his past. You were like a man besieging a castle. First, you weaken the defences and . . .'

'So you made your request . . .'

Kathryn heard the laughter in Colum's voice; even Prior Barnabas allowed himself a slight smile.

'You would have made a good lawyer,' Kathryn murmured. 'Your quick mind and nimble wits. On the one hand, Sir Walter was being attacked by these sinister quotations from scripture, on the other he was being helped by the good brothers of Greyfriars. So, when you made your request for the Lacrima Christi to be exposed here for veneration by the faithful,' Kathryn held up a hand, 'carefully guarded and securely held, your request fell like a ripe apple into Sir Walter's hands. He was eager, wasn't he, Father?'

'Of course,' the Prior whispered, a faraway look in his eyes. 'A man more intent on reparation than anything else.'

'The Lacrima Christi is transferred to Greyfriars,' Kathryn declared briskly. 'Sir Walter is satisfied about its security. The chapel of St. Michael has been carefully prepared.' She tapped her foot. 'Rich red Turkey carpets, the same colour as the ruby, costly altar cloths and, of course, a special receptacle, the same colour as the ruby, to hold the precious relic.' Kathryn rose to her feet and tipped the hook on the end of the silver chain. 'This used to hold the pyx above the altar but now it has been moved further along the ceiling so it dangles down, closer to the door grille. You and your brothers were openly delighted to have such a precious relic at the height of the pilgrimage season. It would increase the revenue of your church, as well as its importance. Pilgrims would be delighted to visit another wondrous object, so everyone is happy: the pilgrims, Sir Walter, Canterbury and, of course, the good brothers of Greyfriars. However, you, Father Prior, had planned something special.' Kathryn paused. 'On the eve of the feast of the Transfiguration you gave the order for the church to be closed in preparation for the great day. The sacred relic was taken down and placed in its locked coffer. At the time I accepted this—but later I thought, why?'

'This chapel had to be cleaned. . . .' Brother Ralph quavered.

'Nonsense!' Kathryn replied. 'It had been refurbished to hold the relic, it was kept locked and barred all the time. Who came in here, apart from Father Prior, to take the relic down last thing at night and rehang it the next morning? No, on that particular day, Father Prior, you carried out the most successful part of your design.'

Standing on tiptoe, Kathryn managed to take the silver hook off the end of the chain. She sat down holding it up between forefinger and thumb.

'I'll be honest, Father Prior.' Kathryn threw the hook from hand to hand. 'At first I wondered if you had been very cunning and skillful, replacing this hook with one fashioned out of some base alloy which then buckled so the receptacle and the Lacrima Christi fell to the ground.' She smiled. 'The solution is much easier.'

201

Kathryn paused. Brother Ralph was now wiping the sweat from the palms of his hands on his robe.

'Sometimes I can be so foolish,' Kathryn continued. 'I face a nagging problem so I look for some subtle solution. Once I had a patient who acted as if he was being poisoned: hideous gripes in the belly, sweating and fever. Did he harbour some malignancy, I thought? Was he being deliberately fed some tainted substance?'

'And?' Father Prior coolly asked.

'He was drinking holy water,' Kathryn replied, 'brought from one of these false leeches, a man called Toadwort.'

'I've heard of him,' Brother Ralph intervened.

'So has half of Canterbury.' Kathryn sighed. 'Toadwort claimed the water was from Palestine, from the well at which Jesus sat. In truth it was from the dirtiest pool in Canterbury and my patient, who'd more money than he had sense, had bought a phial.' Kathryn paused. 'It's the same here, the solution is very simple. We have Sir Walter Maltravers and the Lacrima Christi. You, Father Prior, learn about the history of both the sacred ruby and its owner. You wanted the ruby back, and Sir Walter's illness provided you with the opportunity as well as an accomplice, Brother Ralph the infirmarian. Just as he helped you with the escape of Laus Tibi, so Brother Ralph assisted you in the theft of the Lacrima Christi. This is what happened. On the eve of the feast of the Transfiguration, the Lacrima Christi was taken down for two hours, ostensibly because the church was closed for cleaning. In fact, it was to carry your plot through.'

'How?' Prior Barnabas leaned forward. 'Mistress Swinbrooke, are you taunting us?'

'No.' Kathryn shook her head. 'I am trying to explain my own slowness in this matter. Late that afternoon you restored the Lacrima Christi to its silver chain.' Kathryn held up the hook. 'You then left this chantry chapel, bolted the doors and turned the key in the lock.' Kathryn paused. 'Give me the key, Father Prior.'

Prior Barnabas reluctantly handed it over. Kathryn went across to the door, inserted the key, and turned it once or twice, then crouched down to examine the lock.

'Again, the work of some craftsman,' she murmured. 'Notice, Colum, how smoothly it slides in and out.'

'Of course.' Colum rose and came across. He turned the key himself and grinned at Father Prior. 'Everyone thought you had bolted and locked the door, but only the bolts were drawn across; the lock was never really turned.'

Prior Barnabas closed his eyes. Brother Ralph put his face in his hands.

'It's all an illusion,' Kathryn mused. 'I wondered why such play was made of the sacristan holding the keys, as if he was the one who locked and unlocked this door.' She smiled down at the Prior. 'You hold them now.'

Prior Barnabas just gazed back.

'You wanted to give the impression that not even you, especially when you were performing the sacred vigil, could open the chantry door. When the Lacrima Christi was taken down at night or restored in the morning, you performed the same rite, taking the keys off the sacristan to unlock and relock the door. You established a rhythm which you broke the day the Lacrima Christi was stolen. The church, and this chantry chapel, had to be cleaned: the brothers gather, they are busy with other duties, they witness the same rite though in different circumstances; they were used to it, they'd scarcely notice if the key wasn't fully turned.'

'They might have.' Brother Ralph didn't raise his head.

'No, no,' Kathryn disagreed. 'That explains the mummery of the church being closed for cleaning. Father Prior daren't leave the door to this treasury unlocked all day. Someone might draw the bolts and realise the door was unlocked, a simple accident for which the Prior would certainly be blamed.'

'Of course,' Colum intervened. 'Anyone could have tried that, and with Laus Tibi in sanctuary, it would have been even more perilous.'

'Yes,' Kathryn agreed. 'Prior Barnabas, you had to create the mummery of the door remaining unlocked—but only for that short period of time which coincided with your vigil. On the afternoon of the theft you handed the chantry chapel keys back to

Brother Simon the sacristan. Everyone thought the chantry chapel was bolted and locked, but it wasn't. When darkness fell the church was empty; one of you drew back the bolts, also very well oiled, slipped into the chantry chapel and took down the Lacrima Christi. The alarm was raised, Brother Simon was sent for, great play made of unlocking the door and drawing back the bolts.' Kathryn sat down beside the Prior. 'It simply depends on how you look at what happened. Who would suspect the Prior and a leading member of the Greyfriars community were involved in the theft of a sacred relic? How on earth could they enter a chapel when the door was locked and someone else held the key? So, the mystery begins. One slight flaw.' Kathryn pointed in the direction of the sanctuary. 'Laus Tibi may have seen something; like any felon who has survived so long, he is sharp-eyed and quick-witted. You arranged for Laus Tibi to escape. You also gave him the relic holder: if suspicion was raised, the finger would point to our felon. If he was captured, who would believe his story? They'd say he had accomplices. They'd accuse him of having the receptacle, so why not the relic?'

Kathryn got up and tapped the silver chain.

'What did you intend, Father Prior?' She sighed. 'You must have thought Sir Walter's death was God's blessing on your design. You'd wait for a while, return to your Mother House in Assisi and anonymously arrange for the Lacrima Christi to be restored to its rightful owner.'

'And if I deny all this?' the Prior asked.

'Well, I shall make enquiries amongst your community. Are they certain the key was turned? Did you have a locksmith to ensure both the bolts and lock would slide smoothly? If so, why? Did you pay the same attention to the hinges so the entire door opened soundlessly? Someone's memory will be pricked. Or, there again, we'll have the King's warrant out for Laus Tibi: if he's offered a pardon by Master Murtagh, Laus Tibi might gabble the truth. He may have his own suspicions. Whatever, he will certainly confirm my story of his escape.'

'And I can go to Master Luberon,' Colum added. 'I will get the

Archbishop's warrant, as well as the King's, to search this priory from cellar to ceiling.'

'Father.' Kathryn stepped closer as the Prior climbed to his feet. 'I do not wish to humiliate or disgrace you. I understand why you did it. You are not a thief, stealing for profit.'

Father Prior lowered his head, and when he glanced up his eyes brimmed with tears.

'And if I confess?'

'If we both confess?' Brother Ralph now stood behind his Prior, his determination to be loyal outweighing any personal fears.

'Well, I could look forward to a miracle.' Kathryn smiled. 'The Lacrima Christi could mysteriously reappear in the chapel of St. Michael's chantry. Perhaps the Archangel himself,' she pointed at the stained glass window, 'intervened to get it back?'

'And?' The Prior asked.

'If it's then returned to its rightful owner, the Franciscan Order could present a powerful plea to hold it in trust . . . ?'

The Prior sat down on the steps, face in his hands. At first Kathryn thought he was muttering to himself, but in fact, he was praying. Prior Barnabas took his hands away from his face.

'Do you know, Mistress Swinbrooke, God has given us many gifts.' He grinned sheepishly at Colum. 'You should be careful, Irishman.' He jabbed a finger at Kathryn. 'She has sharp eyes and even sharper wits. You also have a soul, Mistress Swinbrooke. If you lay this information before the sheriff or the archbishop I'd be disgraced. "Confiteor peccata mea." ' He struck his breast three times. 'I confess all my sins.' He breathed out noisily and paused as if half-listening to the sounds in the church. Brother Ralph made to speak but the Prior held up a hand. 'It's my doing,' he confessed. 'I am responsible.' He glanced up at Kathryn. 'It is as you say! Oh, I'd met Maltravers before. He had forgotten about me but I hadn't forgotten him. I followed the armies as an armourer. I made a very good living, it's wonderful what you hear and learn about the great ones and that included Maltravers. I travelled to Towton battlefield where the dead lay piled almost shoulder high, I felt the deepest desolation. I joined the Franciscan Order. I was a very good craftsman but I told them that was all behind me. I went to Italy and stayed for a while in our Mother House in Assisi. I heard about the Lacrima Christi and recalled Sir Walter Maltravers. I forgot about it all until I came here eighteen months ago. I felt angry, as I always do at the great lords of the soil. How dare Maltravers hold the Lacrima Christi which should be held by my Order? At first I thought I should plead with him, but I decided not to. I asked for a sign, and it was given to me. Some time at the beginning of Lent, Sir Walter came and asked to be shriven. He opened a window of his soul. I couldn't resist the temptation to remind him secretly of his past. I had a small book of meditations; I cut them into strips.'

'And you wrote the alleged messages from the Athanatoi?'

'Of course I did.' Prior Barnabas blinked and licked his lips. 'Then it was up with my cowl and into the streets of Canterbury. It was so easy to deliver messages, I knew they would be taken straight to Sir Walter. When he asked for the services of our infirmarian, I thought St. Francis was showing me a sign.' He raised a hand. 'The rest, a few details wrong here and there but, in the main, as you say.' He smiled to himself. 'I arranged for the hinges, lock and bolts of the chantry chapel to be well oiled. I pretended to lock the door and then, under the cover of darkness, slipped in here and took the Lacrima Christi. It took no more than a few heartbeats. I did wonder how much Laus Tibi might have seen, so I arranged his escape: food, clothing, money and the receptacle. I wore an ordinary robe, my cowl pulled up, a mask over my face, Brother Ralph as my guide. Laus Tibi acted like a soul released from Purgatory. I told him he must sell the receptacle, then vanish from the face of the earth. He asked me why I did it. I lied, saying he reminded me of a very close friend. When Sir Walter was murdered,' Prior Barnabas shrugged, 'I thought "another sign," perhaps in the confusion the Lacrima Christi would be forgotten, the years would pass. I'd travel back to the Mother House and the Lacrima Christi would be anonymously returned to our Father General.'

'Where is it now?' Kathryn asked.

'Wait there. Brother Ralph, come with me.'

The two Franciscans left the chapel.

'Is that all you are going to do?' Colum whispered. He gripped Kathryn's hands and stared down at her. 'You look like a dove, Kathryn. In truth, you are a peregrine falcon falling out of the sky onto your unsuspecting quarry.'

'Then we are well matched.' Kathryn stood on tiptoe and kissed his lips. 'Father Prior is not a bad man, just a Franciscan with a misplaced sense of justice. He didn't injure anyone except frighten Maltravers. He didn't steal for personal gain and, who knows, perhaps he saved poor Laus Tibi from a hanging?'

Kathryn kissed Colum again and drew aside as Prior Barnabas and the infirmarian came hurrying down the church and into the chapel. He opened a leather sack and Kathryn gasped at the brilliant ruby he drew out. She took it gently from his hand and held it up against the fading light pouring through the window. The ruby was quite heavy, and resembled in the shape and size a large pigeon's egg. It glowed like blood, a brilliant red with a deeper shade of red within as if there were two rubies, one inside of the other. It was polished, flawless.

'Beautiful!' she whispered. 'Exquisite! A man,' she grinned, 'or a woman could lose their soul over something like this.'

She handed it to Colum who also examined it, exclaiming softly under his breath. He handed it back to the Prior, who replaced it in the leather sack.

'Do I have your word, Father?'

Prior Barnabas shuffled his feet.

'Do I have your word?' Kathryn repeated.

'Tell her!' Brother Ralph urged.

'On the feast of the Assumption of the Blessed Virgin Mary.' Prior Barnabas smiled. 'Greyfriars will witness a great miracle. The Lacrima Christi will be found at the foot of her statue, just as we brothers gather there to sing a hymn to mark the great feast.' His smile faded. 'And, when Lady Elizabeth Maltravers demands its return, I shall hand it back.'

'Amen! Alleluia!' Kathryn replied.

She stretched a hand out, Prior Barnabas clasped it.

'I have given my vow.' The Prior's eyes were now soft, his voice barely above a whisper. 'I have given my word in a sacred place.'

Late in the afternoon Colum and Kathryn returned to Ottemelle Lane. Colum was teasing her about performing miracles, but she swore him to silence, telling him that the matter of the Lacrima Christi must never be discussed, and Colum gave his word. By the time they entered the house, Kathryn was more intent on distracting Thomasina who, if given time and reason, would study her most closely and find out about the grisly business at the old hunting lodge. Kathryn was relieved to find that Thomasina, with the help of Agnes and Wulf, had decided to weed the herbers. Colum said he'd have to go out to Kings Mead; he quietly promised that the corpses at the hunting lodge would be brought into Greyfriars after dark, secretly coffined and given hasty burial. Kathryn absentmindedly kissed him and went up to her own chamber. She took off her gown, dress and underkirtle and washed herself vigorously at the lavarium. She changed all her clothes and sat for a while before the small mirror Colum had bought as a gift, combing her raven black hair, trying to calm her mind.

'The business at Greyfriars is finished,' she murmured. 'But my pursuit is not yet over.'

She recalled the events at the old hunting lodge: Ursula's hate-filled face, that cruel barb pointed at her chest, the Vaudois woman's sleepy eyes; Colum's sword snaking out, a sliver of sun-filled silver; the blood pools glistening amongst the cobbles. Kathryn continued her vigorous brushing. Thomasina brought up a cup of light ale and two manchet loaves on a black wooden platter. Kathryn said she was tired.

'Is there anything wrong?'

Thomasina was at the door; through the mirror Kathryn could see that she was watching her intently.

'Lost in my thoughts, Thomasina. I'll be with you shortly. I need . . .'

'I know what you need!' Thomasina grumbled but thankfully left.

Kathryn went and lay down on the bed. She closed her eyes and forced herself to go back to Ingoldby Hall. She imagined the great meadow, the rambling maze with its tall green hedges, the sun-washed grass, the dark copse of trees. She tried to picture it on that fateful afternoon when Murder had stepped into the maze and taken Sir Walter's head. She could imagine the sunshine, the warm haze, the lazy call of the birds, bees and butterflies hunting amongst the grass. Gurnell's retainers would be sprawled before the maze, the master-at-arms walking up and down. Did he disappear? Thurston coming out of the track, Father John too. Did they return to the hall? Lady Elizabeth and Eleanora in the bower playing sweet music. Sir Walter on his knees, crawling towards the Weeping Cross. A dark shadow slipping out of the copse behind the maze, crossing the grass. And what else? The Vaudois woman and her daughter skulking amongst the trees? Mawsby returning from Canterbury, Brother Ralph leaving the hall. Kathryn smiled to herself. Prior Barnabas had shown great cunning, but she was convinced the Franciscans had nothing to do with Sir Walter's hideous death, so what else was there? Gurnell? Mawsby? They were soldiers who had fought for Lancaster. Thurston had lost kin whilst Father John . . . ?

'A deep pool,' Kathryn murmured, 'with unfathomed depths.'

She recalled the mere near the derelict tower, Veronica's soaked corpse. Kathryn rolled over on her back and stared up at the beautifully embroidered counterpane of the four-poster bed.

'Why kill a poor maid?'

She recalled her own terror in the cellars.

'That's it!'

Kathryn sat up, pushing back the bolsters to rest against. The assassin had seen her examine that mosaic in the library and concluded she'd discovered the map; the same was true of her kneeling at the edge of the maze.

'They thought I was looking for a secret entrance,' Kathryn whispered.

She rearranged the bolsters and lay down against the cool, white linen coverings. From the garden drifted the sound of Thomasina and Wulf chanting some doggerel rhyme. Kathryn closed her eyes and tried to recall every detail of her investigation. Mawsby sprawled in that chamber, the wine drops on the grass. Veronica, did she have that green mask? What could a young woman, who had her chamber at the front of the house, have seen that cost her her life? Veronica had been looking for her locket. Kathryn gasped and sat up.

'Veronica left the kitchen!' she exclaimed. 'She thought Amelia had taken her locket. She wouldn't go back to her own chamber, she went up to Amelia's which overlooked the maze.' The shock of her conclusion made Kathryn gasp. 'Veronica must have seen someone?'

She sat for a while, turning the thought over and over again. Kathryn recalled the story a sheriff's man had told her: how the ghosts of murder victims often haunt the minds of those searching for the culprit.

'You didn't die in vain,' Kathryn declared, quickly crossing herself. 'Oh, no, you didn't.'

She slipped from her bed and finished her dressing, pushing her stockinged feet into a pair of dark purple slippers. She went down to the kitchen for something to eat, then locked herself in her writing chamber. She lit the candles, took a fresh piece of vellum and began to write. Thomasina came and knocked at the door but Kathryn asked not to be disturbed.

Kathryn continued writing lines of neatly formed words; occasionally she would scratch out a line, and she grew so tense she had to stand up and stretch. Thomasina was preparing the evening meal, and the smell of baked meats and a highly spiced sauce drifted into the chamber. A few visitors arrived but Thomasina dealt with them, patients demanding salves or ointments. Eventually Kathryn left the writing chamber and went out to sit near the beehives in the small orchard at the end of the garden; she loved to watch the frenetic activity of these tiny, tireless workers.

'Talking to the bees?'

Kathryn whirled round. Colum stood unstrapping his war belt. He came and sat beside her, kissing her gently on the cheek.

'Colum, a favour.' Kathryn dug into her purse and brought out a small, square piece of parchment sealed with a blob of wax. 'I

210

want you to take this to Brother Ralph at Greyfriars. No, no.' She grasped Colum's hand. 'That business is finished. Ask him to read it and give you an answer. Tell him to express his suspicions. Ask him, is it possible?'

'What's possible?'

Kathryn kissed him noisily on the cheek, her hand combing the sweaty, black tendrils of hair on the nape of his neck.

'Irishman, if you love me truly . . . ?'

A short while later Colum left. Thomasina came out grumbling that she would have to delay the meal. Kathryn wouldn't answer her questions so Thomasina launched the most ferocious attack on a clump of weeds in one of the raised herb patches. Colum returned and Thomasina demanded that they eat. After they'd grouped round the table and Kathryn absentmindedly chanted the grace, Thomasina began to loudly proclaim how meals in this house were delayed, how almond fish stew was an exquisite dish and didn't everyone appreciate it.

Thomasina glared so fiercely round the table that everyone lustily agreed, yet Kathryn found she wasn't hungry. As soon as she could, she excused herself and returned to her writing office. Colum followed her in.

'I gave your message to Brother Ralph. You don't seem interested in the answer?'

'I didn't want to alert Thomasina,' Kathryn replied, 'though I anticipated his reply: it was possible?'

'Is it true,' Colum asked sitting on the stool beside her desk, 'that Sir Walter's stomach gripes were due to poison?'

'Conjecture.' Kathryn nodded. 'A hypothesis with very little evidence. Colum.' She smoothed the top of the desk with her fingers. 'I know what happened to Sir Walter. Why he was killed, when and how.'

'And?'

'I have no real evidence.' Kathryn played with the ring on her finger. 'Indeed, I have very little proof, only conjecture. I know how Sir Walter was killed, why Veronica had to die, why I was attacked and how Mawsby was poisoned.'

Colum stared in amazement. 'But, if you have no proof, no evidence, what can be done?'

'Have you ever,' Kathryn replied, 'met anyone for the first time and taken a great dislike or liking for that person?'

'Yes, I loved you the moment I saw you.'

'Silver-tongued flatterer! You know what I mean. Our humours dictate our actions and, sometimes, there is neither rhyme nor reason. I have patients, people who walk in here for the first time, and I say to myself I like you, or I dislike you. If it's the latter, I feel guilty, for I have no evidence or reason for my feelings. The same is true here, so I am going to trap this murderer by trickery. I am going to fight a lie with a lie and, for that, I need your help.'

'Kathryn!' Colum warned. 'This will mean returning to Ingoldby Hall, won't it?'

'You hold the King's warrant,' Kathryn said. 'You can arrest . . .'

'Kathryn!' Colum rose kicking over the stool. 'Lady Elizabeth Maltravers's household,' he declared, 'are in mourning.'

'I know they are. The old hunting lodge has been cleared?'

Colum nodded.

'I want you,' Kathryn stood up, 'I am begging you, to go back to Kings Mead tonight. You have a clerk of the stables with parchment, quills and ink. I want you to swear out warrants for the arrest of Father John, Gurnell, Thurston and the lady-in-waiting Eleanora.'

'On what charge?'

'Hideous murder.'

'And on what evidence?'

'I shall soon produce that, and the King's Justice will be done.'

'Kathryn! Kathryn!' Colum's hands grasped her by the shoulders and pulled her close. 'Lady Elizabeth Maltravers is very powerful. Father John is a priest and so protected by benefit of clergy.'

'I want you to arrest them,' Kathryn replied firmly. 'You are to take men-at-arms and do what is necessary. I don't want them brought into Canterbury, to the castle or to the dungeons of the Guildhall. They are to be taken to the hunting lodge, given food and drink and I shall join them there.'

'This will take time?'

'Oh, take your time,' Kathryn advised. 'You have to ride to Kings Mead, swear out the warrants, organise your men, journey through the darkness to Ingoldby Hall and arrest those people.'

'If you are wrong?'

'If I am wrong, Colum, then I will purge my guilt. But they must be arrested and taken away.'

Colum was about to refuse but Kathryn became stubborn.

'Colum, time is passing. Gurnell, Father John, Thurston and Lady Eleanora may soon go their own ways. The assassin will escape the net of justice and Sir Walter's blood will be unavenged. Think of him, Colum, sent into the darkness! Poor Veronica struck on the back of her head and drowned in a filthy pool! Your own beloved,' she forced a smile, 'hunted like a rat in that dark, dank cellar.'

Colum stepped closer and, placing his hand on the back of her head, drew her closer and kissed her on the brow.

'If that's the case, sweetheart, I'd arrest the Queen herself!' He stepped back. 'Yet you have no evidence, you are sure?'

'Of a sort.' Kathryn pushed him back on the stool. 'I will leave; remain here until I call.'

Colum sat staring at the candle. He heard Kathryn busy in the kitchen and buttery beyond. He got to his feet and looked at what she had been writing; it was in her own cipher, nothing elaborate, just each word abbreviated, a text Colum couldn't understand.

'You are a mystery,' Colum whispered, making himself comfortable on the chair.

Colum had known Kathryn for over a year. No woman intrigued him as she did yet, at the same time, he felt relaxed, perfectly at peace with her. He thought of her warm kisses and passionate embraces. On the one hand Kathryn could be as self-possessed as any nun and, at others, outrageously flirtatious, but always protected by a shield of her own making. Soon we will be married, Colum reflected, and I'll clear the past. I'll seal the door on it.

'Colum?'

The Irishman grinned and sprang to his feet. If he knew Kathryn, Kathryn certainly knew him. He could lose his temper and sometimes speak or act before he reflected, hence her mysterious ways. He strode out of the chamber and down to the kitchen. Kathryn was enjoying a tankard of ale.

'Pour one yourself, Colum.'

He went across to the small side table. Two of the tankards had already been used so he filled the third and joined her.

'Well?' he asked. 'This evidence?'

Kathryn glanced quickly over her shoulder. Thomasina was still out in the garden crooning softly to herself.

'Evidence, Irishman? You are just drinking it.' She toasted him with her own tankard. 'And tomorrow, whatever happens, remember that!'

Chapter 11

"What is bettre than wisedoom? Womman. And what is
bettre than a good womman? Nothyng."

—Chaucer, "The Tale of Melibee,"
The Canterbury Tales, 1387

*W*hen Colum and Kathryn reached Ingoldby Hall early the
next morning, the Irishman was furious. Muttering under his
breath, he glowered at Kathryn who, acting the minx, smiled coyly
back. Colum had confessed how the previous evening had been
highly unpleasant. He had arrived at the hall and served his warrants. Gurnell drew his sword and had to be restrained by Colum's
retainers. Eleanora had been furious, angrily shaking Colum's
hand off her sleeve. She had collected her cloak and, speaking
quickly in her own tongue, cursed him roundly. Thurston, slightly
drunk, hardly resisted whilst Father John quietly smiled and
pointed out that he was a cleric and so protected by benefit of
clergy. Lady Elizabeth Maltravers was icy in her anger, vowing
that Colum and Kathryn would pay for their insults, both to her
and the memory of her dead husband. In the end, however, Colum
had his way. He did not tell them where they were going and a
fresh dispute arose when they turned off the trackway down to
the old hunting lodge. Nevertheless, Colum insisted that they were
his prisoners and were to stay, at least until the following morning
when Mistress Swinbrooke would visit them. He had then returned to Ottemelle Lane, found the house quiet and Kathryn already retired. She had roused him just before dawn. They had
broken their fast and left but, when they reached the trackway

leading down to the hunting lodge, Kathryn had sprung her surprise.

'We are not going there, at least not yet.'

'What?' Colum had roared back. 'I have provoked a powerful noblewoman, arrested four of her household and you are not even going to question them? Kathryn, you cannot hold them forever. Lady Elizabeth will send messages into Canterbury. The lawyers will be down here like flies over horse dung!'

'A good likeness, but intemperate language,' Kathryn coolly replied. 'First, we must visit Ingoldby Hall.'

She spoke quietly but firmly, then urged her horse on. Colum was still swearing under his breath even as a bleary-eyed retainer opened the front door of the hall and reluctantly admitted them.

'Tell the Lady Elizabeth that I wish to speak to her,' Kathryn declared. 'On the King's business.'

She made her own way into the solar and sat down on the same chair she had occupied on her first visit here.

'Mistress Swinbrooke!'

Kathryn rose as Lady Elizabeth swept into the room.

'Mistress Swinbrooke.' Lady Elizabeth flicked her hand as a sign for Kathryn to sit; Colum she totally ignored. 'I am mourning for my husband. Last night your ruffian, abusing the King's warrants, arrested four of my household. He shattered our mourning, alarmed our guests and now you rouse me from my bed as if I am some scullion maid.'

Lady Elizabeth made herself comfortable in the thronelike chair. She was wearing a nightgown of pure white linen gathered at the neck, and over this a dark blue robe lined with silver fur. Her dainty feet, pushed into red satin slippers, rested on a footstool. She'd parted her hair down the centre, letting it fall to her shoulders; her beautiful, pale face was mottled with anger, and white spittle stained the corner of her mouth whilst her eyes were full of haughty disdain.

'You are much recovered, my lady, from your sickness at Canterbury?'

'I am, thanks be to God, as well as to your ministrations.' Lady Elizabeth's voice was rich with sarcasm. 'I intend to leave Ingoldby later today for London. I shall seek the protection of the King himself. I will ask for the removal of this ruffian.' She pointed at Colum. 'No, sir, you do not sit in my presence!' she yelled as Colum went to occupy the chair next to Kathryn.

'Madam,' Kathryn tartly replied, 'Master Murtagh is a King's Commissioner! He will sit where he wishes whilst I inform you how Master Mawsby killed your husband.'

'What?' Lady Elizabeth clutched the arms of the chair. Her face sagged, the anger draining from her eyes. She turned her head slightly. 'Mistress Swinbrooke, have you taken leave of your wits? Mawsby is dead, his corpse is to be taken to Canterbury . . .'

'Aye, along with Sir Walter's, Veronica's and poor Hockley's. Mawsby will also join the Vaudois woman and her daughter, Ursula. Murder upon murder, eh my lady?'

'The Vaudois woman? What is this?'

'Master Mawsby killed your husband.' Kathryn sat back in her chair, studying Lady Elizabeth intently.

'But he was in Canterbury?'

'No, he went to Canterbury. He carried out his errands. I don't know who for; perhaps you, my lady. He then came galloping back dressed in a new cloak, head and face hidden deep in a cowl. The Vaudois woman glimpsed him; Mawsby was cantering so furiously she thought he was a royal messenger and this stirred her addled brain. She thought he was bringing news about her former lover and son, nonsense of course! Master Mawsby reached the curtain wall of Ingoldby Hall about an hour before noon on that particular Friday, the eve of the Transfiguration. He hobbled his horse in the trees and climbed the wall, as the Vaudois woman did, and followed her trackway through the copse to the edge of the great meadow. On his way he collected a sack taken from the stores and a small but very sharp two-headed axe. Mawsby then crept across the meadow to his chosen point along the rearmost hedge of the maze.'

'But?' Lady Elizabeth interrupted.

'But nothing, my lady. The grass grows longer around the maze and Mawsby had found a gap at the foot of the rear hedge, where the roots of the bushes were not so closely planted together. In the weeks before this hideous murder, unbeknown to some, for that is a lonely part of the manor, Mawsby had worked to enlarge that hole. He possibly snapped a root of one of the hedges, forced the branches further up and kept his handiwork hidden until that particular afternoon. Anyway, on that murderous day Mawsby creeps through the hole with his axe and a sack. Once through he pulls back his cowl and puts on a green mask to hide his face. He then makes his way through the path of the maze to the Weeping Cross.'

'How could he know his way?' Lady Elizabeth's face was flushed, her breathing quicker.

'Oh, he'd found the secret contained within the mosaic in your husband's library. To most people it simply represents strange geometric symbols tastefully displayed on the tiles, but a closer study reveals that the blue cross in the centre marks the middle of the maze. The mosaic is in fact a very clever map. I discovered that and so did Mawsby. He was your husband's secretarius, a man skilled in letters. He would draw up a copy and, unbeknown to anyone, learn the mystery of the maze and how to quickly thread its paths. By the time of the murder,' Kathryn shrugged, 'Mawsby knew the maze as well as your husband did. Sir Walter, of course, on that Friday reached the Weeping Cross. Lost in his own reverie of reparation, your husband may have only known for a few seconds that he was going to die. Mawsby swings the axe, takes your husband's head, puts it into the sack and returns the way he came. The back of the maze cannot be seen by anyone, but Mawsby made one mistake. Once he reached the copse he took off his mask, and his gloves were blood-tinged. Mawsby accidentally dropped the mask whilst making his escape.'

Kathryn paused. Colum's agitation was apparent. He kept shuffling his feet, glancing quickly at Kathryn, then Lady Elizabeth, as if wondering where this was going to lead.

'Mawsby hid the bloodied axe and the sack with its grisly burden deep in that copse amongst the briars and bracken where no one but he could find it. He also took off the cloak and cowl, hid them, climbed back over the wall and unhobbled his horse, not before wiping any foamy sweat from the animal's hide. He would probably let it crop the grass for a while before leaving the trees. He'd travel slowly towards the gates of Ingoldby Hall, to all intents and purposes, the faithful retainer returning from Canterbury.'

'I do not believe this.' Lady Elizabeth drew herself up. 'Master Murtagh, I would be grateful if you could fill me a goblet of wine. I . . .' She touched her stomach. 'Please join me.'

Colum went across to a side table covered with an embroidered linen cloth.

'I do not want any wine,' Kathryn called out.

Colum filled one goblet and took it over to Lady Elizabeth. She grabbed the cup and drank quickly, her eyes never leaving Kathryn as the physician continued her explanation.

'Mawsby acted the innocent, though of course his business was unfinished. Later that night he returned to his secret hiding place in the copse, took out the pole, already prepared, and your husband's head, and committed that blasphemous act.'

'Tell her how.' Colum turned in his chair and winked at Kathryn.

'Oh, the day Sir Walter was killed, Mawsby was very busy. He had the pole ready together with a wineskin full of oil, a tinder and a piece of rope. The pole was driven into the ground and the decapitated head placed on it. Mawsby then soaked that part of the hedge where the secret entrance lay, and using the rope as a fuse, began the conflagration. He not only dishonoured his master but roused the house and destroyed any chance of anyone, including myself, discovering his secret passage into the maze.'

'Mawsby must have hated Sir Walter,' Colum murmured.

'Mawsby breathed hatred and suspicion,' Kathryn replied. 'He resented my arrival here and watched me closely. He glimpsed me in the library studying the mosaic and again, out in the great meadow, on my knees searching the hedges of the maze. He thought I'd stumbled onto the secret and decided to kill me. Mawsby knew the cellars of this house. He followed Hockley and me down, using one of the other entrances so no one might glimpse him. He murdered Hockley and tried to kill me, and when I started that fire he fled.'

'But this is unbelievable!' Lady Elizabeth snapped. 'Then who killed Mawsby? Did he drink that poison himself and commit suicide?'

'No, my lady, you killed Mawsby.'

Lady Elizabeth sprang to her feet, sending the wine cup clattering to the floor, its contents spilling out like blood gushing from a wound. She advanced on Kathryn, fists clenched, face a mask of fury.

'Sit down, my lady.' Kathryn didn't flinch. 'If you do not sit down I will ask Master Murtagh to restrain you.'

Lady Elizabeth's lips moved wordlessly and a strange sound echoed from the back of her throat. Colum half-rose. Lady Elizabeth retreated to her chair, slumping down. She tried to speak.

'What proof?' Kathryn spoke softly. 'Is that what you are trying to ask me? Why, Master Murtagh and I have been busy all night. Eleanora, your lady-in-waiting, has confessed to everything.'

'Never!'

'Never what, my lady? That she never confessed or that she was never involved in murder? Let me tell you,' Kathryn continued coolly; she dare not turn and look at Colum, 'what Eleanora has told us. Mawsby was with you in Canterbury. However, before he left, he met Master Murtagh and me in your husband's writing chamber. I noticed the beautiful wine jug and goblets. Mawsby was drinking from one of these whilst I was studying your husband's papers. You sent Eleanora with a message that you were now departing Ingoldby for Canterbury. So we left your husband's writing chamber and came downstairs. Now I am sure that Mawsby locked the door behind him. However, during the period of waiting, Eleanora quietly returned to the writing chamber. She poured a little wine into two of the goblets and put grains of monkshood in the unused one. She then took the wine jug to the window, opened this and emptied its contents out. She put the jug back on the tray and left the chamber, locking the door behind her.' Kathryn paused and silently prayed her bluff would succeed. 'Later that day,' she continued, 'possibly just before midnight, Mawsby and the others returned from Canterbury. Your husband's chancery was Mawsby's favourite haunt. Now, on that particular night, Mawsby had already drunk a great deal. He was very anxious. He didn't really understand what had happened in Canterbury, so he went up to the writing office.' Kathryn pointed at Lady Elizabeth. 'You made sure he'd go there. Before he left Canterbury, you asked him to look at your husband's will or some other task which had to be completed immediately?'

Lady Elizabeth did not reply but stared hatefully across.

'I shall continue.' Kathryn smiled. 'Mawsby lights a few candles and goes over to the wine jug; it's empty so he orders a maid to bring up some fresh. The jug is filled. Mawsby, and you must remember the light in the chancery would be quite poor, naturally chooses the goblet containing no wine. Everyone drinks from a fresh cup, a stratagem I tried on Master Murtagh last night. Eleanora had stained the other two, forcing Mawsby to accept the cup containing the monkshood. Mawsby pours the wine in and moves round the chamber. What he is now drinking is not the richest burgundy but the most venomous poison. If Mawsby realised what had happened, then he would only have a short while to express his regrets. Death would have been nearly instant. Monkshood is most deadly, but how did it get there? Well, that's how we trapped Eleanora,' Kathryn continued lightly. She held up her hand, fingers splayed. 'There are only two keys to the writing chamber, one held by Mawsby, the other by you! Who else could have put poison in that cup? Who else could have emptied a jug outside that window? Mawsby had been neatly trapped and killed by his accomplices.'

'Accomplices! You forget, Mistress.' Lady Elizabeth fought to control her temper. 'The night Mawsby died, I, too, was poisoned in Canterbury.'

'Oh, a clever piece of mummery,' Kathryn responded. 'I can describe a number of ways to make yourself sick and leave an empty winecup with an acrid smell. Adding salt or some other herbal concoction to wine is one method. You acted the part well: vomiting and retching, collapsing to the floor. As you did so, you knocked your platter and wine goblet into the rushes. The good brothers of Canterbury would be very solicitous. The refectory is a public place. The brothers pride themselves on their cleanliness. The cup had been emptied whilst the rushes, stained and polluted, had to be cleared away and burnt immediately. Eleanora,' she added, 'also confessed to that. Any evidence you'd really been poisoned was swept away.'

'Did Eleanora also confess why Mawsby would kill my husband?' Lady Elizabeth's head went back and she peered at Kathryn through half-closed eyes.

'Oh yes! *"Radix malorum est cupiditas,"* though in this case "cupiditas" is not a love of money but something deeper, more subtle. Let me tell you a story, Lady Elizabeth, about a young noblewoman, namely yourself. You were raised and pampered by your father and brothers, spoilt and indulged yet possessing an inflexible will and a deep resentment of what you term "The iron world of men." Your father gave you everything you wanted; his greatest present was to hire Eleanora as your lady-in-waiting. Only God knows the real relationship between you and that murderous woman. I have heard of such love, a deep infatuation where two souls become one in thought, word and deed. I can imagine you and Eleanora fashioning your own reality in the busy world of men. How one day you would escape it, be masters of your own fate. Nevertheless, you were particular, you cast around for a husband of your choice.'

'You seem to know a lot about me!' Lady Elizabeth's words came in a hiss. Elbows resting on the arm of the chair, fingers laced together, she reminded Kathryn of Ursula holding that crossbolt.

'Sir Walter was a strange man,' Kathryn mused, 'constantly living in the past, persecuted by his own demons. He wasn't hunted by the Athanatoi, that was only a story which others seized on. In Constantinople Sir Walter did what any man would have done. He fled, taking as much treasure as he could find. Sir Walter, however, was haunted by another sin: a massacre of prisoners which took place after the battle of Towton eleven years ago. A group of mercenaries was slain, their decapitated heads barbarously hung from the branches of trees.' Kathryn steeled herself for the next lie, the real lie. 'One of those men, one of the Provencales, was Eleanora's kinsman!'

'She is from Spain!'

'I saw the deed roll in your husband's library,' Kathryn replied. 'Provencale is a general term but this group of mercenaries, according to that roll, came from northern Spain as well as the south of France, territories on either side of the great mountain range. That massacre, blameless though he may be, was Sir Walter's downfall. Eleanora had a blood feud with him, secretive but one she was determined to avenge. Years after the battle, Sir Walter came to London. He moved, as you did, in the glorious circle of the court; the massacre at Towton was well reported. Eleanora marked down the man responsible. She would hold him to account and display his head on a pole. You married Maltravers, my lady, for three reasons: to escape your father's house, to become a mistress of great wealth in your own right, and to avenge Eleanora's blood feud.'

'Marriage for that?'

'I have heard of marriages for worse, my lady. And why not? Sir Walter was personable enough, well favoured by the King and very rich. A man haunted by demons, he would leave you and Eleanora to your own devices. He never suspected the brood of vipers he was nurturing. Sir Walter also arranged for the pardon of Mawsby and gave his kinsman high office in his household. Mawsby, however, was a man who had lost all fighting for the House of Lancaster. He resented what he'd termed Sir Walter's patronising generosity. A man full of hate was Mawsby. Yet he had to dance to the tune being piped: secretarius to Sir Walter was better than penniless exile in the rotting slums of some city beyond the Narrow Seas. They say it takes one soul to recognise another. Elearnora and Mawsby, probably encouraged by you, drew closer together. Mawsby became infatuated with your lady-in-waiting. He began a secret affair, clandestine but deadly. Mawsby would open his heart, let the hate and resentment out. Eleanora would coax him. He fell madly in love with her but, of course, Eleanora loves no one but you.'

'And did Mawsby tell you all this before he died?' Lady Elizabeth asked. 'Did he write out his confession before he drank the monkshood?'

'In a way he did,' Kathryn replied. 'The afternoon when we

were in the writing chamber, Mawsby acted like some besotted lover drinking his wine, sitting in the window seat moodily gazing out. He knew we posed no danger. There was nothing amongst Sir Walter's papers, or so he thought, which could resolve his master's murder.' Kathryn paused. 'He was singing a song, comparing his love to a rose. When Eleanora came to summon us down because you were leaving for Canterbury, I noticed for the first time a beautiful chain with a gold rose hanging about her neck. That was a gift from Mawsby. He was your weapon, your foil, the dagger to strike at the hearts of all who opposed you.'

'And Veronica?' Colum asked, fascinated by Kathryn's revelations. He caught himself just in time. 'Tell her about Veronica.'

'Veronica was nothing more than a country maid who was supposed to be busy in the kitchen. One of Eleanora's responsibilities, as your lady-in-waiting, was to supervise those maids. On that Friday she was determined that they all be busy in the kitchens. No one had to be in the galleries or chambers just in case Mawsby was glimpsed in that brief period of time when he'd run to and from the maze.' Kathryn scratched the back of her hand. 'Veronica was most unfortunate; she'd lost a precious locket. As girls do when they misplace something, she started to accuse others, in this case Amelia, another maid. Veronica, just after noon, slipped from the kitchen and returned to the top gallery.'

'But Veronica's chamber was at the front of the house!' Lady Elizabeth retorted.

'She didn't go there,' Kathryn answered. 'She went up to Amelia's, which overlooks the great meadow. Veronica was unlucky. Perhaps some demon in the air prompted her or, perhaps, she just wanted to see what the view was like. She peered out of the window and glimpsed Mawsby, probably leaving the maze. Nothing more than a sinister shadow flitting across the grass into the line of trees. Veronica would dismiss this as fantasy, more intent on discovering if Amelia had her locket. However, when Sir Walter's murder was announced, she began to wonder. Was it a dream, a vision? She went out to the copse and found a green mask. Now,' Kathryn paused to gather her thoughts. 'She may have been seen doing that or, like the good girl she was, went and told your lady-in-waiting. Eleanora arranged to meet Veronica at that lonely spot near the ruined tower. However, instead of Eleanora waiting for her, Mawsby was. He made another mistake. He didn't first find out what she discovered. Instead he crept up behind her and gave Veronica a terrible blow to the back of her head, then pushed his victim into the mere where she quickly drowned.'

'Green masks!' Lady Elizabeth played with her hands.

'Ah yes, the mask. Eleanora must have been furious.' Kathryn leaned down, opened her writing-satchel and drew out the mask. 'Would you like to examine this, Lady Elizabeth?' She held it out so the blood stain was obvious. 'This is no piece of sacking but two pieces of cloth neatly sewn together. I examined this last night. Mawsby was a soldier. He would be used to mending a girth, or fitting a patch in his jerkin, but stitching like this?' Kathryn shook her head. 'If I compared this to needlework in Eleanora's box, I'd warrant the stitching's the same.'

Lady Elizabeth gazed stony-eyed back, refusing to touch the mask.

'Poor Mawsby.' Kathryn continued, putting the mask away. 'I have yet to discover whether he knew about your role in these matters. Eleanora was his accomplice, his lover, he must have been intrigued by your performance in Canterbury Cathedral. No wonder he returned to Ingoldby Hall eager for a fresh cup of wine. I say poor Mawsby.' Kathryn shook her head. 'But he was a man infatuated with Eleanora, a killer used to the cut and thrust of battle. Human life was cheap to Mawsby. He was the one that followed me around Ingoldby and watched me study the mosaic in the library and then again out in the maze.' Kathryn forced a smile. 'Did he tell you about losing the mask?'

Lady Elizabeth refused to answer, an eerie, calculating look in her eyes.

'Mawsby must have known the Vaudois woman and her daughter were possible suspects.' Kathryn sat back in her chair. 'After all, Master Gurnell had been sweet on Ursula. Did Mawsby know that both women were not as fey and witless as sometimes they pretended to be? Anyway, soon after he had taken care of Sir Walter's head, exposing it for everyone to see, Mawsby took the axe and the blood-soaked sack down to the old hunting lodge and hid them there.' Kathryn shrugged. 'Sooner or later someone would have laid information against the Vaudois woman and her daughter. The old hunting lodge would be searched. We would also find the secret trackway through the copse. The finger of suspicion would point at them. You, of course, were intent on putting as much distance between yourself and Ingoldby as possible. You announced that your household would be dispensed and that included Eleanora. Everyone else would go, you'd then feign some excuse and keep Eleanora with you on your triumphant return to London as a very, very wealthy widow. A woman of independent sustenance, favoured and pitied by the King, protected by all the power of the Crown. How you and Eleanora would laugh at the way you had duped the world of men! And what did it matter to you if Veronica was drowned in a mere? Or poor Hockley lay cold in his grave? Or the Vaudois woman and her daughter, tarred and chained, hung from some gibbet? And Mawsby? Ah well.' Kathryn picked up the mask. 'He'd served his purpose, hadn't he? He could be sent into the dark. The months would pass and, if your husband's murder wasn't placed at the door of others, then it would be eventually forgotten. Who could question it, or your household now dispersed to the four corners of the kingdom?'

'I am sorry about the wine.' The colour had returned to Lady Elizabeth's cheeks. 'And my temper. Mistress Swinbrooke, you do tell a good tale.'

Lady Elizabeth rose, walked over to the wine table, refilled another goblet and returned to her chair, sipping the wine gently.

'A good tale?' Colum queried.

'Let us say it was the truth.' Lady Elizabeth smiled at Kathryn. 'Let us say that Eleanora and Mawsby plotted these hideous murders. And,' she sighed, 'God forgive them for their black hearts and evil deeds. Yet, what proof can you lay against me?'

Colum glanced down to hide his own anxiety. He was certain that this beautiful young woman was a killer, a murderess with a heart of stone. She was now doing what any felon would do, trying to slip through the net and pass the blame to others.

'My proof lies in five parts.' Kathryn's reply was sharp.

Lady Elizabeth's smile faded.

'First, you tried to murder your husband by using poison; that's what gave him the stomach cramp. But when Sir Walter sent for Brother Ralph the infirmarian from Greyfriars, you decided to stop. Only someone very close to Sir Walter could feed poison to him over a long period of time, one of those poisons which grow in strength.'

'Nonsense!'

'Nonsense? When I met you the day you left for Canterbury, I noticed a book about herbs and their properties in your chamber, such works are rare, studied by only those skilled in such matters. I wager you know as much about poison as I do, Lady Elizabeth. Secondly, Mawsby's murder. He locked the door behind us when we left the writing chamber, and the only other person who held a key to that room was yourself.'

'Oh yes, and Eleanora must have borrowed it?'

'Thirdly,' Kathryn continued remorselessly, 'when a jury is empanelled to try you, Lady Elizabeth, they will, as instructed by the King's Justice, be taken out to Ingoldby and asked to sit in the arbour of flowers which stands at the side of the great meadow, where you were the afternoon your husband was murdered.' Kathryn leaned forward. 'Lady Elizabeth, I have studied the plan of that meadow most closely. Anyone sitting there must have seen Mawsby leave the copse of trees for the maze, then return.' Kathryn demonstrated with her hands. 'True, you cannot see the rearmost hedge of the maze, but you do have a clear view of the land between the maze and the copse. Will you explain to the jury how a maid like Veronica could glimpse such a figure in a momentary glance through a window but you and Eleanora never saw anyone either leave or reenter both the copse and the maze, not to mention crossing the lawn in between, on a clear summer's day?'

L'ady Elizabeth's face grew pale and tight.

'We, we . . . could have overlooked it,' she stuttered.

'Nonsense!' Kathryn retorted. 'Two young, sharp-eyed ladies on a full clear day? Mawsby would never have risked it unless you were both fellow conspirators. Indeed,' Kathryn picked up the mask, 'I suspect you were sitting there to protect Mawsby. You were playing a lute, singing: that was the signal. Different verses, different tunes, when it was safe for him to leave the copse and enter the maze and the same for his return. You acted as his spy or sentry. Shall we go to the great meadow, Lady Elizabeth? The jury will certainly be intrigued.'

'You mentioned that your proof was in five parts?'

'Ah yes. Eleanora has confessed.'

'She would never. . . .' Lady Elizabeth's head went down.

'Now we come to the fifth part.' Kathryn's voice was soft. 'Eleanora confessed because of what I have told you. Because Master Murtagh described what it is like to be hanged on the public gallows. Because he offered her a pardon. . . .'

'Never!' Lady Elizabeth shrieked.

'Because he threatened to search both her chamber and yours from floorboard to ceiling. That's why she was arrested so quickly last night. The others were taken into custody to mask our intent.'

Lady Elizabeth put her face in her hands.

'Do you wish to go to trial?' Colum's voice was harsh. 'You will go on trial, Lady Elizabeth! The Crown will not intervene. The King will be most displeased when he hears this news. He will demand the best lawyers, the sharpest attorneys the Crown can muster to pursue this case. In fact, I lied to Eleanora: you murdered your husband, the sentence for that, according to statute law, is to be burnt alive. . . . '

'I . . .' Lady Elizabeth rose, placing the wine cup on the floor beside her. 'I would like to make a full confession.'

She lifted her head. Kathryn was shocked at the change: Lady Elizabeth seemed to have aged, her face was stricken, eyes screwed up as if in pain.

'I truly loved her,' she whispered. 'I favoured her. I married Sir Walter because of her.' She scratched the side of her cheek. 'At first I tried poison. Sir Walter was no different from any other man. My father and brothers were locked in their world of profit. Sir Walter was imprisoned in a dungeon of guilt and remorse. Eleanora hated him: her brother died at Towton. Mawsby,' She shrugged. 'I was jealous of him but he was a fool: full of hate against Sir Walter which he hid so well.' She began to pace up

228

and down. 'Later that afternoon Mawsby watched the great meadow. He glimpsed Veronica going towards the copse: a callow wench with prying eyes.' Lady Elizabeth stopped. 'And what is to become of me?'

Before Colum or Kathryn could stop her, Lady Elizabeth ran towards the door. So surprised, Kathryn was hardly out of her chair when Lady Elizabeth seized the key from the inside lock. By the time Colum had reached it, she'd opened the door and slammed it shut, turning the key in the lock. Colum hammered on the wooden panels. Lady Elizabeth screamed as she ran down the gallery. Colum drew his sword and used the pommel to batter the door, splintering the wood.

'What is it?' a voice called.

'Open this door in the King's name!' Colum shouted.

'But Lady Elizabeth has the key. What is the matter?' a maid, her voice full of fear, echoed back.

Kathryn ran across to the window and pushed open one of the small casement doors.

'Colum!' she called.

He hurried across, gently pushed her aside and thrust his way through. Kathryn, using a stool, climbed out, Colum helping her down onto the grassy verge. They ran round the house. The main door was open and servants milled in the hallway beyond. One of the maids was crying hysterically. Another was halfway up the great staircase, peering after her distraught mistress.

'What is the matter?' A burly stable man planted himself squarely in front of Colum. 'My mistress's household,' his voice was a thick burr, 'are arrested, now she screams like a ghost!'

Colum, restrapping the sword belt taken off when he'd climbed through the window, pushed the tongue of the belt through its loop and drew his sword in a flourish. The stable man stepped back.

'Stand aside!' Colum shouted. 'This is the King's business, though I suspect I will need your help!'

Colum and Kathryn went up the staircase, the servants following fearfully behind. They found the door to Lady Elizabeth's chamber locked and had to use a bench from the great hall to snap it free of its thick leather hinges. Inside, Lady Elizabeth, a goblet of wine on the floor beside her, was already beyond any help: her body was jerking, head going backwards and forwards, eyelids fluttering. A yellowish froth stained the corner of her mouth and the muscles of her face were taut in agony. Kathryn felt her hand and peered closely at the half-closed eyes.

'Poison.' Kathryn picked up the goblet and sniffed at the jewel-encrusted brim. The sweetness of the white wine could not hide the acrid tang. 'Deadly nightshade, monkshood,' Kathryn whispered.

Colum ordered the servants back as Kathryn grasped Lady Elizabeth's hand. The dying woman's face had turned livid. Kathryn was sure the half-open eyes were conscious of her being there. She tried to speak but only the froth bubbled at her lips. Another hideous convulsion and Lady Elizabeth's head jerked, then fell to one side, eyes glazing over, mouth and jaw slack. Kathryn pressed her hand against the woman's neck.

'God have mercy on her!' she prayed. 'She's dead!'

Her words carried to the servants standing in the doorway to be greeted with loud wailings and exclamations, which Colum hushed as he gently urged them away. Kathryn stood for a while gazing down at the corpse. She gently pushed back one tendril of silky blonde hair.

'Such God-given beauty,' she murmured. 'Such a waste!'

Staring down at the liverish face, Kathryn reflected on her own actions—but what other path could she have followed? Indeed, the more she had confronted Lady Elizabeth the more compelling the case against her had become.

Colum came back into the chamber.

'Kathryn, we should be gone. I have instructed the maids to attend to Lady Elizabeth's corpse, to lay it out on the bed. This will cause some flutter in the dove cote,' he added. 'A suicide, they will demand that she be buried at the crossroads.'

'I don't think so.' Kathryn gently stroked Lady Elizabeth's cheek. 'Prior Barnabas of Greyfriars owes me a great favour. He will have another corpse to bury in the Poor Man's Plot.'

Kathryn took one last look at the corpse and left. They returned to the solar; the key Lady Elizabeth had dropped during her flight had been found. They collected their possessions and went out to the stable yard. The sun was now strong, the air rich with the smell of horses, dung, oats, bran and hay. Surly-eyed ostlers brought out their horses. Kathryn and Colum were eager to leave. Once they had passed through the unguarded gates, Colum reined in, dismounted and urged Kathryn to do the same.

'You had no real proof, just logic!'

Colum let his horse nuzzle at his hand. Kathryn gently stroked the neck of her soft-eyed cob.

'Veronica,' she replied. 'Veronica did see Mawsby either enter the maze or leave it. I wondered about Lady Elizabeth and Eleanora. Why were they sitting in the flower arbour? I mean, at that particular time? Why did they stay so long despite the heat of the sun? Surely they must have glimpsed Mawsby? More importantly,' she kissed her horse gently on the neck, 'if Mawsby was acting by himself, a murderer bent on vengeance, would he have left the copse if he had seen Lady Elizabeth and Eleanora sitting in the arbour of flowers? If they were two innocents, he ran the hideous risk of being seen or even apprehended. I therefore concluded that both Lady Elizabeth and Eleanora were his accomplices, if not his masters; they were sitting in the arbour to protect their assassin.' Kathryn held out her hand. 'Once I had that as a hypothesis I began to build. Someone murdered Veronica before she could tell what she had seen or found. Mawsby was a master bowman, that's how he killed Hockley in the cellar. Mawsby's story about being in Canterbury was a cunning way to hide his true whereabouts. And, of course, there was the garbled story of the Vaudois woman, about a messenger galloping along the road. . . .'

'And?' Colum asked.

'Brother Ralph.'

'What about him?'

'Well, according to our good infirmarian, he left Ingoldby Hall just before noon.'

'Ah yes, and he never met Mawsby on the road?'

'That's because Mawsby had already hobbled his horse and was lurking in that copse ready to carry out his murderous task. Other images came back. Mawsby singing a love song. Eleanora's silver chain with the golden rose. I hadn't seen it before and she was supposed to be in mourning. Lady Elizabeth's book of herbs.' Kathryn let the cob graze on the grass, gently wrapping the reins around her wrist. 'The mummery at Canterbury Cathedral, Lady Elizabeth acting as if she had been poisoned but there was nothing for us to examine except an acrid smell, the contents of the cup had been cleared away. What other explanation can there be for Mawsby's murder? Logic, alone dictates it.'

'I should go back,' Colum breathed, 'and search those chambers.'

'Oh, you might find something, but they were a cunning pair. I can't even prove Eleanora made that mask.'

'So, why didn't Lady Elizabeth simply lie?'

'I wondered about that too, but I suspect the love between her and Eleanora was very passionate. Lady Elizabeth is spoilt and vain. Eleanora is the one with the will of steel. They thought we'd never stumble on the hypothesis about Mawsby crossing that lawn unless we had evidence. Once Lady Elizabeth thought Eleanora had betrayed her, what reason did she have for living? Even so . . .'

Kathryn turned her horse back onto the trackway. Colum helped her to remount. She gazed down at him.

'There was a compelling logic against both of them. If a jury was empanelled they would certainly say there was a case to answer and present an indictment.'

'Why did you think Eleanora is the one of steel?'

'Oh, Lady Elizabeth was a doll in her hands. Eleanora could convince Lady Elizabeth that winter was summer and spring was autumn. If we examine that Bede roll, the list of names massacred at Towton, we'll discover Eleanora's kin. In Spain and Italy the blood feud must be pursued, whatever the cost, whatever the means.' She gathered her reins. 'And why should Lady Elizabeth object? She wanted to escape. Maltravers was much older, an ideal choice. I suspect from the start both that precious pair had murder in their hearts. Now, come, Colum.'

He remounted his horse and they went along the trackway, turning off down towards the old hunting lodge. Colum explained how Gurnell had been grieved to hear of the deaths of the Vaudois woman and Ursula, though Colum had not provided details. Just before they reached the bend he reined in, leaned over and grasped Kathryn's hand.

'Why, Irishman, you choose the strangest places and times to do your courting!'

'Kathryn, soon we will be out of this. In a few weeks we'll be married, man and wife. And what then?'

'Why, Irishman.' Kathryn freed her hand and, leaning over, caressed the black hair tumbling down the side of his face, running a finger down his unshaven cheek. 'That's for me to know and you to find out as we go a-courting and a-loving till the end of time.'

'I think we should go away,' Colum declared.

'Go away? Leave Canterbury?'

'Just for a little while. To be alone.'

Kathryn stared through the interlaced branches. For a brief second she experienced what it would be like to be in a strange place, where they were not known, on a beautiful morning like this. Yet, even as she did so, she experienced a slight chill, not of fear but a conviction that, wherever they went and whatever they did, the pursuit of the sons and daughters of Cain would never be far away.

'Kathryn?'

'I'll think about that, Irishman.' She winked at him and urged her horse on. 'But, in the meantime . . .'

They rounded the bend. The old hunting lodge lay before them; from the chimney stack at the side of the house curled a plume of smoke. Colum's retainers were lounging on the ground, one sharpening a stick, others playing a game of hazard.

'Lovely lads!' Colum breathed.

Kathryn thought they were the biggest rogues she had ever met, a group of wild Irishmen, some with hair as black as Colum's, others fiery red, all with swaggering ways and impudent eyes. They hailed Kathryn as if she was a princess, gathering round her, touching her hand, staring up at this 'wise woman' who had captivated their leader. Some whispered endearments in Gaelic. Others grinned admiringly, chatting to each other. Colum they greeted with good-natured insults and, for a while, there was quick repartee in a tongue Kathryn couldn't understand. Two of the retainers helped her dismount, one offering to carry her cloak.

'Lovely lads, Colum!' she called across.

They were all dressed in hose pushed into boots and dark leather jerkins over ragged, stained shirts. They were well armed, sword belts strapped round their waists or across their shoulders; arbalests and crossbows leaned against the outside wall of the house. Colum took Kathryn's hand, chattering to the leader.

'Our four prisoners are inside,' he explained. 'The men took a chicken and roasted it. They have been well fed and looked after.'

'What we have to do,' Kathryn declared, 'we must do quickly. Ask them all to be brought out.'

Colum issued the orders; a short while later Father John, Thurston, and Gurnell, with Eleanora following, were led out of the house.

'I object,' Gurnell stepped forward, 'to being arraigned like a prisoner.'

'You are not prisoners,' Colum intervened. 'You are free to go—except you, Mistress Eleanora!' He pointed a finger. 'By the King's commission to execute justice, both high and low, in the city of Canterbury and the shire of Kent, I arrest you for the murder of Sir Walter Maltravers, Edward Mawsby your erstwhile accomplice, the maid known as Veronica and the retainer known as Hockley. You shall also be impeached and accused of high treason in that you deviously and maliciously plotted against the King's commission . . .'

Eleanora gave a scream and, from somewhere, produced a knife. Grey cloak billowing out, she lunged at Kathryn. Her three companions were too shocked to move but the Irishman standing on Kathryn's right was faster still. He moved, gliding to his left, one hand knocking away Eleanora's knife, the other delivering a punch to her midriff which sent her staggering back, clutching her stomach. She collapsed on the ground, gagging for breath, and was immediately hustled to her feet, her pain being ignored as two of Colum's retainers bound her wrists. Kathryn was shocked by the change: no longer olive-skinned and pretty, Eleanora, despite her pain, lunged forward again, her eyes black pools of hatred, her mouth muttering wordless curses.

'You are guilty,' Kathryn said softly, stepping forward. 'Your mistress has confessed to everything, your former life, your kinsman slain at Towton, the way you enticed Mawsby and then killed him.'

Kathryn gazed calmly into the hate-filled eyes. She felt no pang of remorse. All she could remember was poor Veronica floating face down in that mere, the agonised grief of her father, the brutality of Hockley's death and that sinister attack upon her. Kathryn glimpsed the gold rose on the silver chain still hanging around Eleanora's neck. She felt like snatching it away, but thought differently and withdrew her hand. In sharp, succinct sentences Kathryn described the accusations levelled against lady Elizabeth. How she had not challenged them but had confirmed her proof by taking her own life. At this Eleanora threw back her head, screamed at the sky and then launched into a further tirade of abuse.

'You'll face the King's justice,' Kathryn interrupted.

'I cannot believe this,' Gurnell broke in.

Kathryn glanced at the other members of the household. Thurston was sitting on the ground, head in his hands. Father John stood speechless, staring at some point further down the trackway.

'I cannot believe this.'

Gurnell made to step forward but one of Colum's retainers pushed him back. Eleanora began to curse again and one of her captors put his hand across her mouth. She struggled, then fell silent, her body sagging between the two men holding her.

'Take her away,' Kathryn declared. 'Hand her over to the sheriff's men.'

Eleanora was pushed away. Just near the doorway she struggled, glanced back over her shoulder and screamed a curse before being dragged into the darkness beyond. Kathryn suddenly felt weary. She wanted to be away from here.

'Master Gurnell, Father John, Master Thurston, you are free to go.'

Their horses were led forward and Kathryn was helped to mount. She gathered up the reins.

'Mistress Swinbrooke.' Father John came and caught the bridle of her horse. He stared up at her, his eyes filled with tears. 'I'll go back to Ingoldby Hall, I'll say prayers over her corpse. Afterwards I'll be gone to a place where no hurt comes, the silent cloisters and some sort of peace.'

'Good fortune, Father.'

He still held the bridle of her horse.

'When I first met you, Mistress Swinbrooke, I thought you were most comely. Now, looking at you, I recall a verse from Isaiah about the anger of God bursting forth like fire.' He let go of her bridle and stepped back. 'Mistress Swinbrooke, I just never realised the vengeance of God could come with a smiling face.'

Father John sketched a blessing in the air and followed Gurnell back into the house.

Colum and Kathryn rode down back onto the trackway leading to the crossroads.

'Is that how you see yourself?' Colum abruptly asked. 'The Vengeance of God?'

'No.' Kathryn pushed back her hood to catch the coolness of the early morning breeze. 'Lady Elizabeth and Eleanora were daughters of Cain. I truly believe this, Colum: whatever evil we do,' she pointed to the crows circling high in the sky, 'flies like some bird of the night but always returns to haunt us. It's just a matter of time and place and that's a matter for God's choosing. Our souls are like mansions, they have many rooms and the evil we do in them never leaves us.'

'And the good?' Colum joked.

Kathryn leaned across. 'The good we do, Colum, also remains. I will never leave you my heart. Be assured of that!'

Author's Note

This novel develops a number of very interesting themes. First, medieval medicine was perhaps more advanced than it is given credit for. Like today, quacks and charlatans flourished, but many physicians were keen observers and often diagnosed and, sometimes, even successfully made a prognosis of serious ailments. It is easy to assume that in the medieval ages the status of women was negligible and only succeeding centuries saw a gradual improvement in their general lot. This is certainly incorrect. One famous English historian has pointed out that women probably had more rights in 1300 than they had in 1900, whilst Chaucer's description of the Wife of Bath shows a woman who could not only hold her own in a world of men but travelled all over Europe to the great shrines and was a shrewd businesswoman, ever ready to hold forth on the superiority of the gentler sex.

In this novel fiction corresponds with fact, and the quotation facing the title page summarises quite succinctly how women played a vital role as doctors, healers and apothecaries. Kathryn Swinbrooke may be fictional, but in 1322, the most famous doctor in London was Mathilda of Westminster; Cecily of Oxford was the royal physician to Edward III and his wife, Philippa of Hainault; and Gerard of Cremona's work clearly describes women doctors during the medieval period. In England, particularly, where the medical faculties at the two universities, Oxford and Cambridge, were relatively weak, women did serve as doctors and apothecaries, professions only in later centuries denied to them.

History does not move in a straight line but often in circles, and this certainly applies to medieval medicine. True, as today, there were charlatans ready to make a 'quick shilling' with so-called miraculous cures, but medieval doctors did possess considerable skill, particularly in their powers of observation and diagnosis. Some of their remedies, once dismissed as fanciful, are today, in both Europe and America regarded quite rightly as alternative medicine.

In the Middle Ages, particularly after the fall of Constantinople, relics such as the 'Lacrima Christi' were regarded with great awe and veneration. They were often not only costly in themselves but the source of revenue for cathedrals, churches and priories. Churchmen dreamed of supplementing their revenues with the discovery of a famous relic. Some of these were undoubtedly of great historical value, but to satisfy the hunger for relics, a bogus trade flourished and unscrupulous charlatans were ever ready to trick the gullible.

The fall of Constantinople did influence Western Europe; its borders had been breached and the power of the Turks emerged as a major military threat. Constantinople was looted and some of its treasures and precious books disappeared. Others reemerged in the West and were a factor in the Renaissance both in Italy and Northern Europe.

A Maze of Murders also describes one of the most important effects of the vicious civil war between the Houses of Lancaster and York. The Vendetta became a way of life. A very good example of this was De Vere, Earl of Oxford and a Lancastrian general who eventually defeated the Yorkists under Richard III at Bosworth in 1485. Edward IV realised that De Vere was an experienced and wily strategist; time and again he offered pardon and absolution for De Vere to return home. De Vere, however, could not be bought: he blamed York for the death of his own father and proclaimed that his struggle against York was "a l'outrance"—to the death. Even when the Tudor dynasty was firmly established, Henry VIII was always wary of surviving Yorkist claimants. Margaret of Salisbury, Clarence's daughter, despite her age, was despatched to the execution block, but the charges against her were spurious, her real guilt being her Yorkist blood. Finally, *A Maze of Murders* presents the medieval method of investigating crime. There were no forensic departments. As the novel describes, even books on herbs were rare. Instead, lawyers and prosecutors would follow the same method of investigation as was used in the schools of Oxford and Cambridge. They would deploy a hypothesis and apply logic. Such a method lasted well into the nineteenth century and is still used today. Kathryn follows this method, looking for the flaw in an argument, a system of reasoning taken directly from medieval trials. The jury would finally decide to indict or dismiss on the force of such logic.